THE HOLE BEHIND MIDNIGHT

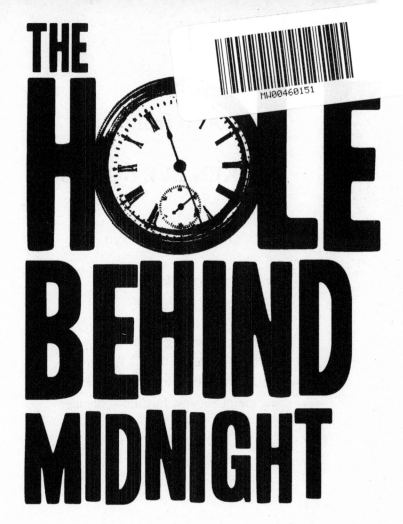

Also from

BROKEN EYE BOOKS

Crooked, by Richard Pett

Anthologies
By Faerie Light

Coming Soon
Scourge of the Realm, by Erik Scott de Bie
Questions, by Stephen Norton & Clinton Boomer
Soapscum Unlimited, by Clinton Boomer

www.brokeneyebooks.com
Blowing minds, one book at a time, with cutting-edge fiction from today's rising stars. Broken Eye Books publishes innovative genre fiction. Fantasy, horror, science fiction, weird, we love it all! And the blurrier the boundaries, the better.

THE HOLE BEHIND MIDNIGHT

A STORY OF THE 25TH HOUR

CLINTON J. BOOMER

Broken
eye
Books

THE HOLE BEHIND MIDNIGHT
Published by
Broken Eye Books
www.brokeneyebooks.com

ISBN: 978-1-940372-06-8

For my Mom.
(despite her very specific request that I not dedicate this book to her)

This work was deeply inspired by,
and is deeply indebted to,
the writings of Uri Kurlianchik.

"The time has come," the Walrus said,
"To talk of many things:
Of shoes—and ships—and sealing-wax—
Of cabbages—and kings—"

—Lewis Carroll, *Through the Looking-Glass*

A BRIEF & INCOMPLETE DRAMATIS PERSONAE

Royden Poole, the King of Jangladesh: our erstwhile (anti-)hero.

Cleon Quiet, the King of Urartu: his estranged mentor.

Ethan Milsborough: apprentice to, and employee of, Cleon Quiet.

Garrick Heldane, the King of Cahokia: a fellow sorcerer.

Tamaka Yun, the Queen of Cahokia: ex-girlfriend of Royden.

Chuck Dawg the Second, Exiled Prince of Minos: also a sorcerer.

Detective Ladislav: a police detective with some history behind the 25th.

Lieutenant Krabowski: an asshole. A fat asshole, specifically. Also, a cop.

Officer Merrick: his young but somehow still long-suffering partner.

Fadey Bohdan: a wealthy and influential Ukrainian crime-lord.

Canio de Pogo AKA **Slappy the Sideways Clown:** a demon.

Gug, Son of Gog, Prince of Majooj: demonic royalty.

Bastard Greg, the King of Majooj: a powerful evil sorcerer.

Simon Humbert Cockalorum, the King of Cocaine: likewise.

The Free Candey Van: a magical van. Yes, spelled that way on purpose.

Kynan & Noel: professional leg breakers.

Frieda Baghaamrita: an ancient spirit who owns an eponymous bar.

Koloksai, Lady of the Sun, Forgotten Queen of Scythia: an elder.

Danya Nedilya: her soft-spoken, gun-toting manservant.

Wendy Tiger-Lily, the Queen of Cocagne: immortal royalty.

Magic-Eatin' Jim, Duke of the Big Rock Candy Mountain: likewise.

Urukagina of Lagash: a feared inquisitor & enforcer of the Forgotten.

Corporate-Owned Christ: his partner. They fight crime.

Rabbi Yehoshua ben Yosef the Nazarene: his twin brother, a comedian.

The Nameless Forgotten King of Gurankalia: their boss.

"Bartender": an employee of "Bar."

The Devil at the Four Way: an ancient trickster-spirit with many masks.

Rick, who is called Chaz: a Boy-Goat Brigadier in service to King Humbert.

… and a cast of **Thousands More.**

PROLOGUE

F uck prologues.

I hate them and refuse to include one.

My name is Royden Poole, and this is my side of the story.

CHAPTER 1

I didn't want to answer my phone.

That should be clearly understood right up front.

And I certainly didn't want to do any of the things that answering my phone at this time of night would inevitably and invariably lead to, like leaving my apartment or getting shot in the face.

What I wanted to do, it should be noted, was roll over and go back to sleep. Failing that, I wanted to get onto the Internet and look at pornography, jerk off, and then go back to sleep. Failing that, I wanted to get very drunk, strongly consider calling Tamaka to tell her that I wasn't dead and to come over, hate myself very much, browse the Internet for porn instead, then jerk off, and finally go back to sleep.

That all of my plans involved going back to sleep is my point.

That was the universal end goal.

Also, I had just found a slick website online with a girl who looks a lot like Tama if you squint just right while either crying or drunk.

Or both.

My phone kept ringing.

Christ.

This whole "being dead" thing was killing me.

I stared at the phone and tried to make it stop ringing by hating it enough, but the call said *Ladislav*, and he's the sort of person who will keep calling until you pick up or, failing that, come over to your apartment and pick you up himself. One of the major flaws of passing for dead in this town is that if someone knows that you're alive and where you're hiding yourself, they pretty much have twenty-four-hour access to you.

Otherwise, I never would have picked up, is my point. It's not like I'm so starved for human attention that I actually wanted to talk to Detective Ladislav.

I sat up, shook out a cigarette, lit up, sighed, and picked up.

"This is Royden, and I hate you for calling me right now."

"I've got a nut for you to crack, Poole."

"I don't do that anymore. I'm playing dead, remember?"

"I have a contract killer here who won't stop crying and a missing persons on two of the richest men in the metro area. There's a busted floor safe here: looks like it was burned open with acid, but forensics can't tell me shit. Half a million in unmarked cash is sitting on my desk untouched, but my guys can't account for a ceramic vase. I have a shooting and no body. There's something brewing here, and I don't know what it is. You know how I get when I don't have answers, Poole. I want you to come down to the station and find out what the fuck my one and only eyewitness knows."

Jesus. Even dead, my life is a mess.

"That's gonna be really tough for me, detective. I can't, you know, leave my apartment right now. Heck, you were the guy who told me to stay dead and all, remember? And then later, you called me? And then I hung up on you? Right now? Okay, so, bye!"

"There's going to be a goddamn squad car in front of your apartment in about four minutes, Poole. If you're not out front to meet it, I'm sending a pair of officers up to your fucking coffin to bring you down in handcuffs. And I will tell them that you are to be considered both armed and dangerous."

"Christ. Why not tell them that I have a kilo of coke in my ass, too? I haven't had a date in months. Can't this wait until morning, Ladislav?"

"It's twenty 'til midnight, Poole. I want you to use your little witching-hour bullshit on my perp."

Christ. You pull the curtains back and show a guy the secret behind the universe, and he still calls it bullshit.

"Alright. Let me just slip into my coat full of doves and hidden handkerchiefs.

But I'll tell you, it's nights like these that make me wonder why I even bothered faking my death in the first place."

"Be downstairs in three minutes, you little wiseass."

Oh, of course.

He saves the short jokes until right before he hangs up on me.

What a dick.

Two and a half minutes later, a squad car pulled up in front of my stoop, lights rolling. The alleyway hookers and my crack-head neighbors gazed at me with newfound suspicion as I stood up, grunting, and flicked the last orange-glow embers of my cigarette butt into the street.

"Don't worry, everyone. This is just a matter of some unpaid parking tickets."

The passenger-side door opened up, and a young-looking cop stared at me, like I was about to do a trick. I tried to make all three-foot-ten of me seem as simultaneously intimidating and disinterested as possible while also pretending that walking down a whole two flights of stairs for the first time in several months hadn't hurt my knees, like I'd whacked them both with a hammer, and made my hip cramp up like it always does.

Here's to hoping that it worked.

"Real subtle there, guys. You know, I have to live around here."

The driver's side opened, and a fat, hatefully familiar face poked over the car's roof. "That's not what I heard, Poole. In fact, I was just telling Officer Merrick here about how we're on county coroner's detail tonight. Heh."

Fucking Krabowski. The only guy I know who can look rumpled and smelly even in freshly pressed dress blues.

"Oh, right. Picking up a dead guy. Oh-ho-ho. Yeah, very fucking funny, lieutenant."

He grinned and flicked a toothpick back and forth with his tongue in that way that makes me want to punch him right in his goddamn balls. "Help the nice, sawed-off sideshow magician into the car, Officer Merrick," he said. "There's a big birthday party downtown, and I guess the balloon-animal guy canceled."

I could almost swear the kid mumbled something about a clown, and then he shut up when I glared at him.

Smart move on his part.

I stormed toward him, and the still-dumbstruck young cop popped the back door open but hesitated on trying to push me in. I took the opportunity to wave at my adoring audience of whores and bums before slipping into the car under my own power, refusing to give the kid the satisfaction of watching me struggle up onto the seat.

My eyes immediately started stinging; someone had puked back here—and recently. I tried to get comfortable.

"So, Lieutenant, is there any use in me pointing out that *you're* the ones who called *me*?"

Three doors slammed, one after another. "Nope."

"Just checking."

I sat back and tried to think while the car took off at about eighty miles an hour, lurching through one gut-wrenching turn after another.

I pulled out my cellphone to check the time, trying not to dislodge the large knife I had hidden in my coat.

If grinning, infuriating old Krabowski didn't get us killed first, we'd be at the station just about on time.

Okay. The detective thought I was going to rabbit. That much was clear. Why else send a squad car or call me mere moments before they got there? That meant something, but I was too groggy to put it together. Also, this was a last-minute panic decision. They would have exhausted every last possibility they had before they called me. Again, that meant something.

What, though, I had no idea.

Also, who the fuck puked back here? And what the fuck had they been eating? Infected sewer runoff?

We pulled right up to the station, and I checked my cellphone. Six minutes 'til. Great. Lieutenant Douchebag hustled me through a sea of blue uniforms and confused looks. Half the force was here tonight.

"Hi. Hi. How you doin'? Special Investigator Magic-Midget Hindu Dead Guy, here. Just passing through. I'll be out of your hair in, like, five minutes, tops."

I was taken directly to interrogation.

Boy, that brought back some memories.

Ladislav was waiting for me, his perpetual scowl cranked up to just past eleven and reminding me of pretty much every other time I had ever seen him.

Even wearing the same ugly yellow tie.

"Poole."

"Evening to you, too. Where's my guy?"

"In there. I'm going to have a camera on you the whole time."

"Not gonna do you much good, but knock yourself out. Well, see you in about," I glanced at my cellphone, "two minutes. Your time."

I reached for the door, then thought better of it. "Hey, you got a cup of coffee?"

Without a word, the detective pushed a steaming styrofoam cup into my hand.

What a guy.

Glad to have him on my team.

The door shut behind me, and I was faced with a horrible little off-white room decorated entirely in a style I like to call Late-Period State Institutional. One metal table, two metal chairs, one over-flowing ashtray, one softly sobbing leg breaker, a half-empty cup of coffee, and a big-ass mirror. One hundred and four thousand seven hundred twenty-nine holes in the ceiling tiles.

I got bored and counted one time. Interestingly, that's also the ten thousandth smallest prime number.

Not sure what that means, but I'm working on it.

I considered the question of the leg breaker. I weigh in at about seventy-eight pounds, so I would put this guy at about five times my total mass. How much did I really want to press this, considering that my best bet was probably to say something along the lines of "Wait! This isn't where I parked my car!" and walk back out?

Dammit, I could be sleeping *right now*.

On the other side of that big-ass mirror, a video camera was watching us. In about ten seconds, it was going to start spitting static at itself, and everything it saw was going to break up into a fuzzy, gray-white wash, rolling up and down, that wouldn't be admissible as evidence on Judge Judy. Those missing frames would last a little less than a quarter of a minute, consolidate themselves back into a semblance of reality, and then I would theoretically go walking right back out of here.

Between now and that moment, there stretched an infinite ocean of potential time. Time enough to walk around the world. Time enough to fall in love, get married on a white beach under purple stars, write a book of poems about truest passion, have a few good and bloody screaming matches, get divorced in a court of autumn elves and gypsy moths, then set the ink-stained, tear-streaked pages of your text ablaze. Time enough to dance around the bonfire naked and cry with a group of friends and finally fall asleep drunk with all of your teeth punched out. Time enough to go insane, just waiting for the thinnest hand of the clock to go *click* again.

Time enough to get killed in any number of horrible ways.

I tried not to focus on that.

The things you do to avoid federal prison.

I set my cellphone down on the table and glanced at the time.

11:59 pm.

I looked at the heavily tattooed leg breaker, and I wondered if I maybe shouldn't have brought a much larger knife.

"Hey, man. You doing all right?"

Red-rimmed eyes, deep and black and not used to crying, glared at me. Well, his first instinct wasn't to assume that he was hallucinating.

That was a start.

"Look. I'm not a cop, but you knew that already. I'm just a guy. I don't know anybody, I don't know anything. I'm here to talk. I have no idea why you're here, and there is literally nothing that you can say to me that will get you in any trouble."

I hopped up onto the chair across from the big bastard and stole another look at my cellphone.

11:60 qm.

Showtime.

Gods dammit, I hate this fucking time of night.

I put my cellphone back in my pocket and fished out a smoke.

"Right now, the guys on the other side of that mirror are watching absolutely fuck all. They can't see us, they can't hear us. Their camera is malfunctioning even as we speak. We're pretty much alone right now, on our own little island in forever."

His eye twitched a little. It meant he was thinking, trying to suss out if I was bullshitting him. Most folks would figure a son of a bitch as big as him wasn't smart, but this guy was cagey. I lit my cigarette and pointed at the door.

"You know what? I say that we go for a walk. You and me, nobody else. I'll take your cuffs off and everything. We'll walk right the fuck out of here, and we can talk."

His eyes flicked to the door. He didn't believe me. But at least he wasn't crying anymore. And he was listening.

"But first, I wanna show you a magic trick."

That caught his attention. I wasn't reading everything, not yet. That was going to take some time because this guy was good at not showing people what he was thinking. But my guess was that he had already seen some magic in the last twenty-four hours.

"Now, most people think that magic is a bunch of bullshit. And most of it is—all misdirection and stage theatrics. But some magic, just a *wee* itty-bitty little bit of it, is as serious as a heart attack. It's killer hard to pull off correctly, but it can be done. And right now, during the witching hour, it's as easy as falling off a log."

I put my cigarette in my mouth, then pulled the right sleeve of my jacket back and up and showed him my arm from hand to elbow. I spread my fingers wide, and turned my forearm back and forth. Simple magician stuff. Nothing up this sleeve, folks.

"Watch. Now, I'm going to pour my drink into my hand, and it's going to vanish."

I curved my right hand, picked up the coffee with my left, and I poured the contents of my coffee cup into my right palm. Sixteen ounces vanished into that space.

"Neat, huh?"

I pulled my cig out of my mouth with my right hand, turned it back and forth. My whole arm still showing.

"Here's where it gets weird."

I showed him the empty cup. Banged it against the table, flipped it end over end, and caught it like one of those fancy flair bartenders. Then I put the cup next to my hand and poured the still-steaming coffee back into it. Then I took a sip and grimaced.

Bad coffee, and now with little grains of sand floating in it.

"Ta-fucking-da."

He looked at me, and a corner of his mouth flickered up. Not a smile although a stupid person might have mistaken it for one and gotten his ass killed for it. This was his angry look. His grimace of frustration and disdain. The classic "I'm about to hit you" look.

He finally spoke. "Fuck off."

Damn. Deep voice, too. This guy was built to be a leg breaker the same way I was built to use step stools and buy children's clothing.

"I'm not fucking with you here, man. I'm serious, as I say, as a heart attack—

there's nothing you can say right now that can get you in more trouble, and there's nothing you can say that's going to freak me out. I've seen people walk through walls, I've seen dead people get up and order room service, and I've seen people peel off their own faces like a mask."

I raised my eyebrows and didn't finish the thought about what was underneath some of those faces.

He looked at me, and I saw something give.

"Yeah."

"Yeah. So, you saw something today. Something that freaked you out. Something bad."

He moved his head a little on the end of a giant neck like you see in action movies and mixed martial arts fights.

Didn't nod but almost.

I was on the money, but there was more than that. Guys like him don't cry because they get freaked out. Something bigger than that. What could make this guy shut down entirely?

"So, we're gonna talk about it. What you say to me here, it's not about you going to jail or you giving me the details of your relationship with your boss or anything like that. I don't want your money, I don't want your confession, and I don't want you to tell me anything except about what weird shit happened to you today."

He nodded. Just a little bit, but he nodded.

"This is gonna suck, kinda, because my guess is that something pretty nasty happened. So I'm not gonna push it, and we don't have to do this here. Believe it or not, I've been on the other side of this. Only worse, even, maybe. You tell me what's going on, and we'll go for a walk. You and I have got all the time in the world."

Just then, the door behind me opened up, and a screaming clown with hollow eye sockets grabbed me by the back of the head.

In one quick motion, it wrapped its fingers around my skull, picked me up with one arm, and pitched me across the room.

It moved faster than anything I'd ever seen.

Especially since I could only see it out of the corner of my in-motion and rapidly watering eye for the half-second it took for the rotting clown to flash across the room. When I landed, I realized that I didn't have my knife anymore.

The leg breaker screamed, and the clown punched my blade into the poor guy's throat a couple dozen times.

Fuck. There went all my good vibes and sexy investigative groundwork with Ladislav.

Lacking anything better to do, I scrambled up, grabbed my chair off the floor, and smashed it across the thing's lower body.

I called upon my crown. The dust of my empire surged inside me, and for one moment, I wielded the strength of millions.

I might as well have whacked the chair into the side of a building.

An explosion of wooden shrapnel filled the air, and now I had two handfuls of kindling. The clown turned to me and started shaking all over. Blood jetted out my perp. The little green poof-balls down the front of the clown's torso jiggled, and its screams went up an octave.

Didn't say it was a plan, or even a good plan.

I said I lacked anything better to do.

It rushed at me, pulling the knife back. I scrambled to the side, but it was on me in an instant. I realized as it crouched onto me that it wasn't really wearing clothes, technically: it was, in reality, a grotesquely deformed naked man painted like a clown with wet little tufts of brightly colored organic fuzz, like flopping sea anemones, jabbing out of puckered bullet-wound-like holes.

Something hard dropped into my hand as the thing tackled me to the floor, and I was too afraid *not* to look. The handle of my knife. The clown suddenly stopped screaming, and I noticed that, despite the otherwise overwhelming amount of nudity my assailant was displaying, he was wearing white circus gloves. I closed my hand around my knife, waiting for the clown to do something—anything.

My cellphone rang. I fished it out of my pocket as the clown hopped up and sprinted out the door. As it fled, I saw that the clown's back was rotten with sores and covered in wet, black stains, like it had been lying in a half inch of water in someone's basement for a month.

If it had wanted to kill me, it probably could have.

But it didn't.

And, at the moment, I couldn't think for the life of me *why*.

My phone kept ringing as I shook there, in shock.

The caller ID said *unlisted*.

"Hi, there. You've reached Royden Poole, Secret King of Jangladesh. I'm not in right now."

"It seems that you've just been framed for murder, Mr. Poole. My advice is to leave town before midnight. This case is closed for you."

"Damn."

"Indeed."

I could hear him. He was just about to hang up. Fuck, fuck, fuck.

"... so real quick, where are you the king of?"

There was a pause, and I heard him start hating me, right there in the silence.

But he had to answer.

Had to. Or forfeit his throne.

"I am the King of Majooj."

"Never heard of you. So, quite a nasty kiddy-scare you called up, Your Highness. You dabble quite a bit in summoning from the Sideways Realms, I take it."

"I have many servants. You've been warned."

Click.

Well, fuck.

I walked out the now-broken door, letting the perp's body cool in the interrogation room. Forensics was going to have a field day with this one: four-foot-tall guy walks into a room, kills a three-hundred-pound guy by stabbing him in the neck until his head nearly comes off, lets the body sit for a few hours, breaks open a battering-ram-proof door, and then just teleports out of a police station all in the space of about thirty seconds.

I kept my knife out, in case you were wondering.

The hallway was deserted, as I expected it to be. In the distance, I could hear the sound of the killer clown's enormous bare feet slapping down the stairs at about seventy miles an hour. Heading for the sub-basement sub-archives, which was probably where his slippy-hole to the Sideways was hidden. Otherwise, I was alone: not a cop to be found in the cop shop tonight.

Well, nothing to do now but raid the evidence locker.

CHAPTER 2

As I went through the evidence locker, trying to find something that might clue me in to what my ill-fated leg breaker was about to tell me before his stabbing or perhaps score myself a sweet new pimp cane, I considered the inherent problems with the 25th Hour and Tama's old love affair with it.

In short, the witching hour is a pain in the ass.

I hadn't used the damn thing in months, of course. Living in that little rat hole pretending at death, there were already too many goddamn hours in the day—it didn't seem like much of a bargain to score myself a little extra time *just for myself* when I was already living alone too much as it was. And sure, I could leave the apartment when the clocks got funny and go wander around for a bit, but the streets were, for the most part, just as empty as my apartment.

And the very few people you do meet in the Nether Time are universally such shit that it's better to be alone.

Come to think of it, that applies to the waking world, too.

The mysteries of stepping between the ticks of almost-midnight and behind the curtain of the real world were joyous to Tamaka, of course. She couldn't believe that I would ever get bored with such a place—couldn't believe that I didn't have scads of magician friends and Sideways Realm pets, a big throne for my kingdom and an amazing new life every night. She wanted to know all about the Totem Empires, and why the most potent magicians choose noble titles of ancient and fallen kingdoms. She drug me out night after night to find misty places a few blocks from our apartment where reality becomes un-anchored and the dreamtime re-writes its own rules—where the streets drift off into forever-after land.

God, I miss that girl.

The truth is that once you stumble into the knowledge of the Other Interval, your best bet is to ignore it and hope that it goes away. There are treasures to be had there only for the sorrowful and the insane. Everything fades to dust except the scars.

Shit.

Look at me here, getting all teary-eyed and morose. Pretty soon, people are going to start mistaking me for Detective Ladislav's weepy contract killer.

Fuck my life.

My one and only real regret, upon further consideration and introspection, is that I didn't burn Frieda Baghaamrita's fucking bar to the ground the last time I was on this side of the Hour.

That bitch.

I kept going through the bins.

Finally, I found the tape of my big buddy's earlier interrogation. It was labeled with this morning's date and a name I didn't recognize: Kynan. It wasn't rewound, but I figured what the fuck, right?

Let's jump right to the good parts.

I tossed it in, rewound a minute or so, and started it up. There in glorious, extra-scratchy black and white was my old friend the detective, and there was my lovable leg breaker:

Ladislav: Tell me again what happened.

Tattooed-Guy: We were supposed to snag this guy named Alexandros. We were told to grab him as he came out of this deli on Clark Street and then bring him to Mr. Bohdan's penthouse.

Fuck. Back when Ladislav said that he had missing persons' reports on rich people, I didn't realize that he meant Fadey Bohdan, the head of Ukrainian crime in the tri-state area. Jesus.

Why do I answer my phone at night?

L: But you weren't supposed to rough him up?

TG: No. He was real clear, the guy on the phone. He said that Alexandros had this nervous condition, where he would freak out if we beat on him and maybe have a heart attack or something.

I could tell that my leg breaker was lying, but I wasn't sure if Ladislav knew yet. And it wasn't a big lie—just a little bit of an omission, with some embroidery on top of the truth. Playing dumb, and he was good at it. Oh, my stars and garters, how I would love to find out what the guy on the phone had actually said.

L: So your job was to take this guy to Fadey Bohdan's penthouse. Then what?

My honed bullshit detectors went off, catching something on the leg breaker. Just a twitch. Something weird. But what?

TG: Just... nothing. He said to take him there. Me and Noel were just supposed to take him to the penthouse. The guy on the phone told us the code for the elevator and everything. Said to make sure the 'package' was unharmed.

L: And this didn't strike you as strange?

TG: No, I... I just figured that maybe this Bohdan guy wanted to have a meeting with Alexandros personally, and he didn't trust any of his guys to do it. We were outside muscle, you know?

Bullshit. This guy Kynan was too smart to have fallen for that. He knew that part of this was weird from the get-go. The money had to have been something amazing.

About that time, I started getting paranoid.

L: So the two of you picked up this Alexandros as he was leaving the deli. And he went quietly?

TG: Yeah. He was real calm about it, just like the guy on the phone said he would be. Put his hands where we could see them, didn't make a fuss or anything. Got in the back of the car with Noel, and basically stared at the gun a lot.

L: And you drove him to the hotel?

TG: It was all real simple. We got there, and Noel takes his coat off and puts it over his arm, covering the gun. The three of us get out and walk to the lobby. There's only this one elevator that goes all the way up to the one penthouse where Bohdan lives, so we go to it and we hit the button and we wait.

Now I could see that Ladislav was getting serious: his frown intensified and it looked like those big bushy eyebrows of his were trying to meet in the middle and then make a run south toward his chin and a new life together. Ladislav had heard this part before. He knew this whole story like the back of his hand.

It was what was coming next that was important.

L: Then what happened?

TG: We fucking get in the elevator, like I told you. And we press the right buttons in the right order, like the guy on the phone said to, and we're heading up to the penthouse. That's all.

L: And then?

TG: And then, I think... I don't know. I guess I got a call on my cellphone, I think.

L: You think?

TG: Yeah. And we're in the elevator, and we're going up, and the guy on the phone, I remember: He said to shoot Bohdan when I get there, block the elevator doors from closing and then leave through the emergency fire exit. It seemed... I don't know. It made sense.

L: Bullshit, Kynan.

This was not bullshit, but Ladislav couldn't believe it. This was, honest to god, a very competent guy trying very hard to piece together something very confusing.

TG: But it made sense! When I got out of the elevator, I remember thinking why else would I be here?

L: Bullshit. So where were Noel and Alexandros during this?

TG: Like I told you before, they just... weren't there anymore. I didn't even remember that they had been there. Christ, I didn't remember that... that either of them even existed until this morning!

He burst into tears. That was the sound of somebody breaking.

Ladislav had that disgusted look on his face that meant he was confused or catching a whiff of rank body odor. Or both.

I had been responsible for giving him that look in a variety of ways over the years.

L: I'm fucking done here.

The detective stormed out of the room, and the tape ended.

I could have rewound it, and checked the tape to see what hotel they had been talking about, but I had a different plan.

If I had to guess, I'd say that the good detective had, by this point, already pieced together that our leg breaker Kynan was in love with his partner, Noel. Or, if it wasn't romantic, he at least loved Noel like a brother. That much was obvious, just seeing the tears. What the detective couldn't believe was that a professional killer and all-around-dangerous criminal like our tattooed guy could get into an elevator with a hostage and his best friend or lover, ride fifty-two stories straight up and then forget that either of them existed or why he was on the goddamn elevator to begin with.

And then, several hours later, have that knowledge come back and hit him hard enough to break him.

Which brought me to my next question: Had this all gone down at around, oh, say... midnight last night? That would make a certain sense—I had assumed that Ladislav wanted me to interview Kynan during the witching hour to save himself some time. I mean, I could spend days with him if I needed to, and it would all collapse back to a tenth-of-a-second burp in time-space as far as Ladislav was concerned. But if someone was using the Enigma Hour to commit clever breaking-and-entering, then it made sense that Ladislav needed me here, now...

Speaking of questions, where were Alexandros and Noel now?

Also: How had my tattooed guy gotten caught? Was the legendary Fadey Bohdan dead, or just missing? And, since Ladislav had mentioned it, what *other* wealthy man-about-town was missing in action at the moment? And what about the vanished vase? And who was the King of Majooj, and why was he framing a dead man for murder?

I glanced at my cellphone.

11:79J3 qm.

Stupid goddamn secret time. Always trickling by when you weren't watching. If I wanted to keep from slipping back into reality, I needed to put some distance between me and all the human anchor points in this building, which meant taking a long walk into the deeper sections of the Epoch In-Between. That meant going someplace unaccounted-for by the masses: abandoned steam tunnels, back alleys without names, all the little places where people don't go in crowds.

Hm. What to do, what to do?

I looked around the evidence locker, scanning for anything else worth slipping into my coat. There wasn't a gun in here that I could trust, and there were no other tapes marked with Kynan's name. There wasn't anything else that I... holy shit! My old hat!

I popped my battered old Yankees cap back onto my head with a smile on my face. Alright, so this wasn't a complete waste of an evening.

I pulled out another cigarette and pondered.

What I really needed to do was retrace Kynan's steps, find out where he had been.

Simple enough. I just needed his shoes.

Fifteen minutes later, I was standing on the front steps of the police station drawing a complex diagram with chalk, waving Kynan's stolen steel-toed Brahmas back and forth like a pendulum and muttering a few magic words. I smudged the diagram with the bottoms of the boots, stained the soles a whitish-yellow with chalk dust and smoke, and then watched a series of faded footprints appear, stretching into the station and backward a full twenty-four hours. He walked into the station, huh? Interesting.

Well, let's hope that he didn't walk too far off the beaten path today. Didn't want to meet any more Sideways horrors tonight.

Actually, I didn't want to meet *anyone* else tonight.

CHAPTER 3

I walked and smoked and muttered to myself and kept waving Kynan's shoes in front of me, dangling by their laces, like a priest in some bad movie about Catholics. *In nomine parti-favor*, or whatever. The footprints were a jumbled, horrible nightmare on the darkened empty streets, compounded by the weird, winding smudge-skate streaks of him getting into, out of, and riding around in cars, making weird striations across the road and out into the distance.

It looked like Kynan had been involved with a busy, shitty day.

Well, at least it had ended with getting murdered. If you're gonna do *bad day*, I mean, you might as well do it right.

Finally, I brought myself to an intersection where the footprints ran every which way: back, forth, around and around. Kynan had done some serious pacing, driving, and general fucking about at this location today. At least three sets of prints headed left, down a street toward the legendary penthouse where I was pretty sure Fadey Bohdan was usually sleeping at this time of night on top of a huge pile of cocaine, money, and Eastern European sex-slaves.

Goody for him, the evil fuck.

I hope his day was worse than mine, for once.

Another set, pointed toward me, kicked backward across the road and out toward the parts of town where three-hundred-pound guys covered in tattoos don't get bothered while they're eating soup.

Here was the real question: was it worth more to me at the moment to see the spot where the magic happened and the mysterious deed was done, or was it better to see where Kynan had spent the earlier part of his day before he suddenly came here and skipped at least halfway to and from one of the nicest hotels in the city a few times before going to the cops?

Oh, yeah, and how was I going to explain a dead suspect to the cops? Also, who the fuck was the King of Majooj, again, and why was he framing me for murder using a monster clown? Also, why had Ladislav kept my hat so long? What kind of jerk does that?

I flicked my cigarette into the street, considered, and then walked toward the hotel, my all-too-stubby legs already starting to cramp. If it had pulled Kynan toward it a half-dozen times today, it had to be the most interesting part of the puzzle.

Across the street, a homeless guy on the other side of the road about a half block down waved at me. Dammit, why do you think I want to talk to you?

"Hail, hail, thou Secret King! A farthing, thee, for an exiled Prince of Minos?"

"Fresh out both of farthings and of giving-a-fucks, guy. I'm just passing through."

He started across a street filled with little more than wind, pausing to look both ways. Yeah, like this town is real well-known for heavy traffic between the hour of 11:8888 and 11:#W2OIJ in the qm.

What an idiot.

"I do know of thee! Thou art the Child Emperor!"

"Look, thou doesn't know jack nor shit. I'm no kid. I'm armed, and I'm off to see the wizard right now, so don't bother me."

"I didst hear that thou wast dead!"

Crap. I turned.

"Alright, buddy. Yeah, I'm dead. How much to keep it that way?"

"Ah, well, mine followers and I do seek some treasures with which to, unto ourselves, raise a mighty army, with which we shall claim back all the dust of Minos from my upstart, usurper brother! And cousins. And also mine nieces and nephews. I do have many enemies which claim my throne."

"Oh, very noble. A good old succession-struggle for the whole family. Glad to help the war effort. So let me guess—minimum donation to the cause is $20?"

"If thou wouldst be so kind."

He grinned at me with a mouth full of black teeth-stumps as I pulled out a crumpled pair of tens. Fuck.

There went my rent money for the week. Being dead is not as cheap as the liberal media likes to make it out to be.

"There. You can probably recruit a strong young warrior by the name of Jack Daniels to your cause now."

"Verily."

Taking a look at the haggard old guy as he bowed to me, I dug into my pocket for a second and fished out another ten.

"Since I've got you here, prince, you wanna tell me a little bit about the local weather? Sports scores, anything?"

"Oh, it would be an honor! Perhaps my guest, this short and traveling king, would care to share with me some of his fine and flavored smoking tobaccos?"

"Yeah. It's real fancy hand-picked Samsun and Izmir Turkish with domestic blend."

He palmed a Camel and lit it with an Elizabethan flair, stuffing my thirty dollars into his back pocket. He exhaled with gusto, and his eyes somehow got more bloodshot. Then the theatrics began in earnest.

"Mine nameless king, there are dark tidings afoot in this land! I warn thee, thou must travel warily and forearmed against the dangers in the All-Night Hour! Formless Magistrates of the Farthest Sideways have set their many eyes upon these very streets! A shadow comes, and the lords of many Emptied Empires shall fall!"

"Great. You hear anything about clowns?"

"Nope."

"Awesome. You know anything about a guy skimming the pocketbooks of the waking world using the Nether Time?"

"Such things are dark, damnable, and dangerous, my miniature and wandering king!"

"And deadly, too. Just wondering. Keep an ear out, will you?"

I passed him another ten. Now, I was all-but-officially broke.

"Of course, ye goodly king! How shalt I find thee if some word cometh mine way? By your sign or another?"

"Please don't. I'll find you."

I stomped off, heading toward Fadey Bohdan's hotel. My amateur medievalist hobo stared at my back, and I hoped to god that I hadn't just gotten fucked by fate yet again. Last thing I needed tonight was word that my death had been slightly exaggerated to filter through what passes for a community in these parts.

And now I was worried that forty bucks in the hand of this asshole wouldn't be enough to guarantee that.

Stupid dire warnings of imminent doom.

They always put me in a bad mood.

Ten minutes later—a bit give or take, considering where and *when* I was—I stood across the street from the gorgeous, opulent, white Le Palace Resplendent, cake-like structure made of glitter and glass and light and fuck-off-you-filthy-stinking-foreign-midget, you.

The tracks had dwindled to a single loop: Kynan had walked in there this afternoon and walked right back out along the same path, right toward his date with the cops and me and destiny and a neck-stabbing clown. Inside that building, I could follow his footsteps and gauge where he went and what he had looked at today. Maybe work out what he had been thinking, roll his motives around in my head a little bit.

Only one problem: That building was made of almost nothing but human anchor points. Overflowing with them. Every damned square inch of carpet in that damned place is accounted for. People have lived and died obsessing over every scrap of fabric and stone and grout on the premises. They host five proms, a debutante's ball, some douchebag's re-election rally, three art shows, a half-hundred-some weddings and the Policeman's Benevolent Dinner here every year, for gods' sake. The picture of the mayor that the chief of police keeps on his desk was taken on the front steps, right there.

Something tells me that there are a few unaccounted-for spots in there, though. Probably up toward the penthouse. But if I cross this street, I'm getting yanked back into the waking world's time stream whether I like it or not. Dammit.

Using the 25th, as I had tried to teach Tamaka, is like walking a tightrope. If you saunter out onto it drunk and without a care in the world, you're not going to be there very long, one way or the other. Probably break something, too. You panic and freak out and lie down and grab onto it and try to keep from slipping, well... you could be hanging out there to dry for a lot longer than is entirely healthy.

You have to keep moving, and you have to keep between the anchor points and the slippy holes—the yin and the yang of mankind's oh-so-tenacious and yet oh-so-tenuous hold on the reality of the waking world. The places where people gather in numbers every day, those places will drag you home. And the places where not even rats hide, where maybe one lone human bothers to check in on once a month? Those slippery fuckers gape open into the Sideways.

Of course, she just wanted to talk about the metaphysics of it all. How the face of the clock each day is really just the curve of rainwater hanging off an infinite leaf of possibility in a haunted forest of the unreal. How you could escape up the bridge of the drop into a true ocean of quantum time between the big hand and the little hand as they squeezed together at the midnight hour and defined, in defiance, another plane.

Fuck damn shit, I miss that girl.

As I turned back toward downtown, I checked my cellphone just to see how much time I had lost for even daring to impugn the dignity of Le Palace Resplendent with my gaze.

11:9F1 qm.

Great.

Unless I headed toward the shittiest parts of town or out to one of the unpleasantly enthusiastic Long Hour holds in the next couple of minutes, I was going to run out of the Unknown Interval pretty shortly.

As in, too soon for comfort.

Well, the best place to re-enter the waking would definitely not be my apartment, what with me being wanted for murder and all.

So I headed there.

CHAPTER 4

So, as I was breaking into my apartment, my emergency backup screwdriver in hand, I considered further the nature of the fractured semi-reality we call 13 Past and the Nether Time and the Secret Epoch and a bunch of other equally bullshit names for a thing that simply shouldn't be.

Point is, there's this weird thing about the Nether Hour that makes using it so damnably frustrating to casual users of the free time and that separates the hardcore addicts who eventually get around to claiming an Emptied Empire as their own from the so-called "hourists"—tourists of the hour. The fact of it is, there's a lot of stuff that you simply can't do during the 25th, and there really aren't a lot of hard and fast rules as to *why*—at least, not that either me or crazy old Cleon could ever quite make heads or tails of.

Oh, hell.

Now *there* was a guy I hadn't thought of in a couple months, minimum. My manic mentor, the esteemed Mr. Cleon Quiet. Just thinking his name and playing it across my lips made me smile. Taught me everything I know, or at least everything worth me knowing, and only asked that I help him sweep up around his miserable little VCR repair shop at nights and not poke at any of the old Betamax cassettes that sometimes shook, howled, and ran blood out of their single, cyclopean spindles.

And then I actually started giggling out loud, remembering the time that I used the term *cyclopean* in front of him. Cleon asked me what, precisely, the cassettes had to do with brick or masonry constructions made without mortar; I, of course, quickly countered that the word also means "suggestive of the cyclops." And he told me to watch my smart mouth while trying not to let me see him smile and be proud.

Anyway, the venerable old King of Urartu had a trick against the Sideways horrors, which he liked to call a black tape exorcism, and kings back in the day used to travel tens of thousands of miles loaded down with tribute in gold and silk to have him perform it on them.

Of course, he also had that weird lop-sided haircut which always reminded me of Sam Jackson from *Unbreakable*, and he always wore 3D glasses for no particularly explicable reason I could fathom. And he still owns a damn VCR repair shop in the third millennium CE, so I feel justified in calling him just the slightest bit bat-shit insane.

Anyway, the point that Cleon impressed upon me about the Hole behind Midnight was this: it all sounds great on paper, but the fine print is a real motherfucker, and nobody can quite make out what it says. Sure, here's this magical extra hunk of time space, tucked away right there at the top of the clock where anybody with an ounce of sense in their head can tell that three hands converging to mark the death of the day has some mystic significance. Yeah, you can squeeze through that crack with a little practice—and you can go walking around in the backstage of reality for hours or even days in the hiccup of time that it takes the audience to blink twice and then go back to the show.

But the place behind the curtain ain't the same as the place lit by the footlights and the spot. There's a whole new set of rules back here, and the farther you step away from the crowd, the weirder it gets. Everything keeps turning, too; that's important to remember. Just because you've slipped further afield from the warm little center of home where all the nice boys and girls have been tucked away into bed by their mommies who love them, all to go creeping around in the ghost lights doesn't mean that the outer rim of the universe is holding still.

If you head around the stage flats behind the curtains and walk past the props table where the old relics from previous scenes are gathering dust in the dim half light, where the kohl-caked characters from old, half-forgotten dance routines are playing at improv and flirting with each other, and skirt the twitching, fraying ropes which hold the stars in the heavens, and sneak past reality's dressing room back to the iron emergency fire doors pressed into the scene shop wall, you can head down forever into the wet sub-basements below everything.

Don't be surprised if whatever you find down there doesn't particularly want to help you sing out the chorus of "Oklahoma," though. If the things that lurch around muttering in the winding boiler room or those that scuttle across the damp, broken-tile floors of the rotting nurseries in the darkness underneath the playhouse even know about the big bright show going on upstairs, they don't much care if you miss your next cue.

In all your lipstick and stage jewelry and big panicked eyes rimmed in mascara, you're just as pretty and sweet as a little doll made of sausage to the boogieman in the bathroom under the basement stairs. And don't forget that if you never come back out on stage for your big number, well, the show must go on.

The crowd probably won't even notice.

Point is, some things from the waking world work just fine during the 25th. And some things don't. And some things that *don't* work during the daylight hours—or at least, aren't *supposed* to work—are the norm during the Unknown Interval rather than the exception. And the real screaming hell of it is that a whole bunch of stuff is in-between. There are scads of cases in the *maybe* category—the *either/or*. The miserable *kinda-sorta, it really depends* factor that drives 21st-century consumers nuts.

Like cash, for one. If you bring it with you into the Nether Time, it's there— but if you walk up to an unattended cash register and pop the bastard open, assuming that you can get it to open in the first place, the till is invariably empty.

You can write things down while in the 25th, but they fade out into nothing sooner or later. You can move certain objects around, at least the ones that *translate* into the Secret Time, but mundane things have a nasty habit of becoming heavier, more stubborn, or just altogether nonfunctional. Some doors are locked and won't budge. Some windows just won't break. Cars simply won't start. A television roots itself to reality, immovable, and plays nothing but static.

Well, if you're lucky, it's just static. Sometimes, it's faces.

A cellphone works, and don't ask me why. Cleon still has this crazy-ass theory about the totemic significance of the clock and the mystic *eye*—that being the little camera—held within the modern mobile phone, along with the quantum nature of a missing cell, which cannot call itself, and the pocket's connection to the root chakra, but whatever.

In his defense, he did once successfully make a long-distance call from a pack of Camels after he wrote *fone* on it in marker, drew in a rough Eye of Providence on top of the pyramid next to the camel's ass, taped a wrist-watch to it and stuck it in his jeans for a week, so I guess he might be on to something.

Also, some people have figured out a trick for using an old-fashioned pocket watch as a compass in the 25th, but I've never gotten it to work. Supposedly, the hands twist around and point things out if you hold it right and concentrate correctly, and it will swing on its chain in the direction of home, but it all looks like a lot of Ouija board mumbo-jumbo to me.

The upshot is this, at least in general:

1) Things that belong to no one, things that most people don't pay close attention to, like dust or magazines in a waiting room or individual pens in a cup or napkins in their dispensers, are all fair game. They show up in the 25th, they can be pocketed, moved around, or whatever. The mass consensus just keeps putting along like nothing ever happened.

2) Things that belong to you, that no one but you is paying attention to, are yours. They click and whir along just fine on either side of the curtain: for instance, a car that you're driving at the moment the clocks get funny keeps going. At least, in theory. The scary part comes when you look over at the guy asleep next to you and realize that he's not there anymore, that the sky has changed color, and then your battery dies along the side of a highway without a name or a spot on the map.

3) Things that belong to someone else or that someone else is paying attention to are either missing or damn near impossible to move on the other side. You can't snatch a food processor or stereo system out of someone's apartment using the Unknown Interval, even if you could get the door open. If someone is watching that TV at the time, same goes—that is, if it shows up at all. More valuable things, like bars of silver, nude photos of exes and celebrities, and paintings by people whose names you recognize only translate to the Nether if they come with you.

4) Things with an intrinsically mysterious technical operation, like a computer (try explaining how one works to the average guy on the street in a single sentence) or a vending machine (same thing) act, for lack of a better term, wonky. Things with a lot of emotional significance invested in them, like teddy

bears and photo albums, also behave really strangely during the 25th. And the more something looks like a person or a part of a person, like a mannequin or a set of false teeth, the worse it gets.

5) Things that everyone knows about sometimes simply don't pop over, or do, but twisted. There's a Statue of Liberty in the 25th Hour, but she looks really fucked-up. I don't know why.

And for every rule, there are two dozen exceptions. Guns are the worst offenders because they straddle several lines of ownership and focus of attention, with the added bonuses of being generally mysterious in their operation (try building one at home!), being emotionally significant to pretty much everyone who has ever seen one, owned one, or had one pointed at them, and being vaguely shaped like a phallus with a part specifically designed for a human hand to hold onto.

A gun that shows up in the Nether Hour either won't work, will work forever without needing to be reloaded but fire hunks of stiff cartilage and super-sonic semen, will fire bullets that fly at about thirty miles an hour making wasp noises and hunting people down, will do nothing but yell "BANG!" in a high-pitched voice just loud enough to wake people up, or will maybe just yank the guy who pulls the trigger through the grip and spit him in a bloody, nine-millimeter-wide spray out the barrel.

Or, quite possibly, something even weirder.

And the other thing to remember is this: I've been doing this for years, and I'm still surprised 99% of the time I step through.

The worst part, of course, is that there are a dozen or more fail-safes in place to prevent things like teleporting televisions and sudden mysterious deaths and vanishing cash-register contents from peeling the curtain back and exposing the average dude to the eternal mysteries of the Eternity Hour, but things happen anyway.

You smell someone close, but they aren't there and never were.

The lights dim for a second and only you seem to notice it.

Someone sets their keys down on their chest of drawers at 11:59 pm, and at 12:01 am, the keys are sitting on the floor.

About half a million people in the US vanish each year and are never found or heard from again.

A cash register rings at exactly midnight, even though no one is touching it—and the drawer stays closed.

Your cat freaks out in the middle of the night, and when you look up, you realize that you apparently didn't close your apartment door all the way. Nothing is missing from your room, but a month later, you can't find that snow globe your grandmother gave you that you put in the back of your closet because you never liked it.

A large man named Kynan gets punched several times in the neck with a knife belonging to yours truly, while everyone in the observation room of interrogation pulls a booger out of the corner of their eye and the camera burps twice and misses sixteen-dozen frames.

All of this is, interestingly enough, what led me to breaking into my apartment. Neither the door nor the hallway of the apartment building technically belongs to me. The whole shebang belongs to some douchebag slumlord somewhere in Idaho, and my key does not turn in the lock when applied during the times of 11:60 and 11:99.

So here I am, as alone in the universe as I could ever hope to be.

Imagine my surprise, then, when I finally busted in and found the King of Cahokia standing in my living room with Tamaka.

CHAPTER 5

Well, hot-diggity shit. I've got the door handle and deadbolt to my front door ripped out of their sockets, a screwdriver in one hand, and a very startled expression on my face.

I did my best to raise an eyebrow ironically.

"Is this a bad time? I wanted to talk to you about Vampire Jesus, but I can just leave some literature downstairs, if that would be better..."

"Royden Poole, King of Jangladesh, I seek an audience with you."

Fuck. Of all the guys in the world for Tamaka to have hooked up with after I died, why did she have to pick the goddamn King of Cahokia? I stared at his perfect, chiseled jaw and his perfect, chiseled physique all wrapped up in perfect, chiseled denim, leather, and raven feathers, trying to decide all over again if he looks more like a blond Aragorn or a manlier, taller Legolas.

I kicked a glance to Tama. She looked pissed and nervous and sad and guilty and disappointed and ten thousand other emotions that made me want to stab myself right in the face with the screwdriver.

Tearing my gaze from Tam, which took actual effort, I watched the King of Cahokia slip his hand into his pocket, putting away a phone so much fancier than mine that I wanted to puke.

Yes, he was standing in my apartment texting somebody.

I somehow actually hated him even more, now.

"Your Majesty. Tamaka. Hope I'm not interrupting. For some reason, I was pretty sure that I had left the stove on, but now that I'm here, I remember that I don't even have a stove. Well, see you later."

"This is not a social call, Royden. My Queen and I require, with you, a word."

Oh, of course, they're married now.

Or "symbolically bonded" or whatever the hippie magicians say nowadays when they're fucking your ex. What, did I think she would wait until my stubby little brown body was cold before she hopped into bed with the first seven-foot Viking Injun chief to pull a coin out from behind her ear and call her *milady*?

"A word. Got it. And so you broke into my apartment?"

"No, it is you who broke in. We merely walked through the walls."

Shit damn, I have to learn that trick one of these days. As soon as Jangladesh gets a shot at the World Series and I've got a pool of power to the name of my throne, I'm going to hunt down one of the old school kings and get him to teach me a trick or two.

"Great. Well, thanks for not busting up the place. I'm really looking forward to getting my security deposit back."

I stepped inside and kicked the door handle and deadbolt so recently removed from my door under the couch. Glancing at the two of them as I pulled the door closed and walked to the couch, I lit a smoke. The perfect blond bastard wrinkled his nose in slight disgust.

"I have entered your imperial territory without your leave, and for that I apologize."

I look at Tama. "Is that what they're calling it now?"

She suddenly hated me very much.

Fine. I'd go ahead and settle for one solid emotion.

"I have traveled many miles and incurred great expense to meet with you, Royden."

"You know, and this is so embarrassing—since we're on a first-name basis and all and you're standing in my office-slash-bedroom-slash-kitchen-slash-television-room, could you please remind me what the hell your name is?"

Tamaka spoke, "Royden, stop it."

"I am called Garrick Heldane."

"Are you, now? Sounds made up. Let's see some ID."

Tama turned and stormed out. She used the door I had just stripped of a handle rather than walking out through the wall, which I considered a personal victory.

"Royden, I have come at the insistence of my queen to warn you of a great danger."

"Yeah, probably the same great danger that a certain very smelly Prince of Minos just warned me off of. You know the one I'm talking about—the homeless jack-off who never misses an opportunity to flap his yap for a few bucks."

"I do not know the prince of whom you speak, Royden. My court has been contacted in this hour by a potent oracle from the Keeps of Cerro Lampay, allied of old with me and mine, who spoke to us of grave tidings—of a foul darkness which now surrounds you. I merely impart my queen's wishes for your safety."

Bullshit. I believe nothing he says. I pulled my knife.

"I have a grave tiding for you, Your Majesty. You get the fuck out of my apartment right now or I'm going to stab you in the cock."

He opened his mouth to say something, so I popped my neck in the most detached way I know how.

"It would be an obvious case of self-defense, Garrick. Big guy like you, little guy like me, in my own apartment in the middle of the night? Hell, there was a break-in, and I have the keys to the door on me. No court on the planet would convict me. Hope you don't have any priors."

"Please heed my warning, King of Jangladesh."

"Please eat shit and die."

He walked backward through the wall of my apartment.

Then I sat down on the floor, threw my knife at the wall where he had vanished, and idly wondered what Tama did first when she found out I was still alive. What was her first thought?

I mean, she hated me now, and with good reason, but... what was her first reaction?

Did she miss me? Did she hate me? Did she want to throw her arms around me?

Then I cried for a little while.

CHAPTER 6

Later, I found myself walking back toward the seedier part of town carrying a backpack and a duffel bag with every one of my worldly possessions stuffed inside, including the last stash of my cash, which I keep hidden from my drunk-self in my otherwise-empty sock drawer. I was following Kynan's other set of footprints, pretty much at this point just to piss off Tama, Ladislav, the King of Majooj, Garrick fucking Heldane and whoever else had tried to tell me what to do tonight.

Oh, yeah, and the Prince of Minos. Him too.

Fuck that guy for calling my ex.

I checked my watch. 11:9@4 qm.

Shit. Here in a little bit, the clocks stop going funny, and we're back to life, back to reality. When it all collapses in on itself like the madman's quantum wave-state that it is and all the monsters take their ball and go home until tomorrow night. On the far side of the curtain, the really degenerate fuckers who live too close to the Sideways are about to experience the reverse of what everyone in the waking world has been enduring for the last Hour That Isn't—they'll blink, and the universe will cram twenty-four hours of good, solid real-people time into the mix.

I should know. I once lost half a month chasing a bastard named Lowell through the mists. I stepped out on a Friday night and came back down on a Thursday almost two weeks later to find that my utilities had been shut off.

But here's the really sticky part, the thing that mucks with the heads of the kids who took a lot of economics and law enforcement instead of philosophy and theoretical particle physics in college: there was still time, even now, to walk to Alaska if you kept to the right roads. There's an infinite series of numbers between 0.9 and 0.91, just like the infinite series of numbers between 0.91 and 0.910001; the trick is just to squeeze them right. I could go back to my apartment and kick the walls for another 16 weeks, if I wanted to. Or I could walk across the street right now and sit down in the bar where Kynan was hanging out this afternoon when he suddenly felt the urge to panic and walk most of the way over to Le Palace Resplendent a couple times.

But walk it wrong, and I won't see another 12:01 until 2021.

Either way, my one eyewitness is still dead by homicidal Sideways clown, and my neighbors are going to notice a busted-open apartment at the end of the hall pretty soon.

Balls.

Halfway across the road to a bar marked simply as *BAR*, things started getting more solid. The sky cleared up from that awful, off-gray ghost-light lunar eclipse color, and I could hear honking and footsteps echo off the pavement. Bars are good places to get out of the 25th because they're full of crowds and open in the dead of night. Establishments like BAR are also good places to get *in*, because there's invariably one stall in every women's restroom that nobody has bothered to look at closely for a few days, weeks, or possibly months.

I sank back into the waking world on the sidewalk, already a part of the crowd. The first reaction of the few midnight pedestrians directly in front of me was that they hadn't noticed the homeless, dark-skinned midget with a Yankees cap standing there just now, but I pretty obviously had been there for at least a moment or two.

They walked around me and forgot me about six seconds later.

I watched a guy glance at his wrist as he subconsciously avoided me and I had to bite back a bitter laugh.

No need to check my clock.

12:00 am, same as it was a second ago.

I leaned up against the wall and dialed Detective Ladislav. He was going to want to hear from me.

No answer. Probably shitting himself at the moment.

Today had been a real downer for him so far.

My fucking heart went out to him.

Beep. Time to leave a message. What to say?

"Hey there, Detective Ladislav. Sorry to bother you because I know you're really busy right now. Call me back any time, and we can talk about the Yankees."

I popped open the door to the bar called BAR, looked at the guy sitting on a stool, and decided that his name was BOUNCER.

He was surprised to see me, and he didn't bother to cover it well. The true test of civilization in the modern age is to stand there talking with someone with a booger hanging out of his nose, a different skin color, a physical deformity or a stutter and to not mention it.

This guy did not see the need to play at civilization tonight.

"You looking for someone, kid?"

"Not a kid, dickless. I've got fucking sideburns. I'm here to wait for Kynan and Noel. Said they'd be here some time after midnight."

"And who are you?"

"I'm the guy with the duffel bag and the attitude, genius. You want to talk about what's inside the duffel bag, or do I guess correctly that Kynan's business is above your pay grade?"

That made BOUNCER want to have me come inside. I walked to the bar and heaved myself up onto the stool. Fucking barstools. Who makes these fucking things so tall? Glancing up and down the bar at a scattered collection of bikers and boozers, now that I was slightly more at their height, I pulled the largest bill I had been able to scrounge from the emergency stash in my apartment out of my pocket and slapped it on the bar: a twenty.

"I'll take a Coca-Cola Classic."

The bartender walked over with a slight smirk on his face. Looked like a snake oil salesman, dressed like a pimp. Here was my guy.

"You say a Coke?"

"Well, I'd prefer a cold can of Kickapoo Joy Juice, but I assume you're fresh out."

He blinked. I continued, suddenly trying to sound serious.

"Plus, I'm driving. Got my Big Wheel double-parked outside."

He smiled wider, grabbed a plastic cup, jammed it full of ice, and started filling it with something dark off the gun. I looked up and down at all of the other patrons: glassware. This guy was an asshole.

"One coke, then."

Trying not to let my irritation show, "And one of whatever you're having. On me. Keep the change."

I slid him the twenty, took my drink, and looked away. Out of my peripheral, I saw him pocket the bill and begin to mix himself a strong drink of Jack with a twist of Jack. Good, an alcoholic with no one but me to talk to. He looked at the side of my head as I scanned the crowd.

"Hey. What's your name, man?"

"I'm called Big Jimmy Jangladesh."

"Heh. That some kind of Arab name?"

"Nah, I'm Hindu, by way of England. Parents moved to the states when I was a kid."

Now, I'm about as Hindu as Ronald McFucking Donald.

And *Poole*, for the record, is a mis-transliteration from *Pulaj* or something from about three generations back, but this guy doesn't need any *part* of the truth, and it beats the alternative where I say Indian and then have to waste time qualifying "dot-on-forehead-for-holiness Indian" as opposed to "woo-woo, come-to-our-casino Little-Bighorn Indian" since this guy didn't seem like he could find New Delhi on a map of the National Capital Territory of Delhi.

So, I guess, Hindu it is.

"You making a delivery?"

"Yep. Why, am I doing it wrong?"

"No, you just seem. I don't know. You do this sort of thing a lot?"

"What, sit in bars and talk to bartenders? Yeah. But if you mean deliver duffel bags, no. Our regular guy got sick, and I got pulled off my usual job to come here and be a pain in your ass."

I had him, now. He grinned wider, leaning over and putting elbows on the counter: "And what's your usual job?"

"I'm a pit-fighter, duh."

A laugh. I took a long draw of soda and glanced around, gauging my audience. No black guys in here tonight.

I spoke a silent advance-apology to Cleon under my breath.

"No, no, man, I'm just fucking with you. Actually, I do porn. A stunt cock, basically—they shoot some big old black dude about to fuck some chick, and then they switch angles, and it's really me plowing her. I'm half the big black dicks you've ever seen rail a little Midwestern white girl."

That got another grin out of him, the racist asshole. "Is that so?"

"Oh, yeah. I may have an arm the size of a dude's dick, but I've got a dick like a dude's arm."

I let him process that as he sipped his drink. A little drunk. Good.

"No, no, man, I'm just fucking with you. I'm in accounting. Real good at math, which means that I'm real good at cooking the books. Plus, I make the boss laugh."

I finished my soda. Fuck, I had been thirsty.

I started calculating how many blocks I had walked today, and suddenly, my leg-cramps spoke up. Ow.

"So your boss has got you making a delivery?"

"Yeah. Buy me another Coke, and I'll tell you all about when I used to play for the Yankees."

He filled my drink, then set it down in front of me. With a coaster this time, I noticed. International bartender sign language for "hang out, man." I dug into my pocket and produced a fiver. Just about my last. It killed me to do it, but I put it on the bar anyway.

"On the house, man. Who did you say you were delivering for?"

"I didn't say, actually. And if my Coke is free, let me buy you another drink. I insist."

He nodded and filled his glass out of the well, stashing my five in his pocket.

"Who you waiting for, if you don't mind me asking?"

"Some guy called Kydan or something. Supposed to be a big fucker, like a head and a half taller than me, minimum. Did a job last night and is supposed to get paid today. I heard he was in this afternoon and took off, but he's supposed to be here any minute."

The bartender's eye twitched. Shit, this guy was better than I expected him to be. I could barely read fuck all off him except that he knew the name Kynan.

"Haven't seen him tonight. Sorry."

That meant, specifically, that my bartender had seen my leg breaker this afternoon.

"He seem a little off, to you?"

My bartender wasn't expecting that. He looked at the door and at the bouncer.

I continued, "Because I've heard that he was acting weird today. All kinds of freaking out. Saying something about Noel."

My greasy pimp-bartender leaned in and looked at me like he was trying to stare me down over his sunglasses. I realized that this guy probably wore shades a lot during the day. I gave him my most innocent look, with a little bit of a not-too-inquisitive quizzical expression—like I was wondering where Kynan was, both psychologically and physically, instead of trying to figure out the series of thoughts and steps that led him to getting neck-knifed by Slappy, the Sideways Clown.

"I wouldn't fuck with Kynan if I was you, man."

"Shit. Do I look like the kind of guy who fucks with anybody? I mean, except little Midwestern white girls?"

"You just be real careful. Kynan hurts people for a living, but I've never seen him like he was today."

I went for it. "I heard that he ran out of here like he was on fire after somebody mentioned Noel."

He actually paused. Something in his head that hadn't turned over yet clicked for him.

"Yeah. He did. Just be cool, is all I'm saying."

"No worries, man. Cool is my middle name."

My cellphone rang. Ladislav.

"Oooh, I gotta take this. It's my mom."

I got up and walked out of the bar, and I wish to god that I could say that I then went down to the bus station, gave the nice lady with the mustache behind the glass my life savings, and went on a tour of all fifty state capitals.

The end.

Instead, I walked outside, slipped into the traffic of the sidewalk, and answered the phone.

"This is Royden 'Cool' Poole, and I'm a little pissed at you right now, Detective."

"Where the fuck are you, you little fuck?"

"In the beautiful Hawa Mahal in Rajasthan, India, sir. After your perp got perforated, I hopped the quickest flight to Jaipur. Oh, look, a tiger playing a sitar."

"What the fuck happened in there, Poole?"

"If I told you that it had to do with a demon clown from the basement of the universe called into service by the King of Majooj, would you believe me?"

"Fuck you."

"Ah-ha. But you *do* believe that I killed your eyewitness for no reason and then teleported out of a crowded police station? I'm just checking, is all."

"I want your scrawny ass in my office right goddamn now."

"There are people who want me dead, detective. Or at the very least violently inconvenienced. People willing to break a few laws of physics to get that done. So I think I'm going to stick this one out on my own."

"I'm going to find you, Poole."

I glanced over my shoulder just to make sure that nobody from BAR was following me, especially not BOUNCER.

I was clear.

"Yeah, waste all of our time with that. Instead, you should be on the lookout for Noel, Bohdan, and this Alexandros guy. Do you have a physical description on him, or have we narrowed it down to guys who hang out in delis at around midnight waiting for leg breakers?"

He hung up on me. I considered for a moment and then dialed him right back.

"Your little brown ass had better be telling me that you're outside my office, or I'm going to strangle you to death when I find you."

"Alexandros did it. I just don't know how yet. Or, I guess, *what.* But he did it. From you, I need a list of every person who has access to Fadey Bohdan's private elevator code at Le Palace Resplendent but who doesn't have access to the combination of his safe. In exchange, I'll find you Noel."

"I already have Noel—he was found dead at the bottom of the elevator shaft."

Then he hung up. Good. I was getting sick of him, anyway.

Oh, and fuck.

Poor guy. Falling down an elevator shaft is no way to die.

Also, poor me. There went one more person who might have been willing to help me solve this stupid case.

I desperately needed somewhere to think, somewhere to sleep, and somewhere to not get arrested. I flattered myself thinking that there was an all-points bulletin about me going out over the radios right now, but either way, a guy like me isn't too hard for Johnny Law to spot.

I considered calling Tama, realized I couldn't do that, and then hated myself the most of any time that I had ever hated myself before.

I went to Cleon's.

CHAPTER 7

All the lights were on at Happy Happy VCR, just like I expected them to be. A guy with no customers, no wife, no kids, no friends except wizards, and an addictive habit of being wide awake at midnight can keep odd hours when he wants to.

I knocked on the front door and waited. After a moment, a dark, craggy, familiar face wearing 3D glasses appeared on the other side of the CLOSED sign.

"Well, I'll be dipped. It's the kid I heard was dead."

"You heard right. Look, us corpses are freezing out here and have had a long night, man."

The lock slid open, and Cleon grinned that gap-toothed grin that I hadn't realized I missed so much until just now.

"Hail, hail, the King of Jangladesh returns to my hallowed halls."

"I bring a gift to the master and the mighty Courts of Urartu, long and ever may they accept a stranger in the night."

I pulled from my backpack a bent sheet cake emblazoned with the bold words *VERY HAPPY ANNIVERSY*: half-off at the all-night grocery store, due to the egregious misspelling. It was mashed from its trip here crammed in my backpack, too.

Cleon grabbed the thing, smiled, and headed into the shop.

"Let's have a drink with our feast, and a proper welcome from the court. How's a nice warm Pabst Blue Ribbon sound?"

Oh, dear sweet god, yes, I wanted a beer.

"Yeah, no. I haven't magically started pouring alcohol onto my thimble-sized liver since the last time you saw me, Cleon."

"Oh, hell no, not for you. You're having a Kickapoo Joy Juice, as per always. But do you think that a PBR would go well with this cake for the grown-ups?"

"Yes. I believe that this cake was specifically designed to be eaten while drinking warm PBR out of a can."

He returned with a pair of plastic forks and two cans. We sat down on the floor behind the counter and ate right out of the box.

After a few minutes, we pretty much had to talk.

"So, uh... Cleon, how's Miss Molly?"

"Good. So. You're not dead."

"Nope."

"Good. Real damn good, actually. You know, I got a case of that Kickapoo shit there in the back, I always hoped you'd come back by and finish it off for me."

"You honestly seem surprised. You hadn't heard, yet?"

"Heard that you wasn't dead? Hell no."

"Seems to be all the rage tonight, knowing that I'm back amongst the living—or what passes for *living* amongst the secret royalty in this town. I paid a homeless guy forty bucks to keep it under his filthy purple and gold knit cap that I faked the whole thing, and had a confrontation with the King and Queen of Cahokia in my own living room mere minutes later."

"Shit. So you know all about Tama and that white boy?"

"Yeah. Ruined my whole night. Well, at least what little bit of it that hadn't already been ruined."

"Damn shame, you going DOA when you did. But I'm glad you're back. Wish I had known you were coming by, I could have put up some streamers and gotten a clown stripper."

"Eugh. What is it with clowns tonight?"

"What?"

"Nothing. Jesus, with all the people who I don't want knowing I'm not dead when he's broadcasting it to the rooftops, the damn Prince of Minos goes and forgets to tell the pertinent info to the one guy who actually wants to see me alive."

"Wait, you talking *the* Prince of Minos? Chuck Dawg the Second? Real scraggly-looking guy, sleeps out on Clark Street during the day?"

"Sure. That's his MO—all black teeth?"

"Yeah, yeah. I seen him tonight. Hell, he was here twice while I was wandering the televisions during the Witching Hour."

Uhg, again.

Cleon is the one and only guy I know who likes to tune-in to a wall of static and try to catch some not-quite human face screaming behind the snow. I always hate hearing what other people do during the Nether Time, but usually, it's because I always have that feeling that I wasted mine.

Like when you hear that somebody taught themselves Japanese over the summer, started a political action group against whale abuse, and went kayaking with a supermodel while you sat on the couch and perfected throwing a dragon punch.

But with Cleon, I mostly just hate to imagine him in here all alone, poking at his screens while the clocks are funny and trying to get the TV to yell *boo* at him.

"He didn't mention me, I take it."

"No. He's a solid guy usually, too. Got the oracle sight and a tight lip; he just wanted to know if I had heard anything about a king skimming tills on the waking world and offered me a brand new Betamax cassette, still in the plastic, if I could clue him in. Wished I had something to tell him, but when I came up empty, he skedaddled. Popped back a bit later to ask me if I ever head the name *Majooj*, but I couldn't tell him enough to get my hands on that cassette."

I decided not to say what I was thinking. "Huh."

"That guy can find just about anything that anyone has ever bought, sold, or put a price on, is what they say. True royalty of Minos by way of Hades, god of wealth and secrets beneath the earth, is the bullshit propaganda. Anyway, his senses are real sharp magic for gold when he's on the sauce, but he can only track a thing that has a cash value on it. Everything else kinda flutters by him."

Which meant that the Prince of Minos had found me, there on the streets because I have a goddamn price on my head. Which meant that after I paid him, my little homeless bloodhound had been half-cracking my case all night while I bitched about the smelly, sorry bastard to the King of Cahokia. Which meant that Tama and her longhaired surfer boy had been telling the truth.

Which meant that there were oracles across the board getting visions about me for the entirety of the 25th Hour.

Which meant that I had stepped in some serious shit.

"That's... fascinating, Cleon. Truly. So, uh—how much for a quick black tape exorcism?"

CHAPTER 8

Cleon stared at me for a couple of seconds, then wiped the frosting from his lips and took a drag of PBR.

"You want me to run a black tape on you?"

I nodded.

"Normally, I would ask why. But since the last time I asked you to explain your motives, back during that shit with the Forgotten King of Eriu and the Warrior-Princes of Builg, you took off in a huff, disappeared for six months, and then died. I only just got my Royden back, so I'm going to let this one go."

"You can watch the tape when whatever is on me is pulled off."

"We'll see about that. Let me call Milsborough."

He stood up and walked into his office. Crazy old guy still uses a rotary telephone.

I got to my feet and shook out a cig.

"Who's Milsborough?"

"He's my apprentice. And you're gonna have to go outside to smoke—you know that."

"Yeah, yeah, yeah."

Shit, since when does a guy like Cleon get an apprentice?

And, while we're on the subject of shit that doesn't make any sense, what's the Prince of Minos doing asking people about the King of Majooj? Also, who the hell is Alexandros, and why does he want a damn vase bad enough to blow holes in the waking world with 25th Hour bullshit? How is this all put together?

And, most importantly, is it possible to hope that Tama hasn't slept with Garrick yet?

I stood outside and tried to think, killing the last of my pack and opening a new one from the all-night grocery store without even noticing I had done it. The real problem here, I decided, was that I had been dead for too long. Hiding in an apartment had cramped my clever muscles, softened my street smarts, and made me doubt my deductions.

I was out of shape.

I stared at the abandoned construction project across the street.

To be completed in 1997, my ass.

A good few minutes and too many cigarettes to be particularly healthy later, a single headlight cut across the parking lot. A skinny kid on a bright blue Vespa: tight faded-black jeans held up by a white belt, overly complicated short brown hair with a yellow streak in it, and a pair of black horn-rimmed glasses. He was wearing a multi-colored scarf over a form-hugging, pink t-shirt with a crappy, low-resolution picture of a moose and the word *Arbuckle* printed across it in chipped lettering. He was carrying a plastic bag labeled *Value Village*.

I wanted to punch him—and not just because he was exactly the sort of guy that Tamaka would have started salivating for.

He parked, hopped off the scooter, and walked past me without a word. Fucking hipster scum. I went in after him, flicking the sparking embers of my cigarette butt at his trendy pseudo-bike, hoping to set it on fire.

I also hoped, idly, that the goddamn exorcism totally fucked up and a Sideways abnormality would pop out of my torso and eat this guy.

Inside, it looked like Cleon had set off an occult-paraphernalia bomb: candles covered every square inch of available counter space; feathers, shining beads and bells on lengths of oddly-knotted, jumbled hemp, wooden dolls, and bird skulls were strewn on piles across the floor, and Cleon was doing something with chalk on the walls as he read from a dog-eared scroll of printer paper with the old perforation things still hanging off both sides.

The carpet was rolled up, revealing a huge circle painted on the bare concrete beneath. And by *circle*, of course, I mean eye-bendingly complex multi-spiral of wrapped Buddhist *oms*, stylized ankhs, Jesus-fish, and less recognizable symbols.

The kid was fishing more crap out of the plastic bag, setting it all right by the door: black electrical tape, cough drops, Precious Moments figurines, sparklers, and a three-pack of blank VHS cassettes. He put his hand in to grab the last few things, saw me looking at the symbol, and grinned a smug and superior grin.

I had to fuck with him.

"What, no holy water and crosses?"

The kid sighed and then rolled his eyes hard, like I had just asked why the sky was blue with my dick hanging out of my jeans.

"Uh, no." His voice was reedy and high-pitched. "The cross is a dangerous symbol because of the unintended weight behind it. And there's no such thing as holy water."

I looked over at Cleon, who was smiling slightly as he read off the sheet. I decided to play the rube a little longer.

"Ooooh, so the cross has... 'dangerous mystical weight'? But it, like, symbolizes Jesus and tolerance and stuff."

The kid couldn't believe how naive I was. "Does it? Tell that to anyone who's ever had one burned in their front yard. The cross was a symbol of Roman rule, a grim device for slow and painful public torture, humiliation, and execution—the opposite extreme from the quick and painless guillotine or lethal injection."

"Neat."

He wasn't finished. "The wails and cries of the crucified are still active across the 25th, as are the memories of those put to the blade by Crusaders, Conquistadors, witch-hunters, and Nazis bearing the Iron Cross."

He was so damn proud of having memorized all of that.

I started clapping, which pissed him off.

Cleon finally piped up, "He's fucking with you, Milsborough."

"This isn't my first rodeo, kid. No crosses, for the same reason we don't use a sniper rifle to evoke the spirit of John F. Kennedy. And the stylized fish are drawn on down there because they were the first symbols of pre-Imperial Roman Christianity; the loaves and the fishes during the sermons, and Jesus calling the early apostles to be "fishers of men". Very few people have ever been put to death with a Jesus-fish. So, kid—you know why Cleon uses Betamax tapes for the really nasty cases?"

He narrowed his eyes at me.

"It's because Betamax died for our sins."

Cleon laughed, finishing the chalk inscription on the wall and turning around. "In 1975, Sony released the finest quality video-recording machine on the planet; superior in terms of picture quality, tape wear, core-system design, and convenience of use to anything produced since. In 1988, they conceded the format war against their far inferior adversary, and Sony started producing VHS recorders. And why was that?"

I finished his thought. "Because the filthy pagans who bought VHS wanted four-hour long tapes, so they could watch sports instead of classic cinema, and because the saintly format of Beta didn't have porn."

Cleon nodded. "Milsborough, this is an old friend of mine. He used to be more of a pain in my ass than you are now. He hasn't lost his way with people, either."

The kid sort of blinked once, and something like a scowl of embarrassment crossed his face, but there was another emotion, which I couldn't quite parse at the moment. Triumph, maybe. He cocked his head at me. "And where are you the king of?"

That caught me off guard.

I started to answer but then looked over at Cleon. *What an odd and surprising question*, I thought idly to myself.

Cleon was making a face like he had bad indigestion.

His puzzling face. His forehead wrinkled, and his eyes went dark behind the 3D glasses. Something was up.

I looked back at the kid, who still had his hand in the bottom of the bag. He had just asked me point blank about my kingdom—my two options now were to answer him straight out or to lose my claim to the throne. Cleon hadn't told him over the phone who I was. And after a single heartbeat, I realized that Cleon hadn't said my name yet.

Things got interesting, then.

"I asked you what your kingdom was."

The next words out of my mouth had to be—HAD TO BE—the name of my dominion, or the dust of my Emptied Empire would leak out of me. I stood as tall as I could and took a deep breath, swelling while I tried to contain in my almost-four-feet of bone and sinew the majesty of every wasteland-dwelling Jat and Rajput chieftain who ever sang a song with blade in hand beneath a bejeweled sky of glittering stars.

The kid pulled a gun from the bottom of the bag, pointed it at me, and started to stand up. I waited until he flicked his eyes to Cleon.

"ME? I'M THE GODDAMN KING OF JANGLADESH, YOU MOTHERFUCKER!"

I rushed him, shoulder-checked him just a bit off balance, grabbed two handfuls of the kid's shirt right at the base of his ribcage, and pulled. He did what I expected him to do—the same thing that anyone not used to holding a gun would do: pinwheel both of his arms backward to keep his feet and spread his legs to keep his center of gravity low.

If he had been competent, by the way, he would have shot me in the fucking skull. Or punted me in the sternum. Or done one of a million other things that would have fucked up my day. It was a gamble I was willing to take, though. This kid was not going to kill Cleon.

With my hands wrapping into his shirt, yanking him toward the floor, and him trying to keep from falling on top of me, it was going to take him a very, very short amount of time to remember that he had a gun and that I did not.

So I leaned back, and with one of my sneakers, smashed his inner kneecap through the back of his leg.

I may be built like a fat, ugly eight year old, but I have the muscle-mass of a full-grown adult man.

Much more than that when I'm channeling Jangladesh.

Or angry. Or both.

The kid's knee exploded. He screamed, and the direction he was falling shifted significantly. I was anticipating this, so I rolled with him. He was not anticipating this, so he flopped to the floor like a screaming hipster who was having a very bad day.

I heard his gun go off, and I considered idly that it was strangely muffled. More like a potato exploding in a distant microwave than a 9mm.

The two of us fell to the ground, him with much more of an oomph than me, and I decided then and there to break both of his arms. As most of your really good firearms instructors will tell you, it's very difficult to wield a gun effectively with two broken arms.

Anyway, I pulled hard at his shirt as he tried to flip over onto his stomach, scrambling up his torso and punching various soft spots as I found them.

The principles of my fighting style, based primarily on the one time I skimmed an article on the knee-twist grappling techniques of Vovinam Viet Vo Dao and some repeated, often-drunken viewings of Royce Gracie winning UFC 1, 2, and 4, suggest that everyone is about the same height when everybody is lying on the floor hitting each other. Okay, so I'm not pulling off leg locks and shit, but if a two hundred pound Brazilian can wrestle a five hundred pound bastard to the ground and choke him out live on national television, I figure that snuggled up against the carpet is the best place for a guy like me to fight.

Something oily, the size of a Q-tip, fell to the floor next to us and started twitching around like an angry, severed human finger.

I let the guy twist over and get facedown as I hauled myself onto his back. He wasn't a fighter. Any competent guy his size wouldn't have tried to stand up right now, not with a blown-out leg.

He should have stayed on his back, focused, drawn down on me, and popped a bullet between my eyes.

But he didn't, thank the Lord Corporate-Owned Christ and his wacky twin brother, humble Rabbi Yehoshua ben Yosef the Nazarene.

I wrapped the fingers of my left hand into the hair on the back of his head, feeling week-old sweat and mousse catch there; I grabbed the soft spot of his right shoulder as he went to an elbow and squeezed that fucker just as hard is I could.

Somewhere, ten thousand forgotten nomad warriors with skin like caramel and eyes like flecks of obsidian cheered as the wind swept around them. Probably from the backs of horses, but I'm not entirely sure. I should really go to the library and look up some historical facts on my Emptied Empire one of these days.

His shoulder and upper bicep crunched like an empty pack of cigarettes. His elbow gave out on the tiles, and he slipped to the ground. I put all of my weight onto the back of his head and mashed his face into the linoleum. There was a satisfying crunch of teeth.

The gun went off again, and this time I watched it. It was about a foot from me, after all.

His hand squeezed, and the whole gun hiccupped with recoil. The sound was weird: not the sharp, ear-splitting crack of a car backfiring or the dense, thick snap that I expect from good-quality guns I'm firing. It was something like out of a movie. If I had to write it out, it would have been *BOOM!*—written in red ink, with a yellow flash around it, like in a fun kid's comic book.

The window of Happy Happy VCR shattered, and something landed way out in the empty parking lot with a wet plop.

I wrapped my right arm around the hipster's throat, slipped my other arm through his left armpit, worked my hands into a fist behind his shoulder blade, and tightened. It was not easy to do this, because my arms are annoyingly short, but Milsborough had a light frame, and I was excited to make the effort on this one.

He convulsed. I felt something pop in his arm, and then he lost consciousness. Awesome.

When I started breathing normally again, I turned and looked around the rest of the room.

Cleon stared at me from around the edge of the counter, ducked behind cover with only the top of his afro poking over the candle-covered surface. After a moment, I realized that he was looking at the wet thing slapping back and forth slowly on the ground next to me like a thin, oil-coated goldfish.

I didn't even know what to say.

"Um. Sorry about all that?"

"It's all right. You got a smoke I can borrow?"

"You smoke, Cleon?"

"Not since before you were born. I need one now, though."

I dug out two cigarettes and surveyed the damage from my perch on Milsborough's slowly breathing back. Out in the parking lot, something the size of a sardine was twitching in the broken glass. I spared a glance at my oh-so-hip assailant's handgun, and I'll be damned if my first thought wasn't *damn, that's so cool.*

"Cleon, you ever see anything like this?"

He lit his cig with a shaking hand, followed my line of sight with his eyes, then considered.

"Looks like a little kid's idea of the *awesomest* gun ever. Like a water-pistol cap-gun thing. Is this what it fired?"

He kicked the slippery tube-thing on the ground next to me, then looked up at where it had dented the ceiling before falling back onto the tiles. It was long and thin, with an X-shaped crease along it and a suction-cup at the front. A rubber dart. It was grayish-black, and covered with a wetness like KY jelly. It skittered across the ground with the force of his kick, still bending back and forth under its own power like it was having severe stomach cramps. Finally, it came to a rest. As we watched, it bent in half right in the middle and stopped.

I stood up and examined the gun in my hipster-assassin's hand. Cleon was right: it was a sort of unrealistic hybrid-revolver with a barrel like an oversized

Glock: half water-pistol, half dart-gun, half impractical hand-cannon from a comic book, and half giant death-dealing phallic object from a shoot-'em-up video game.

I immediately wanted to pick it up and point it at things and make *pew-pew* noises with my mouth. This was Deep Sideways tech.

I looked away. Across the parking lot, someone's apartment light was on. Cleon was walking into his office. Toward his phone.

"That last shot was loud. Cops will be here pretty quick, one way or another, so I'm going to call this in. You're still dead, right?"

"Uh, yeah."

"Then you take the gun and get going, Royden."

Fuck.

"You gonna be alright?"

"Yeah. But this sacred space is fucked for doing anything remotely like an exorcism any time soon. I'll call you when we're clear."

On the floor, the little gray dart was deflating with a thin farting sound, turning into a loose clump of nothing.

I shouted into the office, "What about your apprentice?"

"He's an employee," came from inside. "I'll tell the po-po that he let himself in with a key, looking to hit the register, and that I caught him. Didn't know who he was in the dark, so I hit him with a baseball bat that I keep under the counter."

"No, I mean... what about him?"

"He's been a good kid, worked with me for a while now. I like him. Now I just gotta figure out what's going on here. Who else he's working for and why."

"Let me worry about that, okay?"

"Suit yourself."

He walked out back of his office with the phone cradled to his ear and the cord trailing back inside and handed me a baby blanket with a faded image of Winnie the Pooh on it. I don't know why, but I almost started crying as he handed it to me. Maybe because he looked so old and so tired.

"I'm so sorry, Cleon."

"You got nothing to be sorry for."

I could tell that he meant it, even if I didn't believe him. I didn't know what to say.

"Man, these guys take forever to pick up. Guess it's been a busy night. Your doing?"

"Yep."

"Thought so."

I wrapped the gun up in the Winnie blanket without looking at it and stuffed it in my backpack. Then I looked at all the glass on the floor and turned back to Cleon.

"What about the gunshots?"

He grinned. "Well, I'm just going to tell them that I didn't hear any gunshots. Gonna put some magic behind it, too. There's two options, then. We could get a cop who just doesn't give a fuck, and he writes up the report and never even notices. He hauls Milsborough off to the hospital, tells me to keep it down in here, and goes home. Otherwise, we get your old friend Detective Ladislav. He's going to know that all this shit had to do with you no matter what, and everything I tell him is going to be suspect anyway."

"Huh. You still see Ladislav, ever?"

"Oh, yeah. Used to come by here once a month, ask me if I heard anything from you anymore. I kept telling him you were dead, but he always seemed suspicious about it."

Damn. He was keeping tabs on me the whole time, trying to make sure that I didn't break our "dead, not in prison" agreement.

"Well, if he asks straight out, feel free to tell him that I stopped by with cake."

"Hell, no. I don't say shit to that cop. You know that. Hey, I got an answer. Hello, this is Mr. Quiet. Yes, I'd like to report a break in. I'm calling from Happy Happy VCR on North Calhoun..."

I walked out the unlocked door, lit another smoke, and started walking.

Where to, I wasn't sure.

Too many goddamn questions, too fucking few answers.

And I still needed a place to crash.

I walked out into the parking lot, and stared at the little gray mass on the glittering concrete as it stopped being a dart and started being nothing at all.

A very, very depressed part of me was sort of envious.

I shook off the funk as best I could, hiked out to the road next to a bus stop, and pulled out my cell. There was only one person on the planet I could think of who might be willing to let me crash on their couch.

I called Tamaka.

CHAPTER 9

She picked up on the second ring.

"Royden, this really isn't a..."

I almost hung up. Instead, I got stupid and angry.

"Please, just tell me that you're in town right now, and not in East St. Louis visiting his magical family or something."

"No, Royden, I'm at home, and..."

"And your boyfriend or whatever isn't there, is he?"

"No."

"Okay, I'm coming over."

"Royden, please don't..."

"I just got shot at, Tamaka. Cleon and I almost just got killed. There are cops at his place, there are cops at my place, and there isn't anywhere else for me to go. I don't have any money, and I can't check into a hotel because people are looking for me, and... can I please just crash on your couch tonight?"

She paused.

"Why didn't you tell me that you weren't dead?"

"Because I..."

I wanted to tell her that it was because I loved her and didn't want anyone to hurt her to get to me, that even this felt too dangerous, that I had to stay dead because the bastards who rule both sides of the 25-Hour Curtain are only happy when people like me are suffering, and that gods dammit I loved her so much that me being dead was my greatest and only ever gift to her.

"What, Royden? Because you what?"

Because it was for your own good, I heard myself say, and then foresaw in perfect clarity an entire night of sleeping fitfully in an alley, waking up cold and sore and shitty. Instead, I focused on Tama, and on maybe getting her to heat up a half-dish of lasagna and watching MTV and jerking off after she went to bed and then falling asleep on her couch curled up in her mom's old quilt that still smells like our dog, Piggy Boy.

"Because I'm a fucking asshole."

"Good enough."

She hung up.

I stood in the cold and hated myself and waited at the bus stop and hoped that the police wouldn't pull up across the street and casually walk over and arrest me before the fucking bus got here.

I was not going to be able to play dead much longer.

Really scary people are going to hear about this, and all too soon.

CHAPTER 10

I sat in the back of the bus, as far away as I could from both the driver and the stinky drunk hooker taking up two seats in the middle, and I tried to sort out what I knew about every fucking horrible thing that had gone wrong in my life in just the last several hours. I thought for a moment about George Carlin's old line: "If we could just find out who's in charge, we could kill him."

Now, I just needed names and addresses on a whole list of sons-of-bitches. Starting with the King of Majooj and working backward to Garrick Heldane.

And, of course, I needed a gun.

I blinked, shook my head, and reached down into my bag on the floor and pulled out the blanket-wrapped gun. Winnie the Pooh smiled at me, but I found my attention drawn to Eeyore and his sad-sack eyes. Something started to click over in my head.

I pulled the sucker out, being careful to keep it from either becoming visible from the driver's seat or coming into physical contact with my bare skin. Something about abnormal objects from the realm of the Horrifyingly Abnormal makes me paranoid, I guess. Turning it over in my hands, I noticed that there was nowhere obvious to load it, like it was pressed from a single piece of gray-black plastic.

It looked like a toy.

A very, very, VERY cool toy. Little knobs and dials and stuff stuck off the sides, pointing at little indeterminate symbols, like you could set it to different frequencies or something. As I stared at it, some of them started moving back and forth, twitching like little hairs and making a *click-click* sound like a ten-speed bike shifting gears.

The hammer fell back of its own accord, and suddenly, I had a cocked weapon in my hands. A little bit of smoke that smelled like hot-dogs and fireworks on the 4th of July started leaking out of the barrel, and the whole thing got warm, like buttered toast. As I quickly wrapped it up in the blanket to stuff it back in my bag, I noticed a little inscription set into the butt of the handle, like the word *Tonka* would be pressed into the body of a plastic truck for little kids: *Paese dei Balocchi.*

I don't get out much these days, and I don't know French or whatever, but I had a funny feeling that I had my first clue. I let that warm me up and smiled for the first time in what felt like years.

A few seconds later, the driver yelled at me for lighting up a smoke on the bus. I pretended that I didn't speak English and ignored him.

CHAPTER 11

There isn't much to say about my night at Tamaka's place, and if there was, I sure as hell wouldn't tell you, anyway.

Although, yes, I did get my lasagna.

CHAPTER 12

The next afternoon dawned bright and early and ugly onto Tama's couch, which was lumpier than I had remembered it. Her mom's old quilt was warm and soft, though, and I fought off the effects of the hateful sunlight until almost 3:00 in the afternoon. I got up, coughed half a lung into the toilet, checked once in my overly suspicious way that drives people nuts to be sure that Tamaka had gotten off to work this morning and wasn't tied up in her closet or anything, made myself a bad breakfast of some stale tortilla chips and a mouthful of OJ straight from the carton, left a note on her refrigerator that I hoped would get her in a lot of trouble with her snooping boyfriend if he ever saw it, and let myself out.

Oh, yeah. Also, I stole four-hundred-some bucks from Tama's bed-stand. Asshole move on my part, but as we had established the night before, I'm a real asshole sometimes.

First things first: I wanted to go see an oracle.

Specifically, *my* oracle.

I went to Clark Street, hunched against the rain, to track down Chuck Dawg the Second, the Prince of Minos, and I found him sleeping against a dumpster with a brown-paper-wrapped bottle between his legs.

I prodded him with my foot.

"Hail, friend Prince. 'Tis I, the King of Jangladesh."

He opened an eye, took me in, and smiled.

"Hail, thou Secret King. Privy, how may your humble servant be of aid to you this fine day?"

"I request your ear and aide, good prince. Might this king purchase for thee a feast of the finest meal which fabled McDonald's doth prepare?"

"Verily. Lead on, stout-hearted and gracious king."

CHAPTER 13

We sat in the back of a McDonald's and produced, between us, a deeply funky stink that drove away the wandering masses. Tama had offered me use of her shower the night before, but I didn't want to leave her alone in the same room as my secret new gun.

That girl snoops more than I do.

And this morning I was just too wiped out to care.

When the Prince of Minos was done powering through his pair of Big Macs, I produced a stack of fifteen twenty-dollar bills from my coat.

Goodbye, most of Tama's rent money!

I made three quick stacks of five bills each, topping each one with a ten and a one from my pocket. Wiping the grease from his mouth with the back of his hand, the Prince locked eyes onto the piles of bills.

"Alright. I already paid you good cash to keep an ear out for me on something. You remember this?"

"Assuredly, my king! You hath asked for some word, as you hast said, regarding hourists skimming the pocketbooks of the waking world."

"What have you got for me?"

"Few would join me in palaver, my lord, but those who had some counsel with me spoke of a King of Majooj and some plan which he has enacted which violates the laws of all our kind, including the dread Forgotten. I know near nothing of him, however."

"Fine. That puts us on the same page. So, what about this price on my head? I hear you can see it, right?"

"Indeed! A mark is upon thee, my king, which I can perceive with only some little detail. It sayeth that those who wear the Skin of Demon-Goats have been promised an immortal lifetime of joy should they drag you before a certain throne, of there to be made a dancing-slave."

"... and what the fuck does that mean?"

"I have no idea."

"And the throne in question?"

"Don't know. It is hidden, and by what means, I know not."

"Let's get on with it, then. Oh oracle, I offer thee three boons for three answers; each boon is made of seven sheets, and totals eleventy-all: the Admiral Nelson, who gave one, one, one and all he had, sign also of the Great Bear, the magic constant of a six-and-six magic square built only of primes. Do you see my boons?"

"Verily. Since thou hast mentioned it, with these boons, I shall buy mine self some Admiral Nelson, mayhap. It would be delicious."

Man, all my mystic symbolism wasted on a homeless simpleton.

"Yeah, yeah, verily. So, do you accept my boons?"

The prince's eyes glazed over, and his ketchup-stained hands drifted over the cash.

"I accept these boons. What answers do you seek?"

"First, speak to me of Paese dei Balocchi. Answer me: what is this?"

"Ah. It is a place, I say from glimpses of the cosmos, that is no place; a most non-existent land. *Paese*, in Italian, does mean 'country or land,' but also 'town or village'; it is the name of the Place of Pleasure and Toys in the fictional realm of Cocagne, the Land of Boobies, in the novel *Pinocchio* by the Italian author Carlo Collodi.

"Cocagne, I see, was not invented by Collodi. It is based on older legends still: an alternate spelling, *Cockaigne*, derives from the Middle English *cokaygne*, traced to the Old French for 'plenty' and to the German for 'cake'; the Goliard poetry of the 12th and 13th centuries doth depict it as a place where abbots are beaten by their monks, nuns are flipped over to reveal their naked bottoms, and the skies do rain cheeses.

"Regarding the novel, boys are lured to Paese dei Balocchi by the promise of spending their whole lives in fun and frolic: they play hide-and-seek, whistle at their leisure, watch puppets in canvas theaters, play shuttlecock, bounce on balls, trundle hoops, and rideth wooden horses. They never do any work nor learn anything, and the graffiti which is written upon all the walls is proof of that. As a result, they are become animals, depicted as donkeys or goats.

"But as to your question, it has been made real. Land hath been marked as domain of this place, and a king channels it, as do some rival courts, many and many and more."

Shit. I prevented myself from asking about thirty more questions about that, like "who," "what," and fucking "HOW."

"Second, my oracle, speak to me of Majooj. Answer me: what is this place, and who is its king?"

"The mysterious Gog and Magog, who are seeneth as supernatural beings, including giants or demons, in many folktales from Hebrew to Irish, appear in Qur'an sura Al-Kahf, the Cave chapter, 18:83–98, as Yajuj and Majooj. Although there is little explanation given, here it is said that Gog and Magog are of an 'evil and destructive nature' and that, verily, they 'caused great corruption on earth'; they were sealed behind a vast wall until doomsday by great Dhul-Qarnayn, the one with two horns, and their release shall herald the end of the world.

"Gog himself is king of the nation of Magog, according to extra-Biblical Jewish tradition, but no particular real-world nation is associated with them, nor, forsooth, is any particular territory beyond 'to the north of Israel.' Revelation 20:8 also speaks of Gog and Magog: here, they are 'those nations in the four corners of the earth' who allow them-own-selves to be misled by Satan after he is released from the Abyss. They advance 'over the breadth of the earth' to encircle 'the camp of the holy ones and the beloved city.' A German tradition dated to the 14th century claimeth that a group called the Red Jews, the hordes of Magog, would invade Europe at the end of the world.

"And as to your question, Majooj has a mortal king and court although I do not know how. He is hidden from me—and from all oracles—by great and potent magic."

Fuck.

"Third and last, oracle, tell me of the Secret Kings of these two odd places. Are they in league with one another, and in such league, do they conspire against me?"

"Yes. This I see. Each makes dark plans against you and against all the world. And against each other."

"In that order, I suppose."

He blinked, then snatched up his money. "That wouldst be my guess, mine gracious king. I see also that you are destined to walk, and to be lost within, a labyrinth, although not one built of my house."

"A labyrinth. Great."

"I can give you some little aid. This is a secret of my bloodline: a cutting of He Who Spreads, ally of Pluto, who sleeps in all mazes."

Chuck Dawg the Second dug into a filthy pocket and produced what looked like an ugly, stumpy mass of gray, birch-colored roots, clumped with dirt. He set it on the cracked Formica table, and it seemed to shake for a second and then lay still.

"This will get me out of a labyrinth?"

"Nope. But it will come in handy. Fifty bucks."

"*Will* come in handy, or *might* come in handy?"

"Let's call it a *will*. Forty bucks."

"Shit. Well, better safe than sorry, right?"

"Right."

I forked over the cash with a sigh.

"Speak the name *Pando* while in a puzzle-box, and it is done."

Then he got up and left, presumably to buy a ticket to Detroit or leap under a bus. And if I had possessed a goddamn ounce of sense, I would have followed him.

CHAPTER 14

I walked outside, scanning as not-suspiciously as possible for police, and discovered much to my annoyance that it was raining harder.

Didn't even seem possible, but there you have it.

Dammit, this day was not turning out better than yesterday.

Where to now? My all-too-shallow pool of contacts was already running dry, and the next link in my chain of people who could potentially tell me something useful was not only *not* the sort of person I wanted to talk to but also not the sort of person I wanted to deal with at all. Also, not a person. And most certainly not available until the clocks got funny again in about, oh, eight hours.

My aching feet and sore legs started taking me in the direction of Le Palace Resplendent. I told them emphatically that this wasn't a good idea, what with my lack of a plan and all, but then we kept walking that direction once I realized that we didn't have anywhere else to go, either.

I walked and smoked and stared at people's belt-lines and tried not to dwell on the scenario that was more than likely going to play out when I got to the hotel. Even if there wasn't a whole lot of police tape around the crime scene, the garish yellow and black stuff removed in deference to the delicate sensibilities of the elite and famously finicky clientele, there would still be people watching for unusual activity in the lobby. Like, for example, a dark-skinned midget snooping around.

Fuck.

As I muttered to myself, I caught a glimpse of a movie marquee advertising a four-dollar second run of some big-budget superhero movie that, a few years ago, I would have been first in line to see. Damn, and I hadn't even realized it was coming out. Being dead will do that to you, I guess.

Thinking about it, I realized that people who use the Hole behind Midnight are, for the most part, exactly the same sorts of folks who go see superhero movies. At least, we are in the beginning. Pretty soon, if you're not careful, you can stop going to see superhero movies, stop going to work, stop living under a roof and stop being a person altogether. But the point is, we're just every day, normal folks like anyone else, looking for a little escape. I mean, how many people went and saw that last Batman movie? Shit, a whole lot of them. Made a ton of money.

The whole appeal of the Nether Hour is that it's just like the real world, only way more interesting and just for you. And for people who've always wanted a little bit of power to go along with their escape fantasy—and who doesn't?—it's right there for the picking. "Alone we are kings" is how the old saying goes. You give up a little bit of your time and your energy and your freedom, and I swear to god that it's better than any Facebook application, better than any TV show or web-comic, and better by far than any day at the fucking office.

The scary part is that, once you start being your own superhero, dressing like a vampire and attending Long Hour meetings in shadowed halls built from the bones of a leviathan, meeting interesting people from all over the world, and having unusual sex with them, it becomes more and more fucking difficult to bother feeding your cat or paying your gas bill or putting on a tie in the morning.

The ones with real power, they've checked out completely.

What was it that Cleon used to say? Years ago, he explained the tricks of the 25th to me, talking about how the power flowed. The idea is, as he said, that you just tap into some unclaimed real estate and *POOF*, magic powers. As always, though, the fine print is a mother. The way the reality-warping potency is limited or enhanced, of course, is what people kill and die for.

Absentmindedly, I pulled out my copy of Cleon's old list of rules, and my notes on them, scrawled on the back of an old set list from a Tom Waits show, stapled together backward.

And, let's be honest, you people need to know some of this shit.

Sympathetic Connection: the more you live the role of a king, the more power you get. For some people, this is as simple as just having a little bit of gold or purple on you—even a gold tooth or purple pants will work—and calling yourself a king if someone asks directly. Kings, might I add, always gotta acknowledge their kingdom: refusing the title of your Emptied Empire will immediately cost you your throne.

For others, building a connection means wearing an actual crown (even if it's made of paper), speaking the language of your chosen country, and adopting the other aspects of your divine right to rule. The King of Tlaxcala is gaining power when he spits upon the name of the Meshika-Aztecs, wears feathers, or eats chocolate. A guy with ethnic ties to the Mediterranean has a better shot at claiming the title of King of Etruria than a Mexican guy, but blood isn't the only connection; the real-world Royal Family of Great Britain is ethnically German, for example, and last I heard the current Secret Queen of Pompeii is a Japanese chick. The actual last surviving member of a culture automatically channels his civilization better than any other person (and gets to join the Forgotten Kings Society, too!), forcing would-be thief kings who wanna lay claim to the same Emptied Empire to resort to elaborate rituals of nobility to access portions of that power.

Longevity of the Claim and **Other Claims to the Title:** this is where those aforementioned thief kings come in. There's no limit to the number of people who can lay claim to any single title, but the power is automatically divided among the various claimants to the throne according to their sympathetic connections and how long each has held it. Two guys both calling themselves the King of Dinggong have to split the power of ancient Longshan between them, and the one with the strongest and longest-running claim to the culture gets the lion's share of the magic. Aspects of each king's claim might include actual Mongolian ancestry, relics of the culture, such as pottery made from mud of the Yellow River Valley (even if it was fired after 1900 BCE, when the city fell), symbols of office including falcons, iron shortswords or the color blue, or just having the most people know you as "that one guy, the King of Dinggong"—instead of, for example "that Johnny-come-lately, the usurper."

Brutal underground Wars of Succession are common among certain Secret Kings, as multiple parties all try to lay claim to the really potent Emptied Empires. And *not* trying to stomp out the competition is a losing move: just like in sports, the win usually goes to the guy who wants it the most, and failing that, it goes to the guy who's simply the goddamn meanest. Plus, symbolically, *not* stomping out thief kings is basically the same as abdicating your throne.

Potency of the Empire in Mass Culture: as for how much magic you can theoretically access at 100% "kingliness," well, the stronger the influence of a particular empire in the popular consensus of humanity, the more magic it generates. Whoever can claim the throne of the King of Sparta channels more potency than the King of Catalhoyuk, even though the latter Emptied Empire might arguably have been a more impressive feat of social engineering, arising as it did to dominate what's now Turkey from 6300–5500 BCE without access to full-scale agriculture, craft specialization, a writing system, ceramic production, or even metallurgy.

Anyway, the really clever and devious kings slip references to the glory of their Emptied Empire into the social consciousness to build up their power base; every high school student wearing a t-shirt emblazoned with the word *Spartan* or the number *300* serves to grant the King of Sparta more power. Of course, this attracts other claimants to the throne, which means that the King of Sparta is constantly hunting down thief kings. Of course, the symbolic act of confronting and killing someone who is trying to falsely claim rulership over Sparta generates more power for that king, so only the craziest and most bloodthirsty of bastards ever try to hold onto those particularly famous crowns for long.

Size of the Court: although every wise king fears that his throne and title will be snatched away in ceremonial battle by a direct usurper or drained to nothing in little nibbles by a thousand thief kings with lesser claims to the crown, a lot of kings forge bargains with other hourists for titles of lesser nobility within their court: dukes, barons, princes, and even married couples of kings and queens exist for certain potent kingdoms.

This is a gamble because granted titles of nobility drain-out the resources of the Emptied Empire just like thief kings do, albeit in smaller amounts and without the risk of symbolic abdication. Command of a large and potent court, however, reinforces a king's title in the same way that stamping out a thief king does: the clever king invests some of his power into followers, hoping to reap a sizable reward over time. Various treacherous lesser nobility, of course, will plot to usurp the king and immediately gain control of this investment when they, themselves, ascend to the throne; kings with scheming lesser nobility, of course, are usually planning to publicly expose the dirty bastards, strip them of title and then execute them—all potent rituals of kinghood that can grant a clever manipulator some fat, tasty power.

Keep your friends close, as they say.

Age and Treachery: magic, like Photoshop, can do just about anything... but you have to learn how to use it. I've figured out how to punch my hand through a brick wall, but I couldn't walk through it the way that the King of Cahokia can. Plenty of folks I've seen can step through any doorway on the planet and shift themselves right to their Emptied Empire. Most kings have worked the mojo so that they can't be killed on their home-turf except by another claimant to the throne; there are oracles and diviners galore among the kings. Some douchebags, like the King of Majooj, have trained in the arts of summoning and controlling Sideways abnormalities. There's whatever the fuck Alexandros did to get into Bohdan's penthouse; and I've heard that the King of Wudan can—no shit, honest to gods—turn into a dragon.

It took him seven centuries to learn, they say, but he can do it.

Anyway, members of the Forgotten Kings Society are the most potent of the secret royalty. Most of them are old beyond old, having channeled some portion of their magic into agelessness. They've mastered the techniques of sympathetic connection beyond even the not-inconsiderable benefits of all actually being the last members of their culture (or so they claim), and they're brutally efficient at stamping out thief kings and other claimants. These creepy old bastards pretty much never leave the 25th, and they pull the strings of all of us "lesser" kings; to them, we're little more than children playing musical chairs at a birthday party.

And that's the nice ones.

The truly inhuman ones think of us as dogs playing poker, and imagine the entirety of our "reality" as little more than a third-world nation where poor people live, die, mine for things useful to the secret royalty of the 25th, and work in sweatshops, drug labs, and brothels.

One note on that, by the way: not all of the members of the Forgotten Kings Society are actually the last of their culture, and one of the reasons that nobody in a position of true power likes me is that I happen to know all about that little factoid. The current Forgotten King of Pteria wasn't actually a member of the pre-Hittite society back in 1200 BCE when it fell but was born nearby on the northern edge of the Cappadocian plain in Yozgat province in central Anatolia—that's modern day Turkey—a few centuries later and claimed the already-ruined city-state as his own way back when. Now, does it really matter to the average hourist if this guy is really the last person to live in the ruins of Kerkenes?

Well, yes and no.

He's so old and mean and ruthless that no one else has even tried to claim the title since 547 years before Christ, when Croesus was burned alive on the pyre of boiling gold there. On the other hand, it means that a clever thief king could actually become a member of the Forgotten Kings Society with enough sympathetic connections—which, after all, could include fueling the propaganda that you really *are* the last living member of that society.

Oh, and then there are the Formless Magistrates, the theoretical lords of the Deep Sideways that the Forgotten Kings deal with. Everything regarding them is pretty much entirely speculative, but even then, the less said about them, the better.

Alright, I'll say one thing: they eat gods.

Especially the big, famous ones, which is why gods keep low profiles if they know what's good for them. I heard that they got Thor back in the 80s.

So, the bright side of all this is that while there are plenty of folks wandering into the Secret Time with nothing but childlike wonder and a big hard-on to play magical-powered kings of make-believe land, we don't have anything even close to a four-color superhero with a bright outfit emblazoned in red, white, and blue.

We have a couple-dozen Draculas, a smattering of Saurons, a phalanx of Fausts, a mix of Moriarties with too many Medeas and multiple goddamn Medusas, a score or more of devilish Doctors, Jekyll and Moreau and Frankenstein apiece, and a fucking cavalcade of Mad Hatters, Horned Hunters, Cardinal Richelieus, Invisible Men, Jack the Rippers, and Wicked Witches of the West.

Assholes, every one of them.

CHAPTER 15

I walked and walked and swiftly found myself standing across the street from Le Palace Resplendent.

Again.

In the rain, it lost none of its luster. Hell, the damn thing seemed somehow prettier and fancier and even less likely to want me to come in and track mud through the lobby there in the storm, like the skies spitting cold water in my ears were a form of jewelry for the palace.

Ugh.

I walked across the road, stood under the giant pavilion next to the ashtrays so I could see into the lobby, and decided that, if I was going to do *brutally, borderline-suicidal stupid* this afternoon, I might as well do it right. I pulled out my phone and called Detective Ladislav.

He picked up after a single ring. Boy, that guy can never wait to hear from me.

"Poole."

"Hey, what's up—is this a bad time? I can call back."

"I hope you're ready for some serious jail time, little man."

"Yeah, I'm doing great, thanks for asking. There's this fantastic belly-dancing troupe here in Jaisalmer; they reminded me of your wife. And a levitating guru told me that it's raining back home. Is that true?"

"Your ass is dead meat, Poole."

"No, but seriously, I wanted to ask you about the case. Do you have any kind of description on Alexandros? Maybe like some video footage from the hotel or something?"

"Oh, so you're looking for the real killer now?"

"Well, technically, Alexandros hasn't killed anyone that I'm aware of—it was old brute gravity that did Noel in, and a knife-wielding demon clown from Dimension Q that aced Kynan. I did mention that, right? That it wasn't me?"

"Where the fuck are you, Royden?"

"I'll give you a hint. It's a very famous building in the Thar Desert, built in 1156 by a particularly well known Bhati Rajput ruler. It's made almost entirely of sandstone."

"You're killing me, Poole."

I peeked my head around the glass of the doors and looked into the lobby. No cops.

"Come on, detective. Detect for me, here. I didn't gack your leg breaker, and we both know this. Someone is fucking with me, and that someone is also fucking with you. All I want is a physical description of Alexandros, so I can start making guesses about whether he's the King of Majooj or the King of Cocagne or someone else entirely."

There was a heavy sigh at the other end of the line. I could hear those giant eyebrows being rubbed.

"Yes, detective?"

"... he's real tall and skinny, like a scarecrow or something, with dark hair and dark eyes. Older, maybe in his fifties. My witnesses said that he seemed Greek or Hebrew, maybe."

"Great. That really narrows it down. Probably not from Cocagne, since that's the land of gluttony and all. Well, I'll keep you informed. Also, the answer you were looking for there was Jaisalmer Fort, for those keeping score at home."

"What?"

"That's where I'm at. Beautiful old place—it has 99 bastions and a Laxminath temple."

He hung up on me. Well, good for him.

I stuffed my hat into my backpack, flattened my hair to look something like Donald Trump's, tucked my shirt in and stepped inside to pretend that I was looking for someone who was totally supposed to be waiting for me right there in the lobby. After a moment of craning my neck and sighing like I couldn't believe that I was being so gosh-damn inconvenienced, I pretended that I had just decided to go check by the elevators.

A security guy walked toward me, looking a little suspicious. I walked right toward him, widened my eyes like a curious tourist, and put on my thickest accent. I now sounded like Apu's more hilariously foreign cousin who moonlit on a particularly offensive episode of *Outsourced*.

"Oh, goodness me oh my, my good sir. I was wondering, can you tell me where the lobby is?"

Just to be on the safe side, I also pretended that my arms didn't work very well. The hope here was that this guy had been told to watch out for anything suspicious because of the recent, unsolved murder, and not, for example, to specifically shoot on sight any dark-skinned midgets of Hindi extraction who happened to walk in. The guy blinked once at me, and a whole lot of training in good customer service trumped his much-more-recently-assigned task of being on high alert for vaguely defined "troublesomeness."

"This is the hotel lobby, sir."

"Oh, then I am come to the right place, then, okay. I am waiting for my son-in-law, and have you seen him here?"

"No, sir. What..."

He almost said, 'What does he look like?' and then decided that it might be racist. Then he tried to decide if it was more racist to *not* ask. Oh god, I love a guilty white liberal guy.

I pressed onward.

"I have never met him, this man who has married my daughter, but he has come on a plane to meet our family. I have seen photos of him, on the Internet, and he is a very, very tall boy."

"I see, sir. Well, I can call up to his room, if you like."

"Oh, please do so! I have been waiting now for ten minutes."

"Do you know his room number?"

"No, I do not. I have tried to call my daughter, but her phone is maybe off, I think."

"Their last name?"

"His name is Trent or Kendall or something like this. I will wait by the elevators while you call him."

I walked away, leaving the poor bastard to start quizzing the ladies behind the desk about a white guy, taller than me, who came to the hotel in a cab from the airport. First name Trent or Kendal, or maybe that's his last name? Possibly with a... Hindu-ish woman?

Enjoy that, buddy.

I barely resisted the urge to shout, *maybe it is Trevor or Travis or Clayton or perhaps Steveadore*, over my shoulder as I pretended to limp to the elevators. Actually, I was just a little pissed off that this guy hadn't doubted for a second that I was old enough to have a married daughter. I reassured myself that he probably assumed I had knocked up my arranged-marriage wife at the age of 14.

Hell, it was good enough for Gandhi.

Once I got to the elevators, I found the lift in question quickly enough: the one with the out-of-order sign on it.

I walked over, touched the brushed metal, and felt a little chill go through me. Yes, this had been part of a ritual—and recently. I started to unfocus my eyes, trying to call up some little bit of divination even without the Power of the Hour running in me, and just then a large and well callused hand came down on my shoulder.

Without thinking, still in adorable stereotype mode, "Golly gosh, I think that maybe this elevator is broken."

The hand spun me around, and a gun barrel jammed into my throat. It probably would have been into my chest, but as I've mentioned before, I'm short.

The gun belonged to a large Ukrainian man with a nose that had obviously been broken many, many times and a suit that was worth more than all the money I've ever made, ever.

"You are coming with me."

"You got that right."

No reason to fight it. He pushed the call button, and the elevator right next to the broken-down death-lift opened up. I got in, and the guy with the gun stepped in behind me. He pulled out an old-fashioned key and slipped it into a slot where a button should have been—right there above the top floor and below the penthouse—and the doors slid shut.

I looked at the guy. "My name is Royden Poole, and I'm looking for your boss."

He glared, like he wanted to hit me. Probably pistol-whip me in the back of the head with the gun. Problem is, my exposed neck was at a terrible angle for that.

"Look. I'm not a cop, but you knew that already. I'm just a guy. I don't know anybody, I don't work for anybody, and I don't know anything. I'm here to talk."

Fuck, why do I always seem to say that right before people die?

CHAPTER 16

We rode up in silence: him with his gun and me with a sinking suspicion that today, against all odds, was actually going to turn out worse than yesterday after all.

The doors opened into a room that was pretty obviously not a normal hotel hallway. It looked like a sitting room or a lobby in a very, very nice suite: double doors opened off to the left into a vast bedroom with a bathroom attached and a slightly-more-modest-but-still-impressive doorway off to the right was currently closed. The guy with the gun nudged me with the barrel of his pistol and guided me into the room with a light grunt, and I noticed that another elevator door was right next to us.

Only two elevators come up to this floor, and then there's just one elevator that goes up to Mr. Bohdan's deluxe penthouse in the sky. Restrictive architecture. Oh, how I would have loved to have majored in you in college.

The big Ukrainian gestured with his gun that I should sit. I walked over to one of the immaculate chairs and did so. He strode over, gun still pointed at my face, and grabbed hold of my backpack. I let him take it, while I inspected his gun at close range.

Normal, standard-issue Glock 9mm.

The big guy backed up, dropped to a knee, unzipped my backpack, and rifled through the interior. He was good. His eyes flicked back to me every few seconds, and he wasted no time inspecting things like my baseball cap sitting in the top of the bag. He pulled out my change of socks, an extra pack of smokes, Kynan's shoes, a half-dozen lighters, two sticks of beef jerky, my set of aviator stunna-shades for those times when I'm feeling so extra hung-over that I just don't even give a shit how totally ridiculous I look, and a plastic shopping bag full of what I like to call my St. Willie of Walsh Emergency Fuck-You Kit, for those times when you're not quite sure what you're going to need: a baggie full of ball-bearings, a can of expanding foam, a tube each of Super Glue and wood glue, a twenty-four-shot disposable camera, a small LED flashlight, a tack hammer, a pack of batteries, a black indelible marker, a screwdriver with multi-drill-bit set, a claw hammer, and a three-foot to twenty-five-foot extensible plastic pole.

It's nice to have those things, usually. But not when they're on the floor, five feet from me, and a gun is pointed at my head.

Suddenly, they all seemed really useless.

Then, at the bottom, the giant bastard got to my blanket-wrapped plastic hand-cannon from the Deep Sideways.

"Yeah, I'm just holding that for a friend."

He stared hard at me, and I tried my best to project telepathic *DON'T SHOOT ME* beams.

The guy stood up without fully unwrapping the gun and kicked my backpack into the corner, scattering my stuff everywhere. He said something over his shoulder in a language that I didn't understand, presumably Ukrainian, and kept pointing his gun at me.

Come to think of it, is "Ukrainian" even a language?

Hell if I know. Maybe they speak Russian or something—which, might I add, I also don't understand.

An elderly woman walked into the room through the open doors, dressed in a black business suit like a 1970s funeral director in a bad movie with a big budget. And by *elderly*, I mean that my first guess as to her age would have been about one hundred and sixty. Her skin was like soft, yellowed wax with a few strands of thin gray hair holding onto her liver-spotted skull and pulled back in a tight bun. Once, she would have been beautiful. I would have guessed her about six-foot-two, maybe ninety pounds. She looked about as weak as a four-hundred pound Siberian tiger, and she moved like a ballet dancer.

She opened a mouth full of yellow teeth, and her voice was deep and Slavic: **"Kneel."**

Voice of the King.

It wasn't a request. It was a statement, jumping past the upper echelons of my conscious mind, heading straight back into the lizard hindbrain at the top of my spine, and digging claws in. And it felt like I very nearly broke a knee trying to obey as swiftly as possible.

I heard, rather than saw, the leg breaker drop into a crouch behind me, head bowed low before her.

She glanced around the room casually.

I realized, after a moment, that she was simply checking to see if anyone else was in the room. Someone hidden who would have revealed their presence while falling to the floor at her command.

Jesus wept. Suddenly, I wasn't scared of the gun anymore.

Satisfied, after a moment, that we were alone, she considered me. "Do you know who I am?"

"I'm not sure, but I'm firmly of the impression that you're in charge here. I'm just trying to track down Fadey Bohdan."

"I am called Koloksai, Mother of Mokosh the Earth Goddess, Lady of the Sun, and have ruled the territories north of the Black Sea since seven centuries before the birth of the Christ-child."

Oh, Hell's own bells.

"Your Highness, the Forgotten Queen of Scythia, I beg of you to indulge this humble King of Jangladesh with a moment of your time."

"You may speak, magician dwarf, because it pleases me to indulge you in this."

"I am truly honored, Your Majesty. Rarely do rulers of your august station deign even to enter the waking world, so I must ask, has the disappearance of Fadey Bohdan been of direct inconvenience to you?"

"Yes. He has been my pawn in this place, though he did not know it; a thing in his possession belongs to me, held by his bloodline, and it has been taken by some thief."

"Then you have a vendetta of courts, of blood and honor, against those who have intruded upon your domain. May I ask another question, Forgotten Queen?"

"Speak, dwarf."

"I work for mortal agencies in the waking world, hunting for two kings who have struck against your pawn; I request only what knowledge you might be willing to grant me regarding the nature of the attack and of the missing prize."

She cocked her head slightly and at a speed which would have given most people a sharp headache and a strained neck. It's a completely alien gesture, more like something a bird would do than a mammal, which I've come to take, over the years, as what Forgotten Kings do when they're suddenly really surprised.

Her voice betrayed not a drop of that surprise, I should note.

"You do not work for mortal agencies. You are, in fact, wanted by the authorities."

Fuck. Behind her, I heard something large and scaly begin to uncoil in the bedroom. Well, of course she has a pet.

Trying to remember my mythology, here: the Greeks called the Black Sea the *Euxine*, and it was where the Amazons lived, and where Jason and his Argonauts went to find the Golden Fleece. Shit, she could have a hydra in there, and that's assuming that the old Scythians didn't have even scarier lake-monster legends.

"Ah, yes. Uh, it is by their specific request that I investigate the disappearance of your pawn, mistress, who is by their standards a mighty warlord, and it is by my own duty to the Secret Hour that I preserve the eternal mysteries of your kind from discovery. In the course of my duties, however, to both the edicts of the Forgotten Kings and to the laws of the waking world, I have been framed for murder by the same two lesser kings who have stolen from you."

She considered, then nodded. This, she understood.

She decided that I had not lied to her.

Thus, I got to live. For the moment.

"Continue your investigation, then, magician. My pawns and spies secreted around this inn have not yet contacted the local law as to your arrival, and you may depart safely. My servant Danya will escort you out. Know you this, dwarf: the object stolen from my storehouse here is a potent jar for the holding of souls in transmigration, a thing of antiquity even to me; it will be returned. When you locate my pawn, slay him."

I swallowed. Dammit, how do I get myself into these positions?

"I understand, oh Forgotten Queen of Scythia."

"You shall, in the course of your duties, meet no more resistance from me or from any others of my society."

Which meant that she wasn't going to tell anyone in the Forgotten about this. Because it would make her look weak, and her rivals—and potentially even her allies—would pounce on her. It also meant that I couldn't count on any aid from her, either, because extending any further resources to deal with this problem would overtax her... or, at the very least, would be traceable by the other Forgotten Kings.

Jesus, these people are crazy.

She turned to walk back into the bedroom.

"Mistress, if I might beg of you one last question?"

She stopped, and turned her predator's gaze back upon me. I thought as hard and fast as I ever have.

"Yes, mortal?"

"I believe that the kings who struck against you used a magic with which I am quite unfamiliar: two people were unlatched from time and from space and even from memory for a short while, and the only eyewitness was driven to great confusion and despair, then slain by an Abnormality from the Deep Sideways. Are these the marks of Gog, who is King of Magog?"

She blinked. Once. It was really fucking unnerving.

"You speak of the foul Red Jew?"

Great. She's an anti-Semite. How did I not guess that the ruler of what had finally become eastern Romania, Kazakhstan, and southwestern Russia wouldn't exactly be a huge supporter of Israel?

"I do believe that he is my foe, Lady of the Sun."

"Long have all the Forgotten Kings prepared to face that hidden adversary in combat, for it is said that he heralds the end of the world with the coming of his armies."

"Am I right that his magic is of hiding and of forgetfulness and of disappearance and mischief-making?"

"Yes. Gog is a thief, who turns good to evil with lies and tricks, and his servants, the monsters of Magog, are giants and demons."

That explains the clown. And his hiding from my oracle.

"I hunt him. May I go upstairs to the dwelling of your pawn, and see what clues the King of Magog has left for my divinations to uncover?"

She gestured idly at the elevators, and the doors to the "out-of-order" lift opened. A stink rolled out, like rotting meat.

She turned and departed without a word. The big guy, Danya, handed my still-wrapped plastic pistol back to me and then held me at gunpoint while I stuffed my scattered possessions into my bag and walked to the waiting elevator.

Man, what a dick.

CHAPTER 17

I got into the elevator carefully, looking very closely at the exquisitely carpeted floor as I did so. Unless I had missed my guess, at some point in the last forty-eight hours, a person had fallen right through it.

The big guy, Danya, nudged me in the back of the neck with his pistol. Oh, so he wants to come upstairs with me, now? Fine. Fuck him. I hope that something is hiding up here, and it jumps out and freaks the shit out of him. And then kills him, but not before he kills it.

I was hoping that they would both dead by the end, is my point.

After a moment, the elevator doors closed. I noticed that five of the buttons were lit, like the floors had been pressed. Although, since delicate telekinesis is such a tough trick, it's more likely that the Queen had simply reached into the space behind space with her mind and turned them from *off* to *on* at a sub-reality level.

Dammit, I hate dealing with people who ignore physics.

A quick bit of calculation, and I noticed that the relevant floor-buttons were all primes: 5, 7, 13, 17, and 23. As to what order the code was supposed to be punched in, I wasn't sure.

That reminded me. I still needed to call Detective Ladislav about who has access to the floor code but not the safe's combination.

Man, my life is too fucking complicated.

We went up. There was a *ding*. The doors opened.

It took a very small amount of time.

I walked into the nicest apartment I had ever been in and started looking around for bloodstains and wrenched-open safes and stuff.

I found them easily, in a bedroom to the rear: there was a bed the size of my dad's old car flipped casually up against the wall and the remnants of a Mosler floor safe sunk into the carpeting with a variety of important parts half-melted through.

Yeah, it looked like it had been done with acid, all right.

Except that Mosler safes installed in Hiroshima pre-WWII survived the damn nuclear bomb. This is the same company that Dick Cheney went to for his man-sized safe. Fuck. The CIA uses lock-boxes from Mosler to store shit in Langley, and objects kept in vaults built by the company include the original Constitution and the Declaration of Independence. That's the result of solid old-world Prussian engineering, new-school American technology, and lots of damn money from paranoid fuckers in every country on earth.

So, not burned open with acid from around here, then.

Now, there are a few things lurking about the Deep Sideways that can eat through the densest matter produced in 3-dimensional space like it was cotton candy, and I had a feeling that the King of Majooj had one or two of them on speed dial. The thing is, in order to get an Abnormality of that potency into a place where it could nibble on military-grade titanium, a summoner would first have to get his own happy ass into the room in question, get sideways, get back, and then work his mojo.

Hmm. Easier said than done.

I walked around a little bit, letting my gun-toting Ukrainian follow me around like the world's ugliest puppy, and found a horrifying, bloody little crime scene in a mangled kitchen that was still nicer than mine. I looked at the three bullet holes blown in the drywall, all helpfully marked by those little sticky-arrows that crime-scene guys like so much. Blood on the counter, blood on the floor. Looked like somebody had been shot, slumped to the ground, and then been dragged out of here. Food was splattered on the tiles, not smelling particularly good any longer, with a partial print where somebody had stepped in a smear of what appeared to be a congealed mass of noodles, fried bacon and onion.

This was also helpfully pointed out to me by a sticky arrow.

I owe those guys in forensics a nice fruitcake one of these days.

Anyway, something told me that the shoe in my backpack would not match that print. Kynan was too goddamn smart to have walked through his target's midnight snack on his way out the door. Just be on the safe side, I checked.

Damn, I am so good at this. I'm not much for guessing shoe sizes since I shop in the kid's section, but the print was from a long, thin, over-sized tennis shoe like a Chuck Taylor or something, not Kynan's wide and hefty-sized Brahma. This would have been a red flag for Detective Ladislav, especially if it didn't match whatever shoes Noel was wearing or any of Fadey Bohdan's immaculate Guccis so recently observed in a bedroom closet bigger than my entire apartment. This started to explain why he had called me in the first place.

I weep for that poor man's indigestion.

Okay, then. I walked to the living room, where I spotted the emergency exit. It had, in clear violation of city Fire Code, a dozen dead-bolt locks installed and a three-inch-wide iron bar on a stout chain soldered to the frame, like something out of a medieval castle. This door was intended to be locked down tight, a damn hairbreadth away from just bricking the thing over.

Man, it was almost like Fadey Bohdan was afraid that somebody would come in here, shoot him and take his stuff.

I retraced my steps a second time and then came up with a conclusion. It was, to be perfectly honest, insane.

The Set-Up: the King of Majooj wants what's in Fadey Bohdan's safe, which contains something that doesn't belong to him. He can open the safe by waiting until the 25th and then summoning an Abnormality from the Deep Sideways caustic enough toward physical reality to shear through pretty much any matter in the solar system, but he can't get into the penthouse because of the physical security, which includes the anchor points in the building. No matter which side of the curtain he's on, then, the location is sealed. Now, the safe itself is doubly secure: it probably doesn't even exist in the 25th, at least not for him, and he'd have to use some potent mojo to drag an Abnormality into the waking world when he translates back over and the safe re-appears. That's the sort of power that the Forgotten Kings have in spades, but the techniques involved are tricky even for them.

Okay, so here was his plan: he somehow ferrets out the secret code to the penthouse, which probably left a trail of money, power, and influence. I've got Detective Ladislav on that at the moment, so I'll let him worry about it. Then, Majooj hires a pair of very, very trustworthy leg breakers to kidnap him and escort him, unharmed, to the penthouse of Fadey Bohdan. No wonder old "Alexandros" kept staring at Noel's gun—this was the one part of the plan left very much up to chance. One wrong move, and these guys plug him.

I walked back into the bedroom. Hmm.

Side note: someone has to be running interference on Bohdan's people in the lobby at this point. Sure, the idea of two leg breakers bringing a tall, skinny Hebrew/Greek guy to see Bohdan in the middle of the night isn't weird... except to his top lieutenants, I'm sure. A guy with that much hardware installed in his door and that many precautions installed in his elevator isn't fucking around. So we've got another player here, and my money is on the King of Cocagne.

So, like Kynan said, they get in the elevator. This has to happen almost exactly at 11:59—too soon, and the King of Majooj slips into the 25th and then right back out as the anchor points in the lobby yank him back home. Too late, and they're standing in front of the lifts and it's midnight-oh-one, and now there's no Abnormalities for anybody.

Plus, yeah, he had to be able to predict where Bohdan would be, in his apartment, at that precise time. And that he would be alone. Also, someone had to check, beforehand, that this specific elevator still worked during the Other Interval and wouldn't just get funky—probably due to enchantments put in place in case the Forgotten Queen felt like checking in on her pawn at any time. There were probably other considerations here that I haven't even considered, like making sure that Kynan got away and didn't get nabbed, interrogated, or killed and identified by someone else.

Fuck, with all the planning involved with this, I almost want the son-of-a-bitch to get away with it.

Okay, so on the way up the elevator shaft, things get a little bit iffier for me, but here's the gist: the clocks go funny just above the radius of the last human anchor point in the building, the King of Majooj pulls the whole gang into the Secret Time with him, and then he works some magic. The exact power involved isn't technically important, considering that I have no idea how to work even the first part of it, but the important consideration is that Noel stops existing for a little while. Just, like, *BLINK*—and boom, he's no longer a part of reality. Never existed, and everything rolls on. The elevator keeps going up, Kynan is still doing his job, and soon things get even weirder.

At some point, about the time that the elevator doors open, my guess is that the King of Majooj worked another trick: he swapped the recall of his own existence in Kynan's head for a made-up memory, a little fiction-scene, that the mysterious "guy on the phone" had just called and told our leg breaker to walk in, shoot Fadey Bohdan, block the elevator doors, and walk down the fire escape.

After all, why else would Kynan be here?

I started thinking about that tape I had played, back at the police station. All those little moments when I caught Kynan lying: it was because he had been suspicious of this from the beginning. Which is why he was dead, now: the King of Majooj couldn't let the guy wander around. That hit by the clown was probably set up weeks in advance.

Kynan actually going to the police so soon, however, had been a miscalculation on the part of "Alexandros" or the King of Cocagne or whoever made the call.

Come to think of it, that was the only mistake they had made, and it set off a chain of dominoes that ended with me here, now. If our boy hadn't freaked out and gone to the police, the cops never would have known about this. A dead body at the bottom of the elevator shaft would have been a problem, sure, but things like that get fixed in big hotels in the big city. Someone in the Ukrainian mob would have noticed the break-in eventually, sure, along with the dead boss-man, and there would have been some confused head scratching and maybe some people tortured to death and possibly even a gang war in the wake, but it wouldn't have involved the cops. Not at first—hell, probably not for weeks or maybe months.

Even the Forgotten Queen of Scythia, once she got involved, would be at a loss to solve the riddle: How does an almost three-thousand-year-old stone-cold bitch with only the barest cursory knowledge of the 21st-century investigate something like this without letting anyone know that she was robbed?

Whoever planned this simply hadn't realized that the death of Noel would break Kynan the way that it did.

The plan didn't assume that Kynan was in love.

Interesting.

Totally callous plan, set in motion by totally callous people who neglected to take into account that human factor.

Okay, back to work. What happened next was simple. It was the easiest part of the plan, after all. With his re-programmed leg breaker no longer important, the King of Majooj just lets Kynan slip back into the waking world. He, then, sneaks along, invisibly and between the ticks of the clock, into Fadey Bohdan's bedroom and sets up a summoning ritual to bring in the deepest Sideways abnormality that he can conjure—a demon-storm made of claw-shaped, three-sided translucent planes of super-heated liquid-plasmatic Ununoctium—or whatever.

If this takes him six straight years to build up and contain, who gives a fuck? It all comes out in the wash.

The spell complete, the King of Majooj holds onto his demon and wills himself back out of the Quantum Time. Now, back in the real world, Kynan steps out of the elevator, blocks the doors from closing, walks into the kitchen, and plugs Fadey Bohdan just as he's pulling his midnight snack out of the oven or whatever.

He does not step in the stuff once it hits the ground.

I pulled out a smoke, lit it, and looked at Danya.

"What was that on the floor in the kitchen? The food?"

"A meat dish. Called *kasha hrechana zi shkvarkamy.*"

"Sorry I asked."

He pointed his gun at me a little more, and I decided to keep it polite from now on.

Okay, so Kynan shoots Fadey and leaves, totally professional. He takes the fire escape, which he can unlock from the inside. Now, why did the King of Majooj have him do that? Because just about then, I'm guessing, or maybe in the next couple of minutes, poor old Noel pops back into existence right where he left it, and plummets to the bottom of the elevator shaft. One witness wiped out, Kynan still doesn't remember what the fuck happened, and he'll be dead in twenty-four hours anyway.

So says the King of Majooj while he's planning this, "How much damage could one guy do in twenty-four hours, really? Especially if no one mentions the name *Noel*? Shit, it's not like most leg breakers and professional killers particularly *like* their partners to begin with, and now, it's a one-way split. For the average mercenary meathead thug, even if he catches wind of the weird, that's a 'double my money and isn't that odd' moment. Besides, who the hell cares what he puzzles out, because he's dead soon after."

They couldn't kill him with the demon-clown yet, of course, because Kynan had to leave the 25th to kill Fadey.

Upstairs, meanwhile, wacky old Gog and Magog snap open a safe designed to resist an atomic blast like it was made of melting popsicles. No sense carrying away what isn't worth a fuck, so half a million in cash sits there to be poked at by Ladislav's guys while "Alexandros" pockets the ceramic vase. If the police hadn't shown up with an insurance claim regarding what's in the box, presumably marked as an heirloom with a modest dollar value and some serious emotional attachment to Bohdan in that old-world way of 'you protect this, son, or our whole family is damned for eternity,' more than likely no Ukrainian-crime street-soldier would have even known what was missing.

And hell, without the head honcho of the family around and no spectrographic analysis of the scene, the mob might have assumed that the safebreaker fucked up somewhere along the line and couldn't get into the vault quick enough. Using acid is tricky: my first guess upon wandering into the scene would have been, *Oh look, some idiot set the chemical cocktail and then rabbited when the four minutes it was supposed to take to burn the fucker open turned into forty.*

Alright, so where the shit is Fadey Bohdan? He's there, he's bleeding on the kitchen tiles, and Kynan has every reason to think that he's dead. But his body ain't around, and that means that the King of Majooj did something with it. Or, I suppose, that the King of Majooj did something with *him*—I've met an Abnormality or two that can undo bullet wounds, as well as walk through walls or click back to the Sideways when it suits them, be it Hour 25 or not, and the Forgotten Queen of Scythia seems to think that her pawn is still around.

Oh, and deserving of a good slaying, on top of that.

Fuck. What is wrong with my life that *kill Fadey Bohdan* is now on my to-do list, to say nothing of being near the top of that list?

And then there was the bigger question: coming up on twenty-four hours ago, a particularly hated acquaintance of mine told me that he had a missing person's report on two of the richest men in town.

I had now accounted, in my own particularly useless way, for one of them— Mr. Fadey Bohdan. But my buddy Gog, the King of Majooj, AKA Alexandros, wasn't the other, or the description of the fake-kidnapped mastermind that Detective Ladislav gave me would have been "oh, you know, my other MIA" instead of "dark and skinny and middle-aged and maybe middle eastern." I hated to be a total downer here, but at the very best of all possible scenarios, my case was less than half solved.

Then, there was the damnable ceramic vase. What in the fuck does it do that makes it valuable enough to warrant all of this?

Other than "hold souls in transmigration" or whatever?

I walked over to the elevator, pressed the call button, turned to Danya, and shrugged.

"Looks like termites, to me. Maybe the butler did it."

He did not laugh.

We rode down to the lobby in silence, and I left the hotel.

Still raining.

CHAPTER 18

Now, I really needed to talk to Ladislav. Not just because he knew things that I didn't, like the identity of my mysterious second missing rich guy whom I was secretly hoping would turn out to be dead, as well, which would save me a lot of trouble, but also so I could gloat in his face that I had just been at his crime scene and already solved a significant portion of the case. Hahahaha and fuck you, detective.

The problem, sadly, was that calling him while wandering around was not a smart move. The more time I spent on the streets, the more I was risking immediate arrest and incarceration for a crime I didn't commit.

Dammit, my life is a bad genre parody.

I very briefly considered going to Tamaka's place since Ladislav hadn't busted in last night and was showing no indication that he intended to show up there any time soon. Until, that is, I checked the time and noticed that it was after 5:30 in the afternoon, and realized that (a) she would be getting home from work any minute and that (b) I had stolen quite a bit of money from her, and she was going to notice that.

Man, I burn bridges faster than I can even keep up, these days. In hindsight, my very expensive conversation with the famed, oracular Prince of Minos had not been nearly as useful as I had been hoping it would be. Now I know how old Croesus felt after his trip to Delphi.

Anyway, where to now?

I did what any red-blooded American boy would do—I fucking went to a strip club. I had enough cash for the cover, anyway.

Tastefully dim and well-polished, heavily vacuumed and air-freshened places like Honey Sweet Licks Gentleman's Club and Revue make me proud to be an American, and it's not just because of all the breasts and vaginas available for public and private display.

The building itself is just one giant-ass human anchor point, basically. Open from 4:00 pm until 4:00 am every damn day of the year, including Christmas, the place is cleaned top to bottom every hour on the hour, and there isn't a square inch of the property that a dozen people aren't thinking about at any given time: if not the dancers, then the customers; if not the cops, then the owners.

Oh, sure, there are mysteries aplenty in a good-quality strip club, but a smile and a couple hundred bucks in the right hands reveal all. It's the antithesis of the creepy old abandoned rock quarry or school bus graveyard on the edge of town where the biggest crowd you could ever hope to find is a stinky, half-dozen-strong Broken Human Collective support group huffing paint thinner together and where the slippy holes into the Deep Sideways occasionally start oozing out into the waking world and pantsing people if you're not careful to splash a fresh coat of paint on everything and sweep the dead dogs out every once in a while.

When you absolutely, positively *have* to get your ass back to the time of the real, there's simply no better place than a strip club with a semi-strict dress code.

Plus, nobody looks at you funny if you just sit there just ordering sodas. Or, I suppose, *a soda*. Which is what I would be drinking—despite the fact that I wanted an alcoholic drink so badly that I could feel it in my eyeballs—because I had pretty much no money at all on me anymore.

Now I want to make one thing perfectly clear before somebody gets themselves killed because they weren't paying attention: if the nudie-review establishment you're considering doesn't have a tasteful webpage, bouncers in ties, and high-glossy business cards, stay away while questing the Quantum Time. There's a good chance that secrets, madness, rust, and despair have crept in, and those are telltale signs of the unwatched. And for gods' sake, if one of the walls of the building is just black trash-bags and electrical tape covering a hole, get thee away.

I actually know a guy who somehow survived being washed out to sea during a 25th Hour flash flood that hit a Nether Reflection of a place where strippers with more tattoos than teeth had to put dollars into a jukebox in order to dance on a stage half propped up on a sawhorse.

What liquid, exactly, the flash flood was made of he refused to tell me. So I assume the worst.

CHAPTER 19

So there I sat, bathed in dim neon, letting techno strobe over me, nursing my single watered-down eight-dollar Coke in a very comfy chair designed to facilitate the reaching of one's wallet quickly and without hassle. I was trying to think about what, exactly, I was going to ask Ladislav and how, precisely, I was going to afford to talk to the Devil at the Four Way about my case.

Also, I was looking at naked girls. That should be understood.

I had not gotten laid in months at this point, nor seen an actual, live naked person—unless you count that goddamn demon clown, who should not be considered *alive* or a *person*—in even longer.

What I really needed, I decided, was a hot date, thirty pieces of silver, and a competent magician. Not necessarily in that order.

See, the thing about meeting the Devil at the Four Way is that it's easy. Being able to afford the meeting and then walking away in one piece, on the other hand, rather than getting yourself eaten whole or in part in the bargain, that's the tricky part. Like any manifestation of the Sideways, the devil works in mysterious ways.

Now, folks have been bargaining at the crossroads since, well, time out of mind—back before they wrote down the dates, as far as I can tell. The old Greeks had Hermes, the non-lapsed Hindus among my ancestors have Bhairava—

supposedly an older version of Shiva—the ancient, godless pre-Muslims had the djinn, the Mayans had Underworld Lord Maam—who still shows up to talk to Guatemalans in his Catholic Saint guise of Maximon or Saint Simon—and in Africa, pretty much every group with a name to it has its own version of the crossroads-god, including Legba, Ellegua, Elegbara, Eshu, Exu, Nbumba Nzila, and Pomba Gira, most of whom are still kicking and are all but listed in the mystical phonebook below the Mason-Dixon.

Even the old Anglo-Germanic kids got into it, going way back to Wodan and the pre-Christian, German-pagan woods-devil *Der Teufel*. And the Irish have a whole slew of boggards, fair folk, and bogeymen looking to make a deal at midnight where the paths meet.

About the only cultures I can think of off the top of my head of who don't have "bargaining at the crossroads" woven in are the Japanese and the Native Americans; though, it should be noted, I've heard tell of kappis and coyotes, both, putting in a token appearance at a place where two lonely roads intersect, be it at a small bridge over a stream or along two sand-choked paths through the mesas.

And the big thing to remember is that no matter who shows up to make trade with you once the all-too-easy ritual is complete, be it a trio of grinning, shoemaking elves or a big black man with no face, the devil is a trickster: he'll give you *exactly* what you ask for, at least as he interprets it, always for a price or a risk too high, but he'll deal you fair if you can keep your wits about you.

Oh, and there's only one devil. He wears many masks, but it's all just the one guy being a prick.

At least, that's what Cleon says.

Another theory says that they're a guild with at least two factions.

Point is, the Four Way of the roads is the best damn place to get your deal-making done, as any blues musician can tell you—a no-man's land; it belongs to nobody and no one, and it breaks through the borders of "here" and "there" something fierce. Show up at midnight, slip yourself into the Hour that Isn't, and you're in for a treat.

Or a trick.

Anyhoo, the best way to get on the devil's good side is to bring him nine handfuls or pinches of dirt, taken without being seen, from holy ground: one handful snatched up a day, starting after 3:00 am on a Sunday and all gathered before the sun rises. This is best done during winter, and living near a cemetery or a seminary is the best way to not get caught. If you have the time and energy to get those nine samples of earth, well, you can learn to play the guitar, the fiddle, the piano or the trumpet without ever taking a damn lesson; the fellow at the Four Way has a knack for learning you to dance, learning you to cheat at cards, instructing you in languages you speak, want to speak, or want to forget, and many manner of other tricks regarding babies, pregnancies, marriages, cheating husbands, wayward wives, and lost treasure.

Of course, bringing that devil-pleasing dirt-token means that you can't get what you're after for a full week. That gloomy Sunday morning when you've got eight pinches of dirt, when the rains are coming down and your heart's desire is a day or so away, can be its own special kind of hell. And if you're in a position like mine and can't afford to waste nine cold mornings on errands, you're going to have to bargain with a devil that isn't necessarily predisposed to make you a sweet deal in exchange for something simple like taking the Lord's name in vain seven times.

No, in my current bargaining condition, I would be lucky if the shadow I called up out of the intersection didn't want a pinkie finger, my first born and the memory of my best kiss, all chewed up and spit back into my face as a nightmare, only to cheat me out of my desire with a twist of my words. Half a wish, after all, is a lot like half a kitten.

With thirty pieces of silver, at least, I'd have a bargaining chip that nothing from the Near Sideways could resist; a lot of those critters dwelling *just* on the other side of the Nether Hour's curtain have a certain puppy love for messianic symbolism and its subversion.

And a competent magician would be a godsend because tracking the King of Majooj right now was not in my mystical vocabulary.

And a date would be super-duper purely from a masturbation-fatigue perspective, but that's hardly the point.

Regarding my lack of competence as an hourist, one of the big reasons that I hate the King of Cahokia so goddamn much—and have hated him even since way before he started dating Tama—is that not only is he better looking and better built and taller and blonder and probably smarter and funnier and doubtlessly better hung than I am, he's also better at casting spells, as well as a proponent of the Totemic Magic theory of Kingship.

INTERLUDE ONE: ON TOTEM MAGIC

In a nutshell, there's this old theory, really popular with certain kings, that every Emptied Empire has certain totemic magics; that channeling a certain empire or another gives the king in question certain benefits when it comes to casting or creating certain effects. The theory holds that every king can learn certain very basic spells, like enhancing physical strength, commanding the weak-willed or calling up minor divinations and the like because everyone who ever declared majesty over a group of people for more than about twenty minutes focused a good percentage of their time and energy into having military might to back them up, being obeyed, and predicting the future.

So the theory goes and so proponents such as the Forgotten Queen of Scythia like to claim, certain Emptied Empires have certain totemic magics which they can grant to their kings: someone who rules the crown and throne of Athens is supposed to be better at philosophy, public speaking, logic puzzles, and political-satire-magic than, for example, the King of Sparta, who should theoretically be better than anybody else at fighting totally outnumbered and naked.

Of course, these totems sometimes get all fucked up in the translation: there's an idiot surfer-boy I've heard of supposedly claiming the throne of Atlantis. Seriously, do you think that Atlantis had anything to do with the ocean before it sank? Like, they rode dolphins or something? Idiot. If there's one thing the

Atlanteans should fucking *hate*, it's the ocean, what with the waves having gobbled up their entire world.

But the real problem is this: 99.9% of nations don't have a single totem for what they're best known for, even if the country was primarily regarded in later years for peace or wealth or glory in battle. Every country that ever existed has just been made up of people, plain and simple. Every nation has sinners and saints, heroes and thieves, magicians and hunters, and plenty of poor people. Every fucking nation, ever, has endured famine and gone to war; every nation has made art and built temples; each of them had allies, enemies, trade, monster stories, and a form of law that was occasionally questioned.

What really hacks me off is that Cleon calls the whole totemic magic theory horseshit, and I'm loathe to think that Cleon is wrong. The other problem is that I can't get half the spells I try to work right, and that seems to suggest to people like Garrick Heldane that the totem of Jangladesh must be rank, amateurish incompetence.

Fuck him.

Me, I think it's all self-fulfilling prophecy. A guy who has a hankering for travel magic, so he can pop into the 25th and walk the winding shortcut back roads from Brooklyn to L.A every once in a while, he's naturally going to choose a nomadic culture and call himself the King of Xiongnu or something, completely disregarding the fact that plenty of those pre-Mongolian horse lords built permanent yurts and never left Gansu Province. Likewise, some idiot will always claim that his specific Emptied Empire was the best at ass-kicking until the exact moment that the Forgotten King of Yamato shows up and demonstrates that channeling pre-Imperial, post-Buddhism proto-Japan is a fine way to be able to shatter stone with a sharp stare, a finger-flick, and a whisper.

Which brings me to guys like the King of Majooj and the King of Cocagne— those insane bastards who choose to claim rule over fictional countries. Theoretically, it's impossible.

But apparently people do it.

Now, I've met a very, *very* few folks over the years who have chosen a non-real Emptied Empire, and not one of them has been able to explain exactly how they did it.

Yet, as a very nerdy guy calling himself the King of Gondour once explained to me, the mythic quality of a pretend country is actually quite useful in generating raw power, and more focused power with regard to totemic magic if you believe in that bullshit, than some very *real* fallen nations—the kingdoms of El Dorado and Lilliput, for example, are probably better known to the average American than Tiwanaku, despite the fact that the latter actually ruled Peru, Argentina, Chile, and Bolivia in South America for over four hundred years and the two former nations are about as real as Big Bird's friend Snuffleupagus.

Hell, there's a Forgotten King of Utopia, last I heard, and he honest-to-gods claims that he's the last member of the culture.

Wise-ass people who ask this man to point out on a map where his nation was located, exactly, usually meet with gruesome violence befitting a several-thousand-year-old sociopath. Rumor even has it that the Forgotten King of Utopia has a thing where he yanks people inside out with their tongues.

Point being, the bigger benefit, according to the totemic magic theory, is that the wealth-based magic that the King of El Dorado can churn out is totally unlimited because the city is literally known for nothing *but* being made of gold. It's not like there are recently uncovered accounts of people starving to death in the streets or some little-known historical faction of egalitarian communist Eldoradoites who refused to use money. My own theory, of course, is that only a guy with a mad-on for hard cash would ever bother claiming the crown of that Emptied Empire in the first place, and that the fact that the King of El Dorado can manipulate gold and the stock market is a chicken-and-egg scenario.

The flaw, for those keeping track at home, lies in the way the totem points: Oz may have more cultural resonance to the average guy than even the Roman Empire does, but Oz didn't have a police force. Or taxes or schools or even roads, except for that yellow brick one. You're locked into a very specific paradigm with a fictional empire.

Anyway, here's the real head-trip kicker that the King of Gondour laid on me: the Kingdom of Jangladesh, for example, is just as pretend as the nation of Ishtar from the movie *Ishtar*—it's not real, or at least it isn't anymore. The guy who claims majesty over all the land of the Aztec Empire isn't channeling the very real people who actually live, right now, in Mexico City. There isn't a person in modern-day Bikaner District in the north of India who has ever heard of me, even as I call on the might of everyone who lived there before the 15th century right out from under them.

Of course, this same guy also got really sad when I assumed that he was a Tolkien fan; apparently, Mark Twain created a fictional, merit-and-education-based utopia called The Republic of Gondour back in 1870. To make up for my gaffe, I suggested that he should maybe switch to being the King of Elbonia—because everybody loves *Dilbert*.

And there are a lot more stupid people than there are smart people, which should theoretically make Elbonia more powerful.

He almost started crying.

I'm just not good with people, I guess.

Which reminds me: I need to call Ladislav.

CHAPTER 20

After a few rings, the call went to voice mail. I hung up.

Come to think of it, he was probably in a meeting. Probably in a meeting about me, actually. I sat back, looked at some tits, and imagined someone slapping a manila envelope on a desk and screaming something like, "You're off the case, Ladislav!"

It made me smile.

Since all of my knowledge of police procedural policy comes from 1980s action movies, I like to imagine that Ladislav has a big, angry boss like Dan Hedaya or Frank McRae.

Oh, you know who Frank McRae is.

Fine, just Google him.

Anyway, now I had to call him back and leave a voice mail.

I took a sip of Coke, tried to remember how much cash I had on me, and called the detective again.

He picked up straight away.

"Fucking what do you want, Poole? I'm real busy dealing with your insane bullshit."

"Oh, so you're not off the case, yet?"

"What's that supposed to mean?"

"Nothing. Nevermind. Look, I have some more information on the disappearances and the break-in and the murders and everything. It was all done with magic."

"I'm going to hang up now, Royden. Please do fuck off and die."

"No, look. I just left the crime scene, and your guys did a damn fine job. You called me because the break-in occurred at midnight and because you've got a partial footprint in a sloppy meat dish with a name that sounds like somebody choking on vomit. That print doesn't match any pair of shoes from the scene. Am I getting warm?"

"... yes."

"Okay, so here's what I've got: The one and only mistake these guys made is that they didn't expect Kynan to come to you so soon. Am I right in guessing that unless Kynan had come to you, you probably wouldn't even know about the break-in?"

"No. Maybe."

"Good enough. Anyway, the hit on him was a heat-seeker. He was going to die twenty-four hours after the break-in, pretty much no matter what. Right now, I'm buckling down for whatever gets sent at me next, because I've already ducked one hit in the last day. Point is, the big fuck up here was that Kynan was in love with his partner, and Alexandros didn't know."

"They were brothers."

Shit. Oops. There I go with assumptions again.

Maybe I just wanted to imagine that Kynan died for something truly romantic and beautiful.

"Okay, fine. Whatever. Kynan loved his brother, Noel, all like a brother and stuff. Point is, the crazy bastards who set this up don't think like normal people. They see brothers, and they assume sibling rivalry. They see a family and assume that everyone hates each other, and not in the laugh track, sitcom, *All in the Family, Married With Children* kind of way. I'm talking Corleone family, Hamlet, Cain and Abel, fratricide-as-way-of-life kinds of lunatics here."

I idly wondered, for a moment, how many members of her own family the Forgotten Queen of Scythia had killed.

"What's your point, Poole?"

"That's the only way I'm going to catch these people, is when they make mistakes. The one they already made was waiting twenty-four hours to kill Kynan, and I'm still wondering what on their agenda was so goddamn important that they couldn't bother to bump him off right away. Probably don't have the real-world manpower, and he had to be out of the 25th to make the big hit on Bohdan. Come to think of it, the only other mistake they've made so far was underestimating how paranoid my friends and I are and assuming that I wouldn't immediately hate a certain hipster-fuck-assassin that they sent after me with a magical gun."

"You're the one who put Ethan Milsborough in intensive care. That crazy fucking lying-ass VCR-fucker..."

"You leave Cleon out of this. He has nothing to do with this investigation except following leads for me, and you should be real fucking happy that he isn't dead right now. As for, what, Ethan, is that my assailant's name? You might want to put him under the best protection money can buy because I have a feeling that he's in for a rough night once the clocks get funny."

"Are you threatening him?"

"No, but I have a feeling that the people who hired him are going to be pretty severely pissed off that he failed to put a squirming mass of jellied rubber from the Deep Sideways through my brainpan."

"You are one crazy fuck, Poole."

"Yeah, yeah, I learned it from watching you. Now, I need a name on my other missing rich guy, the one who disappeared on the same night as Fadey Bohdan."

"Who? Oh, no, that's been taken care of. He turned up again."

"That's not reassuring, detective. You have another rich guy disappear at the same time that the break-in is going on, he shows up later, and everything is copacetic? I don't like it."

"You don't like anything, Poole. I can't release the name of the other missing person to you, not only because it's confidential but because you're currently a fugitive wanted for questioning in connection to the murder of a suspect in custody, as well as your admitted assault of Ethan Milsborough, but I assure you that the case is solved."

"Gods dammit, just tell me his name."

"No."

"After all I've done for you, you're not even giving me this guy's name? You suck."

"WHAT? Fucking what, precisely, have you given me, Poole, besides a fucking ulcer? All I've gotten from you is that you've broken into my crime scene and decided that this is a magical conspiracy involving magicians who can teleport and time travel."

"Don't forget memory wiping and demon summoning. Look, I've got this case just about where I want it, and I'm not feeding you a line of bullshit, here. You know what I know, detective, and yeah, admittedly, you can't take that in front of a judge, but I'm working on it."

"This is on top of my dead witness, Poole."

"Oh, fuck you. This again? You know for a fucking fact that I didn't kill him, you asshole!"

I hung up on him, for once. Damn, that actually feels really good. Now I see why Ladislav does it all the time.

I considered for a second, and then called him back.

"What?"

"Just so we're clear, I'd really, really like for you to tell me this guy's name."

"No."

"I'm going to find out, detective. One way or another, you know it, and you do not want to fuck with me on this."

"Keep dreaming, Poole."

"Would it help, at all, if I mentioned that I have reason to believe that our magical break-in artist is involved in a conspiracy?"

"Yeah, you already said that there's a bunch of people behind this, and I've already discounted that."

"By *conspiracy*, I mean exactly two guys. Let me scratch some names off my list, okay? Just tell me this thing."

"No."

Someone walked over to my table. Shit, I have got to learn to be more quiet when I talk to people on the phone. I glanced up, and Fadey Bohdan was standing over me.

Huh.

"Uh, yeah, mom, can I call you back?"

I could almost hear him roll his eyes. "You weird fucker."

The very not-dead lord of Ukrainian crime across three states sat down at the table with me, wearing a pinstripe suit and a fur coat and an expression like a leather saddle made out of frown lines. He looked both ways, then gave me a very un-crime-boss grin and a thumbs up.

"Love you, too. See you at home."

I hung up, stuffed my phone in my pocket, and pulled out my cigs.

"Well, good evening, Mr. Bohdan. You mind if I smoke?"

"Not at all."

Deep, but not as Slavic as I was expecting. I know that voice, or at the very least the inflection.

"I think that this club is non-smoking, actually."

"They'll make an exception. I happen to own this block."

Just checking.

"There's that. I'm speaking to the King of Majooj, I presume?"

"In the flesh, Mr. Poole. The new flesh."

"You told me awhile ago that this case was closed for me. Could you remind me again why I didn't listen?"

He laughed, in a way that didn't quite fit his body.

"Because you are a man who likes to know things, Mr. Poole. To work at things. To pry things open and understand them. A mystery is a delicacy to a palate such as yours, and I am beginning to understand that."

"You're not a man for delicacies, I would expect."

"No, Mr. Poole, I am not. I am a creature of deception, primarily, and of horrors, when it suits me, and I have a need to be feared, but I care for very few things in this world beyond undercooked steak, underground dog-fighting, and underage girls."

"Super. I'm going to go out on a limb here and guess that you and your partner, the King of Cocagne, have already attempted to deal with me in your particular, traditional way. An assassin."

One eyebrow cocked upwards in a manner that simply didn't look natural on Fadey Bohdan's weathered features.

He wasn't sure how I knew about Cocagne.

Now I had one over on him.

He smiled, considered, and continued. "You would be correct although the particular assassin chosen was not mine. A mere boy. And we had already offered to let you walk away after framing you, after all. You were quite rude."

"Got it. No hard feelings, then. Okay, so, the hit didn't work, and now, you're trying it his way again—you're going to make me an offer."

"Hm. I like you, Mr. Poole. You and I have very little in common, but I've found over the years that I particularly enjoy the company of people who are very much unlike me."

"Here's the thing, guy. You know that I can't accept the King of Cocagne's offer, no matter what it is."

"No, probably not."

"Which puts us back to you—your turn again once I don't bite."

"My... turn, Mr. Poole?"

"There are only so many ways that the two of you can try to deal with me discreetly. To be perfectly frank, now you'll have to try to kill me with monsters."

"That is, I'll admit, my intention."

"While we're being honest, I'd just like to admit that I'm scared shitless of the prospect of what you're cooking up to throw at me."

He smiled. "You should be."

"All right, then. It seems like we're at an impasse for the moment, though. You know I have the gun from Paese dei Balocchi on me, you're not equipped with any Abnormalities at the moment, and neither of us wants me to start shooting you here and now."

"Try it."

"... what, seriously?"

"Yes."

He put both of his hands behind his back and inhaled, puffing up his chest with a grin.

I don't like it when people do that. Fuck him. I pulled the gun and shot him in the face.

BOOM.

There was a moment of silence, and by the time I blinked, everyone in the room was staring at me. I watched the little dart bounce off his nose like I had flicked a spitball at him.

His smile deepened.

"Fuck me."

"Well put, Mr. Poole."

He turned and looked around the room, and everyone started looking at something else.

"Uh. Huh. So."

"Yes, Mr. Poole?"

"Shall we... hold off on any further matters of courtly vendetta until the 25th, then?"

"As you wish."

He stood. I considered, and then went for it.

"Your Majesty, a moment if I might be so bold: the suit you're wearing, I've never seen its like before."

He smiled, flicked at his nose once, and then tugged at his lapel with his left hand. "No, you have not."

"One of a kind, then?"

"No. I'll soon have an entire wardrobe."

Oh, fuck.

"Ah. This is the power of the vase stolen from Scythia?"

"This, and so much more."

I pondered as he turned.

"You'll soon have your army, then?"

He paused, smiled, and started laughing. Slowly, at first, then more and more until his whole body shook from the effort of it. Deep, full, throaty, chest-heaving laughter. Hell, I'd call it *maniacal*. People started looking at us again.

"Yes. Yes indeed, Mr. Poole. Yes, indeed."

He walked away, almost vibrating, tears streaming down his face. With half the bar still staring, he stopped by the front desk and said something to the bouncer. The bouncer nodded at me, and in a way that didn't convey that he was about to come over and kick my teeth in.

The laughter of the King of Majooj echoed back, mixed with the sound of heavy rain from outside, as he left the building, still chuckling to himself.

A minute later, a very pretty young lady wearing very little came over and handed me a note—everything in the building was on the house until midnight, courtesy of Fadey Bohdan and his partners.

I ordered another Coke and contemplated head butting the table until I died from it.

CHAPTER 21

I sat there for fifteen minutes and hated and thought and hated some more. Mostly, I thought about that stupid gun and how it didn't work against the King of Majooj. And then I started worrying about curses. And then I felt sick.

You know, there are a lot of folktales and stories and poems about cats toying with mice. It's iconic. The big, bad lion wounds the defenseless little rodent and then lets it limp away just *almost* to safety, only to break another one of its limbs. You know, for fun. And then another limb, and then another, and then finally, when the itty-bitty thing is done thrashing, the predator gets bored and finally aces the little bugger.

There are, I admit, fewer stories about the mouse, once wounded, breaking off one of the lion's teeth, leaping up, and stabbing the monster right in the heart with it.

Still, that's what I decided to try.

I called a waitress over. A new one: a cute redhead. The 6:00 pm crowd was rolling in now, and things were picking up.

"What can I do for you, honey?"

"Hi. You know about my tab, yeah?"

"Oh, yeah."

"Good. Now, you gotta understand, Mr. Bohdan and I go way back. Way, way back."

"Yeah, I figured."

"Way, way, way back. Saved his life twice now. What's your name, sweetheart?"

"I'm Sheridan."

I decided to try out a Brooklyn accent. Like one of the Goodfellas or something—or a guy from Jersey, maybe.

"Sheridan, it's very nice to meet you. Now, do you know what Mr. Bohdan does for a living?"

"Well, I... um. No? No."

That was the sound of her suddenly getting scared. Good. Scared is the point. But I didn't want her *too* scared.

"That's what I like to hear, Sheridan. You see, my thing is, I'm paid to keep people from having to worry about what Mr. Bohdan does for a living. I'm kind of like his buffer, sometimes. Now, we haven't seen each other for awhile, so us coming here is kind of his thank you for me getting into town on short notice, you get me?"

"Yes."

"*Short* notice, get it?"

She pretended to think that was funny, god bless her.

"Alright, now here's the thing. Mr. Bohdan knows that I like looking at pretty girls and that I don't like running errands, you know?"

"Okay."

"My little legs here, I don't enjoy hoofing it all over a town like this. Fuck, I don't even know where a discount pharmacy is, around here."

Sheridan stared at me, silent, biting her lower lip, riveted, waiting for me to order something.

"Okay, so here's what I'm going to do. I'm going to order a Coke right now, and while you're getting that, I want you go check on the specifics of my tab. I'm on a timeline here and got an appointment to keep around midnight, but Mr. Bohdan should have five to ten grand on there set aside for my personal discretion. I assume you have some busboys or bouncers or door guys here who know how to run a discreet errand?"

She nodded.

"Alright. Go get me that Coke, and you check my tab."

My entire body shook with the effort of ordering a Coke instead of an entire bottle of vodka with a chaser of another bottle of vodka.

After a few minutes, Sheridan came over to me, white as a sheet. She was shaking so hard that half my Coke was gone.

"What's he got me down for?"

"N-n-nothing."

Oh, thank god. I was really hoping that he hadn't put a number on there of any kind.

"Nothing... what?"

"I mean, it—it doesn't say any number, Mister... uh..."

"Mister? Oh, yeah, you don't want to know my name, Sheridan. You can call me Big Jimmy Jangladesh, but you never met me, okay?"

"... okay."

"That's what I like to hear. Okay, here's what we're going to do. Mr. Bohdan has done this before, when he's got something big going... well, let's not even talk about it, okay?"

Sheridan nodded enthusiastically.

"This just means that I'm not on a budget tonight. That's fine. Heck, that's good. Means I can do my job now. Okay, you go get me the best guy here who isn't real busy, all right?"

A nod.

"Oh, and thank you. You and me, we're done here, so what I want you to do for me, Sheridan, is you write down this Coca-Cola and one hundred dollars on my bill. You take the hundo out of the register, put it on Mr. Bohdan's tab, and then put it in your pocket. From me to you."

"Thank you."

Oh, with her big, green doe eyes, I just wanted to kiss her right on the cheek. Hell, I almost did.

"Don't mention it. Go get me the guy."

I sipped at my new soda and watched the new girls.

Things were looking up.

CHAPTER 22

Two hours later, I had spent a very sizable chunk of Mr. Bohdan's money, most specifically on things that I intended to use to screw him over and, to a certain lesser degree, I spent some just because, hey, fucking, screw him. Anyway, my helpful errand-runner for this evening had been a young and enthusiastic man named Joe, and I tipped Joe a solid grand right out of the register for his assistance.

You know, I could get used to this whole *obscenely rich* thing.

On the table in front of me, I now had one cellphone charger to replace the one I had forgotten back at my apartment; a carton of Camel Lights to re-infuse my currently dwindling cig supply; one set of high quality night-vision goggles because, fuck it, I've always wanted a set of night-vision goggles because they are wicked awesome; a stack of very flimsy panties, which I had purchased off of various girls this evening at $100 apiece; several soft pretzels from that one pretzel place I like because I had begun to realize at some point during my shopping spree that I had forgotten to eat since last night's cake escapades, this morning's chips, and Micky Ds; and thirty silver coins, each worth about $11. For those last few, I had paid quite a bit more, of course, simply for the convenience of sending a strip club bouncer to a jewelry and coin dealer at 7:00 pm on an old, cold, rainy and miserable evening.

Price, I had assured everyone involved, was not a concern.

Also, just to be sinisterly mysterious, I ordered a set of black plastic garbage bags, duct tape, bolt cutters, and half-gallon of bleach.

That should cement my reputation as somebody not to be fucked with—at least around here.

I was feeling so badass that I even put on my stunner shades.

As I sat, admiring my stack of incongruous items, my phone rang.

Cleon.

"A yo, yo, yo, what it is, my man?"

"I've told you before to knock that shit off, Royden."

"Yeah, but it's always funny. Because you're black."

"So was Redd Foxx, and he woulda slapped the grin right off your face for that shit."

"Please tell me you have good news, Cleon."

"Well, I got some good news, and I got some bad news. The bad news is that I'm having no damn luck securing another sacred space for our little black tape exorcism party. Looks like half the royalty in the city are going to ground for something."

"Storm's brewing."

"Already storming, near as I can tell. Flood warnings across half the state."

"Uh, yeah. I was speaking metaphorically, Cleon."

"Fuck your metaphors—I been trudging my ass around all day in this bleak shit while you're sitting somewhere listening to Miley Cyrus."

"Oh, Jesus, is that who this is?"

"Yep."

"God, and this song is really catchy! This is fucking Billy Ray fucking Cyrus's eight-year-old daughter?"

"I think she's almost legal now, but yeah. Where the hell are you?"

"Actually, I'm at Honey Sweet Licks on North Main. You want to come over? I'll buy you a lapdance."

"You're at a goddamn strip club? In the middle of all this shit? I'm going to kill you."

"Now you're starting to sound just like Detective Ladislav."

"Don't you compare me to that son-of-a-bitch. Man like him always pisses me right off—you pull the curtains back and show that guy the secret behind the universe, and he still calls it bullshit."

"You know, I was just thinking that exact thing a few days ago."

"Learned it from me."

"Yesterday, I think it was. God, my days are blurring together. So. You said you had good news, then?"

"Yeah. I tracked down a little bit more on who my little traitor intern Milsborough has been spending time with. Who might have put a gun in his hand and pointed it at you, I mean."

"Huh. Look, before you say anything else, I just want to say that I think Milsborough might be in quite a bit of danger right now."

"You think that the people who set him on you are gonna want payback 'cuz he fucked it up?"

"Yeah."

"Well, I think you might be right."

"I... I also want to apologize if I acted out of turn. I could have maybe subdued him or something instead of hospitalizing him."

"His own damn fault. I always tell people not to pull guns on you, Royden. You go crazy."

"Still. He was your employee, in your home, and I..."

"And you what? Kept his dumb ass from shooting either of us, is what you did. Enough with the apologies, I haven't got all damn night. Thing is, I'm feeling kind of guilty, myself. Milsborough's been acting weird for a bit now, and I guess I just figured he'd snap out of it. But the more I'm digging, the weirder this seems."

"What have you got?"

"Well, he and his girlfriend broke up a little while ago, I knew that. Cutie little thing, too, real big blue eyes like you wouldn't believe. Anyway, since then, it seems like he's been dropping out of a lot of stuff."

"Like what stuff?"

"Like his band and school and his other part-time job. Hell, I was a little surprised he showed up so fast last night, but I didn't want to say anything about it. Seems like our boy has been spending less and less time with his old friends."

"You talked to them?"

"Yep. Met up with his friend, Stevie, who used to be in a band with him until a few months ago—I went and saw a show they did once, in a basement with a lot of spray paint on the walls and a keg. Not my idea of music, but people seemed to like them well enough. Anyway, this Stevie, he says that Milsborough hasn't just been weird and distant. It's like he's changed."

"Changed for the worse."

"Yeah. Spending a lot of his time out in the 'burbs, is what Stevie said. Some place about an hour and a half from here where there's a rundown old indoor paintball facility or something. Used to be a Laser Tag place back in the late 80s, back before the fad wore off, and then a skate park or some such."

I got a little shiver. I could suddenly imagine the huge, off-white edifice, rust-stained and weed-choked parking lot, graffiti and boarded-up windows for blocks in every direction—a rotting bit of abandoned, forgotten Me-Decade 'burb-sprawl turning gray and rotten in the dampness and recession.

"He's been getting weirder since he started going out there, huh?"

"Yep. At first, he had all these stories about funny-sorta stuff going on there, new friends he'd met, but now he doesn't even hang with his old buddies."

"Dammit. You talk to anyone who's been out to this place?"

"That's the thing. Stevie told me that one of their friends, Trent, went out there once with Milsborough, but when they got there, Trent freaked out and wouldn't even go in the door. Said that the place had a stink to it, like real bad b.o. and unwashed hair. Stale chips, old wrestling mats, and ice-cream stains, were his words."

"That'll do it. Okay, two requests: can you get me an address, and would you please for gods' sake stop investigating my case before you get yourself killed?"

"Hell with you, I'll investigate what I damn well like. Anyway, you're not going out there, are you? That's a sure-as-shit leak to the Deep Sideways and worse."

"And I have a feeling that somebody is watering the slippy hole, rather than weeding it. This case... we've got two perpetrators here, Cleon. I know all-too-much about the one and not a damn thing at all about the other. If I can make a surprise visit to the belly of the beast, I will."

"Suit yourself. I'll have an address to you in an hour, tops."

"Thanks."

"Enjoy the strip club."

"Oh, yeah. Will do. Enjoy the rain."

"Fuck you."

CHAPTER 23

Alright, I had one last thing on my agenda before I got the fuck outta here, and it wasn't a call I was excited about making.

I picked up my phone, set it down, had a cigarette, picked my phone up again, and even though he'd taken the one woman who ever really meant anything to me, I called the King of Cahokia.

He picked up. He sounded pissed.

"Royden."

"Your Majesty. Hey, I want to buy something off you."

"And what would that be, Royden?"

"The best talisman or icon of protection you have. I'm staring down the barrel of a whole mess of feisty Abnormalities, and I want the finest magical armor that money can buy."

"I don't sell magic. Is that all?"

"I've got more than cold, hard cash, Garrick. This afternoon, I stole about four hundred bucks from Tama. You do this thing for me, and I'll put the cash right in your hand, and you can tell her that you got it back from me, you big damn hero, you."

He paused.

"That's right. You'll have incontrovertible proof that I'm a scumbag, that you're the good guy, and that instead of just being pissed about it or saying that you would talk to me or something, you fixed the problem without a worry or a hassle. That's got to be worth some points."

"Where are you?"

"I'm at a strip club up on North Main. You might have heard of it. Tama used to work here."

That wasn't true, but it made him angry. And that made me smile.

"I'll find it. Don't go anywhere."

He hung up on me. It sounded like he pressed the off button on his fancy little solid-plate cellphone as hard as he could. Shit, what is it about me that makes people want to slam a receiver into a phone cradle?

An hour later, Garrick showed up huge with righteous indignity and soaking wet. Damn, but that boy is pretty. He was the best-looking guy in the building by far, and in all honesty, prettier than half the girls.

I refused to take my sunglasses off.

He found me, spared a glance at the bags at my feet where I had carefully tucked away my various ingredients and tools, and set a shirt down on the table. It was a faded, oil-stained, gray and yellow extra-large short-sleeve mechanic's work-shirt. On the front left pocket, above the heart, it had a little yellow patch that said *GIL*.

On the back, a huge yellow and black patch advertised *AEGIS AUTOMOTIVE of Mt. Olympus, Hollywood, California* with a bright, gold, shield-like logo.

"Oh, let me guess... magic bulletproof shirt?"

"No. It will not stop any mundane bullets. This is a potent item: ancient and perhaps the only of its kind. The name *Gil* originally comes from the Greek; it means 'shield bearer.' In Hebrew, it means 'happy or bright.' In older English, it is short for *Gilbert*, meaning 'brilliant pledge, steadfast, or trustworthy.' The word *Aegis—*"

"Means a cape worn to display the protection provided by a religious authority or a badge bag that holds a shield. Originally derived from a breastplate in Greek myths. Shows sponsorship, protection, or authority derived from a higher source or a deity. Duh. I'm not an idiot, Heldane, and I only slept through math class, not the fun stuff. So let me fill in the rest: Hollywood is where the gods live now, and I assume that the yellow symbolizes the golden-threaded aegis of Zeus, crafted by Hephaestus and held by both Athena and Apollo in the *Iliad*?"

"This garment will turn back the claws, horns, teeth, and spittle of any Abnormality. It is proof against burning breath and poison blood alike, and it is said that it will even unweave itself, in sacrifice, to protect your flesh against the gaze of a basilisk or the bite of a hydra."

"What about spells?"

"Very few Abnormalities use ritual magic. If any of them are after you, you're going to die with or without that shirt."

"Great. What if an Abnormality throws a car at me?"

"A magical car?"

"Sure."

"Then I hope you have fucking health insurance. It might work, and it might not. Give me Tama's money, so I can get out of this cesspit."

"Man, you don't want a beer or something?"

"No, Royden, I do not. I am loathe to deal with you at the best of times, and you have done nothing but provoke my anger."

"Fine. Here's your money. It's all in singles because I've been stealing it out of g-strings all night. You can count it, if you like."

He stormed away.

I sort of absently felt guilty about being such a prick.

I strongly considered yelling *Thank you, dad!* very loudly, and I foresaw Garrick ignoring me, too proud and dignified to flip me off.

My feeling of guilt passed.

All right, great. I've got my magic armor and my magic gun and thirty pieces of silver to pay the Devil at the Four Way, with almost three hours to spare before the clocks got funny.

I felt, honestly, like I deserved a lapdance.

CHAPTER 24

Iwas in the VIP area, getting a very pleasant lapdance from a very pleasant young lady named Chloe when my phone rang.

Cleon. Oh, yeah, he was going to be calling about that whole stupid haunted Laser Tag place.

Man, how time flies when you've got a naked girl on your lap.

"This is Big Jimmy Jangladesh, and you better hope this is worth my time, motherfucker."

"Oh, great tough-guy act. You trying to impress somebody?"

"Yep. What have you got for me?"

"Well, I tracked down Trent. He isn't looking so good these days."

"Fuck. So the Sideways is really eating into the local reality, huh?"

Chloe looked at me funny, so I handed her a fistful of twenties and asked her to come back in a half-hour. She left without hesitation. That's a work ethic you've got to admire.

"Yeah. Trent's got something that looks a lot like the flu, but the vomiting is worse than I've seen in quite a while. He doesn't have any cash for a doctor, so he's been trying to wait it out for the last week on knock-off NyQuil and chicken soup."

"How long has it been since he went out to the place?"

"About a week exactly since he went to MacSherman Hollows. That's the name of the 'burb, but he couldn't remember a street address."

"Of course he couldn't; it broke half his brain just going there. Jesus, fantastic. He's this sick from Sideways backlash, and he didn't even walk in. Did he say the words *Paese dei Balocchi* at any point?"

"Is that what you're calling our mysterious Sideways spot? He said that there was something weird spray painted over the door in a language he didn't understand. Words looked like *Place de la Bologna*."

"Yep. That's exactly what I was worried about."

"Royden, I assume that you know that you'd be insane to go there. It's a damn deathtrap."

"I have a feeling that it's a trap for wayward boys who don't want to grow up, actually, and I'm getting a little bit nervous about what the kids might turn into. You know the story of Pinocchio, right?"

"Great. We've got ourselves... what, like a Sideways reflection of Pleasure Island?"

"That's the thought. Apparently, though, it wasn't an island in the original book—it was a town or something in the land of Cocagne."

"I've heard of it, although I don't know of any royalty channeling it. Let me get my books."

I hated to do this, getting the poor old guy further and further into my case, but if I didn't give Cleon something to worry about tonight, there was a good chance that he would try skipping off to investigate the problem himself. I took a sip of my Coke and admired the decor for a few minutes.

The decor included boobs. That was nice.

"All right, Royden?"

"Yeah. That was fast."

"I have a near-photographic memory for my books. You know that as well as anybody."

"Still, it's very impressive. I had just figured that you might be getting senile in your old age."

"Blow yourself. All right, here's what I've got—according to Herman Pleij, from *Dreaming of Cockaigne*, it's a place where 'roasted pigs wander about with knives in their backs to make carving easy, grilled geese fly directly into one's mouth, where cooked fish jump out of the water and land at one's feet. The weather is always mild, the wine flows freely, sex is readily and freely available, and all people enjoy eternal youth.' Sounds like quite the place."

"Sure does. You have to wonder why it isn't more heavily contested amongst the Secret Kings."

"Probably a curse or two bouncing about, if I know the lay of the land among our more vicious colleagues. Echoes of madness and death kind of stuff. The problem with a fictional Emptied Empire like that is that people don't tell stories about perfect places where nothing ever goes wrong; it's always sugar-coated poison, to teach your kids the value of doing their schoolwork."

"Better to choose black-and-white Kansas over the Emerald City and all that. But, if you don't mind me saying so, you're starting to talk like a totemic magic proponent here, Cleon."

"The problem isn't that the theory is wrong, Royden. The problem is that people have anecdotal evidence that it's true and, more importantly, that they *want* it to be true. People don't want to believe that they have free will once they start channeling a potent and fearsome empire—they want to believe that the mystery of the dust moves through them and that their cruelty and callous disconnection from the mainstream is the fault of the magic, not of themselves."

"Okay, so you're saying that even if Cocagne isn't cursed, driving people to insanity and gluttony and terrible physical transformation and all that, anyone who would choose to tap the power has to be the sort of person who wants immediate, consequence-free pleasure and, in their heart of guilty hearts, knows that there's no such thing. And it turns a nice kid with a broken heart into an attempted murderer."

"On the nose. Like a pothead who grows his hair out and starts listening to the Dead; it's not the chemical doing it, it's the paradigm. At least in theory. All right, Royden, I'll see if I can come up with anything else on the topic. Come to think of it, there was a drifter who wandered through a few years back, name of Magic-Eatin' Jim, who called himself the Duke of the Big Rock Candy Mountain. Sounds like a lead."

"Try to track him down, would you?"

"Got it."

"And, Cleon, if you don't mind terribly, how would you feel about checking on a missing-person report from last night that mysteriously stopped being important to Detective Ladislav?"

"Huh. Not my usual thing, but you're saying that this would piss him off, me finding out?"

"That is correct."

"I'm on it. What are your plans for the Witching Hour?"

"I've got thirty pieces of silver, a few esoteric questions for the Devil at the Four Way, and all but a signed affidavit from the King of Majooj that he's going to send a horde of monsters after me as soon as I poke my head behind the curtain."

"Huh. You didn't mention the King of Majooj before. The same one that the Prince of Minos is looking for?"

"Oh. Yeah. I was kind of hoping that you wouldn't have to find out about all that, honestly. He's my problem, not yours."

"Shit. Your problems have a way of fucking with people who are close to you, Royden."

"Christ. See, this is why I was dead."

"No, you fucker. You were dead because it was more convenient to you to be dead than to tell me what the fuck was going on. And, might I note, the basic reason that your problems have such as nasty habit of latching onto the throats of people who are friends of yours is that you never goddamn tell anyone anything."

"Are we really having the conversation now?"

"Yes."

"Great. Look, this thing about me not keeping you up to speed, that's... not entirely fair, Cleon."

"Oh, I'm sure you got a million good reasons to keep my ass in the dark, and if I get killed because of it, I just know that you'll be real sorry about it. But I haven't seen you in months, I thought you were dead, and then I leave you alone for less than twenty-four hours to track down a new sacred space, and the shit you get yourself into has to do with the damn King of Majooj, whoever the fuck that is."

"Actually, that's why I wanted the black tape in the first place and why the Prince of Minos was looking. I was pretty sure that there was a price on my head, mystical or otherwise, and I was hoping to get it stripped onto cassette. Yank the divination or the mark or the scent or whatever off of me."

"And?"

"Well, now I know for a fact that I'm all but a dead-man-walking, and the guy after me doesn't even need to bother looking that hard, so I don't need the exorcism."

"You're a real asshole, Royden."

"I didn't want you getting hurt in all this, Cleon. I'm sorry."

"You got a goddamn funny way of showing it."

I didn't know what to say.

"... sorry?"

"Oh, fucking save it. I'm a big boy, and every member of the secret royalty knows that you don't open the hall of your court to the King of Jangladesh unless you want trouble."

"Is that really what they say?"

"Yes."

"I'm... I'm flattered, actually."

He laughed. Oh, god, how I've missed that.

"Oh, yeah, you should be. Earned every bit of it."

"All right, then, I'll come clean. I'm thinking that I've stepped in some real shit on this case and don't want you getting hurt or killed."

"Then tell me everything you know."

"That could take awhile. And I'm not sure, to be honest, exactly what I know."

"We'll have ourselves a proper court, then. When you're done with the Devil at the Four Way, you come to my place."

"... you just really don't want me going to your turncoat helper's Paese dei Balocchi by myself, do you?"

"Fuck, no, I do not. You'll get yourself killed, Royden."

"Well, I don't want you going, either. And I also don't want you coming with me."

"Fine. We'll send Ladislav."

"That's a bad idea, and you know it."

"We'll send the King of Cahokia, then."

"I'm hanging up now, Cleon."

"You're no fun anymore. See you after midnight."

Click.

And then, right there, ended the very best part of my day. I think that maybe, just maybe, talking to Cleon like old times was exactly what I needed. I hadn't realized it at the time, but our reunion last night had been all too brief and all too strained and all too polite.

I guess I just needed someone to see my bullshit for what it really was, call me an asshole and still like me afterward, despite the fact that I am, unfortunately, exactly who I am.

Speaking of me being who I am, I had about two hours before the Quantum Time, and I was aching to go ruin somebody's day.

Since staying here any longer, especially until midnight, would be tantamount to falling asleep right before the executioner's blade came down, I decided to leave.

My phone was done charging, after all.

And so, now, I was going... where, again?

Well, how about nowhere in particular? I've heard that it's nice this time of year.

CHAPTER 25

As I walked and smoked and hated the rain and got used to the weight of my now nearly overflowing backpack full of goodies, I began to contemplate the genius of the plan the King of Majooj and the King of Cocagne had cooked up to deal with me.

The way the deal worked right now, all I really had to do to stay safe was simply not use the 25th Hour.

Ever again.

If I just sat in that strip club and bathed myself in human anchor points, even a guy as trained as myself would have a hard time kicking back behind the curtain to the Nether Hour at midnight, and the trip wouldn't last very long even if I crept between the hands of the clock successfully. Maybe a few seconds, tops.

Nowhere near long enough for a horde of Abnormalities to descend on me like a Biblical plague.

And I'm good at slipping into the Dreamtime. Heck, there are competent people who couldn't have made the slide back in the police station. It's chock full of anchor points, but—and this is the scary part—not as many as John Q. Public would probably like to believe. A building with plumbing problems or a stain on some carpet somewhere or an unexplained draft or even just a few lights that really ought to be re-wired as soon as somebody gets around to doing it... that's all it takes. Most cops are a lot more worried about real life than they are about how recently their garbage can has been taken out or what's fermenting in the back of the fridge.

And a part of me was wondering if having the demon clown on Kynan's tail had helped pull us through, so it could kill him.

That did not make me feel better.

Point being, these two bastards were all but letting me go, if I wanted to go. All I had to do to avoid a mauling by some Sideways spawn with human excrement for blood, a carapace made out of shattered glass, and a hermit crab for a face was stay on this side of the Quantum Time indefinitely. Hell, the two of them could afford to set me up in style, now, too. Unless I missed my guess, all I had to do was say *Please, sir, may I have some more boobies?* and the King of Cocagne would fall all over himself to throw me lavish parties the likes of which I had gotten only the littlest taste of tonight.

And I would be safe, secure, and bought right up until the exact moment that the King of Majooj, riding Fadey Bohdan's puppet-body, decided to have me killed.

Pincher maneuver; hammer and anvil.

Let the little bastard get comfortable on the anvil, and then bring the hammer down when he stops being funny.

Fuck them.

I was muttering hateful curses and complex, deeply offensive threats against the two of them when the cop car pulled up next to me, lights rolling.

Dammit, why do I always do these things, like leaving my apartment or leaving a strip club or, well, leaving the womb?

I was so happy there, I seem to remember.

"Royden Poole, you are under arrest."

"Evening, Lieutenant Krabowski. How's it hanging?"

"Put your fucking hands up, you little piece of shit."

"Is this about those unpaid parking tickets?"

CHAPTER 26

Lieutenant Krabowski leaned over the roof of the car, taking aim at me using both hands, and the passenger-side door opened to disgorge the still-surprised-looking new guy, Officer What's-His-Name.

"Cuff him, Officer Merrick."

Oh yeah, that's his name.

"Nice to see both of you boys again. Have you been working out, lieutenant? Your abs look huge."

Dammit, I hate getting arrested.

One of the many emotionally calming sayings that gets me through the day when the skies are spitting flaming arrows and there's dog shit on my shoes is that a person can get used to just about anything, given the chance. Hell, folks have been surviving and bitching about the weather and thinking about the nature of man and pumping out babies for something like fifty thousand years now, and we've only had hot and cold running water indoors for, like, a century at the most.

When the human race reaches out and pokes its curious little nose over the edge of the known universe, people will have gotten used to all sorts of things that would have freaked out humans only maybe a half-generation before.

Still, there's something about being arrested that's just plain miserable, and I'll probably never get used to it.

I mean, there I am, with a large angry guy pointing a gun at me and telling me to keep my hands where he can fucking see them, a kid barely old enough to shave creeping toward me with cuffs in one hand looking like he's about to try to disarm a live nuclear weapon, and my first instinct is to check my cellphone just to see what time it is.

Oh, but no, I can't do that! Nor can I ask them to just let me go take a leak. What a drag.

"I said to put your hands up, Poole!"

"Got it. Hey, Krabowski, real quick, you know what time it is?"

"Time to shut the fuck up."

"No, but seriously, I have a date with your wife later tonight. What time is it?"

He refused to tell me, so I glanced around as non-threateningly as possible until I spotted a bank sign up the road with the time and temp.

11:28.

"Damn. I've been wandering around out here for almost an hour and a half? No wonder somebody spotted me."

"You're not real inconspicuous, Poole. I'm just happy that I'm the one who caught you. I've earned it."

Officer Merrick walked around behind me, pulled both of my arms down real hard, and locked my wrists into the cuffs. He started mumbling my Miranda rights with a nervous Southern twang.

And yes, cuffs fit on midget wrists. I hate it, which is why I've gotten good at breaking them.

"Uh, guy, not to be a pain in the ass, but maybe you should have had me take my backpack off, first."

The kid blushed. The lieutenant holstered his weapon. "You shut the fuck up, Poole. Merrick, get his ass into the car."

Oh, crap, now what? The back door locks, and then the car drives to the jail. And then those doors lock, too, and pretty soon, I'm behind a whole lot of locks.

Fuck it. I decided to go for broke.

"Maybe you should *have me sit in the front*, officer."

I felt the power of ancient Jangledesh surge in my throat, mojo ran in my veins, and without thinking, the kid turned and opened the front passenger-side door for me.

Gods dammit, I'm not good at this at the best of times, and I'm both out of practice and low on juice. Please, by the ash and dust of every mad bastard who ever roamed the grim deserts of Churu, Ganganagar, and Hanumangarh stabbing anyone who wasn't a clansman, just keep me safe until I can catch the crazy train through the Hole behind Midnight and get myself into a whole new world of life-threatening bullshit.

The kid pushed me into the front seat, and the lieutenant blinked twice. "Hey, what the fuck?"

"Uh, it would be better if *I sit in the front*."

He blinked again and then looked real suspicious. "Then where the fuck is Officer Merrick going to sit, smart guy?"

Crap.

"*He should*, uh, *stay here and look for clues while you take me in*. That would be the best idea."

He squinted at me and then raised his chin. He looked over the top of the car, where the kid was still standing, holding my door open. "Officer Merrick, you stay here. I'm going to call this in, get this fucker behind bars, and have someone come pick you up once you've secured the scene."

The officer slammed my door shut. Great.

Now, every member of the secret royalty worth the title can wrap their words up in power and force their will on the unsuspecting masses. The King of Cahokia allegedly refers to it as the *great voice of king's command*; Cleon just calls it *hey, fuck you, I'm in charge here*, and I used to call it the *Bavarian fire drill* back when I used it a lot—but the problem is that people have buckets and buckets of that pesky free will, and it's damnably hard to get people to do something they don't already want to do unless you're pushing harder, and far more expertly, than I know how to do.

Officer Merrick didn't want to get in the car with me. Presumably, he's been hearing horror stories about my various criminal escapades for the last twenty-four hours, and if he got himself a good look at the way I left the interrogation room before somebody came in and cleaned up several pints of arterial spray, he had a right to be nervous. Telling him to stay behind fit his truest and deepest desires perfectly.

And, of course, Lieutenant Krabowski had every reason to want to bring me in all by his lonesome. After all, hadn't he just told me that he was happy that *he* was the one who caught me?

Hell, he'd probably like to stop on the way to the station to beat the hell out of me. I could talk him into that, I'm sure.

But convincing him to, say, drop me off at a steakhouse right now was out of the question. Oh, sure, there are people out there—and for the most part really callous fucks who no longer think of humans as particularly worth a damn— who could have talked him into loaning them his gun, his keys, his badge, his wife and kids, and a couple hundred bucks before swallowing his own tongue, but I'm not one of them.

Fuck, fuck, fuck.

So I braced myself against the seat back, popped the metal of my cuffs out of shape with a grunt, and put my foot through his radio right as Krabowski got in. I kept my hands tucked underneath my ass and put on my most innocent grin.

"The... the fuck just happened?"

"Huh. I think your thing is broken, lieutenant."

"Did you just break my fucking two-way?"

"Uh, no. I kicked it, and it's broken, but I think *it's pretty damn obvious that I'm not the one who broke it*. I weigh, like, fifty pounds."

"Shut up. Fuck. All right, sit your ass still."

The car started up, and we pulled out at quite a few more miles-per-hour than I felt was entirely safe.

Now, this was going to be interesting.

I didn't want to slip behind the curtain with Krabowski, but I also had no intention of getting thrown into jail. I had a date with the Devil at the Four Way, and there're places in holding that are anchor-heavy enough that I can't slip into the 25th.

Hell, even if I could, there are simply too many doors between lock-up and freedom, and not a one of them likes to move.

Dammit, what would Jesus do?

"So, uh, lieutenant. You know it's coming up on midnight. Aren't you worried that I'll just, you know, slip out again?"

"Nope. You're getting processed with a fucking nightstick, if I have a damn thing to say about it, and then you're going into the tightest cell we've got, you little shit."

"Bah. None of your co-workers has half the balls it takes to fight me, and there's no cell on earth that can hold me. I'm the fucking Hindu Houdini, and you know that as well as I do."

He glared at me, taking his eyes off the road for far longer than I thought was particularly safe, given our current near-eighty-mile-an-hour velocity. "We'll see about that."

"Aren't you the least bit curious about how I got out last time?"

"Nope."

"Okay, that's fair."

I let a minute pass: "But... aren't you the least bit curious as to why *I let myself get caught just now*?"

He stomped on the brakes and fixed me with a nasty and paranoid look as we skidded to a halt. Okay, great, now I had his attention.

"Fuck you."

"No, really. If I'm the fucking master of illusions and trickery and all of that like you think I am, how the hell did I wind up on the exact right side of the road at *exactly* the right time for you to snag me?"

"Bullshit."

"This is all part of my plan, lieutenant. How about this, if you're so incredulous: why am I sitting in the front seat, and *you know that I have no cuffs on*, while your partner is standing a couple dozen blocks back there, scratching his head and picking his nose... and you haven't even called my arrest in, yet?"

His eyes went wide and flicked back and forth between his broken radio and me. He wondered about the fact that I was in the front seat for about an eighth of a second and then decided not to think about it before the migraine hit. He settled on the one thing that he could wrap his brain around: trying to guess whether or not I was bluffing about the cuffs. For some reason, it seemed really credible.

"Show me your hands."

"Did I say that I'm not wearing cuffs? I meant that I totally *am* wearing cuff, and they're so super awesome. Now, please, drive me to the police station."

He stared at me, one eye twitching, trying to decide what to do next and hating it.

Here's the thing: a part of me really went out to the poor bastard. There I was, damaging his sanity, potentially quite irrevocably, and all Lieutenant Krabowski wanted to do was lock up a dangerous career criminal, wash his hands, punch out, and then probably go home and watch some sports team or another doing some kind of sports thing while drinking a beer.

The American dream, and all that.

Technically, I think that's the Canadian dream, too, but with a different sport. And a different beer. Maybe the Australian dream and the Mexican dream, too, now that I think about it.

Perhaps, with only minor variations, it's the *human* dream.

The real problem, of course, was that I wasn't even trying to poke holes in the guy's sanity just yet. If I was being a real dick, I would have punched all of his teeth down his throat, dragged the both of us out of the car and down a blind alley, and then jumped into the Nether Hour where I could feed him to abnormalities.

Ugh, the terrible things I do when I'm trying to be nice.

Not my fault that me having magical powers was such a problem for the lieutenant. And come to think of it, where the fuck was I going to go once I escaped custody? Just keep avoiding cops forever and sleeping... where, exactly?

There's an old line from a friend of mine named Seanbaby that goes, "If police were allowed to believe in the supernatural, they would be shooting people all day long. Meth addicts would be shot as goblins. People lined up for *Twilight* would be gunned down as vampires. And like I mentioned before, gay prostitutes performing deer necromancy would be... actually, I think they already shoot you for that."

Like so many things Sean used to say to me, it was sort of vaguely applicable to the situation at the time.

Also, later.

I made a decision.

"All right then, Krabowski. Let's do it this way: you're not sure if I'm handcuffed or not, and we both know that the door next to me isn't locked. You don't want to check to see if I'm handcuffed because that would take putting your right hand under my ass and that puts you close enough that I might do something dangerous.

"If you started driving right now, you might be able to get your gun out of your holster and pop me before I decide to slip out that door, assuming that I'm not cuffed and, thus, that I can get the door to open.

"But if I'm not cuffed, you also can't go for your pistol right now, because I could come across the seat and knife you, just like I knifed that big guy last night, before you got it out of the holster.

"But you also don't want to shoot me just yet because killing a cuffed, unarmed midget in the front seat of your car is not a good way to build credit with the Police Chief."

He glared at me.

"That is, if I'm still cuffed. So, then, we're at an impasse. You can't call for backup, and you can't keep driving, and you can't check to see if I'm cuffed. But here's the even stickier part: you already know that I want you to take me to the police station, but maybe I'm just saying that I want you to take me to the police station, so you'll not take me there. But how about this: where else the fuck can you take me?"

He licked his lips, trying to hate me to death.

"There's nothing you can trust in this situation with the exception of one thing: it's almost midnight."

"What the fuck is that supposed to mean?"

"You've heard the crazy rumors. Read all the police reports. Half the weird shit I've ever been involved in has had something to do with midnight—before it, during it, or right after it. My disappearing act last night? Midnight on the dot. Hell, I'll bet that Ladislav told you to get me to the station by 11:55, and don't spare the horses. Shit, that's probably why he picked you, beyond the fact that you already know how dangerous I am when I'm feeling cornered. You drive like a spastic fuck."

"Your point, asshole?"

"You don't believe that I can do magic tricks. All this little small-time, con-game bullshit that I'm pulling right now, telling you one thing and then telling you another, trying to get you worked up so you make a mistake, this is as deep as my vaunted mystical powers get. But there are people who do believe in my amazing ability to walk out of any cell on the planet, teleport across town, pop open a pair or two of cuffs, and stab a man three to four times my size to death all just at the stroke of midnight. Detective Ladislav is one of them. And so am I."

"Because you're crazy."

"And you're not. Only a really crazy and unhinged guy believes his own cult's hype, just like only a very stupid drug dealer uses his own product. What I'm saying is that for all you know, *my crazy plan rests on getting to the police station by midnight*, so I need you to drive me there right now."

He stared at me, and then a little smile creased his lip.

"Fuck you, Poole. No, I think that you and me are going to sit right here for a little while."

Oh, lordy lordy no, don't throw me in the briar patch!

"What? Seriously? We're just going to sit here?"

"That's right. And your little witching hour is going to come and go, and you're still going to be here in the car. And then I'm going to drive your ass to the station and book you."

"Fine. Fuck it. You mind if I smoke?"

"Yep. Don't mind one bit if I have one, though."

CHAPTER 27

So there we sat, two guys both real pissed off and each thinking that we were so much smarter than the other one. Without my cellphone in front of me, I had to be careful to feel for the shift in Quantum Tide, but the neighborhood couldn't have been more perfect: cold, quiet, lonely, with old leaves and cigarette butts caked in the gutters and neon glaring down on us, a flickering sodium lamp about a half-block up keeping time with the wind.

This was middle ground: claimed territory of the waking world, paved over with human attention, with plenty of little cracks in the mass consciousness splintered and scattered through the asphalt like frozen lightning bolts. I kept looking up and down the block, watching for the signs of the sky shifting imperceptibly into the Nether Hour.

"Well, guess you got me, lieutenant."

"Shut the fuck up, Poole. You got another thirty seconds."

"Great. Hey, I just realized: since the world has, like, twenty-four different time zones, does that mean that I could have used my midnight magic at any time?"

"Eat me, you little fuck."

"I'm just now realizing, it doesn't even make any sense. I mean, would the magic not work if I crossed state lines and jumped forward an hour? What about on a plane going from New York to LA? And what about daylight savings time?"

"Shaddup."

"Hey, do you want to know how magic works? Like, *really* works?"

"No."

"So, you know how they say that we only use 10% of our brains?"

He did not bother to indulge me by responding.

"Well, that's totally not the case at all. We use 100% of our brains, all the time, same way that we use 100% of our spinal columns, digestive tracts, and toes. Otherwise, head wounds would be pretty insignificant, don't you think? People would be like, 'Hooray, only a head wound! Thank god because I wasn't using a full ninety percent of it!' So, if..."

"Shut. The fuck. Up."

Fine advice. I closed my eyes and tried to center my thoughts on the black ocean of time hanging just above us—that place on the dark side of noon. Everything around me got a little crisper, as if the wind was blowing through the car.

The one thing I didn't want to do was yank Lieutenant Krabowski through with me although it would have been all too easy. Hell, he was keeping focused on me hard enough that it was going to be all but impossible not to yank him along with me up the spout into the Other Interval. But I also didn't want to bring the car with me, or any of the bullshit sticking to it, like the guns in the trunk or the anchor-heavy license and registration. The weight of those materials held onto the real world and peeled off of me. Krabowski stuck to them, hard.

Good cop.

The seat started to feel soft. *Whispy*, you might say. Without looking, I let the wind press against my back as I extended my legs through the bottom of the floorboard and started walking forward along the street.

I opened my eyes, and I was alone on a deserted road under a sky the color of a million bruises piled on top of each other. Large sections of tar and cement were missing on this side of the curtain, and moist black earth spilled up through the holes.

Ahead of me, the intersection with flickering sodium lights was now shining half a shade more gray, if that's at all possible.

I performed a minor-at-best ritual involving no more than three languages I don't speak and the burning of one paper doll with my name on it. Then I spat on the ground.

Suddenly, five figures stood in a circle surrounding me, wrapped up in long black robes.

Awesome.

I pulled off my backpack and rummaged around for my baggie full of coins.

"Hail, hail, thou dwellers at the crossroad. The King of Jangladesh comes to the Four Way at midnight to barter with whatever devils he may find and brings thirty pieces of stolen silver to make trade."

The five looked up at me and grinned.

Shit. Skull-faces.

With one voice, they spoke. "We are the curses which beset all who live, mortal and immortal alike; pale Disease and vengeful Worry, and Hunger that persuades to crime; death-dealing War and mad Discord, and we alone hold court this night."

"You, devils, will barter for answers to my queries."

I made sure that I didn't make that a question.

"Indeed. In silver and in blood and in bondage-pledge to us, we will barter you for what you seek. We are the doormen of Hades and know all things that the living share with the dead: what secrets the dead alone keep are beyond us, things known only to the living are shrouded in mist, and the secrets of those never born are best left unspoken, even by ones such as us."

"I bow, and seek to know three things, and three things only."

"We see. Your thirty silver pieces will purchase three answers, but beyond that, the price will be in blood. A pound of flesh for each answer, and when you are no more, a year apiece of your soul's servitude. Now, then, what... *things* do you seek to know, oh King of Jangladesh?"

"First is the nature of a certain weapon, stolen from my enemy and held in my armory; it is a strange device, and I seek to know its curses."

"The second?"

"I wish to know the secrets, each, of my two enemies, the Kings of Majooj and of Cocagne, regarding how they wish to use the jar stolen from the Forgotten Queen of Scythia."

"And the third?"

"Nice try. That's three questions right there: the nature of one weapon, one enemy, and a second enemy. I wasn't born yesterday."

"Hmm. You are a cautious magician, little King of Jangladesh. We shall not attempt to deceive you again."

"Oh, go fuck yourselves. Of course, you will. Now answer me my goddamn questions."

"Very well. The weapon you carry in your pack was wrought of daydream-stuff and jellyfish stings, of snips and snails and of puppy-dog tails, made strong and plastic by the weave of a waterfall-dwelling dvergar shapeshifter and gold-sorcerer called Pale Alberich of Niflung; also known as Dwarf Andvari, the Careful One; also called Auberon, the Lord of Fairies, the crowned and tailed child-taker Erlkönig, ancient brother-foe of Loki and consort of Titania, the daughter of King Cronus. It is one of many brothers, all forged together in a squirming litter, and it carries no curse except that it longs to be used in play, to shatter windows and break tin cans and knock over vases and numb the flesh of those it bites."

"Fantastic."

"Shall we speak more of this weapon? You have but to ask."

"Get bent. Answer me my second question."

"He, the King who bears the Crown of Majooj, was once called Gregory Howsgrove, also called Bastard Greg the Kitty-Cat Killer. He channeled the might of his empire, in early days, without knowing it—making himself a secret monster that delighted in the anguish of those from whom he took most precious loves in the dead of night. The totems of Magog are, then, to be always hated by every other; to be persecuted and sealed up but never forgotten, to be hunted and denied and spoken against in all places. He gains strength when he is watched for but not seen; his power is in lordship over monsters via unspeakable acts. He seeks and gains a jar to gain ever-more-powerful bodies and make these bodies his own."

"Neat. My last question, please."

"There is no King of Cocagne."

I very, very, very nearly spoke the word *what* out loud.

"Wha... well, isn't that... sure is interesting. Yep."

"Hmm. You are cautious indeed, King of Jangladesh."

"Piss off. Answer my fucking question."

"No single soul bears the Crown of Cocagne at this moment, for the Emptied Empire is in mighty flux. The jar taken from the Queen of Scythia factors into this war of succession, but none who know have yet died—and thus, the details are hazy to us."

I resisted the urge to ask about a dozen questions.

Like, how the fuck do you have a war of succession without any dead people? How can there not be a King of Cocagne right now? What are these assholes up to? Where did the old king get the resources or the balls to barter with a legendary dweller in the Near Sideways that has appeared in a Wagner opera, a Shakespearean play, a Goethe poem, and a Middle High German epic after leaving the Norse myths?

Oh, and what the fuck is wrong with my life that I have a nemesis known to the Devil at the Four Way as "Bastard Greg the Kitty-Cat Killer"?

Instead of getting any answers and spending the rest of the night carving pieces off myself, I dropped the silver and left.

CHAPTER 28

Still in the Nether Time, I stormed toward Cleon's place to meet up and talk shop, pulling my fancy new curse-free gun out of my backpack and hoping idly to get attacked by some monsters, so I had an excuse to kill something.

It felt heavier than before. I stared at it, watching the little dials crank back and forth. I noticed that one of the knobs had two settings: a smiley face and a frowny face. The little plastic piece was set to the angry mode but was twitching as if it was trying to crank even further away from *happy* and into a theoretical *super-pissed* setting.

This was my kind of gun.

For no good reason, I fired several shots down the street, feeling the gun thud in my hand and hearing glass shatter somewhere off in the distance like I had just hit a home run out on the sandlot. A dog started barking, completing the illusion.

It was a semi-automatic. Sexy.

A little bit of smoke came wafting out of the gun with a scent somehow familiar. It smelled like hot Vaseline. Weird.

CHAPTER 29

The horizon is always an interesting thing to observe during the Nether Time.

Hell, the first few months when I started using the Interval In-Between—still calling myself an hourist because I didn't know any better and because I hadn't laid claim to Jangdalesh, yet—when I was slowly dropping out of my boring real life and spending more and more time every day giving myself a crash-course education in what Cleon calls "postmodern meta-mythology," I could sit on a rooftop with a sketchpad for an eternity, just watching the horizon shift and warp, watching the comings and goings of kings.

One of the weird, takes-getting-used-to things about spacetime during the Unknown Hour is that everything seems a lot closer, somehow. I don't mean that it actually *is* closer although there are certainly some tricks that I've never quite picked up properly that can get you from point A to point B more swiftly than any waking-world conveyance, like the folks who can step off of a curb in Singapore and have their feet hit the street in Madrid or find the vaunted Labyrinth behind the City that the innumerable Heirs of Minos are eternally squabbling over.

I just mean that it all *seems* closer, like how the moon is always huge in the sky right when it comes sailing over the edge of the world, the planet's best-loved and most famous Ponzo illusion.

As I flipped my gaze over the tops of buildings tonight, I could see the huge, bone-white hull of the giant-carrying Naglfar crest around a series of skyscrapers in the distance. Hell, it could be hundreds of miles from here: the King of Jötunheimr out on a late-night pleasure cruise with old Captain Hrym, hunting for Scylla and Charybdis and their children, that chattering clutch of Catch-22s.

I walked and smoked, taking the back road toward Cleon's. I had a careful balance to maintain tonight—didn't want to get yanked too close to home and slip out of the 25th until I got back to the squad car, didn't want to get caught out in the open and jumped by whatever monsters the King of Majooj had cooked up for me, and most certainly didn't want to sink deep into the unnoticed spaces and get yanked Sideways.

The gun in my hand was reassuring, at least.

And knowing that it wasn't cursed... oh, that felt good.

See, the thing about checking your stolen goods for curses is that it's always the smartest move, and just the act of having done it, like getting tested for STDs, sometimes spins your whole perception of the universe right around. And the thing about unaccounted-for magical items is that you start getting paranoid about every little stray thought that pops up—and the scariest part is that concluding that you must be under a curse is sometimes dangerously reassuring, just like the totemic magic theory when taken to a logical, damnable extreme.

For example, I'm striding along the Dark Ways of the Unknown with the awesome aegis the King of Cahokia sold me wrapped like a robe underneath my coat, the hem of the XL shirt brushing back and forth over my shins, and a heavy chunk of bone-shattering Sideways tech in my hand when an idle, casually hurt thought about Tama and how she never paid attention to me when I was trying to be serious happens to cross my mind.

Now, there are a million explanations for this. Maybe it's because I'm nervous, and my brain is trying to distract me by bringing up stuff that will make me usefully sullen, aggressive, and trigger happy. Maybe it's because, subconsciously, I'm trying to remember every piece of good advice I ever filtered from Cleon to Tama, and I'm coming up short. Maybe I'm just pissed at the fact that the both of them would know better than to have gotten themselves into this stupid situation in the first place. And maybe, just maybe, it's because I'm wearing

Tama's new boyfriend's shirt, and I'm relying on him actually being as much more competent than me as everyone seems to think he is to save my bacon.

Maybe a lot of things.

But if I wasn't sure in my heart of hearts that the gun wasn't cursed, I might just attribute the feeling to the pistol.

Sure, why not? Maybe the gun is a misogynist. Makes as much sense as anything, I guess. It's a gun made out of the clubhouse with a "no girls allowed" sign posted outside, designed to be fired while letting out war-whoops and playing in the mud with your best friends. And, then, if it's not *really* my fault that I'm getting a little angry, now, about that time I tried telling Tama about the whole shitfest brewing with the Forgotten King of Eriu and the Warrior-Princes of Builg and all she could ask was if this "was about leprechauns," well, fuck it. And, if I'm getting a little pissed off now and kind of want to shoot her, well, hey, it's not my fault!

Yes, bitch, it was about fucking leprechauns.

A person can get themselves into some dangerous situations if they think they don't have control, when they can abdicate responsibility to an outside, unknowable force. I have a feeling more people have been done in by made-up, all-in-the-head curses than by the real thing, honestly. Here, you can try it at home, using a trick a very frightening guy named Max used to pull: next time some stranger pisses you off, just look them real hard in the eye and tell them, without blinking, that tomorrow will be the worst goddamn day of their life.

You have to sell it, sure. Any good confidence man can tell you that delivery, clear-headedness, and timing are worth at least as much as a solid plan. And remember, you can only bring 50% to any relationship: if the other party isn't emotionally investing a damn thing in the exchange, you can push as hard as you want, and it's still going to come up a failing grade, whether you're picking up girls at the bar, building a solid relationship with your dad, or pretending to put a hex on somebody. So, sure, maybe they'll laugh you off, and maybe something really exciting and wonderful will happen in the next five minutes, and they'll forget all about you.

But it has happened.

You push them, just enough, with that seed of doubt. Hell, if you really sell it, throwing everything you've got into it, it only takes that other person a few little foibles and fumbles in the next day before they start investing a little bit of belief: 10%, then 20%; pretty soon, you've got yourself a C average. Push someone at the right time, like they teach in cult-school, waiting until someone is stressed out and full of grief, and you'll be amazed what you can do.

I'll bet you good money that the real original Hercules got nothing more than a nasty dose of somebody's *witchcraft*; the sort of thing that we would just call neurolinguistic programming today. And, by the by, I'm talking about whatever sad, backwoods Greek bastard the legends were based on, way back before a Roman-looking guy with the same name took up residence in the Near Sideways to start performing feats of legendary strength in exchange for women and booze and then got himself devoured whole and crispy by the Formless Magistrates.

My point is, you put a few heavy drinks in a meat-headed, country bumpkin rage-case and tell him that he's been "driven mad by the goddess Hera," you need just stand back and watch what happens.

People tend to forget that even in the most shining mythological accounts of the guy, old Herc killed his music tutor Linus with his own lyre after the guy reprimanded the kid for making mistakes, back around 1264 BCE; that's *well* before the murder of his family or the subsequent "famous labors." It's treated like a footnote in the more modern stories or ignored altogether; but seriously, if you knew a kid who, during a routine guitar lesson, beat his music teacher to death with said guitar, your first instinct would probably be to put him in solitary forever. That guy only needs a poke in the right direction, and pretty soon you've got piles of dead people.

Anyway, my point is that telling yourself you're being mind controlled is powerful and seductive stuff. Just ask anybody who's really into the S&M scene—letting go can be fun. And the hint of a curse is sometimes just as dangerous as the real thing.

Oh, and in case you're wondering why I didn't have the Prince of Minos check my cool new gun for curses, well... oracles open themselves up to a lot when they read ahead in the programming language of the Secret Universe. If there had been a nasty bit of bug-fuckery somewhere in the system, I didn't want him getting swallowed whole.

Probably because I'm such a nice guy.

As for the Devil at the Four Way, well... he can go fuck himself as far as I'm concerned.

On my way to Cleon's, I'm thinking about how awesome that would have been. If I had actually tricked the infamous, immortal crossroads-dweller into opening a virus-filled psychic-email from Loki's dick brother buried inside a magic gun, well, I would go down in history as the cleverest bastard of all time.

And that's when the screaming swarm of striges fell upon me.

CHAPTER 30

The thing about a strix is that it's really not that dangerous. Oh, sure, it drinks blood, and it looks like a multi-winged over-sized mosquito crossed with a barn owl and a very shriveled, ugly old woman's face with raptor talons coming out the top of its head—and it howls a lot. And if you give it an opportunity to pump anticoagulant saliva into you and then disembowel you, it will take you up on it.

And, yes, they can grow pretty big: I've seen one the size of a rottweiler, winging around and cackling and rolling its bloodshot eyes.

But, considering some of the shit that roams around at this time of night, a strix is a minor annoyance.

Except in swarms. A mass of striges is bad fucking news.

There was an ear-shattering *wooo* sound, like a hundred firetruck sirens and train whistles going off simultaneously. A shadow fell over me like somebody threw a refrigerator-box full of heat-seeking rabid chihuahuas off the roof above the alley, and then a mass of wings and teeth and claws wrapped around me.

Thump, thump, thump thumb-thump-thum-thum-tum-tm!

A couple-dozen sharp beak-stingers punched through my coat, hit my magic shirt, and stopped cold, like a greyhound sprinting into a brick wall. The strix, like a sort of omnicidal hummingbird, puts everything it has into a bite. I'll say this now, with not a moment of hesitation and no small hit to my ego: if I hadn't bought the aegis from Garrick fucking Heldane, I would be dead right now.

Sadly, the shirt did not a damn thing to stop a mass of striges from jabbing serrated hooks into my exposed arms, neck, and face.

Ow, ow, ow.

I wheeled around, trying to shake the fuckers off and lashing out with my arms to crush shutter-flapping wings and gnashing claws in my grasp. I called on every ounce of my power, roaring almost loud enough to be heard above the howl of the swarm.

Dark bluish blood spattered to the alley floor.

Yeah, that was mine.

I don't know why, exactly, but the blood of kings usually shines a weird off-blue color in the light of the 25th, and the really old bastards who run the place have a black tinge to the stuff, suffused with a glow like a sterno-flame, that simply isn't human.

Even as I killed masses of the things, swiping my arms through the air with every ounce of my strength and feeling the ones I caught burst as if I had smashed them with a baseball bat, I could feel my arms getting heavier. Already? Christ, paralysis from blood-loss is no way to die. I started running, head down and blind, and the little bastards plucked at me, trying to pull me into the air with them.

I've heard that they like to pick up and drop people who fight back too hard. That's how they killed that one cyclops, I think.

I could not survive this much longer, dammit.

And that's when I spotted the abnormality I was running toward.

Hell.

It was skinny, spiny, and tall; taller than anything even remotely real-world could have been, partially wrapped around a telephone pole at the edge of the alley and smiling at me with three sets of teeth—at least that I could see at the moment. It looked sort of like a long, emaciated squid, except with bony plates covering its tentacles and a set of not-quite-human faces nested inside one another like Russian dolls. It flexed, and foot-long spider-fingers that would have given Lovecraft heart palpitations grew out of its limbs.

This was from the Deep Sideways. For all the horror the striges were causing me at the moment, they're at least Near Sideways dangers, susceptible to myth and codification and all the rules that creatures with something approaching an anatomy have to follow. Hell, the story goes that the first of them were cannibal bear-people cursed by Artemis or Apollo or Aphrodite or somebody to become, I guess, even more horrible.

The gods are weird.

Anyway, I decided to run the other direction. I also decided to set myself on fire. This only required one hand, which was nice.

Now, there are a million good reasons not to set yourself on fire. Anyone who has ever taken a basic court-mandated home-safety course knows this. But there are those times that even really good life coaches don't teach you about, like when you're running through an alley bleeding to death in the Time between Midnight and monsters are chasing you and giggling.

I yanked out my lighter, trying to be sure that it wouldn't slip through my gore-slicked fingers, and spoke a few panicked, ancient words of power that couldn't have conveyed even the slightest bit of information to anyone except, possibly, "I am desperate for a miracle."

Then I squeezed the fucker hard enough to crack the plastic.

And hoped.

The thing detonated like a hiccup of wet heat with a spray of fluid and a blinding flare of white-hot flame. I felt, rather than saw, a wave of flailing things around me collapse to ash, and I could hear the thing at the back of the alley recoil.

I stopped, blinking the afterglow out of my eyes and trying to peel my burned fingers off shards of melted plastic as I looked around for any other attackers. None. A hard tongue-like thing, formerly of a strix, was embedded in my neck, but it hadn't hit an artery.

The thing at the edge of the alley looked at me, cocking its head back and forth like a bird. The smaller head, inside the creature's mouth, cocked its head the other way. That was unnerving. The innermost head only had one eye, so it just blinked at me and chattered its teeth.

"You want some, you big fucker? I'm the King of Jangladesh, and I'm just getting warmed up."

It spoke with inhalations instead of exhalations, its voice sharp like someone catching their breath while huffing anti-freeze. "... warmed up... burned skin... *hahahaha* funny..."

"Oh, yeah, I'm a goddamn laugh riot."

"... little king, big magic..."

"That's me. You tell the asshole who summoned you that I wasn't as easy prey as he promised you I would be."

"... could still kill you... bleeding bad..."

"Not as bad as it looks, I assure you."

For emphasis, I punched the brick wall next to me, hoping against hope that this wasn't somebody's favorite wall in the whole wide world and that I wouldn't discover that it was human anchored, waking bound, and borderline indestructible at the exact moment my entire forearm shattered. I broke a finger against the mortar, I think, and tried not to wince, but my fist blew a good-sized hole in the brick and kicked up an impressive cloud of dust when I pulled it back out.

Cool.

"... *hmmm*... hunt you..."

It spit something at me, faster than I had time to react. A wet, jagged sliver of bone, like an over-sized knitting needle, bounced off my chest harmlessly. It hit the ground, twitched itself into a shape halfway between a comic-book lightning bolt and the world's nastiest fishhook, and then lay very still with a line of web-like saliva running out the back of it in a slick trail to the thing's inner jaws.

The monster looked a little surprised.

"Oh, fuck you."

I shot the thing. The gun seemed very, very excited about this, and the darts that came leaping out of the barrel each had a weight like a twenty-ounce bottle of Kickapoo Joy Juice fired out of a howitzer.

BOOM BOOM BOOM BOOM.

Pieces of the thing clipped off in sputtering jagged coils the way I imagine it would look if you tossed a fancy glass chandelier down a flight of cement steps. It screamed and fled in a direction that I can only describe as "not up or left or backward, but yeah, kinda sort-of."

Goddamn multi-dimensional critters from the Deep Sideways.

Okay, now what?

I pulled my backpack off, snagged out one of my spare lighters, lit a cig, and called Cleon.

"Royden. I was worried you got held-up in the waking world."

"No, I'm here. On my way to your place."

"Yeah, do that."

"I... "

"Yeah, good call."

"Fuck. There's somebody else there, isn't there?"

"Alright, yep, see you soon."

"Tell me to pick up pizza if it's the King of Majooj."

"Sure. Get one. Hey, grab some beers on the way over here, will you? At least a twenty-four pack."

"Shit. If you think I can take these guys, tell me to hurry."

"No hurries, man. I'll see you when you get here."

Click.

Dammit, this night just keeps getting worse.

CHAPTER 31

I stood there, smoked my cigarette, and let myself get good and angry for a little while. Safely and harmlessly, mindlessly mad, I roared and cursed and hated and let my blood pressure spike into a range that would have given my old doctor ulcers.

I shook with adrenaline and balled my burned, bruised, and aching hands into fists. I breathed hard and set my jaw and scrunched my face up into a mask of abject rage, and I may have punched a few walls, broken finger be damned.

I also screamed.

I pumped shots into the air and howled and kicked the bodies of the dead striges on the ground, and I cried a little, too.

Fucking bullshit, them coming after Cleon. That man never hurt a living soul. You gotta be some kind of absolute monster to want to threaten an eighty-year-old retired janitor just to piss off a trigger-happy Hindu midget.

I made a thousand vows to hack the bodies of the King of Majooj and all who served him into a spray of unidentifiable meat, burn the entire mass to ash, and then salt the earth where the bone-chunks landed.

Then, I calmed the fuck down and started planning revenge.

You see, I have this philosophy: a wise man can learn from his mistakes. The average idiot, immortal or not, spends a lifetime making the same damn mistakes over and over again, and I'm living proof of that. I've spent decades doing the same fucking thing a thousand times in a row, disappointed every time that the results are always "oops!"

The time had now come to not make the same mistake again, which in this instance meant that I had to *not* go charging headlong toward Cleon's place, gun blazing and dick swinging, trying to take on the army of the damned. Also, as soon as I survived this and saved Cleon and the world and all that, I intended to quit drinking for good and sort out my love life and maybe get a job.

But the path before me was clear, and it involved getting medical attention. For one thing, I had first-to-second-degree burns across most of my arms and face on top of the bite-sting wounds, and I couldn't feel my eyebrows.

I started walking toward a hospital.

See, the thing about getting emergency care in the 25th Hour is that, just like the real world, you've got a couple of options, and they all suck some real ass.

Oh, sure, the truest Forgotten Kings and the highest muckety-mucks of the Nether Hour will tell you to drink a bottle of ambrosia, lay down on a bed of moss on holy ground, and sleep it off for a century or two, but for those of us with pressing business and things to do in the here-and-now, the options involve much less pleasant alternatives.

I contemplated this, angrily, as I stood in the parking lot of a darkened hospital and drew, with my own blood and saliva, a very rough caricature of the Rod of Asclepius over a caduceus painted on a door while time slipped all-too-quickly between my fingers and into the human anchor points inside.

You see, in order to walk Sideways into one of the floating asclepeions, you need to track down a good-quality picture of two snakes entwined around a staff—a universal symbol of medicine ever since the US Army Medical Corp put it on their uniforms back in 1902. But the two snakes themselves have, if you'll pardon my French, absolutely fuck all nothing to do with Hippocrates or the field of healing. For that, you want the single serpent frozen on the staff, an ancient and potent rune, and it has to be drawn in fresh human tissue. Blood, semen, whatever.

No, seriously, you can look this up.

Anyway, I traced out the shape of one of the serpents, watched a dim light come on somewhere down a hallway on the other side of the door, illuminating a space slightly less than parallel and slightly more than perpendicular to the door itself, and pushed through.

I hate going to the free clinic.

CHAPTER 32

I sat and waited in an orange-lit, shag-carpeted, smoke-filled lobby approximately the size of the inside of a Volkswagen, listening to the snores of the receptionist and to the three-fingered guy across from me practice making Spanish guitar music with his mouth, pointedly ignoring the large, swastika-adorned Viking sitting next to me, who introduced himself as the King of Rerik.

He had an arrow buried in one eye, but that didn't seem to bother him much. At one point, he tried to strike up a conversation that went something like this:

"Hey, man, you hear that they're remaking that Tom Hanks movie where the little kid turns into a grown-up?"

"Fuck the fuck off, you dumb fucking shit-fuck."

"Yeah, but they've got that rapper guy Ice Cube or somebody in the role of Tom Hanks."

"If you speak to me again, I will kill you."

"It's this little white kid, and he wants to be a black guy."

"Oh, Jesus, what the fuck is wrong with you?"

"You know what they're calling it?"

"I formally declare vendetta between my court and yours. As soon as we leave here, I am going to dedicate my life to hurting you."

"They're calling it Nig. Get it? Because he's a nigger?"

"Oh, fuck off."

"So, you hear about that Obama? He's a nigger, too."

"So am I. And a Jew and a homosexual. Shut the fuck up, and leave me the hell alone."

"Yeah, but you seem nice."

"Does your culture have a word for what's wrong with you?"

"Fine, be that way. Just making conversation."

"Go power-fuck your own mother."

The guy across from us, to his credit, was actually pretty good at imitating a Spanish guitar. I have a feeling that he probably used to play before he lost all those fingers.

When the doctor finally had time to see me, he was, as I expected, disappointing. Some poor 3rd-year med student wiped out of his skull on sleep deprivation, anxiety, depression, and caffeine pills, not even remotely awake, sleepwalking through his 4th-shift rounds at the behest of a minor medicine-spirit. Wrapped around his neck and perched on his shoulder, there in the middle of his twitching slumber, was a small, ugly creature combining the least pleasant aspects of a fat rattlesnake and a too-skinny house-cat.

The doc's too-heavy head lolled back and forth on his neck as the spirit-critter worked the guy's jaw with its tail, and the glimmering eyes of the too-silent cat-snake burned into me as I wondered how sore this poor bastard was going to be in the morning.

"And how are we feeling today?"

"Terrible. I woke up, and I'm way too tall. You have something that could make me about a foot shorter? Something involving a circular saw, maybe, or an arc-welder?"

"Very droll, sir. So, Mr. Poole, it says here on your chart that you were bitten by a strix?"

"Oh, yeah. Whole bunch of them."

"Strix attacks are down in the last seventeen centuries, and no major incidents have been reported on your home continent since the late 1400s. Curious."

"Yep. Guess I got lucky."

"I suppose. Your blood sample also came back negative for strix venom although you do have an elevated rate of anti-toxin for their saliva, probably produced naturally by your body."

Huh. Guess my magic shirt worked against their blood-thinning poison, after all. I owe Garrick Heldane a nice thank-you note.

"Cool."

"Still, your wounds are otherwise entirely consistent with those traditionally made by striges, and thankfully, I see no nerve damage. Most of your wounds are superficial although I'll give you a mild sedative and I'll want to put that finger in a cast."

"Great."

"As to the strix, perhaps it was a non-toxic breed, or they were very young. If a group of adults had caught you in a swarm, well, then you would very lucky to be alive, young man."

"Goodie for me."

"I don't suppose that you collected any of their feathers, did you? They make excellent ingredients for love potions."

"Didn't know that. I'll try to remember that for the next time."

"Well, more's the shame. I see here that you are also suffering from some severe burns."

"Ooooh, what tipped you off? The various severe burns on my face, maybe?"

"No need to be rude, Mr. Poole."

"Yeah, I get that a lot. Look, could you give me some ointment or something, send a bill to AWAK, and let me be on my way?"

"Ah, you're a member of the Alone We Are Kings organization?"

"That was a joke, but yeah."

"Hmm. I'll have to inform them that you're here, obviously."

"Why?"

"A state of emergency at the moment, I'm afraid."

"Christ. Great. Well, I'm gone."

I walked out while he was trying to decide if I was joking or not and stole some tongue depressors, cotton swabs, and a bottle apiece of some generic painkillers and a topical creme, which I later discovered was actually for hemorrhoids, from behind the receptionist's desk.

Still, there's something reassuring about sitting in a doctor's office, something that always makes me feel better. Maybe it's just the ritual that's important. That and some soup, which I decided was next on the agenda.

Plus, if I'm not entirely mistaken, the act of telling a neo-Nazi to power-fuck his own mother has deep totemic significance to Jangladesh. I was probably swimming in all kinds of power right now, at least according to some batshit crazy organization or another.

Feeling sufficiently rested and having assuaged the guilty part of my brain that was trying to make sure that I didn't run headlong into terrible danger without a plan, I swiftly devised a brilliant scheme as I built my own homemade splint for my hand out of electrical tape and some tongue-depressing devices that always remind me of Popsicle sticks; I decided to immediately go to Cleon's and to set off the King of Majooj's little trap by shooting everything that moved.

Foolproof.

CHAPTER 33

I applied my makeshift bandages, constructed of spare socks and electrical tape, to the most grievous of my wounds and popped a couple of painkillers, washing them down with a warm Coke purchased out of an abandoned-looking vending machine that offered, in a low voice like a chain-smoking Jessica Rabbit, to suck me off for ten bucks.

I decided not to stick my dick in the change-slot to see what would happen. This is what I get for wandering around the slums near the hospital and interacting with glowing objects in the glass-strewn parking lots of motels that rent rooms by the hour. There were more cars parked along the streets, here—the sort of automobiles that drift into the nether are the ones no one is thinking about anymore, where you could shatter out one of the windows and nobody would notice for a week, minimum.

I put one foot in front of the other, heading toward Cleon's Happy Happy VCR by the most circuitous and poorly lit route possible. I wanted some time to think, to come up with any kind of plan at all, maybe, and I was also secretly hoping to be assaulted by one of the King of Majooj's monsters, so I could vent my aggression on somebody.

My cellphone rang.

Tama.

Oh, hell. Probably calling to bitch me out about... well, any of the various things I deserved to be bitched out about. *Eeech*.

"Hi. You've reached Royden Poole, Secret King of Jangladesh. I'm not in right now."

"Oh my god, Royden, are you okay?"

Boy, I can never predict how that girl is going to react to things.

"Yep. Got bit by some striges, and I set myself on fire, but I'm fine. You get a call as my next of kin?"

"Royden, the whole town is freaking out! Everything's on lock-down right now! Tonight's AWAK gathering at the Long Hour hold was canceled because of a bomb-threat or something, and Garrick just got a call from Cleon telling him to come meet him at his place!"

"Oh, wow. That's... okay. Good to know. Hey, I'll have to call you back, okay?"

"Royden, what's going on?"

"Routine end-of-the-world kind of stuff. Don't worry, this is just some nutty guy named Greg with a penchant for killing little girls' cats and more skill at summoning demons than common sense. Seriously, I have it on good authority from a very classy guy at the Brahma Kumaris World Spiritual University that the world won't end until 2036."

"Royden!"

"Okay, sometime *around* 2036. It's not an exact science."

"Please be serious, Royden. Please."

"I am being serious. Look, I have to go shoot a guy in the face right now, but when I'm done, I'll explain everything."

I heard footsteps behind me. I looked around and noticed that two people were following me, both about a half-block back and walking slowly on opposite sides of the street.

One of them was my killer clown from the other night, slapping along on his giant bare feet and looking forlorn. The other was a barrel-chested, heavily bearded guy in a long, patchwork greatcoat that looked like he had raided the wardrobe of *Stalag 17* and worn the coat every day since, all covered in patches, buttons, and colorful bumper stickers, wearing a paper crown from Burger King and sipping out of a paper bag wrapped around some kind of bottle.

I waved, and they both waved back.

Tama said something over the phone.

"Sorry, what?"

"I said be careful, okay?"

"Yeah, I can't promise that. Or, honestly, even promise to try. But I'll promise to think about trying, okay?"

"I hate you, Royden."

"I get that a lot."

She hung up on me. Yeah, I get that a lot, too. I turned and shouted over my shoulder. "Hey, man!"

The big grizzled guy hollered back with a lazy Appalachian drawl: "Hey, man, you've got an abnormality after you."

"Yeah, that's a bad one, too. He fucking with you?"

"Not no-more. Nasty guy here saw me following you and tried to pull a bit of mojo on me, which was a bad idea on his part. He's feeling about as weak as a newborn kitten right now, I'm happy to say."

I stopped walking. The bearded guy and the naked clown-monster were still heading toward me, and I could just faintly make out a thin whistle emanating from the throat of the grease-painted, brightly tufted rotting mass.

It was trying to scream at me.

"Well, thanks, man. You, uh... ?"

"Oh, I ate his magic."

"Ate his..."

"Oh, yeah. Lapped it up like it was beef stew, I did! He's mostly made of magic, so he ain't real happy right now."

"Cool. I think I'm going to kill this thing and be done with it, if that's alright with you."

"Oh, absolutely! Yeah, I'd give you a hand and all, but Deep Sideways things like him always give me a nasty spot of indigestion."

"How about I buy you a drink?"

"Sure! Let me finish this one first, okay?"

The guy took a draw off his paper-wrapped bottle, and I shot the still-approaching clown about seventeen times. As it collapsed into a spray of charcoal, wet confetti, and silver and orange ribbons before dissolving into the street, still walking toward me, it growled at me one last time.

The guy sidled up casually, like he was taking a stroll down the beach. I looked him up and down, taking in his beard and his semi-stoned grin and his prodigious gut. I nodded to him.

"Looks like I owe you one, partner."

"Don't mention it, my friend. Hey, you're the guy, the friend of the King of Urartu, huh?"

"Royden Poole, King of Jangladesh, at your service. Friend of Cleon's and of yours."

"Yep. I set my feet on walking toward you, and this is where I am. I'm Jim, man. They call me Magic-Eatin' Jim, on account of my mojo, but you can call me Jim or Jimbo or Slim Jim or whatever. Just don't call me James—that's my pappy! I'm one of the dukes of the Big Rock Candy Mountain, where we hung the jerk that invented work."

"Nice to meet you, Jimbo."

He took a swig and considered. "Well, heck yeah, it is. It's always nice to meet me, man. Hey, you want any of this before I pitch it?"

I lied as convincingly as possible. "No. Never drink when I'm on a case, man. Sorry."

"No worries, no hurries, no apologies, and suit yourself. Hey, sorry to be following you around and all, but the Boxcar Court got word through the lines that the Kings of Urartu and Jangladesh was looking for me, on account of having something to do with the trouble brewing, and you seemed like the cat in question, but I wanted to be sure before I bugged you and all, 'cuz I hate to be a nuisance."

I pieced that together as best I was able.

"Okay. It's cool, man. Guess the Boxcar Court is really on their game these days. I didn't expect to hear from you so soon."

"No?"

"Nope."

"Well, man, there's civil war in the lands of Cocagne right now. All us folks 'round the mountain are keeping our eyes peeled, trying to keep us from getting ourselves tossed in the pokey."

"... the *pokey*?"

He shivered. "Worst thing on earth, man. It's a place, from what they say, where a man is locked up and, if the legends are true, deprived of things like warm stew and booze and smooches and naps. Every citizen of Cocagne fears the pokey the way a mortal man might fear death."

"Okay, got it. Hey, how about I buy you that drink and you tell me a little bit more about Cocagne and the Big Rock Candy Mountain?"

"Well, that just sounds swell. Lead on, MacDude."

CHAPTER 34

Iknow what you're going to say—me, a recovering alcoholic, out on the town looking for a drink with a quite-possibly-insane and most-certainly-stoned homeless man from a fictional country, prowling around in the middle of the Between Hour while Cleon presumably endures heavy torture or, at the very least, a rambling and discursive villain-lecture from the King of Majooj, that prick.

My rational, responsible side kept telling my angry, ball-punching side that this was the right thing to do; even a hint of info on Cocagne was worth more to Cleon and to the case than me getting killed for being stupid. My more passionate side, of course, just wanted to strangle the prim little bookkeeper in the back of my head and then kick all his teeth out. Also, it wanted some beers.

I decided to compromise and do the only logical thing I could think of: head deeper into the further Sideways, slip away from the anchor points and the incessant tick-tocks of the Secret Time, ebbing us all back toward normalcy, and find a bar in the backstage of reality where me and Magic-Eatin' Jim could have a lengthy conversation about the troubles of his homeland over a few drinks in the space of time it would take Cleon to scratch his nose.

Sadly, that meant going to Frieda Baghaamrita's, about the only bar in the 25th where I wouldn't be shot dead just walking in. Since getting killed would, of course, save the King of Majooj a whole lot of trouble, and, specifically, trouble that I was deeply looking forward to making him eat slowly, painfully, and soon, this seemed like pretty much my only and best course of action.

Yet somehow, after carefully considering where, exactly, we were headed, I strongly contemplated just shooting myself first.

It's just... a bad bar, you know?

Seems like those are the only places I'm welcome any more, sadly.

And yet, I could literally think of nowhere else to go.

We walked down streets that don't exist during the day, going perpendicular to the city, passing stranger and more esoteric landmarks with every block. Pretty soon, we found the hideous old place: a big, crumbling stone temple-auditorium in vaguely proto-Hindu, pre-Classical Greek style, draped with red silk banners depicting various stages of semi-human debauchery and covered in graffiti in over a thousand languages.

I noticed a new one written in English: *Dick-Girls Gone Wild!*

Great.

Inside, I could hear some sloppy drunken idiot on a brass and glass karaoke machine butchering a slobbering country-western version of Jimmy Buffet's *Why Don't We Get Drunk (and Screw)*.

This was going to be a long night.

My guest looked at the building with something approaching religious admiration. "Huh. What kind of place is this?"

"Ueegh. It's a mish-mash of left-over mythological flotsam from about a half-dozen theologies all dead by 400 BCE, pulled together by Sideways tides of batshit insanity and the immortal desire to make a quick buck. It's run by the handmaidens of an old Greek goddess from the Dark Ages, a precursor to Bacchus with a Sanskrit name that roughly translates to God the Androgynous or God who Comes—the lord-lady of sexual force, sexy foreigners, music, ecstasy, epiphany, and intoxication. She-he's the manager, and an old... associate."

"Huh. They got booze and dancing here?"

"Yep. They've got home-brewed honey mead and special blood-red doves that they milk for a kind of piss-weak ambrosia, and there's a floor show every half-hour that you probably don't want to see."

"You had me at 'yep.' Come on, let's go meet some chicks."

He patted me on the back and burped, and suddenly, this didn't seem like such a hot idea any more.

"Well, they're not really chicks, is the thing. Oh, hell, you'll see."

The olive-skinned, heavily-pierced bouncer, clad only in an over-flowing, unzipped leather jacket and an equally-overflowing g-string, stopped us for all of a half-second, looking the two of us up and down with a grin before gesturing for us to enter by tossing a head of luxurious, curly black hair over her shoulder. Considering the attitude here toward barfights, spills, underage drinkers, and public nudity, I'm not entirely sure why they have a bouncer, come to think of it.

Maybe to keep out good guys.

Jimbo was impressed. "Oh, man, she was a looker."

"Yeah, I think she liked you, too. Didn't you see her adjusting her *giant cock*?"

"Huh. This seems like my kind of place. The whole Boxcar Court would love it here. Wonder why I never heard of it before..."

"Oh, that's pretty simple, actually. This place was founded on the principles of a mystery cult. That means that they charge for things, here."

He recoiled the way I've always imagined vampires, if they existed, would shrink back when presented with a cross, if they worked.

"Wait. You mean, like, *money*?"

"Yep. Don't worry, though. I'm buying. I'm flush with cash from robbing a strip club."

We found a mostly unoccupied table, shoving a sleeping guy to the floor where he would be swept up with the broken bottles, teeth, and various liquid residues staining the stone in a few "hours," or what passes for them around here, by the blue-skinned satyrs of the cleaning crew.

Okay, fine. I'm the one who shoved him. Jim seems like he would be too nice to do that; fortunately for me, he was too busy staring at the place like a rube.

In his defense, it's pretty wild. Imagine a bondage fetishist's dream of some rotting pre-Columbian, South American temple retrofitted into something halfway between a speakeasy and an old west saloon, if there was a lot more neon. Oh, and *everyone* on the waitstaff looks like a mostly-naked Selma Hayek—or, depending, Jessica Alba.

Or maybe Kate Beckinsale or Monica Bellucci or Eliza Dushku or Jennifer Connelly. All dolled up in lingerie like something out of the world's silliest fan-fiction. Oh, and also imagine if every smoking-hot brunette in the room had a dong like a military-grade cucumber packed—mostly—into a pair of skintight Speedos.

Our waitress sauntered over. From her too-skinny waist and up, she looked like an exceptionally well-endowed and slutty Lucy Liu. From her prodigious hips and on down, she more closely resembled a very excited John Holmes, albeit without the hair. I tried to look her in the eye, but in my peripherals, I could tell that she was trying to poke Jim in the face without using her hands. He didn't seem bothered.

"I'm Jase. So, what can I get for you boys?"

"Hi. You have any specials?"

"Only thing special in here tonight is you two handsome fellas."

"Super. My buddy here wants the best drink you have, and unless you have Kickapoo Joy Juice, I'll take a Coca-Cola Classic on the rocks."

"Oh, no. Don't have soda, sugar. How about a beer for a hard-working, hard-drinking, hard-as-steel man?"

Dammit.

"Glass of water?"

"No. How 'bout a beer?"

"Cranberry? Tomato? Orange juice or lemonade or something?"

"Two cold beers with a shot of ambrosia and vodka for two good-looking guys, coming right up."

Fuck. Okay, we better make this quick. I cannot sit there with a goddamn beer in front of me.

"Alright, Jim. Here's what I'm going to do. I owe you a drink for saving my life, and I owe you a drink for coming to see me at the request of the King of Urartu. Now, I gotta dash and go save my buddy's life, but before I go I'd like to buy you another drink in exchange for a little bit of info on the whole nature of this conflict in Cocagne right now."

"Well, alright. Hey, you think that waitress was flirting with me?"

"She's flirting with you, yes. She's flirting with you in a bad way. She's flirting with you the same way that a fifth-year-senior fratboy flirts with a recently rufied freshman women's studies major."

"Huh. So you're saying that I have a chance?"

"I assure you, Slim Jim, you've got a better chance of hooking up with our waitress tonight than you have ever had with anyone before, ever. Hell, you play your cards right, and you might go home with half the staff."

"Cool. Can you buy her a drink from me?"

"I think she'd love that, Jim. In fact, the first two rounds you buy her are on me. Now, tell me what you can about the troubles of Cocagne."

"Well, where should I start?"

"Assume that I know nothing about Cocagne except that it's where you're from and that it's the sweetest and bestest place ever."

"Alright, well, there's a bunch of different sections to it, is the thing. Like how America has states, Cocagne has them, too. Except that they're smaller, and they're not states. There's a whole bunch, like Down-in-Kokomo, and Sweet-Home-Alabama, and Mount Penglai, where the Eight Immortals all have their banquets, and then on the other side of the border there's Mount Hokrai or something, which isn't as nice from what I hear. But there's a place called Freeland, and a place called Elysium, and there's the Strawberry Fields and Scarborough Faire, and there's Pan's Arcadia and Fiddler's Green and Neverland and the Pastoral Idyll and the Hundred Acre Woods, and there's other places, too."

"But you're from the Big Rock Candy Mountain. Tell me all about it, if you would."

"Well, hell! Like the man say: It's a land that's fair and bright!"

He began to sing, then, with a clear, strong, twangy voice that would have made David Allen Coe weep with joy:

> *Where the handouts grow on bushes and you sleep out every night*
> *Where the boxcars are all empty and the sun shines every day*
> *On the birds and the bees and the cigarette trees*
> *Where the lemonade springs where the bluebird sings*
> *In the Big Rock Candy Mountains*
>
> *In the Big Rock Candy Mountains you never change your socks*
> *And the little streams of alcohol come a-trickling down the rocks*
> *The brakemen have to tip their hats and the railroad bulls are blind*
> *There's a lake of stew and of whiskey too*
> *You can paddle all around 'em in a big canoe*
> *In the Big Rock Candy Mountains*

"... and there's more, too, but I can't remember it'all."

That got me giggling. Which got Jim giggling.

Damn. I had tears in my eyes and a grin on my face. I looked around, hoping that no one had noticed. Mostly, they hadn't.

Philistines.

"Okay, then, Jim. So, tell me about the King of Cocagne."

"Oh, there ain't a king! Well, I mean, we have ourselves a bonfire every once in a while there on the beach, and people come from all over Cocagne to say how-d'ye-do or whatever, and sometimes we'll crown a king for a night or something if people are in the mood after the skinny-dipping and the horseplay, but it's not like we pay taxes or buy war bonds or anything. Nobody's in charge, like."

"But you say there's a civil war on?"

"Oh, yeah, it's terrible. People are getting locked up, man. It's fairly and rightly inhuman."

"So, someone declared themselves king?"

"Well, I mean, every man is king in Cocagne, you know? But I guess that somebody might have went and declared themselves, like, the One True King after winning a big pork-and-beans eating contest or somesuch. We place pretty high stake in that sort of thing."

"Got it. Look, I guess what I'm asking is who's doing all the locking up that people are so afraid of."

"Oh, them? It's the Boy-Goat Brigade. Everybody knows that."

I was about to ask him what the hell he was talking about when a shadow fell over the table. I turned to take my beer from my waitress and suddenly found myself staring at a sneering Rose McGowan look-alike holding a gun just like the one in my backpack. She was also sporting breasts like something out of a cartoon, straining against her 36DDD bra, with a thirteen-inch erection jutting out of her bikini briefs.

"Huh. Hi, Frieda. Been a long time."

"Royden. How about you take a little walk with me, now?"

"Eek. Is this about my bar tab? Because that wasn't me. It was an evil doppelganger summoned to Earth by a vile wizard. I can prove this. I have documentation from my priest."

"That wasn't a request, Poole. Stand your little ass up."

Dammit. If my life is going to be genre parody, why does my femme fatale have to have a dong like one of my thighs? I looked past her, where two well-endowed figures who could have been Katy Perry and Selma Blair were scowling and holding what appeared to be huge, elaborately styled, gray plastic Fisher-Price katanas.

Also, their penises were quite menacing.

The threat of imminent physical harm notwithstanding, my first instinct upon seeing the swords was "oh, dude, sweet! Wish I had one!" I immediately wanted to grab the thing and swing it around and make whooshing noises and whack ninjas over the heads with it and maybe swordfight my best friend.

Dammit. More hardware from Paese dei Balocchi, and just before I got a chance to ask the only guy I'd met so far who might know a damn thing about Cocagne.

Magic-Eatin' Jim did not seem to be as concerned with the danger as I was. "So, how did the two of ya'll meet?"

Frieda and I both glared at him.

Simultaneously, we said, "Long story."

She growled. Jim burped. I stood, trying to be casual.

"Frieda, I'm serious. Go on one date with me, and you'll swear off becoming a nun, I promise you."

"I think I'm going to shut you up, Royden. I've been wanting to do this for years."

She stabbed me in the throat with baby's-first-switchblade. The tip was dull, and the plastic edge was soft, like getting poked with an eraser, but I felt my entire neck go numb, from my jaw line to the top of my sternum like... well, like I had been stabbed in the throat with a knife.

My air passages seized up, and I suddenly couldn't breathe except in wheezing, dull gasps.

Paralysis seeped into me.

I fell to my knees as Jimbo stood up.

"Hey, that's not fair. You're not supposed to hit people if they're not ready—or hit hard in the neck or the face or the swimsuit areas."

Oh, my hero.

Frieda was equally unimpressed. "Kill the hobo."

From my new vantage point on the stone floor, I watched both women charge Jim—they whacked him in the arms, stomach, and head, swinging for the bleachers. The light plastic blades bounced off him like they were waffle ball bats.

"Ow! That stings!"

He flinched, letting the blows rain down upon him, then went wide-eyed, belched, blinked, and turned to run toward the door. The two ladies both looked surprised at this development. One of them cautiously touched the edge of her blade and then wiggled her finger as if confused as to why her pretend sword didn't work.

Lacking the ability to feel my lips or tongue, I sent out thought waves: *run, you beautiful bastard, run! That's right, Magic-Eatin' Jim, run!*

Jim looked over his shoulder at me and then burped again, like a heavy smoker trying to sprint while eating a chili-cheese dog.

Holy shit, I actually shot thought beams at him.

I didn't know that I could do that.

"KILL HIM!"

A reasonable facsimile of Megan Fox leapt from beside the bar and flying-tackled the big man, her throbbing member jutting out the top of her underwear and bouncing repeatedly against her wet lower sternum.

Ew.

Also, dammit, why did I expect Jim to be good at athletics?

She sat on his chest hard, casually slapped both his hands to the side as he put them up to ineffectually shield his face, and then she wrapped both of her hands around his neck.

Dammit, why was I hoping that Jim would be good at fighting?

"Oh, oh no, please don't put me in the pokey!"

That plea really confused the girl on Jim's chest. She had a much different interpretation of the phrase *put in the pokey* than he did, and she was trying to puzzle it out. Also, she appeared to be getting smaller as she sat there, like a very unnerving Alice after drinking from the bottle in that one story.

Night of the Living Dead, I think it was.

Jim burped again, and the girl was now no bigger than me.

Frieda laughed. "He's a glamervore, almost like one of the true Ancient Formless. He takes in and digests power—I've not seen a mortal one in some many ages. Ladies, disembowel him, and we'll have ourselves a lovely supper tonight."

A swarm of well-hung brunettes fell upon his prone form, and sharp, manicured nails came down on him again and again. A spray of red came out of my friend Jim, his boots twitched, and then he was very, very still. Just like me, drooling there on the floor.

"Royden, you and I are going to have ourselves a little chat. You are not going to like it."

I tried very hard to say something witty, or even think it, but my brain was as seized up as my mouth.

CHAPTER 35

Freida, with a small squad of big-dicked spirit-brunettes in tow, dragged my paralyzed, dead-weight frame into the back rooms of the bar, way past the well-locked beer and liquor room and the laughably primitive bead curtains hanging across the doorway to the communal bathroom. As if to spite me, the music stayed on and most of the customers didn't leave.

Jerks.

We went down a flight of steps. And then another. Down, down down, for days, forever, into a dank basement lit with that low, amber, nectar-rich candle-glow that only creatures from fables and the crazy people who hang out with them can see very well in.

It's times like this that I wish I was a really huge guy.

Like, minimum five hundred pounds, just so that dragging me around would be a huge inconvenience to people instead of just casually annoying.

We took a sharp turn and I was tossed unceremoniously into a small, dirt-floored cell. Actually, I think it was supposed to be a kennel, at least judging by the stench. God, why am I never tossed unceremoniously anywhere nice?

I landed on my side, and with considerable effort and some small amount of luck, I succeeded at turning myself very, very slightly. I felt really good about this until I realized that Frieda was stripping off my backpack and that I hadn't actually moved myself after all. She tossed my bag in the corner.

"Welcome."

I wondered: *so, this the little chat? So far, not so bad.*

"No, not so bad, yet. You'll have visitors soon, Poole. In the meantime, Gia here is going to keep you company."

A girl knelt beside me and absently petted my head. She looked kind of like that one chick from *Gilmore Girls*, Alexis Bledel or whoever, except after an epic boob job sponsored by the Michelin Man and barely able to keep a nightstick-sized dork tucked into her shorts. She was smiling with a dangerous light in her big blue eyes.

"Hi. I'm Gia, and you're really hot."

"Leave him in one piece, Gia. We've got totemic kings paying a lot of money for him."

Frieda left, winking at me as she walked away with a theatrical sway to her hips. Dammit, I hate her.

"So, you're Royden, huh? That's a totally great name. I think it's really sexy. Is it Mexican or something?"

British, actually, you dumb bitch.

She giggled, rolled her eyes, and started pulling my shirt off, and I could feel something that felt like a two-liter bottle of very warm, slightly slimy soda flop against my leg.

Oh, please, dear god, whoever you are, don't let me die like this.

"Die? Oh, you're not gonna die, probably. I mean, sometimes it might happen, if I get all carried away excited or if you're like a bleeder or whatever, but I just want to have some sexy fun with you."

Oh, neat, she can hear my thoughts.

"Yeah, they kind of tickle, like you're putting your tongue in my ear or something, but like, both at the same time. It's dirty because now I'm thinking about if there were two of you."

The lump against my leg started getting bigger and bigger. Oh, hell. She started pulling my pants down and flipped me onto my stomach.

"So, you don't, like, talk in peoples' heads much, huh? God-Mistress Freida, she said that you're like a totem king or something, so maybe, if you talk a lot normally or always think sort of out loud, maybe that's your totem, and like, because you can't talk right now, you can use your power to like, get words across anyway."

Yeah, that would explain it.

She started biting the back of my neck. In the unsexiest way possible, for fuck's sake. Ouch.

"Yeah. You know, like, I really like how you do that, all in my ears and stuff. You're making me want to be naughty, mister. So, you want to play the baby-making game with me?"

I'd rather not, actually.

"Oh, neat! I always really like it when people don't want to play the baby-making game, but then we play anyway. I usually win, then. Now, you can't move, I guess, so I'll go first. Feel free to keep talking in my head and stuff. I like the nasty talk, like 'no, no, no' and things."

FOR THE LOVE OF ALL THAT IS HOLY, SOMEONE PLEASE HELP ME!

"Yeah, just like that! Keep talking while I fuck your ass."

I tried to decide whether this counted as what the Prince of Minos would call a puzzle-box or not and very quickly decided that I didn't actually care.

Well, here went nothing:

PANDO.

And then something very weird happened. My bag shook, a low keening rolled through the room and a whole metric shitload of tree branches suddenly began working their way up through the dirt floor, all of them a mottled grayish-greenish-white, and marked with black horizontal scars and knots.

"Woah! Wha— "

Gia was suddenly wrapped up in a mass of lightweight, iron-hard coils of living tree; the bark rubbed against me, and I felt my strength begin to rush back into me. I took my first good and solid deep breath in what seemed like ages.

Still weak as a kitten, I managed to find my voice:

"Hello?"

"Hello. I heard you crying out, young friend, and I came to see if you were all right. You carry my cutting of old."

The voice came from beneath the earth and filled the room like thunder. I looked over, and Gia hung erect and unmoving.

This called for plenty of politeness on my part.

"Yes, I am all right, thanks to you. Who are you, so that I might know who to thank?"

"I am called the Quaker Pando, friend. I am glad to help; I am old beyond old, and I stir only rarely even in the Secret Time, but you seemed very frightened, deep within the blackness I swim, and I owe, of long time gone, great debt to your college."

"I was, indeed, very frightened."

"I recognized the scent of it, and the sound, and I also know your aegis of centuries past. Many great heroes have worn it, and I aid you now as once the young Zeus and his valiant squire Hades aided me in my time of struggle against the Wurms of Nemesis."

"Thanks."

"You are welcome."

I looked over at Gia. She had stopped breathing with a totally innocent look of surprise on her face.

Dammit, why did I suddenly feel guilty?

I knew why. Because she's dumb and naïve, and she couldn't help wanting to butt-pump me any more than I could help wanting a beer right about now.

No, worse than that—because Gia wasn't human. She was a spirit, and that's what spirits *do*: what they're made to do, nothing more and nothing less. She couldn't stop herself from wanting to stick it in me any more than I could stop my heart from beating. I had walked into her lair of my own volition, and I had become her new sexy friend.

I might as well have hated a mother bear for snapping at me after I blundered into her cave and poked her cub with a stick or hated a bat for flying into my apartment.

"You seem anxious, friend."

"I regret the death of my attacker, Pando. Nothing more."

"Oh, she is not dead. To you, she appears as frozen, but we are deep now in Midnight's Midnight: the space outside of space itself and even the tenth-dimensional bubble that holds it, the Time Beyond, removed even from the Secret Time. We have now been here for two weeks, waiting while your weakness elapsed from your nerves and your mind contemplated the nature of spirits. Your mind has moved, in this time, as mine does."

"Oh."

"Your wound was dire, and you shall carry some part of it until you die. Much of your strength has returned, but not all—and not all of it ever shall. Your chest will always be tight, and your throat sore."

"I'm a smoker, so that's nothing new."

Suddenly, I was a little pissed that Gia was still alive. She had, after all, considered my terrified panic quite fun. While I might not hate the bat in my house or even the mosquito on my arm, I'll kill the fucker just the same and without shedding a tear. "So, what about Gia?"

"I think I take your meaning, friend, but I cannot harm her. Although I am a true giant, more than twice your age, it is not in my capacity to kill."

"More than twice my age? Like, 70?"

"Twice the age of your species, friend. I am the vast heart that beats once a century, that sips upon the sunlight and the rain in my sleep. I am miles of knots in rich soil tempered by flames, my skin makes a feast for the butterfly; my powdered flesh when prepared by magic is a panacea, alchemical proof against fever, malaria, pain, and inflammation alike. My hair is transformed by men into books and furniture and houses; I am a friend to all who live, and I forever tremble at the voice of the gods, heard in every breath of wind."

"Ah. Well, I thank you very much for saving my ass. Literally."

"Your thanks are appreciated although they are not necessary."

I decided to go for broke, hoping that the answer was no. "Might I give you some gift or token of my appreciation?"

"Since you have offered, I would have you travel to the place where I dwell in the waking world and pour some ambrosia among the trunks. It would bring me great joy, for I have not indulged in ambrosia dreams in some many centuries."

Dammit. "Got it. Where are you at?"

"It is called Fishlake National Forest, and it is in a land called Utah, in the United States. Tell them that that you wish to see Pando, and you will be brought unto me."

"That might take some time. I mean, first to get the stuff and then to find you, and I've got a whole end-of-the-world thing going on."

"Ah. An end-of-the-world. I have seen many. Do not fret, friend. I cover over one hundred acres, and you will find me in due time. Now, if you will excuse me, I have grown very tired."

"Okay, then. Well, I ought to get going."

"Be well, friend. I hope to perhaps wake and see you again before you die. If not, give my regards to Zeus and to his father."

And with that, the branches began to recede, and the semi-reality of the Near Sideways slowly sped back up. Shit. I felt bad that Pando didn't know about Zeus getting served up rotisserie-style by a crew of Formless Magistrates a few years ago.

It was for Christmas, I think.

I looked at Gia, hanging there totally harmless, and felt less than comfortable about the options I had before me for dealing with her.

Then her erection throbbed at me, and I didn't feel bad any more.

I wasted absolutely no time in diving for my backpack, pulling my gun, and popping the bitch a dozen times.

CHAPTER 36

I caught my breath, pulled my pants back up, and watched the comically oversexed caricature in front of me deflate into a mass of black hair, semen, and milk, idly considering all the while that maybe firing a dozen shots in such an enclosed space wasn't such a good idea. Well, the best way to fix this problem was to put my magic shirt back on, grab my backpack, and leave.

I checked, and the clump of Pando's cutting was gone.

Eerie.

I sprinted out the door, headed up the hallway, and after a few steps, I whacked my knee against a table that I hadn't noticed in the dim amber off-glow. The pain was a hell of a lot more impressive than I had expected. Felt like I had cracked something in there.

A part of me was just happy to know I still had enough strength in me to dislocate my fucking kneecap against a stationary object. The rest of me was pissed about the spike of pain running through my leg.

When I looked up, I was lost. Dammit. Too dark in here. I fished out my new night-vision goggles and tried them on.

Nope. Even worse.

"And where do you think you're going, Royden?"

I yanked my goggles up to my forehead and looked up and down the hallways, watching the floor warp and twist in the jack-o-lantern light. After a moment, I could make out five doors crowded around me. Fuck, I was out of my element. I couldn't see shit.

"Hi, Frieda. Just looking for a bathroom. Also, do you have any moist towels?"

"There was an intruder in my domain just now, Royden. And here I thought you didn't have any friends."

"I don't, really. What just happened was the equivalent of a Fortune 500 billionaire on his way from New York to L.A. stopping on the side of the road at an abandoned gas station in Kansas to break up a fight between a six-year-old and an overly aggressive poodle."

"Boy, you get mouthy when you're panicking. I would hardly call that *glib*. Maybe *clunky* is a better description."

"Fuck you, Frieda."

"Oh, that's the stuff I love. Sounds more like you."

Shadows kept moving around and around at the edges of my peripheral vision. I tried to concentrate and focus on the path out, but now I couldn't remember which direction I had been heading. Also, whatever I had whacked my knee against was gone now.

"Yeah."

"Something old and slow, like a wave of continental drift made from raw life, poked a barest eyelash into my domain to help you, and that was the worst and last mistake it will ever make. I have its scent now, Royden, and I am going to track that creature down and fuck it to death. I've never eaten the intestines of a creature eighty thousand years old."

Sorry, Pando. Hope you're better at fighting than old Magic-Eatin' Jim was. Also, sorry, Jim.

"Look, the intruder didn't kill Gia. I did that, myself."

"Oh, I know you did. And it amuses me that you did so."

Crimeny fuck, it sounded like she was right behind me. I spun. Nothing. I started trying to remember a spell, ANY spell, that could get me out of here, and all I could think of is how pissed I was that Garrick Heldane can walk through walls, and I can't.

Well, magic loves pain. I gritted my teeth and re-broke my semi-splinted finger, trying a very simple divination asking the cosmos only for the path to most immediate safety.

The result came back. *Bite off your own dick and eat it.*

Gee, what a fantastic universe I live in.

I bluffed. "You can't hold me down here like this forever."

She laughed. "Can I not? You are locked now in the Mists of Thing/No-Thing, and a mortal who walks the path of either male or female can scarce clear this fog. Wiser men and braver women than you have gotten lost in the coils down here long enough to starve to death, amongst their number a certain Forgotten King—one, sadly, I am too much a lady to name at this time."

"Oh, shit, please tell me it was the Forgotten King of Elymi, that filthy Carthaginian-lover."

"Ah. But I'm afraid that you do not have time to die here today of an empty, howling stomach nor to choke on fistfuls your own severed reproductive organs in vain attempt to satisfy the Way Between Him and Her. I present to you your buyer, little slave: the Prince of Majooj."

The mists parted, and a broad figure stepped toward me, a slice in reality shaped like a jet-black business suit, a sharp-white dress shirt, and a blood-red power tie. Thick brown hair was sculpted across the top of his head like a TV weatherman's, and his shoes looked more like polished obsidian than leather. His glowing golden watch cost more than my car—or at least it would, if I owned one. He looked like every prick I've ever hated, like the classic 80s greed-is-good stockbroker somehow wrought more huge, except that he had no face.

The front of his skull was just a ragged vertical wound of flesh—half drooling fang-filled maw and half gaping, abused vagina, running from the center of his forehead down to the top of his immaculately sculpted goatee. His hands were buried in his pockets, and his shoulders seemed about as broad as I am tall.

Those hideous lips burbled, "Weep. For this, slave, is Gug, son of Gog, keeper of the hounds and general of the armies of Magog."

I looked him up and down for a moment, raised my gun, and fired everything I had at him.

I hit fuck all.

In a blur, Gug drew two of those cool plastic samurai-swords from behind his back, and without flinching, he swatted the hyper-sonic darts from the air with careful, practiced ease, like something out of a movie. I could swear that the fucking darts actually slowed down for him.

I'll note that his hands did not leave his pockets when he did this. At the elbow, his anatomy *forked*, for lack of a better term, leaving him with two sets of hands. He posed, and crossed the blades.

What an asshole.

"An asshole? Indeed, Gug is. Madame Baghaamrita, have its girl-thing servants secure Gug's property, and this business will be concluded."

Oops. Didn't mean to think that so loud. This new magic of mine was going to take some getting used to.

Specifically, I was going to have to come up with a way for it to be in any way useful besides screaming for help.

A dozen very feminine arms suddenly wrapped around me from out of the shadows, and I felt a mass of semi-hard dicks press against my back and sides. Spinning, I recognized faces that were reasonable facsimiles of Jennifer Lopez and Angelina Jolie, plus a few others. One of them might have been Kim Kardashian. A plastic blade about as sharp as a box of Altoids was pressed against my throat.

I dropped my gun.

"Okay, okay, let's get not go crazy here. Mr. Gug here didn't pay good money for you to manhandle and ding the merchandise."

"Yea, for Gug's new property speaks true. The king wishes it to arrive unharmed, the better for his entertainment."

"Boy oh-boy then, Mr. Gug, you sure are lucky that an eight-hundred-century-old Utah Quaker grove spirit saved my bacon before you got here. These ladies were looking to void your warranty something fierce. You would have gotten chewed out, for sure."

The guy casually walked up and smashed me across the face with a lightly curled-up fist. Christ, I think he knocked a tooth loose. Strength like a bulldozer. From up close, he was even uglier.

"It does not speak to the royalty of Magog, bloodline of Majooj, ever again. Now, move it to the van."

I quickly sized up the prince as the brunette demi-girls dragged me away through winding halls carved with unspeakably profane images. Not a big guy. I'd guess him five-foot-seven, maybe a hundred and twenty pounds. Of course, my tricks for fighting a guy just under two feet taller than me and twice my weight always assume that I've got more strength, more speed, more willingness to win the fight, and, pound for pound, more of what I like to call *fuckyouitude*.

These things, I was afraid, might not rate against the prince. He was a Near Way spirit before he took up residence in a court; there are few myth-things in the Sideways that dabble in power the way kings do, and they're universally dangerous.

The ladies hauled me along, letting the toes of my sneakers scrape against stone. They also kept grabbing my ass, and more than I think was entirely necessary.

We finally stepped around a corner and then out the side of the building in a Sideways manner that probably wasn't entirely healthy. The sudden light of the raw 25th Hour, rushing down from the sky like the waves of an MC Escher portrait of the aurora borealis, very nearly blinded me and set off a nasty headache.

It was an alleyway behind Frieda Baghaamrita's, and there was no door behind us. In the alley was a beat-up, dust-covered white van with no side windows and "Free Candey" scrawled on the side in black spray paint. Oh, awesome.

Standing before it were four figures: my much-loved neck-stabbing clown, looking hardly any the worse for wear since Jim's mojo-drinking and my multiple gunshots, and three skinny-built, beer-gutted guys with nasty acne decked out in black-ops strike-team outfits, like something out of a cheesy FPS video game. All three of them, each over seven feet tall, were sporting super-sweet, unbelievably complex night-vision goggles that made mine look like total crap and huge assault-rifle versions of the gun I had dropped inside, along with massive plastic sidearms, grenades, and a dozen-or-more other cool gadgets strapped to them or bulging out of pockets.

Damn, they looked badass.

They also appeared to be suffering from what I might term acute, late-stage were-goat-ism: elongated faces with jutting jaws, patchy gray fur, awkwardly bent legs with hairy hooves, oversized furry ears, creepy rectangular-pupil eyes, bulging on the far sides of their heads, and small horns. They were staring at my captors, whispering and huddling together in a way that much more suggested fifteen-year-old *Star Trek* fans alone at the big homecoming dance than ultimate fighting badasses.

"Hi, everybody. So, you guys must be the Boy-Goat Brigade. Well, all right: Paese dei Balocchi or bust, huh?"

The painted, eyeless monster opened its mouth and made a "REEE" sound at me, flexing its hands as if it wanted to put them into me.

"Got it, Slappy the Sideways Clown. So, who do I talk to about getting a cigarette around here?"

The three guys looked a little unsure of themselves until one guy, whom I decided to name Extra-Acne-Man, stepped forward and spoke, never taking his left eye off the girls. Specifically, their racks.

"We wait here for Prince Gug to complete the transaction."

I glared at him, memorizing his face, or at least the semi-human parts of it that I might recognize later. That's when I noticed the t-shirt he had on under the trench coat, which had "Surprise Buttsecks!" on it.

I spared a glance at the girls holding me.

The one he was ogling, in the guy's defense, looked like Sasha Grey with the chest of Dolly Parton. Also, she was licking her lips in the least subtle way humanly possible.

Or, I suppose, inhumanly possible.

All of a sudden, I actually had a goddamn plan. Neat.

"No prob, dude. We should just chill here until Gug gets back from, you know, getting his balls drained."

One of the girls let out an audible moan at that comment. I felt more and more dick pushing on my back. Well, here went nothing.

As an aside, there's something that they teach you for dealing with tense and illegal prisoner or hostage-exchange programs. Or, well, at least they should, because I figured it out, and it seemed pretty goddamn genius at the moment. The fact is, if there weren't a minimum of two sides, they wouldn't have to have a fucking exchange in the first place. And if everybody trusted everyone else, it wouldn't be all tense.

I started calling up every drop of power I had in my system, letting the potency of Jangladesh stop trying to rebuild my shattered finger and summoning to my words the dust of every square inch and square mile of ash of my Emptied Empire.

Suddenly, I really wished that I had killed that shot of ambrosia and vodka earlier. Not just for the vodka, which sounded fucking fantastic at the moment, but for the ambrosia.

That shit will turn you into a goddamn sexual Tyrannosaurus, and that's what I needed at the moment. Oh, and speaking of which, where in the name of holy living fuck was I going to get a bottle of ambrosia to pour over Pando's roots? Shit, last I heard, the going rate for a bottle was something like seven immortal souls.

I decided not to dwell on the fact that he might be dead pretty soon anyway and chose my next words very carefully: "Well, since we're waiting and all, **you guys should all get to know each other better.**"

The effect was like tossing a handful of M-80s into a bonfire.

For about a half second, I wasn't sure that it was going to work, and then I was covering my eyes with both hands and trying to prevent having any important limbs taken off.

Considering that most of my weight was actually being supported by the brunettes, and that my legs, especially that knee I cracked earlier, were not feeling very cool about standing up, I went toppling to the ground like a four-foot-tall sack of bruised potatoes. The girls rushed the boy-goats, screaming in a creepy register right between pubescent girls at a boy-band concert and shore-leave sailors rushing a whorehouse marked "2-for-one-special for men in uniform."

Several pounds worth of total dick met somewhere next to the van, and a lot of clothing came off really quickly. In fact, for about two seconds, everyone was having fun except Slappy the Sideways Clown, and I'm pretty sure that he doesn't even speak English. Now that I noticed it, he seemed really intent on killing me or, at the very least, just breaking all of the bones on the right side of my body, so I couldn't go anywhere.

That part of the plan, unfortunately, I hadn't gotten to yet.

Then, like the graffiti on the front of the building says, we had "dick-girls gone wild." There was some screaming, and I felt pretty bad for everyone involved. Well, this is what you get for meeting me, I guess.

And then it was just me and the clown, mano a mano.

Wait, is that right? I'm trying to say "hand-to-hand." I think that *mano y mano* means "hand-AND-hand," and it's the funny way to say it if you're trying to be funny, which I'm not.

Anyway, the clown charged me like a bolt of lightning.

Before I got a chance to stand up, the clown rushed over so fast that I heard the oxygen molecules slapping together behind him as he ran, and he punted me in the chest with a bare, red-painted foot that I might have guessed to be in the range of a size forty-two.

I was immediately grateful that he hadn't kicked me in the face although he was probably just worried that my head might actually snap off of my shoulders if he did, and as far as I know, he was still under orders to bring me back alive.

I mean, he wasn't exactly being nice, but twelve sets of broken ribs is a lot easier to survive than a decapitation.

Anyway, he plowed that foot into me like he was kicking a field goal or, you know, whatever sports metaphor would be best, and I heard a whole lot of things go *crunch* inside his leg. Everything from the middle of the femur on down popped, and his toes turned into what I might politely call bone-and-meat jelly.

With the aegis wrapped around me, he might as well have stuck his leg out the window of a speeding car and roundhoused the side of a parking garage. From my end, it felt like somebody had farted very softly through the fabric. And just then, I came up with a plan for how to deal with the clown.

Well, something kind of like a plan. Let's not go crazy, here.

Quick as I could, still on hands and knees, I scrambled over to where my captors had so carelessly dropped, during their mad dash toward sexual fulfillment, the plastic knife that had been held to my throat. Careful not to grab the blade, I snatched it up and turned on Slappy.

He was visibly angry, weeping blood in streams from empty eye sockets, and to his credit, his plan now appeared to be to hop over to me on one foot and continue killing me. That takes some dedication. I would have fallen over and started crying for sure. And just about then, holding my knife out, I realized that I had fuck all in the way of proof that this blade would actually harm something from the Deep Sideways.

Dammit.

Also, just then the wall behind me vomited out a very angry, slobber-faced Prince Gug.

CHAPTER 37

I took a good, long look at Prince Gug, now suddenly bathed in the moonless-moonlight of the Nether Hour rather than wrapped in the shadows and incense thrown by the nectar-candles. I tried to call up my mythology and also not puke.

Damn, he was ugly. Although his hair *was* really nice—not a strand out of place. The day I'm willing to pay more than six bucks for a haircut, I am definitely going to get it styled like that.

I could now faintly make out a pair of blackish, cigarette-burn-sized holes in the sides of his head, about where a normal person might have temples or cheekbones. They weren't ears, because his ears were perfect and right where people usually have them, so my first assumption was that they were nostrils. Although, come to think of it, it's not like he lacked a hole through which to respire, and they kind of looked like eyes. Little inky pools of piggy eyes, maybe, with itty-bitty dots—pink like baby's toenails—wiggling in the center.

So I decided to go with *eyes*, at least for the moment.

The weirdest part about him was definitely the arms. I take back what I said earlier, now that I could see him better: it wasn't his anatomy that forked at the elbow, because I couldn't for the life of me make out a seam or anything where that immaculate black suit stopped being normal and started going Sideways. It was reality itself that forked.

His suit just bent in two directions simultaneously, heading up all four of his forearms and ending in $10,000 cuffs without a hesitation or so much as a wrinkle.

Oh, also, he had my gun in one hand, two of those cool katanas that looked even more awesome now that I could see them better—one in each of his two "lower" hands—and his final hand was adjusting his tie.

Slick mamajama. And pissed at me, if the wrinkles of his gash-face were to be read correctly.

"Hey, prince. Look, are we about ready to go, or what?"

He shot me several times.

The gun made a soft little *pff-pff-pff* sound as it fired, a sharp contrast to my preferred *BLAMMO* noise. The things kicked through the air all but silently, slapping into me like swift gray spitballs.

The first couple of darts bounced off my shirt harmlessly, leaving greasy stains on the fabric. Thank you, Gil, whoever the fuck you are.

He traced a line across me with shots: the last dart caught me right in the wrist. It stung for about a half second and then my entire hand and forearm went numb.

That was nice, at least, because I had been expecting the suction cup to blow through my arm in a spray of crimson ruin.

Ah.

The "non-lethal" happy-face setting does the same thing that the plastic knives and swords do. Good to know.

"Fine, then, dick. We'll do it your way. Hey ladies, **this pretty guy over here is a virgin.**"

That bought me about twelve seconds. A wave of jiggling tits, flopping wet dicks, and unrealistically taut flesh pulled off of the three prone and bloody boy-goats and surged toward the Prince of Majooj; a howling sound came out of the whole ensemble as he tore into the group with a blur of soft blades and suddenly loud gunshots. I rolled away from the hopping clown monster creeping toward me, using my momentum to get my backpack around to my stomach and unzip it.

Digging into my pack and pulling out a black magic marker wasn't as easy to accomplish with one hand as I had been hoping. I managed to yank the bastard out, tear the cap off with my teeth, and draw a very simple symbol on the back of my numb hand.

For those wondering, it was a branch-like image composed of six lines, first seen in a letter written from HP Lovecraft to Clark Ashton Smith in 1930. The toughest part is remembering that there are three lines pointing up and slightly to the left on top, one in the middle going across diagonally, and two sticking straight right on the bottom.

The last of the girls fell to the ground, some of them thrashing around and some of them creepily still. I now had the undivided attention of Gug. I presented the back of my numb hand to the prince as best I could; I looked like I was a damsel in distress, presenting a dangling limb to an approaching knight or maybe a priest or king offering to let him smooch my ring finger.

"Now, by Koth, you fuck right off."

He took a step back, flinching. Good. I was really hoping that would work. I'm pretty sure that he's supposed to be taller.

"That symbol. It is not the Sign of Koth. It cannot... cannot ward against Gug."

I stood up slowly, feeling like Sherlock goddamn Holmes. "Yeah, but I can never remember how to draw the Sign of Koth. Anyway, I think this will work just fine. It is the Elder Sign, after all, and that does give me a significant amount of leverage. And by *elder*, I mean that it's the first, not that post-40s stuff. Just so you know, there's a town called Koth in Gujarat, only a few miles south of what used to be Jangladesh, so I've got you spiked on the totem, there; Mahatma Gandhi was from around those parts, so it's thick with anti-corruption power, and I notice that you haven't stepped any closer yet, asshole."

"Ungh. Where did it learn that sign, slave? How does it know of me and mine, of Gug, Son of Gog?"

"Oh, yeah, like I've never read *Dream-Quest of Unknown Kadath*, dick. Sure, I never masturbated to the idea of growing up to be ST Joshi someday. No, I was way too busy playing sportsball for the Sportsville Sportsteam and banging cheerleaders to have brushed up on pretty basic early 20th-century horror-fantasy."

Hahahahaha, goddamn, that felt good.

And people said that my obsessions would never come in handy.

"The sign will not save it forever, slave. It has only a single dagger wrought by Pale Alberich, and the accursed sign it possesses has no power over dread Canio de Pogo."

He gestured to the clown, who was still hopping toward me. Dammit, that was one very determined monster. Shit. I also happened to look at the van, which was still running, keys in the ignition. Something very much like a plan popped into my head.

In case you're wondering, it was based on some half-remembered ideas about Viking rune magic and a running theory that neither the Prince of Majooj nor Canio de Pogo knew how to drive. And yes, I would have classified this plan, if pressed, as *desperate.*

"How about this? I'm going to get in your van and leave, and you're going to walk the fuck home, and we're going to save the little ass kicking you've earned from me for tomorrow night."

"It is mine, slave. It will not forget that."

Not entirely certain if he meant to say "you are mine" and "you will not forget that," respectively. I decided to try my luck.

"Hey, you! Free Candey Van. Get over here."

The thing dutifully backed up and drove over to me, carelessly crunching over the prone boy-goats and then slowing down, being certain not to hit the clown.

Oh, thank you, Northmen, you crazy, hairy, fermented-goat's-milk-drinking, semi-literate berzerkers, for establishing in song that writing an object's name on it gives it magical powers and a personality.

The prince looked incensed, in a way that only a guy with a sputtering slash-wound full of ragged teeth and leaking membranes for a face can look, "Impossible. Van, this prince commands it to stop."

The thing screeched to a halt. I dashed over, threw the side door open and jumped into the seat. The prince surged forward the moment my arm moved, and then came to an uncomfortable halt when I spun back to point it at him.

It was like playing the world's least sane version of Red Light, Green Light.

Out the window, doing my best to flip the prince off with my numb hand while still presenting the Elder Sign. "Let me guess: it's a fun car that answers to the King of Cocagne. But since everyone is King in Cocagne, it answers to everybody."

"Van, bring the slave here, so Gug might kill it."

The thing started to idle forward.

"So I just have one question for you: where are you the king of?"

I watched a million little angry emotions run across what passed for his face: "I... am Gug, the Prince of Magog."

The van stopped moving.

"Then you have no power or command over this object. Van, drive away very fast."

The thing sped off at about fifty miles an hour, picking up speed as we rocketed along. I jammed fingers into my ears, closed my eyes, and started screaming. In all likelihood, Prince Gug shouted a question at me as we drove away.

But I'll tell you this: if he asked me where I was the king of, I didn't hear him.

CHAPTER 38

My enemies gave chase, and for a moment, I wasn't sure that I was going to get away. I'd put old Prince Gug in the top ten fastest people I've ever seen, and he kept up with the van in a nerve-wracking fashion for at least three blocks.

If I hadn't pressed the back of my still-numb hand to the rear window, he actually might have caught me.

He stopped dead in the middle of the street, sputtering with fury, and we vanished down dim streets, taking one corner after another and blowing through the few stop signs that live here.

Now, there was no way that the van could have outrun crazy Canio de Pogo since he probably ranks in the top three of all-time sprinters and, in a dead heat, could probably outrun an Andy Pettitte fastball, but with a shattered leg, he wasn't going to be winning any races in the next couple of hours. Speaking of shattered limbs, I sat down on the shag carpeting in the back of the van—careful not to touch the dirty mattress set up next to the television—and took stock of my injuries.

My cheek was swollen from the prince's right hook, and a black eye might be forming, but it was livable. My knee, upon further examination, seemed all right. Sore and prone to making popping noises but, otherwise, mostly fine. Of course, I was still burned across my face and neck and those bite-stab marks were feeling nasty, but two weeks' worth of relaxation in the care of the Quaker Pando had calmed the worst of it, and the bleeding was over and done with. Other than all that, plus the savage fire in my repeatedly broken finger and a wave of exhaustion like I couldn't believe, I actually felt pretty okay.

I mean, not great by any stretch but okay. Compared to Jimbo, who I considered with a stab of guilt, I was doing just superduper.

I decided not to dwell on that.

Back to my injuries: my wrist seemed fine. No breaks, no sprain. Hell, I was even getting a little bit of feeling back, tingling like it had been asleep. Those darts packed a wallop, but I swiftly deduced that they were meant, on low setting, to temporarily subdue rather than permanently paralyze. Same with the blades, would be my guess—but a stab in the throat is a stab in the throat. A chick like Frieda could jab somebody in the jugular with a bag of marshmallows and make it hurt.

Poking at my wrist, trying to get it to move by concentrating with limited success, I could actually imagine having a lot of fun with a bunch of those guns—assuming I had a big group of friends to arm up and play with. It would be like paintball or something, except that where you got hit would actually go numb and freeze up when shot. Pop a guy in both knees and watch him collapse to the ground—not in pain but only because he can't move them anymore.

Yeah, this whole Boy-Goat Brigade thing actually made a lot of sense, in a creepy way.

I looked around the interior of the van, still hauling along at something approaching eighty miles an hour down empty Sideways streets. The inside was really big. Supernaturally big. About the size of my apartment, actually. You could have fit two dozen or more people in here, if everyone felt like getting cozy.

Lot of pictures from porno mags taped up on the walls, along with pictures of professional wrestlers, some creepy Polaroids, and a few unspeakable pictures printed off the Internet. Audio-video equipment was plugged into the flatscreen TV, looking like the ultimate dorm-room fantasy. A high-end digital video camera about the size of my fist was set up on a tripod with a DVD-burner attached and pointed at the mattress. A glass-fronted mini-fridge stocked with energy drinks and cheap off-brand beer sat in the corner with a large bong on top. There were several video game systems, including one with a weird design and a top-loading cartridge system stamped with the Paese dei Balocchi logo and an infinity symbol. The game plugged into the top was called *Gangrape Fuckpunch 2.*

Wow.

The floor was littered with jammed-out cigarette butts and crushed, empty packs of smokes; there were drifts of discarded candy bar wrappers and greasy, destroyed bags of chips and a few comic books and several articles of clothing.

Some of them had bites taken out of them. Hungry goats.

There was also a sizable weapons cache, slung with body armor and assault rifles that looked like decked-out 22nd-century AKs drawn by a gun-fetishist fanboy and hung with plastic katanas in slick black sheathes.

I got up into the driver's seat and thought for a little bit. Eerie bits of half-city whipped past us on both sides. The speedometer kept going up, up, and up—one hundred twenty miles an hour, now. The gas gauge sat on empty, bumping up to indicate a quarter-tank every time we hit a bump. The clock in the dashboard had gone funny, like it does when you're heading in too damn deep.

11:@#$% qm, it said.

Fuck.

I thought up a plan—or at least its non-union, third-world counterpart.

"Free Candey Van, honk twice for *yes* if you can understand me and answer my questions."

BEEP BEEP.

"Great. From now on, honk once for *no*, got it?"

BEEP BEEP.

"Van, do you know how to get to Happy Happy VCR?"

BEEP BEEP.

"So you've been there before. Did you go there tonight?"

BEEP BEEP.

Huh.

"Did you take someone from inside Happy Happy VCR to Paese dei Balocchi tonight?"

BEEP BEEP.

"Was it two people—a black guy and a white guy?"

BEEP BEEP.

"Were these two guys taken at the same time?"

BEEP BEEP.

"Huh. Did you drive the King of Majooj there and then back?"

BEEP BEEP.

"Did you leave anyone at Happy Happy VCR?"

BEEP.

"So, then, Happy Happy VCR is empty right now."

BEEP BEEP.

"Take me there."

CHAPTER 39

We got to Happy Happy VCR a few *minutes* later, taking a shortcut that would have made the city planner go cross-eyed and maybe puke blood.

The place looked dead. Like, as in, actually dead—the windows stared like empty eye sockets, and the kicked-in door gaped open like a screaming mouth.

The clock next to the dashboard said 11:8X9 qm.

Not much time left. I hopped out and slammed the door, walking around to the double doors in the back and throwing them wide.

"Alright then, Free Candey Van. I'm going to load up with weapons, and then I want you to drive back to Paese dei Balocchi, got it?"

BEEP BEEP.

I started hauling out guns. And thinking, hard. This next part was going to be interesting.

"I want you to drive there like a bat out of hell, and I want you to **_drive through the door as fast as you can when you get there_**. Got it?"

BEEP BEEP!

Oh, neat. It's both susceptible to suggestion magic and always wanted to go inside.

"Just, like going crazy with speed when you get there. Ram through the doors and keep going as far as you can with your horn honking the whole time. Maybe turn on your stereo really loud. Can you do that?"

BEEP BEEP.

"Okay. Huh. Now, can you make a phone call to me, like by using your radio antenna or something? I'm the... "

And no shit, honest to god, there for a second I almost told the van that I was the King of Jangladesh. Which would have fucked my plan sideways, up, down, left right, and center.

Fuck. Close call. I'm getting tired and sloppy.

But now, dammit, I also couldn't lie about who I was. Can't say that I'm *not* the King of Jangladesh, unless I want to see every drop of power I've ever managed to scoop up into my hands and my blood go washing out of me in a torrent. And claiming another kingdom is verboten... although, obviously, I'm allowed to let the van assume that I'm a king of Cocagne, such as every citizen is king there.

And, honestly, if there's one country that might be willing to offer a guy like me citizenship just for the fun of it, it would have to be Cocagne. After all, I bought Magic-Eatin' Jim a beer.

Even if, you know, he didn't get to drink it.

Fuck.

BEEP BEEP?

Shit, shit, shit. I pulled out my cell.

"Um, sorry. Look, this is the phone of the King of Jangladesh. Can you call it?"

There was a pause. My cellphone rang. The caller ID said "Free Candey Van."

In the van's defense, that *is* how it's written on the side.

I answered.

BEEP BEEP.

I hung up.

"Okay, great. Here's what I want you to do. It's like an hour and a half drive from here to the Paese dei Balocchi, right? Out in MacSherman Hollows?"

BEEP.

"I mean, for other people. Not for you."

BEEP BEEP.

"Okay. You call me when you're almost there, okay?"

BEEP BEEP.

"Alright. Let me get the last of these weapons out and lock up the back doors, and I'll send you on your way."

BEEP BEEP.

"I'll miss you, Free Candey Van. Be sure to call me, okay?"

BEEP BEEP.

Fucking creepy-ass haunted vehicle. Ugh.

CHAPTER 40

I brought all the gear inside and then watched the van squeal away.

My haul: six assault rifles, four katanas, three sets of body armor, two-dozen grenades, a pair of alien-looking headsets sized for goat-faces marked "Everything-Vision Goggles" and a copy of *Gangrape Fuckpunch 2* that was going into a blast furnace.

I stepped over the broken glass inside Happy Happy VCR and went to Cleon's office.

I needed to do two things, and after a quick glance at Cleon's desk clock to confirm from the red LED lettering that it was now 11:9X qm, I needed to do them very fast: find a handful of dirt or something from Urartu, and then figure out how to officially make a doorway part of that Emptied Empire.

No pressure.

CHAPTER 41

I popped open drawer after drawer, looking for something from Cleon's famed kingdom. Finally, I found a coffee can wrapped up in rubber bands with a little hunk of stone in it and a yellow sticky note inside with faded writing in pencil that said "Peak of Mt. Ararat, 1967."

That's the old Iron Age Akkadian name for Urartu, I think. Shit. I set it on the floor, flipped open Cleon's duct-taped three-ring binder full of rituals, and started looking for spells.

What would it be under? Spell of... consecration? No, that's for churches. Ummm... conquest? Rite of conquest, right there. No, that's for executing other kings and taking the dust of their empire for yourself. Command, maybe. Oops, that's for keeping your men fighting during hopeless ass kickings. No, no, no... dominion and domain. "For claiming unbound territory as empire, to last until seven dawnings of the waking hours." There it is.

I breezed through the formula, looking at my ingredients, wishing that this thing was written up just a little more like the back of a cheap microwavable chicken pot pie box and a little less like a theoretical particle physics textbook from 1700.

There we go: candles, check; blood of a king, check; a sword and a crown, check and check; soil of the empire... well, mostly a rock, but whatever.

Most of that shit was right there in the desk—paper crown, candles, matches, all the good stuff. Hell, half of it I had already thrown on the floor looking for the coffee can. Except for the sword and the blood, I mean—and I had one part of that pair pumping through me, and if I needed to, I would cut my own heart out right now to save Cleon.

Plus, my new stolen magic sword in the other room might make the spell work better.

Still scanning. Fuck me. A problem ingredient: "the corpse of a bird, black of feathered [sic], preferably a raven or a bat."

Fucking idiots. Who writes these spells, anyway? I scanned the room, trying not to dwell on the desk clock shining that ominous crimson 11:98 qm. I needed to get further Sideways, wrap myself in magic, or I was going home, and soon.

My eyes fell upon a nature magazine sitting on Cleon's desk. Well, uh... a magazine is made of wood pulp. That's a kind of corpse, I guess. And I'm only trying to claim a single doorway as domain, after all.

Hoping against hope that there was at least one picture of a blackish bird in there—and if my luck held out, a raven (or a bat)—I dropped it into the doorway, tossed the chunk of Mt. Ararat on top of it, set up the other ingredients, and started chanting the spell. The room got thick with power, building around my tongue as if I was inhaling ozone.

I looked over to the clock during a breath. It said 11:9999—and then, as everything got mystical, it started scrolling, ...99999999, just like that.

Damn and double damn, I was cutting it close.

I glanced ahead, reading with only one eye and mumbling the incantation. Shit. I have to state my empire before I can dedicate the land as my own. Crap, crap, crap. Oh, like no king has ever wanted to claim some empire for a friend, I'm sure. Shit.

I lit the candles in proper sequence, doffing my crown and stabbing myself in the correct order, still looking ahead in the spell. Ah, there, I found it: I could claim the land for more than one empire, but one of them has to be mine, and we have to have engaged in friendly court or treaty within the last full moon.

Yep, got it. Thank god for that cake last night.

Finally, I had to ask a bunch of stupid questions out loud and answer them in turn, using, and I quote: "a voice more feminene [sic], like that of the castrate or the invert, but never of the Lesbite."

I wanted to punch the guy who wrote this right in the face.

Oh, well, on with it.

"What empire does claim this land?"

"Urartu and Jangladesh both."

"What offerings to the claim are made?"

"Blood and crown, sword and soil and feathers black."

"Who makes this claim?"

"I, the King of Jangladesh. By bond of friendly court, the King of Urartu. We claim this land, us both."

"It is done."

That last sentence echoed, and I distinctly heard at least two other voices speak it along with me.

One of them was Cleon's, and the other might have been my dad.

There was an audible pop, and everything except the stone was gone, and a thin line of steam was escaping from a one-inch-wide line of sand now drawn across the base of the doorway. Well, hope that Cleon was done reading that magazine.

Oh, wait. Shit. I didn't put any soil from Jangladesh on there. Also, my head felt like I had been kicked in the temples.

This plan of mine sucked.

CHAPTER 42

I walked out the back door to get some air, stare at the abandoned construction project across the parking lot and keep myself from getting yanked back home by all the human anchor points in Cleon's place.

Most of them were mine, I realized after a moment.

I tried to light a cigarette and belatedly realized that my hands were shaking too hard.

My phone rang: "Free Candey Van."

Click. I could hear the song "Let the Bodies Hit the Floor" by Rob Zombie or whoever blaring through.

"Hey. You're almost there?"

BEEP BEEP.

"Cool. Hey, have fun, okay?"

BEEP BEEP!

I hung up, grinned through my headache and dialed up the King of Cahokia.

A very measured, very even, very furiously angry voice picked up. I recognized it as the body of Fadey Bohdan doing a passable impersonation of the King of Majooj.

What a dick, picking up a hostage's cellphone.

"Hello, Royden."

"Hi, is this the King of Cahokia? I'm calling for Cleon. My guy at the psychic friends' network said he'd be there."

"Oh, the two of them are both right here, I assure you."

Thank God. Okay, next step. "Wait, is this... well hey, Greg! How's it hanging?"

"Ah, I am... what the fuck did you just call me?"

"Greg, right? Gregory Howsgrove? Bastard Greg the Kitty-Cat Killer? We went to high school together! You were voted most likely to kill cats or something!"

"I'm going to fucking murder you."

"Oh, you've already tried that, and what has it gotten you? A headache, and that's about it. I'm like a pit bull or a honey badger, Greg. I'm about half your size, but if you get close enough to grab me, you better hope I don't bite something off, first."

He started to say something else, and a crashing sound like a van driving through the door of an auditorium sounded in the background. I heard screaming.

"You should probably check on that, Greg."

Now this next part, I was going to have to time very carefully. Also, it was going to require use of a power I wasn't entirely sure I knew how to use properly. Also, I regretted pretty much everything I had ever done, especially since picking up that call from Ladislav.

I listened. A door opened. NOW.

With everything I had left, I crushed my eyes closed and focused on the appearance of my name on the other end of the phone. I knew what Garrick Heldane's phone looked like, tried to picture it. I imagined my name, "ROYDEN, KING OF JANGLADESH," written huge there, all encompassing, in glowing letters.

That was me. That's where I was. Right now. Right here.

I screamed, with my throat and my mind at the same time, channeling every bit of command and of telepathy at once.

CLEON, RUN THROUGH A DOORWAY AND THINK OF YOUR OFFICE!

I blacked out for a second.

I thought about Garrick Heldane, still trapped.

I felt guilty, leaving him, but there was nothing I could do.

That didn't make me feel less guilty.

When my eyes came open, I was falling over, the parking lot behind Happy Happy VCR reaching up like a sparkling asphalt wave to slap me in the face, rushing in like a hand of the gods.

My nose broke as I hit the ground, too lightheaded to stand, staring *up* across the empty pavement at the twinkling city lights that make up the tips of god's fingers. I coughed up blood that was running down my throat and felt my teeth with a dry, alien tongue.

From inside the building, "Royden?"

"... out... out here, Cleon."

Oh, damn, it hurt to talk. I heard him shuffle out, managed to turn to see the silhouette of his hair making a halo against the light of the door. I couldn't tell how hurt he was.

"Man, you suck at casting spells, Royden."

"Fuck me. It worked."

"Just barely. Singed my goddamn nose hair off coming through there, and got a migraine to boot. What did you use to establish domain, that bat guano I've got tucked away in my bottom drawer?"

"Bats aren't birds, Cleon. I learned that in, like, third grade."

"Well, old Pliny the Elder disagreed with you and so did the guy who wrote that spell."

"Those guys... were assholes."

I tried to stand.

I failed.

I stared up at the sky, which had gone back to being black with millions of stars, bathed only the faintest orange in the city's low-glow.

"Yeah. Alright, here, let me help you inside."

"Thanks. Hey, Cleon, what time is it?"

"Little after midnight. Same as it was a minute ago."

"Fuck. Alright, well, I'm supposed to be in a squad car right now, so we might have to make this quick. Some people are gonna check around to see if I scampered off here. I'm in custody at the moment."

"Yeah."

"I don't like being in custody, Cleon."

"I dig."

"But I think I have to go to jail tonight."

"Well, you'll definitely get your chance. The police are gonna be here pretty damn soon anyway. My security alarms just started going off. Hell of a lot of good they did me against them goat-kids."

He picked me up, and I could see the ragged wounds carved into him and a torn-open handcuff hanging from a swollen, bloody, probably fractured wrist. Damn. He looked like I felt. Somehow, though, he still had those goddamn red-and-blue 3D glasses on.

"Maybe they'll let us go to the hospital together."

"Let's hope."

CHAPTER 43

We got inside, turned on all the lights and waited for the police.

We sat on the floor in one of the few places not covered in broken glass, tried not to stare at the bruises and bleeding holes covering each other, and pretended that we were both okay.

Finally, he broke the silence. "You sure you want to go to jail tonight, Royden?"

"I've thought about it, and no. But there's really nowhere that I would possibly be any safer. I have a magical plastic knife in my pocket and a multimillionaire crime lord slash demon summoner on my tail, and I'm sick of running from the cops."

"Have it your way. I'll come visit you tomorrow, and we'll talk. Case work. Sort some shit out."

"Got it. You're going to want to move all the magical munitions hardware in the other room. I stole it from the King of Majooj, and I don't think the cops will like that very much."

"Huh. Not cursed, is it?"

"Nope. Found that out from the Devil at the Four Way, his-very-own-damned self."

"Good enough for me. How's the old bastard doing?"

I actually had to laugh.

"Fantastic, thanks much for asking. Christ, Cleon, why you like that guy, I'll never know."

"Always been friendly to me. It's just different for us colored folks, Royden. You wouldn't understand."

"Oh, I'm the same color you are, asshole."

"But you isn't *black*, is you?"

"Met a guy who thought I was. He had an arrow in his eye, though, so it might not count."

"Shit, I've met people who think I'm Sam Jackson. Doesn't make it so. You're about as black as Rick Astley, and you know it."

"Who?"

"Damn, you are out of touch."

"What?"

"Forget about it."

Cleon started laughing, and suddenly, every terrible thing I that had ever happened to me seemed worth it.

"Uh-huh. Look, can you lock the shit up or not?"

"No problem. I got a spot downstairs, in the vault-vault."

"The vault. Shit. Forgot you had that although I couldn't tell you how that might have slipped my mind."

"The vault-vault is very sneaky, Royden."

"Yeah. Yeah, I guess it is."

I considered for a moment. "You don't really have the Hitler suicide on video down there, do you?"

"You'll never know. I'm just gonna say that he was a cinephile, and he was depressed in that bunker, and he owned a camera, and he owned a gun, and we know he used both of them, and I watch that video every Christmas. And no, you can't see it."

"Fine. Then I want a beer, Cleon."

"... you don't drink, Royden."

"Actually, I *shouldn't* drink. I'm a recovering alcoholic."

He kind of stared at me. "I didn't know that."

"I don't tell many people."

"Now I feel like an asshole, sitting here always having a beer while you watched. Man, dammit, I used to offer them to you."

"It's all right, Cleon. It's part of my condition, as you know all too well. I just don't tell people things, sometimes. And I'm sorry about that."

"Okay, fine, now we both feel bad. Look, you really want a beer?"

"If you'll have one with me. And then, if you please, you can have one of my cigarettes."

"Huh. Seems like a damn fine way to end a damn terrible day."

He got up, limped to his kitchenette, popped two warm PBRs, and handed one to me. I took a sip. Jesus, that tasted terrible.

I decided to finish it as quickly as possible.

Half the thing gone, I lit two cigarettes and passed one to Cleon.

"I got somebody killed tonight, Cleon."

"Who?"

"Real nice guy. Your contact, that Magic-Eatin' Jim."

"Shit."

"Yeah. He didn't deserve it, man. Got tore down and gobbled up at Frieda Baghaamrita's, just about the time that I was almost killed, myself."

"Dammit. She's on the King of Majooj's payroll, then. I might have guessed it, that heartless, beautiful, big-tittied bitch."

"You forgot well-hung."

"She ain't *that* well-hung."

"Yeah, sure. Look, I was gonna see if maybe you could get a hold of Jim for me. Let me talk to him."

"In death? Huh. Well, he was royalty, so I might be able to ring him up with some work. Not gonna be a cheap call, but yeah. So, you really think he's wandering around in the wastes between here, there, and the unknowable afterward?"

"I'm saying that he probably wouldn't walk toward the light unless it smelled like Twinkies and was shaking tequila-soaked tits at him. He was a genuinely good guy, and he left a place that was basically already heaven to come deal with me and my bullshit. And now, he's dead, and I don't know where he's supposed to go, and I doubt that he does, either."

"Could he really eat magic?"

"Yep. Gobble it down like beef stew and without even knowing it. Spells just slid off him sideways... and then he burped."

"Damn. Did he have a bellyful when he died?"

"That's another reason I think he might be sticking around, on top of lacking a red cent to pay the ferryman."

"Shit. Ferryman's a myth. There ain't no toll for the dead."

"Oh, yeah, sure. Tell that to the people stuck on the side of the River Lethe right now, going through their pockets for loose change. 'Oh!'—they cry in their torment—'Cleon said that poor people finally get a break in death, no matter how unlikely that seems after a lifetime of poverty. But now, we have no cash, and we're stuck here! Boo-hoo!' That's really terrible of you, Cleon."

"Terrible, my ass. I ain't no preacher—you take what I say for what it is. One busted-up old man talking. But shit, you're gonna feel real lucky if they won't let you into hell because you're too broke to pay the toll and your ass has got to sit on the bank of a river for all eternity chatting with people instead of enduring some much-deserved torment."

"Heh. There's that."

We were quiet for a while, and then we finally heard sirens in the distance. Soon, we would be seeing the red-and-blues flashing on the buildings across the parking lot. Took their sweet-ass time.

"Last call. That's my ride."

"You want one more for the road, Royden?"

"Nah. I'm not even going to finish this one."

That was a lie. I had already killed my beer, and I wanted another one so bad that my whole body hurt.

Okay, fine, it hurt more than even my grievous injuries might have otherwise suggested.

"Alright, help me with these magic guns and shit."

"Got it."

We carried things downstairs in silence, passing through a door that no one would have noticed in a million years except that once it opened, it was pretty obvious that it had been there all along. On the door was a little note, carved into the wood and then painted over: "TV Man Wasn't Here."

At the bottom of the stairs and around a few corners, Cleon opened what looked like a meat locker with a key from around his neck. Inside were hundreds upon hundreds of black VHS tapes arranged on the shelves like books, all without labels.

Then I thought of something.

"But seriously, Cleon, who the fuck thinks that bats are birds?"

"Huh? Man, look, Pliny the Elder wrote a lot of shit that people believed in for centuries, and he was always going on about how bats were the only birds that suckled their young."

"That's dumb."

"Is it? Okay, you know that whole thing about ostriches sticking their heads in the ground to hide from shit?"

"Yeah?"

"They don't actually do that. Pliny the Elder said they did, probably because he saw some ostriches eating gravel or something just like chickens do, and he decided based on their itty-bitty heads and itty-bitty brains that they were probably so dumb that they stuck their heads in the ground when they got scared, thinking they were hidden."

"They don't actually do that?"

"No, it's all bullshit. But you thought it was true, just because you never considered that, logically and based on evolutionary terms and what we know about how fucking dangerous an ostrich is and how fast it can run, it doesn't make any sense."

"Huh. I hate that all this stupid shit is important. It's so random."

"You love it, and you damn well know it. Hell, you probably could have gotten away with a picture of a bird or a black t-shirt or something, in an emergency. I wouldn't want to risk my life on it, but if I hadn't had that bat guano, you might have tried that."

"Yeah. Huh. Well, that's good to know. Hey, uh, could I also throw my backpack in there, too?"

We did, along with all the items from Paese dei Balocchi, and Cleon locked the thing back up. Then we came back upstairs and shut the door and watched it not be there anymore.

"Hm. There's no way I could hide behind that and not get arrested, is there?"

"You want to stay in my basement for the rest of your life?"

"No."

"Good because the spell isn't real strong. You'd be just safe as houses until just about the time your ass started making noise down there or some mildly competent diviner decided to come looking for you."

"I think that it's likely that either one of those things or both will probably start happening within the next twenty four hours."

"Yeah. Let's go see the police."

We walked into the front lobby of Happy Happy VCR, both of us with our hands out in plain sight and squinting against the harsh glare of spotlights and rollers shining in through the busted windows.

There were easily six squad cars out there.

"Wow, Cleon. The security of your store apparently rates pretty high for the local PD"

"Damn skippy. I've paid taxes several times."

"Either that or Krabowski thought I might be here."

He smiled. "Oh yeah, that would explain it. He'll make detective in no time— just you watch."

And people wonder where I get it from.

A bullhorn:

"ROYDEN POOLE, COME OUT WITH YOUR HANDS UP."

"They're playing my song. Hey, Cleon, seriously—come see me tomorrow."

"Will do."

And then I walked toward my date with the law.

CHAPTER 44

I don't remember much about what happened right after that because I was
semi-drunk, in a great deal of pain, and felt like I had been up for about
seventy-two straight hours running marathons one after another.

But here's my best recollection: I walked outside with my hands up, squinting
around my swollen eye, blood still running pretty freely from my nose. There
were about a dozen people in uniform all pointing guns at me there in the
spotlights; it felt like I had just walked on stage to perform my hit Broadway
solo performance *Worst Night of My Goddamn Life*.

Hell, I could almost hear cheering.

Come to think of it, that was probably the sound of the radios squawking
back.

Me and my whole disappearing-out-of-Lieutenant-Krabowski's-squad-car
act and leaving behind nothing but a busted set of handcuffs and a crushed two-
way had apparently caused quite a stir.

"Don't worry, officers! You should see the other guy!"

Then my one busted knee went out, and I fell down.

"Jesus! Get him up!"

Oh, neat, Detective Ladislav is here.

I was pulled to my feet. You know, of all the times I had been pulled to my feet tonight, by the girls at Frieda's and by Cleon and by everybody else, well, this one was the least unpleasant. Probably because I was so numb all of a sudden.

Then I puked.

Dammit, I shouldn't have drank that beer so fast.

In defense of the local PD, they didn't immediately drop me. I probably would have. These guys are pretty well trained.

I started shaking all over.

"Oh, don't worry about all that blood in that puke, guys. That's from when I blew out my throat casting magic spells."

"He's going into shock! Get an ambulance here now, lay him down, and *keep* him down!"

Suddenly, I was looking at the sky. Someone stuck something under my head. It felt like a wadded-up jacket.

Detective Ladislav appeared above me like a very, very ugly angel.

"You're in a lot of shit, Royden."

"Good to see you too, detective. Hey, look, I've got a couple of leads for you."

"I'm going to put you under twenty-four-hour surveillance in a secure medical wing at the hospital."

"The same one where Ethan Milsborough died earlier tonight?"

He wrinkled his brow. His giant eyebrows suddenly became the central point of the universe, glaring down at me like two angry gods.

"You know, the one who used to work here with Cleon, who looked even worse than this last night? Seriously, call the hospital. If he's alive and well in his bed, I'll go. Otherwise, you take me and lock me up in general population. Brightly lit and full of people, if you don't mind."

"I can't do that."

I struggled to sit up and then struggled to stop the parking lot from spinning around.

"You've got a lieutenant with something like sixty years on the force who can corroborate, if pressed, that I broke every law of physics he knows about only a few minutes ago, and now, I look like I came through a goddamn thresher. We can chalk this all up as swamp gas and mass hallucinations or whatever you want, but if Ethan Milsborough died on your watch, then I'm not going to the hospital."

"Lay your ass back down."

He stormed away. Good for him. I would have, too.

I looked over my shoulder to see Cleon discussing the break-in with an officer. I couldn't hear them, but I was hoping that he was pinning it all on me. If I were him, I would have told the guys that this crazy brown-skinned midget who used to work here came in all hopped up on PCP and goofballs, throwing chairs around and stuff—that the little monster should be locked up forever.

He wasn't, though. He was going to feed them some line of bullshit about gang activity or whatever: how he had seen me outside getting beaten up by a group of neighborhood guys and how he had yelled at them. Then, how they had thrown some stuff through his windows until he came back with a baseball bat, and how they had beaten him up pretty good but eventually left. Then, how he had rescued me and given me a beer and how we had waited for the police together.

Then he was going to thank them kindly and ask if he could come visit me tomorrow, and, oh, no, he didn't know that I was a wanted criminal, but Jesus loves everybody, and he knew what it was like to be in trouble with the law, sometimes, because he had been a kid once, too, and please, would they let him come visit me tomorrow?

And then the officer was going to tell Cleon that, yeah, okay, no problem, sure.

And then Cleon was going to offer the officer a beer, and when the guy declined it, Cleon was going to offer him a card for 50% off any VCR repairs he wanted, good until Christmas, and the officer was going to be so humbled that he wasn't even going tell Cleon that he couldn't accept gifts, and he certainly wasn't going to mention that he hadn't owned a VCR in ten years and didn't know anyone who did.

He was going to shove that card in his pocket and forget about it.

And then Ladislav was going to read the report that this officer filed, and he was going to get really pissed and crumple it up and storm down a hallway and throw a door open and ask the officer why the fuck he thought there were six goddamn squad cars at that little shithole VCR place to begin with, if we weren't looking for a criminal who had already escaped custody at least once, and that VCR-fucker was in on it the whole time, dammit.

Now, this was a headache that Cleon didn't need. Because at that point, the officer was either going to shrug and say, "He said he didn't know the guy," and then go on with his day or he was going to go "Hmmm, you're right, that is weird," and then drive over and fuck with Cleon a whole lot more and force Cleon to feed the man another line of Voice of Kings bullshit, theoretically forever.

Better, in my opinion, to just cut the midget loose, be done with the thing, and maybe move to Key West.

But, as I may have mentioned before, Cleon is truly a much, much better man than I am.

So I laid there and waited for Detective Ladislav.

I also patted myself down real quick: in my pocket, I still had my soft plastic knife stolen from the girls at Frieda Baghaamrita's, which I pulled out and slipped between my butt-cheeks as subtly as possible. Working with the thing, I figured out that it was collapsible, like baby's-first foldaway hunting knife or something.

While doing this, I also discovered that my wallet full of money stolen from Fadey Bohdan and Honey Sweet Licks was missing.

That explained the girls grabbing my butt so much while they dragged me to meet Canio de Pogo and the boy-goats. Suddenly, I didn't feel so bad about Prince Gug having killed them all.

Also, as soon as I get home, I'm going to Google that name. "Canio de Pogo and the Boy-Goats" would be an excellent name for a very loud, shitty punk band.

"All right, Poole, you're coming to the station with us."

Fuck. I hate being right all the goddamn time.

"Eugh. So Ethan is dead."

"Guys, pick him up and get him in the back of a car."

"So he's not dead? Missing, then. Got up on his destroyed leg and calmly walked out of a secure medical wing at or around midnight, huh? All of ten minutes ago, and now nowhere to be seen? And I'd just bet dollars to donuts that no one saw nothing."

"Shut the fuck up, Poole."

"Oops. Shouldn't have mentioned donuts. Sorry."

He stormed away, and I stared at the sky some more.

Eventually, I was tossed in the back of the squad car with another important question on my mind: the boy-goats. Are they always horrible half-man monsters, or do they shift back to human form during the waking hours? And was Ethan Milsborough one of them?

"Hey, did it look like a goat had eaten anything at the hospital?"

No answer. Just as well.

Also, how bad should I feel that I didn't save Garrick Heldane?

We went to the station, but I missed that part.

I fell asleep in the back seat, and the cops had to wake me up. They were surprisingly nice about it. I guess that after Detective Ladislav stormed away, the story about me being beaten up by a gang was spreading amongst the people who didn't already know me. Actually, pretty much everybody was really nice to me once we got there.

It was, in all honesty, because I looked really fucking pathetic. You ever seen a sleepy, beaten-up midget put on the puppy-dog eyes?

Yeah, you would be nice to me, too.

Okay, maybe not *you*. You know me too goddamn well.

Anyway, I was ushered through the booking process quick, and shunted into holding. The few guys who were awake didn't bother to fuck with me, and I didn't fuck with them.

About that time, I thought of a really funny line that I should have used on Detective Ladislav about how I had just gotten back from India, and I was going to get him a gift, but the only thing I saw there that reminded me of him was a particularly nasty foot fungus, and I wasn't sure how to ship it.

Damn. I'll have to use that one next time.

Note: the cops did not find my plastic knife.

There's an advantage to having a butt that's only a foot or so off the ground, and it's that people very rarely feel comfortable grabbing at it.

As the door slammed shut and locked, I found a relatively quiet corner, pulled my knife out of my pants, curled both hands around it while clutching it to my chest, laid down on a bench, curled up, and went to sleep.

CHAPTER 45

I'm pretty sure that I had a visitor that night.

Someone who couldn't be seen by most humans. Someone who could walk through walls by aligning themselves with the brickwork just right and could step between the ticks of the second hand when no one is looking. Someone who doesn't show up on cameras and who stood over me in lockup with huge black eyes like ebony holes cut into nothingness and pale skin the color of faded hospital hallways at night, watching me breathe and hating me for it.

The problem, of course, was that I was hallucinating pretty badly as I came out of shock—as I processed all the power I'd taken in and then burned up and then taken in all over again throughout the course of the night. The longer you're in the Nether Hour, the more dust of your Emptied Empire you soak up. You start rolling in it, breathing it, letting it seep into you until your tears and skin and hair are the same scent as the earth and the wind and the water there.

And this last trip behind midnight, it had been my longest jaunt in months. Hell, if you counted the alleged two-week recuperation with Pando, then this was my lengthiest trip behind the curtain, well, *ever*. I was washed dry with the power of the Other Interval—my throat gone red and raw not just from that last, panicked exhalation-command to Cleon and my stabbing. It was like I had been walking through an eternal dust storm full of ghosts, all of them chanting my name. Breathing a spray of hot sand caught in the whipping frenzy of forever and letting it fill my blood with something more potent than mere oxygen.

I heard someone whisper, "They lived, some fifty centuries ago, in the great desert to the west of the Indus, and have been at war since before there were words to describe strength, anger, pride, or indomitable will. They protect you now, king, for your totem is to be ever outmatched, to be always without friend or family, to live each day hungry and thirsty and in pain, to spend each night cold and alone. They choose you as their king because you do not relent, never relent, never ever. But you will grow coddled someday, king, and then I will have you."

Still shivering, I screamed.

"FUCK YOU! I'LL RIP YOUR FUCKING THROAT OUT!"

But then there was no one there, at all.

So, like I say, I'm pretty sure that I had a visitor that night.

But I don't have any proof of that.

CHAPTER 46

I slept for a long damn time, and I would have slept until about the next week if I hadn't been in jail.

They get you up at a certain time in jail, is the problem.

So the next morning, I sat in general holding, and I made notes in my head, and I met a very nice staff nurse named Fred who fixed up my nose as best he could and patched up the rest of me with a sort of confused shrug, and I bummed some smokes off a Hispanic guy whose name I don't remember now, and I drank possibly the worst coffee ever inflicted on sentient life.

And, more than anything else, I thought very, very hard.

There's an old story about some guy who wanted to write a book and just couldn't do it. Things kept coming at him: he always had to deal with other people's problems and go to work and come home and make dinner and then wash the dishes and run errands and do all the other stuff that you're not allowed to do when you're in lockup. So he stole a carton of cigarettes in broad daylight, got caught, and went to jail so that he could write his book in peace.

I'd like to say that the book he wrote was really good. You know, it would be cool to have some great ending to a story like that, something like, "And that man's name was Donald Trump" or something.

But I don't know.

Come to think of it, I might have made that story up.

Anyway, here's what I do know: when you're in jail, you sit there a lot, and you're not allowed to go home.

That's the basic premise of jail.

For people who are all whacked out on meth or are freaking out because they owe serious money to scary people or are climbing the walls because they *really* need to go back to their house and finish burying that dead hooker, it can be a nightmare. The guilt alone can eat you up and drive you nuts, if you're the sort of person who dwells on that sort of thing; and the dread of being told to sit the fuck down and shut the fuck up and wait for other people to decide how badly fucked you are can fill you with an existential malaise of hellish proportions.

At least, that's the idea.

Jail, optimally, is supposed to put the fear of authority back into people who've stepped out of line just a little bit—remind the work-a-day Joes who would otherwise never break the law that, no, drinking and driving is not okay, even on your birthday. And no, you're not allowed to throw beer bottles into the street or through windows, even if you're really mad. And no, we don't hit people. No, seriously, you're not allowed to hit people. Not your wife, not your coworker, not a police officer.

No, you're not supposed to throw things at them, either, even if you weren't *really* trying to hit them.

And also, yes, you're supposed to pay speeding tickets.

Alternatively, jail is supposed to keep really dangerous people off the streets. If a dude just really won't stop hitting people, then, okay, let's put him somewhere isolated where there's nobody to hit and let him think about it for a while. As a society, we civilized humans have a whole series of smaller and more isolated places to put these people, depending on how fucked-up they are and how little we trust them.

The point is, there are really good reasons to put people in jail, but I wasn't in jail for any particularly good reason, and I could take some solace in that.

You know, just like that one guy who only wanted to write a novel or whatever, who I'm really very sure I read about somewhere and didn't just totally make up off the top of my head. Me and him were compatriots: I had a case to solve, and he had his book to write, and both of us realized that stealing a bunch of cigarettes and hanging out behind bars for a while without all the day-to-day distractions of non-jail was the best way to do it. Like two peas in a pod.

Except for the cigarettes thing, obviously. I mean, I haven't stolen cigarettes in years.

Anyway, it wasn't like I was some guy who just couldn't be bothered to follow the law, who really needed to cool his heels in a steel cage for a bit and kind of think about what he was doing with his life.

Okay, fine.

Maybe I am, to a certain degree, a habitual law breaker. That's a fair assessment, and I thank you for noticing it. But it's not like I'm a deranged lunatic who might pose a danger to himself and others.

Well, I mean, not a lunatic like, say... you know what? No more of this. I don't have to explain myself to you. Fuck you.

Point is, I didn't feel bad about being in jail because I hadn't done anything wrong, and I'm not going to bother giving you a rundown of all the various ways I was able to convince myself that I hadn't done anything wrong because the day I want to deal with all of that, I'll hire a very expensive therapist.

I'm not a bad guy. I'm a good guy.

I kept repeating that to myself.

And that's what jail is like. You just sit there and think about it.

There I sat, wishing that my feet touched the ground when I sit in institutional chairs and smoking a cigarette I borrowed from Jose—just remembered the Hispanic guy's name, by the way: it was Jose—and thinking about how I was going to kill the King of Majooj when a very friendly officer came over.

"Mr. Poole, you have a visitor."

My first reaction was to tell him that it wasn't technically visiting hours and to fuck off, but I had met so very few genuinely pleasant people in the last... ever... that I didn't bother.

"Okay."

"It's your lawyers, Mr. Poole."

Now *that* was surprising. I immediately tried to remember the last time I had spoken to a lawyer, and I came up short unless you counted that one time at that bar that I flicked a lit cigarette at that guy who turned out to be a lawyer and also a huge pain in my ass.

"Super."

"Right this way, Mr. Poole."

I finally looked at the guy. *Really* looked at him, I mean.

Huh. This guy was scared shitless.

So, no, not being nice. Or at least, not *just* being nice.

Not everyone would have caught it, but I did.

The officer unlocked the cell door. Away we went down a series of all-too-familiar hallways, and I got to like this guy more and more even though he was just being nice because for some reason he was terrified nearly into tears, and I didn't even feel that it was sort of a violation of our new friendship that he had insisted on putting me in handcuffs.

We got to a conference room only slightly marred by the inclusion of military-grade steel mesh in the very, very small window, where a pair of officers stood outside trying not to act nervous.

"Hey, everybody. The lawyers finally showed up, huh?"

One of the guys swallowed very hard.

We went inside, where two inhumanly attractive, familiar-looking people were sitting behind a steel table: a man and a woman, each with a face like something based on a series of pictures of mannequins and then carved from porcelain, both with long black hair and dark eyes hidden behind sunglasses. They were both dressed in sharp black business suits with glossy black ties and were both slightly marred by what looked like the sort of cuts you might get from running through the woods in the dark, letting branches hit you in the face.

"Leave us, officer."

The man gestured dismissively with one hand, causing my escort to leave hurriedly, while the woman behind the table casually attempted to sip coffee from her mug with a stirring straw. Also, I noticed at that point that the two of them were holding hands under the table.

That's when I placed the two of them: the dual male and female aspects of my much-hated, bar-owning enemy Frieda Baghaamrita.

Man, what a bunch of idiots spirit creatures can be.

Note: there are a lot of conspiracy nuts out there who have witnessed or heard eyewitness reports about or claim to have heard from a very close friend who has recently stopped taking his medication about some kind of surreal encounter with what are colloquially called "MIBs"—the quintessential Men in Black, those creepy, slender, sinister bastards who work for some "superior agency" and who always wear black, drive shiny, dark-colored cars, show up when weird things happen, and so often seem a little bit *off*.

Stories about the MIBs go back to 1947—or even earlier, if you happen to believe that the "black man" from Washington Irving's short story "The Devil and Tom Walker" from 1824 was actually the same damn critter with a slightly different disguise.

Oh, and for the record, I *do*.

Point is, these conspiracy people will rant and rave about how *they*—that is, whoever it is really behind the MIBs—were oh-so-clever in subtly working into the cultural zeitgeist a basic, universal knowledge of a benevolent, charming, and slightly wacky organization called the Men in Black, which—according to a pair of hit films and a popular children's television show—actually employs popular actors Will Smith and Tommy Lee Jones to hunt down evil aliens and save the world.

This was all a clever plan, say the conspiracy nuts. Oh, this was a *genius* move, say the tin-foil-hat crowd, meant to soothe the "sheeple" into compliance. This was a crafty trick, a great scam, a piece of perfectly pitched propaganda, say the folks who think the CIA clones spy cats: lies meant to undo the damage done by a far more realistic and government-damning television show starring a young David Duchovny and Gillian Anderson which was very popular in 1997.

All I can say is this: if the shadowy, sinister people behind the sinister shadow-people behind it all are that good, we're doomed. I mean, we're talking good enough at cultural manipulation to produce propaganda so popular that references to the films broadly eclipse every other citation regarding the phenomenon on Google. Hell, they're savvy enough to have grossed close to a billion dollars worldwide just from the two films alone, not counting soundtrack sales or action figures or the cartoon.

If somebody did all that *on purpose*, just to cover their tracks, well... those of us fighting the MIBs are pretty damn well fucked.

I prefer to take a different view—MIBs are borderline retarded when it comes to human interaction because they're not human.

As if to prove my point, the man behind the table leaned back in his chair far enough to briefly lose his balance, then caught himself and leaned forward and tried to be intimidating from a different angle.

He raised an eyebrow at me.

The woman, meanwhile, was trying to figure out how to open a sugar packet with only one hand. No, she did not think to try letting go of the guy's hand, and eventually she just started biting at the packet.

"Okay, let me guess—first time out of the 25th in a few centuries?"

The guy glared at me. "We bring you an offer from two totemic kings, Mr. Poole. It will not be repeated."

"Great. An intermediary. Just what this vendetta needed. So, what do I call you guys?"

"We are Fred and Anita."

"Awesome."

Sugar started spilling down Anita's perfect chin.

She spit the packet out onto the table with a grimace and then glared at me. "Do you wish to hear the terms, Mr. Poole?"

"Hmm. Yes. Yes, I do. I wish to hear your terms."

CHAPTER 47

Fred and Anita looked at each other, trying to replicate in their waking world translation the instantaneous left-brain to right-brain cross-firing that it/they was/were used to, using only hand squeezes and facial tics and whispers and empathetic telepathy or whatever the hell mind magic the creatures of myth get in their goody bag of inhuman tricks.

They looked like the two silliest G-men on the planet, gazing lovingly into each other's pitch-black sunglasses and grimly muttering sweet nothings under their breath.

I leaned back in my chair and considered for a moment, trying to sort through all of the bullshit bureaucracy of the Alone We Are Kings society and the miles of red tape and etched-in-stone rules that attempt to govern us squabbling fucks down from absolute anarchy to mere constant internecine blood feuds.

Dammit, now I wished that I had gone to more meetings, or at the very least had brushed up on Robert's Rules of Order when I did go, instead of hammering down a few mouthfuls of vodka and then heckling the Long Hour kids from the back.

Okay, so a formal offer from two courts to a third was about to be put on the table, and I wasn't even sure if there was capital-letter type of *Offer* that all us kingly types were supposed to recognize. Was this technically *Parlay* or *Treaty* or *Drawing of Grand Vendetta* or some other such thing altogether? *Declaration of War*, maybe? *Negotiation of Courtly Hostilities*? *Formalizing of a Duel*? Maybe a cease-fire? And would that get capitalized, or no?

Probably.

Kings love capitalization almost as much as they love symbolism.

AWAK has rules for everything from spirit marriages to no-strings-attached sex, and they're all equally dumb: a mess of centuries-old decrees from paper-pushing councilmen amongst power-mad tyrants, all formed with the goal of making a motley assortment of self-destructive, social-misfit, escape-fetishist magicians behave ourselves like we're a boarding school Model UN or something. A bunch of addicts and bums playing dress up, putting on the big shoes and the makeup and pretending to be more like the genocidal, abusive, insane forgotten father figures who lord immortality over us.

Dammit.

I needed a backup.

There's a reason why real-life kings traditionally have advisers and seconds and seneschals and named hands. Problem was, AWAK doesn't allow for those sorts of niceties: we're supposed to be kings *alone*, after all. If I had a proper court, though, with barons and dukes and such, I could probably insist that they be here.

Or at least that they listen in on speakerphone.

Then I had an idea.

Kind of an idea, at least.

Sure, maybe not a great idea, but I took what I could get.

"Lord and Lady Baghaamrita, have you prepared a scribe for this formal event?"

They looked at each other, then looked at me. Fred spoke, "There is no need for a scribe, Mr. Poole—this is merely an offer made, not a Courtly Declaration."

Wow. It's so neat how I could actually *hear* the capital letters in that particular sentence.

"Yeah, well. Be that as it may, you are acting as intermediaries between three courts engaged in open feud but without formal Assignation of Vendetta. I presume that you are empowered to, you know, take any of my official statements back to the courts in question. Maybe I want to do something covered under important AWAK guidelines."

Smug-ass Anita this time. "You wish to have a scribe? It is your responsibility to provide one."

"Oh, really, is it? Duh, thanks for the update—now we're really getting somewhere. Look, not a one of us wants to get the Forgotten King of Gurankalia involved with this diplomatically, or god-help-us wind up getting dragged naked in front of Urukagina of Lagash on a technicality, so we're all agreed that we do this by the book, yes?"

Fred, then, looking much more angry than nervous: "All proper proceedings have been followed, Mr. Poole."

"Yeah. And now I want to summon my scribe. There's a reason that Bastard Greg and the Poacher King of Cocagne aren't even here right now, and it's *not* just so that waking world shit stays on one side of the curtain and Nether Hour shit stays on the other. They're trying to play me like a bitch by staying hidden. If they don't want me asking questions they don't want to answer or want me getting a good look at either of them, fine. Fuck them. But I also know how to play the rules, and I want a copy of what's said here."

Anita responded. "Hm. Have you access to such a summonable scribe... *Your Majesty*? You must produce, of your own power, a tongueless and sightless transcriptionist or other muted and notarized secretary of your court within one hour or forfeit your right."

I started bullshitting. "Oh, yeah, got it. AWAK recognizes the use of automated recording devices for use as a scribe. It fits the letter of the law because it doesn't have eyes or a tongue, and it can repeat only what it hears."

Fred chimed in, "You have one of these devices?"

Then I started outright lying. "I do. My cellphone happens to have a tape recorder on it. You know, a cellphone? The magic box that hourists use to talk to each other across distances, ever since homing pigeons went out of style?"

"Then produce your device and we will begin," replied Anita.

Oh, thank god for your incredible incompetence, you beautiful bitch, you.

"I don't have it on me because I'm in jail. They turned it off with a key, so I can't make phone calls, but I also have naked pictures stored on it, and they don't let us look at those in here."

Fred questioned, "Then how will you summon it?"

"Easy as pie. Have a cop go get it for me. That's within your purview, right?"

Fred pushed a button on the desk. There was a barely audible buzz from the hallway, and the door opened to reveal a sweating, smartly dressed young cop.

"Yes?"

"My client requires use of his cellphone. Fetch it and bring it here to him," Anita demanded.

"Uh, well..."

Fred drove it home. "This is not a request, lawman. This is a matter of national security. Go now."

He left.

"Oh, nice, guys. Very subtle. I assume that you have some fancy badges, huh? CIA, NSA, Secret Service? IRS? Walmart? Homeland Security?"

They pretended not to hear me.

"Oh, I get it. You're not gonna say another word until it's on the record. Fine. Now I wish I hadn't mentioned Urukagina of Lagash."

Nothing.

"At least I didn't bring up Corporate-Owned Christ. That guy is the worst. And, you know, I should really be pissed at you for stabbing me in the neck and selling me to the King of Majooj. And I am."

Nothing.

"So, how was your date with Pando? Looks like there was some turbulence."

They glared. I smirked and shut up.

We sat in stony silence for a few minutes.

Which was fine by me.

CHAPTER 48

The door clicked with the sound of a deadbolt being thrown; it swung open and produced the cop, coming back with my cell. Then, he suddenly looked really nervous because he didn't know what to do with it. Set it on the table? Put it in my lap? Maybe hand it over to the creepy MIBs?

Realizing that I didn't want to try explaining how to use the non-existent recording device in my phone to Fred and Anita, I solved his problem by swiftly wrenching open my handcuffs and holding out a hand as casually as possible.

"Oh, my phone."

It's always fun to destroy handcuffs, and I'm better at it than most people I know. The trick is to yank really hard until you hear the metal make a little *pank* sound; alternatively, you can grind your wrist against the steel until something inside your hand gives, which is what happens when most people other than me try it. If I believed in all that totem magic bullshit, I would probably attribute my skill at snapping chains and locks to something about the wild riders who roamed free and unfettered along the borders of modern-day Pakistan, but I prefer to imagine that I've just got a knack for breaking things.

"I'll take that. Have a nice day, officer."

He left, still wide-eyed.

Fred and Anita looked at me, all alien and pissy.

"Oh, come off it. That was way more subtle than your "national security" line. He'll chalk that all up to me being improperly cuffed by someone else and imagining the sound effect of metal bursting open because he was surprised. Now if you'll excuse me, I need to turn on my Dictaphone."

I took a deep breath and prayed that Cleon was up and in a feisty mood. Then I turned on my speakerphone and turned down the volume on my earpiece.

Shit. Home or cell? Where would Cleon be right now?

Fuck it. I went with the one that's listed as "DO NOT CALL THIS NUMBER, ROYDEN."

Pretending that I was accessing a program, I dialed Cleon's number and then coughed a few times to cover the sound of ringing without putting the earpiece to my head. I stared at the screen like I was working a calculator, holding the phone like a Geiger counter. The moment the little thing showed him pick up, I started talking.

"Cellphone: access recording device."

There was a small sound from the earpiece, barely audible even to me, as I pretended to angle the phone to see the screen better.

I hoped to fuck that Fred/Anita had human-level hearing in their waking world translation(s).

"Royden?"

"Cellphone, begin recording process now. Ahem. This is Royden Poole, King of Jangladesh, here in jail, now entertaining an offer from two as-of-yet unnamed AWAK courts under the accepted auspices of designated intermediaries Fred and Anita Baghaamrita."

Cleon, speaking loudly over my phone but still very quiet: "bleep bloorp bloop, recording in process!"

"Thank you, cellphone."

I set the phone on the table and looked at the pair of black-clad spirit creatures. They had the impassive glares of people who are getting tired of being yanked around by bureaucracy but, thankfully, not the pissed-off glares of two people who have just figured out that they're being totally scammed.

"All right, kids, let's get down to this shit. I think that we just established that I am interested in hearing your terms."

"Very well. Let the record note that no offer has yet been made, nor have formal introductions of courts been engaged," injected Anita.

"Noted. Let the record also show that the chosen intermediaries have allowed my use of an AWAK-authorized scribe for purposes of this not-yet-formal courtly exchange and that I have requested use of a scribe on the off chance that I wish to make some formal declaration of Vendetta, Treaty, or Parlay toward the as-of-yet unnamed courts after hearing this specific offer."

Fred followed, "Now then, Mr. Poole. Are we ready to proceed?"

"Yes. Let's hear it."

Fred continued, "An offer is made to you, Mr. Royden Poole, to be removed from this mortal incarceration facility immediately in exchange for an agreement on your part to be barred indefinitely from the Nether Hour and to remain under the extended protection of one Mr. Fadey Bohdan and any waking world agencies chosen by him or acting under his orders. Should you accept, you would be transferred from this facility to an airport where you would be given a passport, an unlimited line of credit, and transport to this island in the Dominican Republic."

Anita slid a glossy pamphlet across the table. I picked it up.

Nice picture.

"... okay. This appears to be a resort."

I flipped it open. More pictures and a business card.

"Ah. A resort full of scantily clad Ukrainian fashion models."

Anita explained, "It is a full-service, all-inclusive holiday, Mr. Poole. For you, an indefinite holiday on a tropical island with a personal five-star chef, an open bar, and a minimum of twelve erotic escorts available twenty-four hours a day, with two girls leaving and two or more arriving each month."

"Huh. This is my retirement package?"

Fred pressed on, "The island has golf, boating, hiking, snorkeling, satellite television, a casino, live theater, and several places of interest, including a world-class shopping district within a short drive of the resort proper. At your discretion, the resort could be opened to additional guests or even made public. You would be treated as guest and part-owner, able to make managerial decisions, but removed from day-to-day operations."

I flipped to the back of the brochure.

"I see. Uh, is this a picture of Paris Hilton in a hot tub?"

"Indeed. The resort has been open to select private clientele for a number of years, but is currently awaiting your exclusive arrival," assured Anita.

"Ah."

Fred picked up again, "The resort can host as many as twenty guests at any one time; further construction projects on the island would be yours to approve or deny. Two flights leave daily to Miami and New York, and the airfield also has access to much of Eastern Europe."

"I wouldn't be allowed to leave, obviously."

"That is correct. You would be monitored. Discretely, of course."

"Great. May I ask the names of the courts involved in this offer?"

Back to Anita, "No. It is believed that you are fully familiar with the other courts and that you understand the needs of the individuals making this offer to you."

"Of course. Let me spell it out, then: I stay the fuck out of both the 25th and all of the waking world except for Fadey Bohdan's private paradise island for the rest of my natural-born life. All on Majooj's and Cocagne's dime."

Fred added, "You would not be alone. Any of your companions could join you at any time; you could surround yourself, there, with the rich and beautiful of the waking world or live the life of a hermit. You would have access to the finest amenities, Mr. Poole. Girls, drugs, sun, sand, and water as far as the eye can see. I encourage you accept this offer."

"Let me think about it."

Anita, set her coffee down. "You have only until 10:00 tonight, when the car leaves to take you to the airport. This offer will not be repeated."

Then something weird happened. She nodded at me subtly and did a little thing with her hand, twisting it back and forth with her fingers and thumb clenched like she was asking for a tip or turning a page.

Very casually, I looked at the brochure. And the business card, which was embossed with a very sexy silhouette and had only a single line of text with a URL. I flipped it over.

Loopy, feminine handwriting: "Incapacitate Fred"

I shifted in my seat, leaning forward like I was really interested and putting both feet on the ground, so only the very edge of my ass was still touching the chair. "Okay, so what if I don't want to go? I sit here and rot in jail? Right up until I get shanked?"

"It is not my place to make threats," said Fred.

"But it would be bad, right?"

They both nodded.

"Huh. Well, that seems really... *FUCK YOU, BUDDY!*"

I jumped across the table and spear tackled Fred in the chest.

It's not as easy as I make it sound here and involved a certain amount of supernatural power that I really didn't want to give up. Also, I whacked my knees on the edge of the table as I went over it and that hurt like hell, but it sure was a lot of fun.

OOMP! We hit the ground hard as his chair flipped backward. Anita let go of his hand and backed into the corner.

Fred, startled and suddenly full of adrenaline and pure alpha-male anger, grabbed me around the throat. I punched him in the face, not connecting nearly as hard as I wanted to, as he pushed me backward with fingers locked around my windpipe.

Now I was almost vertical, sitting on his chest with all-too-strong hands choking the life from me. I brought a leg up, right across his sternum, and kicked him in the chin as hard as I could.

His head cranked back and pounded into the linoleum with a sharp crack. He went limp.

I turned. "All right, bitch, what's up?"

She had pulled one of the plastic handguns and was pointing it right at me. I scooted off Fred's body and ducked under the table as she fired with a little *fftff* sound. Tagged me right in the meat of my calf, and after a nasty sting, like a cigarette burn, I felt myself go numb and limp from knee to ankle. I got myself to cover and looked at her feet from my vantage point on the ground.

"Dammit, ow! What the fuck?"

"Turn off your recording device, Royden."

"What?"

"Tell your device to stop recording."

"Oh. Yeah, got it. Cellphone, please stop recording this."

Cleon's voice sounded from the phone. "Recording ended. Now processing recording. Do not press any buttons until recording is finished processing."

"There. Okay, we're off the record. Now, are you going to shoot me again or what?"

"If you move from under that table, yes."

I looked at the door, right through the steel-mesh window. Nobody. We were locked in, and the guards appeared to be on break. I could maybe bust that door down. Maybe not.

"Then let's talk."

"Let us speak plainly, Mr. Poole. I need to make something clear to you, and my male half cannot be privy to it."

"So you had me knock Fred out, and then you shot me?"

"I did not shoot to kill, only to remind you as clearly as possible that I am still in charge."

"Got it. You're in charge."

"You are dangerous and unpredictable, Mr. Poole. I will let no further harm come to Fred; you must understand that I cannot allow you to cause him any further damage."

"Jesus. The fuck is wrong with you, lady?"

"In my immortal incarnation, I am of two minds about my current situation; as this waking flesh, my division of thought is more pronounced. When I step back across the curtain, I will remember two sets of events and my reasoning for both."

"Great. So you're going to be pissed at me about how you tricked me into beating you up."

"My feelings regarding you are of no importance, Royden, although I assure you they are not kind. The issue at hand is simple: I must urge you not to accept the King of Majooj's offer."

"*Not* to accept? You've got a funny way of showing it."

"My aggressive, paternalistic side believes that I can control the situation in the long run; another, more conservative side of me believes that I must act directly to neutralize the King of Majooj and his unnamed compatriot, and immediately."

"Men are from Mars, huh?"

"I am not human, Royden, and never have been. That is known. I do not understand the theoretical dichotomies of the mortal male/female thought processes, even though their overlap is my channel of influence. But yes, I am at the moment more female than male, tinged with an eternal aspect of taboo desire. If it serves you to make sense of my actions, imagine that you are currently talking to my incarnation as an angry woman in fear of losing her lover and child."

"Got it. So, your feminine side is telling you to use me to kill Bastard Greg, King of Majooj, and his buddy the Usurper of Cocagne, whoever the fuck that is?"

"Yes. I have some reason to believe that neither party is being completely honest with the other, nor with me; there are more variables and betrayals in play than I can reasonably allow myself to commit to. In the long run, I am a survivor and have no intention of allowing an end-of-the-world scenario or a massive Nether Hour upheaval that would lead to investigation by forgotten powers or the god-killing formless."

"Very logical. But you allowed yourself to be used in the waking world, where you're a lot more vulnerable. That doesn't seem very, you know, *conservative*."

"True, but it was a risk that I was prepared to take. As a creature once worshiped, I have the ability to pull the strings of human loyalty and have little to fear here."

"Let me guess: your badge just says "GOD" on it."

I could hear a smile in her voice. "Or the closest approximation the individual mind can accept."

"Great. Okay, so let's make this real simple. You want me to kill these guys, and I want to kill these guys. The more you tell me about what you know, the better off I am trying to do what you want me to do. I don't like you, but we're on the same team for now. Are we agreed?"

"Yes."

"All right. So what can you tell me about these sons of bitches?"

"Little. He who rules from Paese dei Balocchi is all but unknown to me although plainly his weapons have made their way to my armory. I do not even know, truly, what Emptied Empire he claims. Though many continue to call him the King of Cocagne, that place is mysterious to me, and I doubt that even what little I know of his motives are true."

"Fine. Give me some wild guesses."

"I believe that he is attempting to ride the chance symbolic link between two unrelated etymologies to near godhood."

CHAPTER 49

"H uh. Wait... come again?"

"The word *cocaine*, meaning in this instance the illegal crystalline tropane alkaloid stimulant, is named for the words *coca* and the alkaloid chemical suffix of *-ine* because it is produced from coca leaves and has a nitrogen base, much like the chemical caffeine."

"Uh huh."

"It is pronounced the same way, in some dialects, as the completely unrelated mythical kingdom. Alternate names of said kingdom include Ko-Kanye, but that is more archaic."

"And he's, what... building a bridge between the two of them? *Cocaine* and *Cocagne* and all that?"

"Yes. That is my belief. He is linking a $77-plus-billion-a-year worldwide industry with the core of a medieval escape fantasy lasting all the way to the modern day, creating along the way an army of mutated demon-animal men with superhuman reflexes to serve his whim."

"Yeah, great. My next step is probably going to be burning down a certain indoor paintball skate park. So what about Bastard Greg?"

"The totem of Majooj is the world-ender; a nation of twisted monsters locked away until Armageddon, which might be hidden anywhere, lurking, always hated and spoken against. The post-Roman British thought that Gog and Magog were giants in Ireland while the ancient Israelites thought that Gog was the king of the Magog demons from the north. The medieval Germans thought that their foes were Red Jews. The scholars of 14th-century Islam thought that the Great Wall of China held Ya'Jooj and Ma'Jooj at bay, according to the records of Ibn Battuta; symbolically, that links the ancient Mongols to Magog, as well. It is even said that in 2003, then-President Bush told Jacques Chirac that 'Gog and Magog' were at work in the Middle East. All men cringe and scowl and point fingers at the uttering of Magog's name."

"It's the slasher movie of nations. Awesome."

She gave me that uncomprehending, disdainful look like you get when you show a dog a card trick. I started to giggle. Seriously, how can a demigod be intimately aware of the chemical makeup of cocaine but not know what a slasher movie is?

"A story with monsters in it. It has pictures that move because this is the future, now. *Move-ie.*"

"I see. Yes, that seems to be an appropriate comparison. Still, it is important to remember that Gog and Magog, despite being monstrous and unrepentantly evil, are not always seen as purely negative. The mortal Lord Mayor of London uses the images of two demon-blooded giants in his yearly procession, for Gog and Magog are depicted as guardians over that city. Similarly, in the 1600s, Queen Christina of Sweden, she who dared to challenge the Sun King Louis XIV, proudly traced her own line back 250 generations to the Goths and eventually to Magog."

"Great. So there's a totemic tradition of people using Gog and Magog as a sort of boogie-bodyguard: don't fuck with us, the good guys, or the monsters will get you. Again, that gives Bastard Greg power."

"Indeed. Most troubling, to my mind, is this Gregory's use of the Arabic term *Majooj* instead of *Magog.*"

"... okay, you've lost me again."

She sighed. "It is said that there are none on Earth who hate quite like the followers of Muhammad. It can be seen even now in the strength and power of their ideology: the mightiest living nation of the planet's long history now contends with Muslim warriors in the great Graveyard of Empires. Although the president unified the vastest and best-equipped of all worldly armies to fight the scourge of Magog in Afghanistan more than half a decade ago, he has still not yet succeeded. The war outlasted his reign because those he fought would rather blow themselves up than submit."

"Okay, so your point is that suicide bombers in Afghanistan are angrier than American kids. Got it. What the fuck does that have to do with this Majooj fuck?"

"I believe that this Gregory has named himself as the enemy of Islam to tap their rage against him while also taking an Islamic name to channel the rage of America."

"Fuck."

"But that is child's play compared to what I suspect to be his final and eternal goal."

"Okay, which is... ?"

"The final destruction of America and the claim of it as his Emptied Empire."

"... Jesus. Fuck. What? How?"

"All he must do is link inextricably, in the totemic consensus, the nation of the United States with Gog and Magog. This has been done for him already, in some ways. The great cities of New York and LA might represent the two heads of the demon-born giants, and the fact that the US is, as a nation, defined as a plural is symbolically useful: the *States*."

"Hell."

"Yes. In some places, America is already called the Great Satan. This mortal King of Majooj must only shift the nomenclature to a pair of scriptural monsters, not transform it utterly."

"But... fuck, how the hell is one guy going to bring down the entire US of A?"

"No nation can stand forever, as only an immortal can attest. He need only wedge at the fractures already in place, cracking along the seams of separatists and secessionists, until the *United States* is truly no more. Although the foolish late-coming sorcerers of AWAK seem to assume that a nation must perish in fire, riot, and disease to become an Emptied Empire, it is not true. There are many among the Forgotten who were simply the last to proclaim citizenship of a land overtaken with schisms and conquest. While some of the towers of Babylon still stand, there are none who pay fealty to the King of Babylon except himself."

"So on the day that the US stops printing money and delivering mail, it becomes a claimable Emptied Empire; the last guy to self-identify as a citizen gets the lion's share of the claim. Interesting theory."

"America would be a powerful empire to channel, with potent totems and far-reaching influence. Planes, bombs, internment camps, and vast cities. There will be many who will wish to claim the spoils, just as the succession war still rages in the East over who will ascend as the Forgotten King of the USSR... but if this Gregory can link the States with Gog and Magog, he will have great advantage in this conflict."

"Because he was already channeling it. At least in part, because he linked a fictive empire to it. Secret Chief of the US."

Her voice was grim, "Exactly."

"Jesus, my head hurts. Okay, but I still don't get how he's going to bring down the States. There are survivalist loons out in rural Alaska and Utah and Michigan and all the other backwaters talking about overthrowing the government, I'm sure, but nothing even close to a workable plan."

"Perhaps. But he now has the great Scythian Queen's stolen Jar of Shifting Souls, which will allow him to plan on a multi-century scale. In addition, because of the powers it grants, he can now begin to manipulate things at a much more macro-level: arming terrorists or even fomenting anti-US sentiments across the world."

"The jar. Right. Explain it to me."

"The pot itself is a thing from well before the time of history, said to have been thrown from the enchanted clay of Lemuria's pale soil some twenty million years ago by the Dragonflesh Men of Dzyan. In later epochs, it was held holy to the Hyberboreans who dwelt far to the north even of Scythia in the gold-drenched lands where the sun shines eternally and the crystal cities reflect back the Northern Lights. I do not know the truth of these rumors, but I do know that the jar is real: it allows a user to exchange souls across the borders of flesh, to live for thousands of years untouched by disease or age. The Forgotten Queen of Scythia has held it for nearly three thousand years, but none knew where she kept it."

"She wasn't using it? She didn't look so good, last I saw her."

"Few mortals, ageless or no, have the energy or wherewithal to perform routine maintenance for longer than a few centuries although the fresh heart of a virgin, properly prepared, would restore the look of youth to her. The body she currently wears, to my understanding, is as potent a form as any that has been born in the last three millennia."

"Fine, fuck it. So she got her perfect body, and then she kept the Hyperborean jar for funsies. As to that, okay, wait, I know this part. The Greeks and Romans talked about Hyperborea, right? It's where the sun god Apollo spent his winters, if I'm not mistaken."

"Correct. One of the famous terrae incognitae of writers including Pliny and Herodotus, Virgil and Cicero."

"But it wasn't one of those 'here be dragons' kind of places, was it, full of cyclopses and monsters that bleed scorpions? No, it was a magical land of happiness where nobody ever worked or suffered or died."

She was becoming bored. "Correct. It is said that the only battle there was between the Muses: which could inspire the greater beauty with flute and lyre and chorus and dance."

"Fuck. That explains why Greg needed the influence of the King of Cocagne. Only he would have the totemic power to track down a holy relic of his nation."

"Indeed."

There was a little grunt. Fred was waking up. Damn and double damn, spirit creatures are tough.

I pulled my magical plastic knife out of my pocket.

"I think that Fred's about to wake up real pissed off, Anita."

"My male half and I must depart, Mr. Poole. Remember what I said. Do not accept this offer."

"Great. Look, I'm going to scoot toward the door, you can tell him that you shot me a bunch of times, and there's no reason to beat the shit out of me, okay? Tell him I'm going to think about the offer, and then the two of you can leave."

"Very well."

"Also, leave my cell dictaphone here but tell the police that you took it with you, okay?"

"Agreed. I will leave a sealed letter at the front desk of the police station. Upon your request, it will be opened and will give the details of your immediate transfer from this facility to the car waiting to take you to the airport. It also has our cellphone number on it."

Oh, of course they have a cellphone.

She spared a glance at Fred. He was out of it.

She whispered, "Again, I urge you *not* to accept this offer."

"Right. Got it."

I quickly scooted out from under the table and backed my way to the door: the feeling in my leg was slowly starting to come back, but I didn't want to give away how much mobility I was capable of.

Anita shot me a bunch of times, the gun making little *fft* sounds with each shot.

"OW! Bitch!"

And then I realized that it didn't hurt. She had fired center mass: the gray darts all bounced off my magic shirt without doing a damn thing. I decided to play possum, falling over as if I had gone floppy from the neck down.

"Damn you, devil woman! You shot me!"

She grinned.

Oh, thank god that I'm so good at lying.

With me sprawled there on the floor, she walked over and helped Fred to his feet. He shook his head and started coming to, blinking behind his askew sunglasses and trying to get his feet underneath him. Little bits of cracked linoleum fell out of his hair.

"Now, Mr. Poole, we will leave you to consider our offer. Accept it. A policeman will be along to collect you shortly."

"Fuck you."

Propping her limping male counterpart up, Anita walked to the door and made a simple pass with her hand in front of the knob. There was a click inside it, and then she casually opened it.

Fred kicked me in the ribs hard enough to make a *thud*. Through the shirt, it felt like a kitten curling up against me, but I hope to hell that he broke a toe doing it.

I faked an *oof* as best I could. Then they walked out into the police station proper, and I heard the weird sound of a deadbolt lock throwing itself inside the door. Cha-clack.

After giving Fred and Anita a moment to make sure that they had gone all the way down the hallway and weren't coming back to kick me again, I hopped up and ran to my phone.

"Hey, Cleon! Is this a bad time?"

"Not at all. I'm actually at the hospital right now, bored out of my damn mind, so this was fantastic. The television daytime dramas are awful, and Judge

Joe Brown ain't on till later. You all right?"

"Yeah. Magic shirt. Proof against magic darts and spirit rib-kicks alike. Long story."

"Cool. You live one interesting damn life, son."

"Thanks. Sorry again to keep getting you involved with all this."

"I wouldn't have picked up if I wasn't interested in being involved. And now it's personal, what with me getting tortured and all."

"Eeesh. Yeah. By the way, have I apologized recently for getting you kidnapped, tortured, and almost killed?"

"Oh, hell, it was barely a slap and tickle. I fought the Krauts in WWII, for gods' sake."

"No you didn't, Cleon."

"Well, I tell people that I did. Anyway, I'm glad you called me. That little Anita girl has some fascinating damn theories."

"She's insane."

"Be that as it may. An immortal who dodged the deaths of two pantheons, by my count, is a cunning bitch by any standards. Anyway, I've been looking up a little bit more stuff on the King of Cocagne based on what I saw last night. Added to the other stuff I'm going to look up here from what Anita said, I think I'll have a pretty good dossier for you when I come visit this afternoon."

"Cleon, don't come visit me this afternoon. You're in the damn hospital for a reason."

"Yeah, to score some drugs. I ain't in a hospital bed, dummy. I'm sitting in a waiting room watching soaps. All the boy-goats did to me was some bruises, shallow cuts, and one broken rib. I'll be fine as soon as I get some more painkillers."

"Seriously, Cleon, get bedrest."

"Fuck you. Last night, you couldn't wait to have me come visit you. Anyway, I'm also bringing you something so your ungrateful ass can call up Magic-Eatin' Jim and tell him you're sorry."

"... thanks, Cleon."

"Don't mention it."

I heard footsteps in the hallway and looked up. Cops.

"Got to go."

"See you soon. Don't drop the soap."

"Ha fucking ha."

CHAPTER 50

I stuffed my phone in a hip pocket, slipped the plastic knife into another pocket, and then tried to pull my oversized shirt out and kind of slouch over so that it wasn't real obvious that I had pants full of contraband. To add to the illusion, I stuffed my hands in my jeans and started whistling.

I needn't have bothered.

The door swung open hard, and Detective Ladislav suddenly stared at me with three armed officers behind him.

"Poole."

"Well, hey there, guys."

One of those huge and terrible eyebrows started creeping up Ladislav's forehead, driving deeper and deeper wrinkles before it on a march up into his white and gray hairline. It looked like the top of the right side of his head was fleeing from his nose.

I didn't blame it.

Then his left eyebrow cranked down, and I recognized his 'you have got to be fucking shitting me' look.

"Let me guess. The nice G-men told you that I was having a heart attack or something."

"Yeah. Something. You attacked a federal officer, Poole."

"Oh, really? What agency?"

Ladislav blinked at me. The frown, impossibly, deepened. Oh, it was on the tip of his tongue. Not FBI, not NSA, not Secret Service...

"Ugh. Don't bother. Here's what's important. Those two were lawyers, yeah? Real dick-swinging lawyers. Working for somebody even more powerful, like the Pope or McErrent downtown or somebody."

"Yeah, your ass is real important all of a sudden, Poole."

"Great. And they left an envelope with the principal's office and said that it was okay that I kicked that guy, right?"

"Yeah. Said that they had been sent to talk with you on behalf of a client and that, despite your outburst, everything had been dealt with."

"Because I had been subdued. And that I would recover, in time."

"Yep. That sounds just like them."

"Well, they sure as fuck subdued me pretty good. Oh, look at me, all subdued. Woopie!"

One of the officers was looking at the floor next to the table, where I had dropped the now-crumpled pamphlet. I scooped it up and waved it at them.

"Just planning my next vacation, guys. Nothing to get nervous about. It simply involves an open bar and some escorts."

I then remembered the destroyed handcuff still looped around one wrist.

"Ooh, yeah. Also, I'm going to need a new pair of handcuffs. These ones broke."

"Cuff him. Get him back to holding. Private cell."

Ladislav stormed away. Oh, I love getting that look. It's nice to know that you can still surprise a man who prides himself on being unflappable after twenty-some years of facing down scumbag crackheads and one crazy night wandering around on the wrong side of midnight.

On our way to my cell, I realized that even after being told that I was paralyzed or dying or whatever after a meeting with the super lawyers, Ladislav's first instinct was to call in three armed cops and check on the room himself before he dialed for a paramedic.

Huh. I wasn't sure whether to be flattered or horrified.

CHAPTER 51

I sat there for a few hours and waited for 3 pm—so I could see Cleon—and worried idly that maybe he wouldn't make it for some reason. I fiddled with the pamphlet and thought about the case a little bit and tried to work up the energy to make some good solid notes on what the fuck was wrong with my life. All I could do was think about accepting the King of Majooj's offer and living in a paradise in the sun until he got around to sending someone down to shoot me in the head or, potentially, the world ended.

Here's the thing. I don't believe that everybody has a price.

There are folks, you just can't buy 'em.

They're not for sale. You talk to the great musicians or the truly amazing athletes like Tiger Woods: they don't do it for the money or the fame or anything else. Those are just perks. They would work at Kinko's for a living and fuck around on the weekends, and it would be all the same thing but on a much smaller budget. And it goes for bad stuff, too. There are some guys who will never, ever stop cheating on their wives. Just ask Tiger Woods. Not gonna happen, no matter what. There are guys who can't stop gambling. Or stealing. Hell, I think that most serial killers are like that.

It's a compulsion. It's a fact.

If you put a gun to the head of some folks and tell them to stop what they do, they might bullshit you an "okay," and they might bullshit themselves that they could really stop, and maybe they even *could*, for a while, but... shit, the really honest ones, they would tell you to just pull the damn trigger already and get it over with.

And it's not just "stop or I'll kill you" scenarios—you want to talk carrot-and-the-stick here? There are people out there who don't need any more money. Just flat out *do not need it*. They could flush handfuls of hundreds down the shitter by the minute and wash out the pipes with Cristal, and still die long before the cash ran out. And these bastards are still writing, hammering out code, or making up new recipes because they just can't stop. Ask a guy like Bob Dylan or Jimmy Buffet or Tom Waits why he keeps making music. Singing and song writing, I'll tell you, is not easy. It's hard work. And these guys sure as fuck don't have to make any more music to stay afloat, even in today's ever-changing business world.

But for the damn life of him, ol' Steve King just can't walk away from that typewriter.

Now, me? I'm no musician. I'm no writer. I'm no artist.

I'm just a pain in the ass.

I'm a contrary little fucker. I have a compulsion to get in the way, to work shit out in my head, and to rub people's faces in it. I see, I build theories, I grumble, I break things.

On the other hand... just about everybody has something they desperately want. Something they would be willing to do just about anything in order to get. Maybe it's to be young again, and maybe it's a dad's forgiveness, and maybe it's just to get out of that fucking wheelchair. But if you're human and you're reading this, there's quite likely something that you would kill an orphan for.

Don't believe me? Just ask the fucking Devil at the Four Way. He's been making Faustian bargains for centuries upon centuries, ever since they had words for the idea of barter. Hell, they're lining up for him. Half the folks who've read this are probably wondering if I'm bullshitting about meeting the old fucker at midnight.

But the fact of the matter is, there's a delicate balance between what you truly want and who you truly are. And that's where the real power is, there on the tips of the scales: to offer the secret prize, in exchange for only the choicest of self-betrayals.

The question I had in front of me right now was simple. Could I truly and honestly give up this goddamn case? Could I go on hiatus for an eternity of paradise, or at least until the King of Majooj won? And if not, what the hell does that say about my priorities?

The problem is, my price has always been too high for people to afford me. I can't be bought for a grand. Or ten grand. Or fucking a million grand. I'm too full of hate. But I've got a soft spot in my heart for desert islands full of free booze and hookers.

I really do.

And the fact that this was an escape—and by that I mean a true and real and actual escape, not a pretend walk in the park between midnight where you come back and you're still a loser wearing a paper crown—had something appealing about it, too.

I stared at a picture of the nicest fireplace I had ever seen, right next to a glass patio door looking out on a moon-drenched beach and a hot tub and a blond with thighs you could base a major world religion on, and the words *OPEN BAR* flashed in my mind's eye... and goddamn.

And I sat there and tried to remember why I needed to look up that monster clown's name—Pogo-something-or-other—and I listened to a guy a cell down from me take a piss while crying, and I tried to remember the last time I actually enjoyed slipping behind the curtain. And suddenly, I was not very interested in pursuing this case.

In fact, there was a chance that the only thing keeping me even partially interested was my overwhelming and only-recently-remembered guilt at having abandoned Garrick Heldane to his fate.

I tried not to think about that.

Upon further examination of my brochure, it appeared that this resort also featured some Asian and Hispanic women. One girl kinda looked like Tama.

Well, she would if I was drunk.

Disgusted, I flipped the thing over to pitch it on the floor, and there was Paris Hilton grinning at me.

I imagined kicking her out of my club, her in tears, and me laughing about it. I imagined sitting in that hot tub with Cleon and a beer and a few pretty girls. I imagined walking along a beach barefoot in a thousand-dollar white tuxedo fitted just for me, skipping rocks and killing a bottle of Absolut and fucking not even caring when it dropped into the surf. I imagined finding the same bottle five years later, worn down into something beautiful. I imagined staying up that night and making myself a sandwich in that giant, giant kitchen.

For all his many flaws, the King of Cocagne had done his damn homework. He knew what I wanted.

I crumpled up the brochure into a tight ball and whipped it against the stone wall and then got pissed that it didn't make a more satisfying sound. I could barely hear it over the rain hitting the building.

"Fuck."

"You know, Mr. Poole, that aggression really isn't very healthy."

I spun in place. Standing right outside my cell was a young woman with dreadlocks and a sly smile. Never seen her before.

"Yeah, well, neither are cigarettes, and yet, somehow, I still manage to smoke."

"I see. You know, I might also mention that if you keep breaking the handcuffs, they're probably going to start charging you for them."

"Put them on my tab."

"You're funny, Mr. Poole. I like that. To set your mind at ease, I don't work for the people with the handcuffs. I'm just trying to help."

"And why is that?"

"Because I want you to be well-damn-ready when you kill the King of Majooj for me."

"Huh. So who are you, then?"

"My name is Wendy, and I'm the Queen of Cocagne. Let's you and me talk, eh?"

"Oh, yes. Let's do."

CHAPTER 52

The woman outside my cell smiled—big enough that I could see she was missing one of her front teeth—rubbed her hands together and then stepped into my cell. She pushed the bars to the side as if they were dangling hippie beads in a head shop; they fell back with a little clacking sound: *click-click, click-click*. When the bars came to rest, they weren't quite straight anymore, like they had gotten tangled up with themselves.

I started hoping that no one would notice.

She whispered something under her breath while she stepped. I only caught it because I was half expecting it. "These bars are made of tin. And you can walk right out again…"

I looked her up and down as she took a seat on my cot: dreadlocks; rough wooden beads on a frayed hemp necklace; chipped nails; a knee-length, off-white skirt stained with tea and dirt and mustard; faded Birkenstock sandals; a worn-out, red-pink t-shirt with the words *Pikinini Pik* still faintly imprinted in flaking, crooked white letters; and the deep, earthy scent of Patchouli oil. Big wooden plugs in her earlobes. She had a nose ring, but not one of the fashionable ones: this one went right through the middle, like a bull's.

I might have guessed her between the ages of 16 and 36. Not much taller than me. Maybe four-foot-ten. Wide in the hips, small in the chest, with a little bit of what I might call a beer-belly.

Also, somehow beautiful. A strange combination of mother and child, spirit and dirty, nature-loving human all at once.

"Wife of the esteemed King of Cocagne, then?"

"No. Wife to nobody, especially not that poacher fuck."

"Well, in that case, come right in. Make yourself at home. Let me put on a cup of tea."

She laughed and sat down.

A cop walked past and looked at me funny. I nodded at him seriously and gave him a big thumb's up sign. He walked away.

"Yeah, the grown-ups can't see me."

I looked back to her: she was sitting cross-legged. And not wearing underwear. I tried not to gaze too long at her bare anatomy and, finally, settled on staring at a wall.

"Uhh..."

"Uh, what?"

"Umm... well..."

In my peripheral, I watched her hike her skirt up to see what I was looking at. I got a better look. Bare as a baby's bottom.

"Oh, yeah. Sorry. It's a tough channel, the eternal youth thing. I taboo totem by shaving, but hair on the kitty is also a no-no. I like this look, though. Makes me feel like a little kid."

She was still inspecting now, extending one foot and leaning back against the concrete wall. I put a hand up to shield my eyes, trying not to let her see me blush.

"Would you be so kind as to...?"

Laughing aloud, Wendy dropped her dress and leaned forward. It became obvious even with her slight build that she wasn't wearing a bra.

"The famous Royden Poole. Suddenly without a witty comeback or a wry observational comment. Hope you're better at scrapping than you are at banter. Or is that just rumor, too?"

"Christ. The fuck do you want?"

She leaned back, producing a joint from nowhere, as if she pulled it out of one of her dreads. She lit it by miming the action of a lighter. The dank scent of good, quality weed permeated the cell.

"I'm in the market to get somebody killed. I heard that you're the guy to come to for that. Wind you up and point you in the right direction is all it takes, is what they say."

"Engineering an assassination? Not very Wonderland of you."

She laughed, letting the action transform into deep chest-coughs. She recovered with one last wet hack, wiping a tear from her eye.

"Is that so? I seem to remember that Tinkerbell once told Tootles to shoot Wendy. The eternal mystery of woman is allowed to be a little vindictive, even in a fairytale."

"Wendy. Got it. So that's you?"

"No, although she's part of my totem. If anything, I'm Tiger Lily, Princess of the Piccaninny Injuns. We fight with them Lost Boys, and we drink with them Lost Boys, but we ain't never going back to London like them Lost Boys. We some real-ass noble savages—they're just righteous unbaptized looking for home. Here, have a puff."

She passed me the joint. I stared at it, wondering if it would be visible to the police.

"Huh. And you're the Queen of Cocagne?"

"Yep. Earned it my own damn self. Ain't a lot girls in Cocagne to begin with, and most of them wind up being Alice or Dorothy or Cinderella or a good witch or a wicked witch or even The Queen of Hearts, but can't handle the whole thing all at once. It's a tough totem—you gotta be a little girl and a big-sister and a girl-next-door and a mom and a lover and a plaything and a house keeper, and better."

I took a drag and considered. My head went light.

Damn. Strong stuff. I started thinking, and this is what came out. "So, then... you're not the Queen of Hearts?"

"Naw, man. The chopping-off-heads thing is a trap. The folks of Cocagne don't much like a tyrant although they'll put up with a funny one, so the executions never quite stick. You wind up being a little queen of nothing, shouting orders that your soldiers humor you by pretending to obey, while the King of Hearts pardons everybody behind your back. It's like the gryphon says, 'They never executes nobody around here.'"

"Huh. How's that different from you?"

She snatched the joint back from me. "I'm the real deal. I play along. Get captured by pirates in the morning, have tea with the Hatter in the afternoon, read bedtime stories to Peter in the evening, and still be ready for the fairy orgy when the moon comes up. It ain't easy. You think the 21st century has some issues with strong women? Go back less than a half-century and see what you find. Shit, I'm den mother, little sister, fuck buddy, best friend, babysitter, fairy godmother, love interest, and personal chef to the goddamn cast of *Lord of the Flies.*"

"Man. So you're the girl in charge of maintaining the frat house, including the fun parts. Complex damn totem."

She took a drag and let the smoke roll out of her nose slowly, like a dragon. "Damn right. And I wouldn't have it any other way. When I jumped out that bedroom window at midnight, oh those many years ago, I didn't want to die. No. No, I wanted to live. Well, I flew away, and where I landed, I've made a better life than I ever could have hoped for. Now, the problems of Cocagne are mine alone. But I like winning fights, so your ass is going to even the playing field. You're gonna kill the King of Majooj for me."

She handed me the joint again.

"Is that so?"

"Yep. That is so."

I took another drag. Started coughing. "Huh. You know, I'm getting real tired of women telling me to kill that guy."

She paused, taking the joint back from me. "How many women?"

I considered. Counting the Queen of Scythia and Frieda...

"Well, you would be the third."

"Well, now ain't that interesting. Mother, maiden, and crone?"

"Huh. Actually, yeah. Or close enough, at the very least."

"An old woman, a married woman, and me—the little girl who couldn't grow up. Maybe we're channeling a big totem without knowing it. I think someone is trying to tell you something, Royden."

I shook my head, trying to clear the fog. "Yeah. *Something*, indeed. The question, now: are you the bloody Norns, the Moirae, the three-fold Parcae with their power over even old Jupiter himself, or just the Weird Sisters from MacBeth?

"Does it matter?"

"Yeah, it does. I don't believe in fate, I don't believe in the Fates, I don't trust manipulations just because they're mystically significant, and I sure as hell don't trust big, scary totems with or without secret royalty fronting them."

She suddenly sat forward, and her eyes flashed fire. "Fine. Maybe we're Virgil's goddamn Erinyes. You can call me Tisiphone the Avenging Murder, if you want to. But the fact is that you've got plenty of reasons to do what I'm telling you to do. As a side note, you got something that sure as hell looks like the Fates or the Furies or something older still, all pushing you in the direction of kicking off the King of Majooj, and if I were you, I'd pay goddamn attention."

I folded my arms.

"Whoever told you that the best way to get me in your corner was to kick me a few times and then make some vague threats was fucking with you, lady. Looks to me like you and your poacher king, whatever his name is, deserve each other, and I don't much feel like sticking my neck out for you. See, for me, this is personal. You just want me to take down one of the guys in your enemy's goddamn crew. I may want to kill the bastard, but who I fight, and why, is my own goddamn business."

She blinked. Her legs crossed at the knee. Suddenly, her whole posture changed into something quite like a Victorian nanny. Or, more accurately, something like a very precocious child's silly parody of one.

"My deepest apologies, Mr. Poole. I suppose that I'm simply not accustomed to interaction between grown-ups any longer. How about this, then. I'll tell you a story. If it turns out that the tale I have to tell has something to do with your predicament, I'll give you a magic feather. If not, then I'll go away."

"... okay."

"All right, then. Our story begins with an enchanted place called the New World. It was home, in ancient days, to amazing things: fountains of youth and cities of gold, savage men with blood-red skin and astonishing creatures unlike anything a gentleman had ever seen before. It was hot and wild and altogether unusual. They called it Asia and India for a time until, with a shock, they discovered that it was more far-off and stranger still than even the wonders of the "Hindu Lands"! The Bard himself said that this New World, called America by the cartographers who dwelt in the ruins of Rome, was the secret place where the fairy king Oberon spent his winters and where Titania's boy, the root of all that trouble with the four lovers at Midsummer's, was born among the natives. In the flow of centuries, this New World gained new titles: the Land of Opportunity; The Country Without a King; The Land of the Free, and the Home of the Brave."

Shit. I could see where she was going with this.

"I tell you now, the American Dream was the living embodiment of Cocagne.

This land was the first to set foot on the moon, of all the silly things! The first without an official church! The first with many states and more all the time: some full of gold and others of wheat, some full of snow and others of cows, and one that is an island paradise beyond where the sun sets. And yes, certainly, there were stumbles. Slavery and genocide and poverty and cruelty and assassinations and an un-civil war between brothers among them. But the *Real* and the *Ideal* have always been confusing bedfellows, and the poets, from Kerouac to Hunter S. have never given up their hunt for America's dream, that strange promise. For a time, the Elected King of the States, of old Irish-hills blood and a playboy's charm, called his reign Camelot—and what is Camelot if not a part of my domain?"

Fuck. An ideological struggle between two made-up countries over the soul of real-world real estate was not what I needed.

"Once, I could have been called Miss America. Perhaps now, I might be called the Queen of the West with my boots and my pistols, riding into the sunset. Or maybe I am just Dani California now, the spirit of Haight-Ashbury, the secret daughter of Emperor Norton living barefoot in the shadow of Golden Gate Park. Maybe all I have left is a quiet corner of the Red Victorian, a book on world peace and a cup of tea. But I will not give up my lands to a usurper or to the courts of Majooj without a fight, I tell you this."

"So you know about Bastard Greg's plan."

"I don't know who Bastard Greg is, but I do know that the Poacher King of Cocagne wants to rewrite our adopted homeland's totem to better match the movie *Blow* or *Traffic* or maybe *American Gangster*. That's not going to happen. If he's in league with a guy named Greg, then you should kill Greg."

"Yeah. I believe that you promised me you would leave, now."

She stood, considered, and then with a flutter and a sigh she dropped theatrically across the floor of my cell, the back of her hand pressed up against her forehead and her other hand fanning the air.

"Nope. Now, I play the damsel in distress, tied to the tracks in a penny dreadful. Please, oh mysterious rider with no ties to our little town, save our fair city from this dastardly villain!"

"Christ, lady. Stand up."

Without looking at me, she began fanning herself as if she had the vapors: "You're supposed to say, 'Lily, please. You are making a German spectacle of yourself.' That's from *Blazing Saddles*."

"I know what it's from."

She took another drag from the joint and began rolling back and forth, kicking her legs like she was fighting in slow motion: "Well, I'm not getting up until you say that you will help me. Oh, goodness, goodness me, whatever will I do!"

"Lord. Okay, how about this. I tell you I'll think about it, and you leave me the hell alone?"

She paused for a moment, taking one last hit off the joint, and then smudged it out on the floor.

"Not good enough. Hey, do you want to hear how loud I can scream? I'll bet that the cops could see me, then."

"You're a real pain in the ass, lady."

"Well, have it your way, then. MOM! DAD! ROYDEN IS SMOKING MARIJUANA WEED IN HIS CELL!"

"Oh, fuck my life."

I heard cops coming up the corridor. Wendy grinned, hopped up, and stuck out her hand.

"Ooo, ooo, HE ALSO SAID A SWEAR WORD! So, what do you say? Partners?"

"I do not need this right now."

"I'm not sure you have a choice."

"Fine. Fuck it."

"That's my favorite sentence."

We were shaking hands when the cops came around the corner. She tucked a feather into my palm and kissed me on the cheek.

And then she was gone.

CHAPTER 53

The cops showed up, and I got them to go away by telling them I had no idea what was going on.

It helped, I think, that the smooshed joint on the floor and the haze of smoke had disappeared along with Wendy and that nobody except me could seem to remember why in the hell they were checking on the cells in the first place. Strong mojo. In fact, the bars of my cell had even straightened back to their original positions.

Well, *mostly* back, upon closer examination.

For a while, I sat and considered that the bars being forever bent, even just a little bit, to mark the passage of a true free spirit through them was a powerful metaphor for the human condition. I immediately wanted to go visit the Birmingham jail where Dr. King wrote his famous open letter. Maybe commemorate it in some way.

"Injustice anywhere is a threat to justice everywhere"—I pulled out my plastic knife and tried to carve that into the wall.

That got me thinking about how a plastic knife can't cut stone, which was pretty profound at the time, and that somehow led me to thinking about Jean-Paul Sartre and his comments on the paper knife and how humans are condemned to be free. I had already started trying to carve the words *Existence*

Precedes Essence into the wall when I finally realized that I was really, *really* high.

Stupid high, even.

Part of me was pissed because I couldn't remember how to spell any of the words in my fancy new Sartre quote. Part of me was trying to close my eyes, so I could better visualize the words. Part of me was trying to keep my eyes open, so that I didn't lop anything off with my knife while I jammed it into the wall and wiggled it back and forth. And another part of me was trying to reconcile the cutting nature of a real knife with the numbing power of a magical plastic knife and wondering what would happen if I slipped and poked myself in the eye with it.

Why, I would poke my own eye out, kid.

Then I started wondering what it would be like if I poked my brain with it. Then I was thinking about how interesting it is that people can understand words and meanings but not remember how to spell them.

Also, another part was reminding me why I don't fucking smoke weed anymore.

Ugh. I felt like my numbness-knife was already buried in my skull, jabber-jabbed into my frontal lobe.

I started mumbling "numbness knife" over and over, feeling the words run over my tongue like cold molasses down a dry dishtowel. I said "this is not really a knife" under my breath, and then I started giggling and saying "Ceci n'est pas une pipe" and wondering if I spoke any other French.

Then I got really thirsty, and right before I took a nap, I started thinking about how Wendy had totemed-away the smoke from the room but not from my blood, and then I thought of Tim Curry in drag: "I'll remove the cause, but not the symptom."

I started softly singing bits from *Rocky Horror Picture Show* and making observations out loud to my captive audience of Plastic Knife and Magic Feather, which was still in my hand, all sweaty and crumpled, and that was weird, something about how Sartre said that man makes himself, but Dr. Frankenfurter had made himself a better man just using some leftover Meat Loaf.

Then I giggled until I blacked out.

CHAPTER 54

Fucking bullshit Wonderland ditch weed.

I woke up in a sweat with a throbbing headache and a raging hard on, thinking about the time right after we first met that Tama and I went to see *Rocky Horror* at midnight. She dressed up as Columbia and tried to get me to go as Riff Raff, but it was too silly for me. And anyway, Columbia and Riff Raff aren't really a couple, and a midget is already pretty wild even if he isn't in costume, and we made out in the bathroom, and it was so great that I didn't even mind missing the 25th for a night.

Then I felt guilty about not saving Garrick Heldane.

I scratched my forearms, smelling my own sweat and feeling a little bit too much like a heroin addict for my own comfort, and I tried not to be nervous about what Wendy's supernatural joint had probably been laced with: magic mushrooms and faerie dust and moonlit unicorn jizz and gods-know-what-else. The scabs from the strix bites came off in rust-red flakes, showing unblemished cocoa-colored skin beneath.

Huh. Neat. Ambrosia. Maybe that Wendy girl is all right, after all.

The pounding in my head got louder, and then I realized that a cop was banging on my cell door.

"Poole. You have a visitor."

"Oh, sweet. Take me to him, Mr. Cop."

A very rude police officer shoved me into the visitor's area, which I've always been a little pissed off about because it kind of reminds me of that one place from *Arrested Development* but not nearly as well lit, and nothing fun or funny ever happens there.

I got to sit down and talk to Cleon.

He had several books with him, and his hair had been transformed into a mass of cornrow spikes, and I immediately had to reconsider the idea that nothing amusing ever happens in jail.

"Holy shit, Cleon. You look like Old Man Coolio."

"Fuck you. I spent the night on my niece's couch. Her grandbabies did this to me, and it was a small price to pay for a warm, home-cooked meal afterward."

My stomach growled. I decided to change the subject.

"Oh, it's super cute. It suits you. Didn't know you had any family around here, Cleon."

"Don't have many, don't talk about them much. But there's a few folks who'll let me crash on a couch after I get mugged, and that's about all I need family for."

"Well, all right. So, down to business, then—they're gonna kick me back in my cell before too long."

"Business, it is. So, you gonna invite me to your new island?"

"... what?"

"English, motherfucker. Do you speak it? *Are you. Going to. Invite me. To your new island?* You know, the one you're thinking about running off to?"

"I'm not... Cleon, I'm not going to take off to the island."

"Well, shit. Here I was hoping to show off my new hairstyle to some pretty island girls, maybe score me some free drinks on account of how I saved the boss-man's life a few times. Walk on the beach in my old sandals, see that big sun, maybe get out from under this rain. But we're not going?"

"No, Cleon. Jesus, why would you think that?"

"Because I know you. I know how you operate. I know how you think, you contrary little fuck. You had no goddamn intention of taking that obvious bait from the King of Majooj until the fucking moment that Anita told you *not* to do it and then shot you. Shit, if I was trying to talk you into doing something, I'd hire a woman to do exactly what she did. You flinch from carrots and bite at sticks, boy. Always have."

I considered for a moment.

"Wait, are you saying... it's a double-cross? Fuck, a triple-cross, maybe? Anita is trying to get me to go?"

"I don't know a goddamn thing about what Anita wants you to do or does not want you to do. What I do know is that you're thinking about getting on that plane to the Dominican Republic. Maybe not hard and maybe not a lot, but you're considering it. And I just want to tell you, in case you weren't aware—as you so often are not—that it's because you want to spite Anita. And that's fine."

"Dammit, Cleon. How the fuck do you...?"

"I can read you like a book, son. Learned it the hard way. Now, the real question is, do you want to get a rundown on these bastards, or do you want you and me to go shopping for some new swim trunks?"

"You want to go?"

"Shit, yes. Best offer I ever heard."

"But you don't think it's a good idea."

"Not one goddamn bit. I'll retire to the Caribbean as soon as all these fuckers are dead, and not one goddamn minute before."

"We're on the same page, then. Let's get our notes clear here, and then we'll take these bastards on. Then maybe we'll take some well-deserved vacation. Hell, we'll do a *Shawshank Redemption* thing, what do you say?"

"Shit. You ain't half as good looking as Andy Dufresne. Anyway, the two of them got off to the Pacific, not the Caribbean."

"Great. Awesome. You're a total film nerd, Cleon."

"Did you know that the reunion on the beach in Zihuatanejo at the end was only added because of studio pressure? It's actually not in Frank Darabont's original script or the novella."

"Can we focus for a minute on this? With the bad guys and all?"

"Man, I'm gonna watch that when I get home. That and *Count of Monte Cristo*. The 1934 one, I mean. The one from *V for Vendetta*."

"Cleon, tell me what you know about the King of Cocagne, or I'm going to tell all the girls at the resort that you're Coolio's granddad."

"Well, fine. Here, I thought a young man like yourself, sealed away in prison, might take some especial kind of solace thinking of *Shawshank*—or at the very least, of *Monte Cristo*."

"This is jail, not prison. I won't be off to prison until they get around to figuring out exactly which laws I've broken, and that could take some serious time and a spreadsheet. Now, I see that you've brought books and such with you. Educate me, dammit!"

"All right. First and foremost, we're gonna start with a little historical background on the king you haven't met yet: There's a whole wealth of information on the *King of Cockaigne* out there. Type it into Google, and you get a shitload of results, almost as many as you get for searching the *King of Atlantis.*"

"Fuck. Are you serious?"

"As a heart attack. A lot of the references go back to the 1100s, but calling someone a *King of Cockaigne* was something of a roundabout insult, suggesting flightiness, excess, incompetence, or gluttony—this is up through the time of John Keats. It's used here and there thousands of times throughout Western Literature until about a century ago, and then it pops up again in Umberto Eco's *The Name of the Rose,* like it was never gone. But here's what's really weird: the guy always has a title, but I could never find a proper name. Even when he's acting as a sort of bizarro anti-Santa Claus in Grimm-style Christmas stories from the 1300s, chasing naughty kids around, trying to get them to eat more pie, so Krampus can beat them with rusty chains. He's only ever called the King of Cockaigne. Anyway, there's only one place that I could find a first name listed for the king: a pantomime called "Jack in the Box," written by E.L. Blanchard from around 1873, which calls him *King Cockalorum.*"

"Oh, awesome name. *Cockalorum* here meaning a self-important little man, right?"

"Yep. From the Flemish. You're good."

"Yeah, guess how I happen to know that one."

"Ha-ha. Now, those two words, one from the Old German for 'cake' and the other eventually leading, through the Dutch, to the modern terms for 'to crow' and 'cocky,' are etymologically distinct—but they were successfully linked in the mass consciousness."

"I don't know if I'd call it *mass* consciousness, Cleon. Never fucking heard of this Blanchard guy or his play."

"Well, pantomime isn't what it used to be in popularity. But back in the day, newspapers like *The Times of London* couldn't get enough of the stuff. Neither could John Ruskin, the Sage of Brantwood. He had this to say about seeing the show 'Jack in the Box' at the Drury Lane Theater, also featuring the King of Cocagne, where it was children playing fairytale characters like Tom Tucker and Princess Poppet for the amusement of adults..."

Cleon pulled out a sheet of paper and read:

"*Inside the Circus, there have been wonderful Mr. Edward Cooke, and pretty Mademoiselle Aguzzi... and grave little Sandy, and bright and graceful Miss Hengler, all doing the most splendid feats of strength, and patience and skill. There have been dear little Cinderella and her Prince, and all the pretty children beautifully dressed, taught thoroughly how to behave, and how to dance, and how to sit still, and giving everybody delight that looks at them; whereas the instant I come outside the door, I find all the children about the streets ill-dressed, and ill-taught, and ill-behaved and nobody cares to look at them.*"

"... I find that mildly creepy, Cleon."

"Yeah, you're supposed to. We're looking at two very different views of children, here. A fairytale one where they sit still and pretend to be magical princesses and another where they're poor and starving and borderline feral. And here's where it gets even weirder; although the word *Cocagne* comes from the German for 'honey cake,' it was linked with the word *cuckold* during the reign on Marie Antoinette; *that* word comes from the French, and starts off an oblique reference to the legendary infidelity of the cuckoo. I also found some research to suggest a link in the word to the Cockneys of London because they lived as if there were no consequences—or, at least, they did so in the perceptions of the upper class. Think of the singing dad from *My Fair Lady*, or Dick Van Dyke from *Mary Poppins*."

"I try not to."

"Basically, when I compare what I saw during my time in the custody of the nameless usurper-king and what I heard Frieda say over your cell, I get that he's building a post-modern interpretation of the word *Cocagne*: equal parts *cocoa* and *coca* from 1700s Spanish and 1970s Miami drug culture with little bits of pre-Revolutionary through Industrial Age literary wordplay, all built on a medieval escape fantasy."

"Why must my head hurt all the time? Ugh. So... meaning?"

"Meaning that he's a cocky, cockney cuckold coke-head with a chocolate fetish. Or, at least, that's the mask he's wearing to channel a new totem of his own design."

"Oh, Jesus. I hate puns."

"So do I, and I got tortured by one. He sat there in a hoodie and a tracksuit, nibbling cookies and doing lines and looking at lolcats and Japanese drawings of kiddie porn while a group of freak-monster teenagers tagged me with box cutters and beat me with wiffleball bats. Those things sting like a motherfucker after a while."

"Hell. Is that what it was like?"

"It was like seeing a much darker take on the Artful Dodger from *Oliver Twist* or a kind of a cartoon villain from an 80s anti-drug public service announcement brought to life. King Humbert—or Simon or Cockalorum—whatever they call him: he's this sort of vaguely Hispanic-looking, skinny guy with a huge pot belly, gold teeth because brushing isn't fun, and long greasy hair that smells like stale corn chips. He wears this ridiculous pair of "brass knuckles," all gold and set in chain with the words *FEEL GOOD* set in fake diamonds. His accent is all over the place, but bad Southie-Londoner is the core. Hell, he might actually be Welsh or even Roma, but I couldn't tell you."

"And he's setting up a landgrab."

"Yep. Him and his demon-summoning buddy Gog."

"I'm going to kill both of them."

"Hoped you would say that."

CHAPTER 55

I spared a glance at the clock on the wall, set behind a mesh of wire. Shit, visiting hours were running out on me. I considered, then fished out a smoke and lit it up.

"Okay, so I have my targets. What can you tell me about King Cockalorum's demon-summoning buddy?"

"Historically? Not much. Toss the word *Gog* into a search engine, you get literally *millions* of results; only a handful of them have even the slightest thing to do with what we're after, unfortunately. Hell, I found everything from the Gynecologic Oncology Group to a website with old video games. I narrowed it down a lot with a couple of private emails to some biblical scholars I know, but all I got was a half-dozen rabbis with messianic studies backgrounds falling all over themselves to point out that prophecies in Ezekiel aren't meant to be taken literally."

"Awesome. So where does that leave us?"

"This guy is an asshole, and he's named himself after a satanic monster-king intent on destroying all the people of goodness and light. One interesting thing, though: he never took a swing at me—and neither did the King of Cockagne. Just let their minions and monsters do it. Greg-Gog, for one, just stood there with his hands in his pockets the whole time."

"Huh. Might be that Gog, King of Magog, breaks totem by actually getting into a fight. Didn't somebody tell me that his symbol was darkness and sneakiness?"

"Sure. Makes as much sense as anything else. Of course, I wouldn't put too much stock in that little theory unless pressed. According to legend, the goddamn Forgotten King of Kidane-Mehret isn't allowed to touch people—unless, of course, he's killing them with his hands. Maybe it's something like that because I was being used as bait for you. Or maybe he just didn't want his prints on the scene."

"About that, did you see the King of Majooj in his new borrowed human-suit?"

"I was actually going to ask you about that little factoid. Because last night, he freaked out when you called him Greg, but that motherfucker was Fadey Bohdan. I looked him up."

"Oh, shit. Yeah. I keep forgetting what little chance we've had to talk about all of this. The real life King of Majooj used to be some vaguely Jewish or Greek-looking guy named Gregory Howsgrove, AKA Bastard Greg the Kitty-Cat Killer. Then he got a hold of the Jar of Shifting Souls or whatever, and now, he's gotten himself a much more politically connected and wealthy body."

"Well, I'll be dipped in shit. Wish I had one of those."

"Yeah, the ability to trade bodies sounds pretty damn enticing."

"It's going to make him a hell of a dangerous opponent, too. If he can wear his Fadey suit to boardroom deals and a much scarier one to a fight, we're in trouble. Do you think he can switch into the body of something from the Sideways?"

"I don't know if a lot of stuff from the Sideways even has a soul to shift, but if anybody could come up with a way to do it, it would be Greg. I don't much like the idea of somebody with his power and smarts in the body of a nigh-unkillable monster."

"Hmm. Something like that monster-clown of his?"

"Oh, shit, Cleon. You met his pet clown?"

"Yep. He tossed it an uncooked steak at one point. Bit into it like a rabid pit bull and fought with it."

"The one member of his court that I met, Prince Gug, called it Canio de Pogo. That ring a bell for you?"

He considered. "I think so. From the opera *Pagliacci*, the murderous clown is called Canio. Or, at least, that's the name of the husband and the actor. He stabs a couple of people on stage—it's kind of a play within a play. And unless I'm totally off, *Pogo the Clown* was the name of John Wayne Gacy's persona when he dressed up in the makeup and the balloons."

"Oh, shit, awesome. So he's made out of every subconscious fear of murderous clowns going back, what, how long?"

"I don't know. 1890s, maybe? As demons go, it's a young one."

"Yeah, but with a totem referenced in everything from *The Simpsons* to Steven King to *Seinfeld*. Jesus. Okay, so what else do I need to know?"

He sighed. "Here's the bad news: all of this is above board. At least officially. I talked with a few people since last night, mostly on condition of anonymity, and word is that the Forgotten King of Gurankalia has formalized a Conquest by these two kings within AWAK."

"Huh? The fuck is that supposed to mean?"

"It means—and if you remember, I warned your ass over and over—that you never took AWAK shit seriously. And now it's biting you in the behind. Basically, these two have the right to claim territory if they have the strength of arm to do so. In other words, get the fuck out of the way if you don't want to get run over. I don't know if these two have earned themselves some leverage with the Forgotten Kings Society at large or if the crazy old bastards in the FKS are taking a hands-off approach until they can bring the hammer down in their own sweet time, but the bomb threat at the Long Hour hold last night has been declared a non-issue."

"Shit. Okay, so... what bomb threat? Tama called me last night to tell me that people were freaking out. What happened?"

"You didn't hear. Oh, shit, Royden. I... I don't know how to tell you this."

"What?"

"Your homeless buddy, that oracle, the Prince of Minos, uh... he was stuck to the door of the hotel ballroom with a note on him saying that the AWAK meeting was canceled until further notice due to threat of imminent death. He had a big fake bomb, made of these construction-paper and duct-tape tubes that looked like sticks of dynamite, stuck in his mouth and in his shirt and down the front of his pants, all wired to an old alarm clock stuck at midnight."

"Christ."

"People freaked out. Called each other, packed their bags, headed out of town. This whole city and most of the tri-state area is pretty much empty of hourists at the moment."

"Every goddamn secret king but you and me and the bad guys ran for the hills, huh?"

"Across the board. Hourists, kings, even the non-court friends and family of pretty much everybody who has ever stepped behind the curtain to do more than peek."

"So what about Chuck Dawg the Second? Where's he now?"

"... he's dead, Royden. He was crucified, nailed to the doors with railroad spikes and a couple-hundred industrial-grade staples. They think it had to have been done before the 25th even started, by a crew of a least a dozen."

"Fuck. Oh, fuck. This is what he gets for talking to me. Great. Jesus. Hell. And the one guy who could jump an oracle..."

"Would be the King of Magog. Yeah. All the Courts of Minos are in an uproar about it, but you know how they are. Half of them are blaming the other half, calling it an assassination or a coup; the last half are so wrapped up in paranoia that they've retreated into their little labyrinths with guns and axe-wielding, half-breed minotaurs to wait out the next wave of hits."

"... that's three halves, Cleon."

"Yeah, you'll have that. This reminds me... here."

He slid a hand across the table, keeping an eye out for a guard. I palmed whatever he had in it. Something small, light, and plastic.

I peeked at it as I slipped it into my pocket.

"A pink toy cellphone?"

"Picked it up at a gas station on the way here. It was full of candy. It should help you get a hold of Magic-Eatin' Jim."

I felt the thing, running my fingers along it.

"What's taped to it?"

"A two-dollar bill from the 1930s: the serial number is a prime. The bill represents the two coins on the eyes of the dead, and the picture of Monticello on the back, printed during the Great Depression, symbolizes the power of cash to overcome all obstacles. Also, I wrote the words *call-anywhere* on the bill with a pen from a bank."

"Fantastic."

"Just to be on the safe side, I wouldn't try calling him until the 25th. And if you can get your hands on something he likes, like a Twinkie or a beer or something, it might help when you ring him up."

"Yeah, I'll do that. I'll order something up from room service."

"Man, you are one sour little son of a bitch, today."

"I just found out that my buddy the Prince of Minos is dead."

"Well, then, you can call his ass, too. He had a thing for money, and he was royalty, right?"

"Shit. Yeah, I suppose."

A loud siren blared. A guard started shouting that visiting hours were over.

"Buck up, motherfucker. We got people who need killing, and I need you in a fighting mood."

"Yeah, that's... that just what a girl named Wendy told me. Hey, can you do a little scouting on a girl, calls herself Wendy and Tiger Lily? Queen of Cocagne, but not married to the bad guy?"

He grinned and stood. "Got it. See you tomorrow."

"Call me, if you need to. I still have my phone on me. And a magic feather, funny enough."

"Magic feather?"

"Yeah."

I pulled it out of my pocket, just enough so that we could both get a look at it. For the first time, I really examined the thing—bright red, almost a neon. Little highlights of an intense orange, like you only see in marine-rescue equipment and artificial, cheese-food products, with the most unnatural color of yellow imaginable streaked across it, glaring hot enough to make a banana look pale.

It fit in the palm of my hand, and then stirred a little.

It was soft and light, almost weightless, like something stripped off a gaudy feather boa that would sting the eyes in anything except candlelight. I tried to imagine a whole mass of these draped around someone and got back images of little kids in pancake makeup, playing dress-up in floppy hats, tottering in giant high heels eight sizes too big.

This was a six-year-old's idea of fashionable.

"Damn. Phoenix feather, maybe? Vermilion fire bird?"

"I don't think so. I mean, it could be, but it doesn't have any heat coming off it. And this was given to me by an insane fairy princess, not a Greek-era heroine or a Chinese empress. I'd guess it's from a song, a cartoon, or something even goofier."

"Might be from the parrot, Captain Flint, in *Treasure Island*. Or maybe off something from *The Jungle Book*, like the kite, whatever his name was, although that would probably be more brown. Hell, there's flamingos aplenty in Wonderland. Might even be from Billina, the magic yellow chicken, in the Emerald City."

"Now you're just making shit up."

"Dead serious. There's a magic chicken in *Ozma of Oz*. She's the Toto character. Haven't you been studying up on any of this shit?"

"No."

"You're an idiot."

The guard walked up and very specifically indicated with his shotgun that Cleon should leave.

"Well, bye. Thanks for coming to visit."

"Yeah. If it's from Wendy, ask Magic-Eatin' Jim about it."

"Got it."

He left, looking over his shoulder just once to nod at me as he disappeared out the door.

I sat at our little table and was sad for a while, and then I was taken back to my cell to be sad there.

CHAPTER 56

I sat in my stupid cell and listened to rain hit the building and slowly drifted from sad thoughts to angry thoughts.

I flicked by knife open and closed a whole bunch of times.

The time had come, I decided, to make a list of what I knew and what I was semi-certain of and what I was wildly guessing about and what I was completely in the dark on. As old Dick Cheney might have put it, I needed to calculate my "known knowns" and my "known unknowns" and even a few of my "unknown unknowns."

Wait, or was that Rumsfeld?

Fuck, I need to start reading the news again.

I turned my cellphone off, crossed my legs, sat down on my cot, and began to run down my mental checklist.

Currently known: the two Kings of Majooj and Cocagne are temporarily in league. Their goals involve landgabbing the entire US once it collapses into an Emptied Empire; they each have a small army. They do not trust one another—nor should they, might I add. Once the prize is shared between them, they can squabble over it all they like. And they're competent: so far, they've robbed Koloksai, a powerful member of the Forgotten, in order to steal a body-swapping artifact and run circles around every other member of AWAK and mortal law-enforcement in the book. Now, the Forgotten Kings have given the two of them free reign to take what they can get, and AWAK as a whole is on the run. These two, however, have reason to fear me, so far, because I'm very famously a dangerous asshole, and they also want me alive, according to the late Prince of Minos. Their first plan once I got mixed-up with their scheme involved framing me for murder and trying to get me to run away—quick reaction, considering that I was officially dead only minutes before. Since then, they've sent a gun-toting minion, probably a member of the Boy-Goat Brigade and already working deep cover with Cleon, to kill me; they've attempted to scare me off after bribing me, then sent several monsters after me; they involved Frieda, now Fred and Anita, an old... associate... of mine to turn me over; and after failing to kill or capture me several times have made another overture of peace. Once I fail to accept their new offer, they'll try to kill me again. They might actually succeed this time; if I hadn't gotten that magical shirt from Garrick Heldane, I would be dead many times over by now.

Currently semi-known: speaking of that guy... the Secret King of Cahokia, Garrick Heldane, ran off to Happy Happy VCR to save Cleon. He was subsequently taken by the evil kings and dragged to Paese dei Balocchi. For some reason, when Tama called me to tell me this, she didn't seem upset that I had stolen money from her. Which, come to think of it now, leads me to think that Garrick never told her that I stole that cash and must have secretly replaced in the drawer, which makes him a much better guy than me and makes me a *real* fucking asshole for not having saved him yet. Speaking of a rescue, that's on my to-do list, which is okay because I'm pretty sure that he's being held at an abandoned skate park and laser tag facility outside of town with deep connections to the Sideways, and I'm heading that way right now anyway, if only to burn the fucker down.

Currently unexplained: I still have no fucking idea what's up with that second missing rich guy, suddenly returned and considered all solved now by Detective Ladislav, which I don't trust for a minute. Also, the real nature of Freida's—AKA Fred and Anita Baghaamrita—involvement in this shit is still real iffy to me. Then there's the Queen of Cocagne and her little vendetta, which seems all cut and dry until you remember that no, fuck you, I don't trust her.

What I really wanted to do, to be honest, was to call Magic-Eatin' Jim and run Wendy's name past him. Also, I wanted to apologize for getting him killed and maybe just shoot the shit for a little bit.

He was a good guy.

But, as Cleon had said, the best time to make that call would be at or around the midnight hour when the clocks go funny. And unless I missed my guess, whatever part of the building they're keeping Garrick Heldane in is probably only accessible during the 25th. That made me feel a little better because if that was the case, then he was currently experiencing a little time burp while tied to a chair and was not actually getting tortured at the moment. He was un-phased from reality and had been since I fell down in the parking lot and broke my nose.

Which, just for the record, still hurts like a son-of-a-bitch.

I opened my eyes and glanced at my cell.

It was almost six in the evening.

I was getting restless. I wanted to get up and punch the walls and go out and walk around and find some random bar I had never been in before and buy everyone a drink. I wanted to go meet a girl, tell her stupid jokes, lie about my middle name, and jump in a fountain with her. I wanted to stand on top of a building and yell at people. Maybe learn to kayak. If I believed in all that totem shit, I would have started attributing my wanderlust to something inherent in the windswept Emptied Empire of Jangladesh and her nomad princes, but I can't actually think of *anyone* who likes being locked up.

I checked my cellphone again.

Gah, less than a minute since I last checked it? Fuck.

I was going to be climbing the walls any second now.

Okay. I had just over four hours until the magical 10:00 pm time when the car dedicated to taking me to the airport would leave. And I had more than *six* fucking hours before I could slip the waking bonds of this mortal prison and, hypothetically, still be stuck in this fucking jail cell because the universe is designed to fuck people like me over and the locks and human anchor points in this place are built tough.

I considered for a moment.

The more I thought about it, the more I had to appreciate the elegance of the King of Cocagne's little trap. Me, sitting stuck in a fucking concrete and steel cage, solves his problem. I'm no threat locked up. And being here would be enough to make me go batty; taking his escape route is the only obvious solution. And if I did that, I was useless against him: either he has somebody kill me when I get into the car, or the car drives me to the airport and somebody kills me there, or I fly to the Dominican Republic and somebody kills me *there*, or… what?

Well, I go to the beach, and I'm happy, and then I'm in the fucking Dominican Republic and no threat to him at all.

That last one seems like the simplest solution, especially since he's cleared all of this with the great and powerful Forgotten.

I mean, there was no way I could get back here from the Dominican Republic.

Then I actually sat and considered that for a moment.

Yes, actually.

Yes, I could. I could get back from the Dominican Republic, if I really wanted to. I could step to Jangladesh, no problem. And going elsewhere would just involve using powers of the 25th that I'm not well-practiced at, and it would be a pain in the ass and dangerous, but I could do it by temporarily marking some place that I wanted to teleport to as property of my Emptied Empire and stepping toward it through a bounded doorway, but… yeah, I could do it. Fuck it, I had helped Cleon do exactly that within the last twenty-four hours.

Not a particularly uncommon trick. Almost everybody knows it, and anybody could learn it. Certainly not on par with unhinging yourself from reality while in an elevator, is what I'm saying.

Okay, now, the sort of thing where I could step to a pre-marked domain of mine would only be possible within the 25th Hour. Couldn't do it during daylight, unlike some of the Forgotten bastards with their eons of potency and chains of conquered sites made permanent with the blood of thousands and hallowed by worship.

But there was a possibility that come midnight, I could just pop through to the Secret Time, and then step through a doorway and wind up right there in Cleon's office. *Poof.* Ta-da, please hold your applause. Okay, so I wouldn't be able to do that while in jail because I would need to step through a doorway, and the bars in front of me are about as human-anchored as anything on the planet, with the sole exception of maybe the Wailing Wall, what with the hours and hours every day that people spend staring at them, but since Wendy had already used a little bit of freedom-mojo to walk through them, there was a chance I could do the same.

Or at least shoulder-check the fuckers out of shape and slip my slim-ass through to the other side.

But while on an island in the sun, I could hop away like nothing. I mean, there are doors at most resorts. Assuming, of course, that I had a prearranged spot to hop to, it would be easy. And I did, pretty obviously: the dust in Cleon's place.

So what was I missing, here? Had the two asshole kings that I was targeting in on somehow already accounted for this, or was I tumbling at this exact moment to an overlooked hole in their defenses? Maybe this was an instance that, like I had told Ladislav earlier, I could only beat them when they made a mistake?

That would be one big, silly, dumbass mistake. And these guys weren't famous for those.

I pulled out the last of the smokes I'd bummed from Jose and lit it up. No, we're not supposed to smoke in here. But fuck it. The worst they could do at this point was come in and take my cig away from me. And to be perfectly honest, I'd like to see them try.

All right, so how about this: the villain-kings hadn't expected me to align a doorway with the Kingdom of Urartu and let Cleon make his escape. That probably came down to an assumption of callousness, incompetence, or cowardice in me; the Kings of Douchebaggery wouldn't have guessed that I would try something like that to save Cleon because that's not how they think.

Honestly, it's not like I'm well-known for saving my friends, as Jimbo, Chuck Dawg, and Garrick could attest, and I'm not known as a great spellcaster, as everyone else likes to attest, and me contacting Cleon with a newly made domain during a cunning pre-engineered distraction was pretty damned clever if I may attest so myself.

But since Cleon hopped the bitch already, it made damn good sense that the two of them would have accounted for the ability to hop doors from that point forward.

And the offer to let me walk out and drive away and fly off to the big island full of vodka-soaked sexy girls was made... this morning.

Hm.

Okay, let's assume that they're watching the spot where I could hop to because it's the same place that Cleon hopped away to while in their custody: his office. Any relatively good detective could make a decent guess about where Cleon wound up, and even if they didn't have a diviner handy to trace the thread of his passage, it wouldn't take more than a few hours before a team could check his place and inspect the dust trails there for magical residue.

And it would show up.

So... huh.

Sure, Cleon could have moved the dirt. But seeing that the dirt was moved would only add to their paranoia.

Huh.

Huh?

I didn't have an answer on this one. Also, where was Cleon now? He had spent the night at a family member's house, he said, and then gone to the hospital. He wasn't going back to Happy Happy VCR, was he? Was he in danger?

Shit.

I pulled out my phone to call Cleon, and noticed that I had nine missed calls.

Interesting.

With the bastard still on silent, I flipped the fucker open and checked the missed calls: all from Cleon, and all in the last fifteen minutes while I had been sitting here ruminating. No messages.

Weird.

I called him.

CHAPTER 57

Royden! Jesus!"

"Hi, Cleon. I was just about to call you."

"Fuck, man, I was afraid you had your cellphone taken. You turn your ringer off or something?"

"Yes, I did. Hey, look, can we make this quick? I'm not actually supposed to have this on me."

"Yeah. It's all over the news, man: there was a huge drug bust out in the 'burbs. Something like twenty-five or thirty kids with coke and meth and heroin and a hydroponic grow-lab and all sorts of other shit just got raided by the local PD; there was an anonymous tip called in, and half the fucking county showed up to grab the little bastards!"

"Wait, so the skate-park got busted?"

"Nope. But the same 'burb, MacSherman Hollows or something. A little pizzeria about a block away. They grabbed a quarter-million in drugs, they said, and thirty kids."

"Wait one fucking minute. Where are they taking the kids?"

"That's why I'm calling you, you stupid asshole! The local police station doesn't have the room to hold all of them, so they're getting shipped into your holding, downtown. They've got a set of three vans heading into the city proper as soon as the kids have been processed here. The local mayor out in the 'burbs just had a fucking press conference, thanking the city for being so accommodating in this time of crisis; talking about how although most of them are first-time offender juveniles, seeing the big-city lockup would be good for them."

"Shit. Shit shit fuck shit. That's the fucking Boy-Goat Brigade. They're coming in here to kill me."

"No fucking shit, you little Sherlock. And how much you want to bet that they'll each be loaded up with one or two plastic-ass weapons apiece that won't get noticed by the PD in either jurisdiction and won't set off alarms?"

"Why do you say that?"

"Because I just got a look at the 'burb-mayor on the TV, and there's a guy standing right fucking next to him who's a dead ringer for Fadey Bohdan. I'm not sure of it, but I think that when the camera guy panned across the mayor's entourage, I saw a dude who's probably the King of Cocagne wearing a fucking suit and tie. Looks like they're already putting that jar to good use."

"Oh, shit."

"Hell, the guys driving the vans look like they could have been kids at the skate-park. Real young cops, man."

"Oh, fuck."

"Classic hammer and anvil. Get your ass comfortable in jail, thinking you're safe there and only there, then send the brigade in to get you."

"Oh, Christ. I have to get out of here."

"Yeah, good call. How are you going to do that, exactly?"

"Hm. Actually, I may have a plan."

"You mean a plan, or a plane?"

"Either or. Somewhere in between, maybe. It involves a quick bait and switch. Hey, thank you, Cleon."

"No problem, man. Don't mention it."

I heard a guard come walking up the hallway. That was okay. My new plan also involved me getting caught with the phone. And smoking.

"Oh, Cleon, real quick—one other thing."

"Yeah?"

"I'm wondering about that dirt from the domain ritual I did last night during the 25th. What did you do with it?"

"Stuck some of it in the vault-vault, got some of it in my coat pocket. Why?"

"I'm wondering if you can think of any way that the King of Cocagne or the King of Majooj could prevent me from using it?"

"Use it? What do you mean?"

"I mean, like, if I had you sprinkle it somewhere and maybe repeat the ritual or something, I could use it to teleport to it just like I did last night, right? Or, I mean, like I had you do last night. Fuck. Look, I don't even know how all this magic-shit works. Basically, what I'm asking is, is there some way the kings have out-thought me on me using that dirt as a destination?"

"Jesus, you're fucking paranoid."

"You taught me well."

The cop came around the corner and stared at me. With my ear to the receiver, I nodded at him and held up my cigarette to give him the international sign for "one second, I'm on the phone."

He did not find it as funny as I did. "Hey! What the fuck are you doing?"

I glared at him. "Fucker, can you not see that I'm on the phone?"

Cleon, on the line. "Shit, do you have to go?"

"Not until you tell me what you think about this. Is there any reason that I couldn't have you put that somewhere and let me 'port to it?"

"Not that I can think of. Can I call you back with an answer?"

"Sure."

The cop started to come toward my jail cell, hand on his baton. With practiced ease, I clicked the plastic folding-knife out of my pocket and pointed it at him, hoping it looked steel-like. He froze.

I looked him dead in the eye. "Get me Ladislav. Get him now."

The cop went bug-eyed and left.

Cleon chimed in, "All part of your plan?"

"Sure, let's call it that. One other thing, if you don't mind?"

"Okay, shoot."

Sirens went off across the facility.

I tried to straighten my thoughts.

"The mayor, on the TV. Would you describe him as, say, about five-foot-seven, a hundred twenty pounds, pretty broad in the shoulders, with a really nice suit and hair like a local news weatherman?"

"Yeah. Maybe a little shorter than that. And, well, his shoulders aren't exactly the broadest I ever seen."

"No, that makes sense. Flesh translation, and all. Still, a pretty unremarkable face? Just, like, the sort of face you would expect any rich white guy to have? But with a really nice goatee?"

"Yep."

"Damn. I think I just found our other missing rich guy. The mayor is the soul-shifted host-body for Prince Gug, a spirit-creature that should have a head about the size of a barrel and hands two-and-a-half feet across, according to Lovecraft. Can't believe I didn't think of that before. There's no way that a gug could have gotten down into those caverns under Frieda's without some magic."

"Oh, you and your fucking Lovecraft. Racist old asshole."

"Cleon, goddammit, for the last time, Lovecraft wasn't racist the way that, like, a modern-day racist is racist. He was born in 1890, for fuck's sake, on the upper East Coast, and he married a Jewish woman. That's pretty much the definition of open-minded, man. Okay, sure, so he was scared of black people. So was everybody. It's not like he was a member of the Klan or something."

"Whatever, Royden. You ever read his poem 'On the Creation of Niggers,' by chance?"

"No."

"Also, what are we doing? Don't you need to get off the phone?"

"Not until they make me. It's part of my plan. And no, I haven't read that stupid poem with a racial epithet in the title."

"Oh, it's a doozy. And for the damn record, Mark Twain was born 55 years earlier, poorer, goofier looking and less well educated on the Mississippi, and he makes Lovecaft look like a fucking neo-Nazi. You're not convincing me on this one."

"Fine. At least Lovecraft was racist against the Irish, too."

"Of course he was. The Irish barely rate as sub-human."

"Yeah, there's that."

And just then, a whole bunch of uniformed guys with shotguns came around the corner.

"DROP THE FUCKING KNIFE!"

I did so. "Gotta go, Cleon."

"Have fun, man. Thanks for calling and all."

"You too. Much love."

I dropped my cell and the cig, too, and I put my hands where the cops could see them.

"Hi, guys. There's a note up front with the desk from a couple of federal agents I'd like you to read. Also, seriously, get me Ladislav."

CHAPTER 58

With several shotguns pointed at various parts of me, in a triple-set of handcuffs, I was walked to a meeting room.

Ladislav was sitting there, his huge-ass eyebrows hovering and twitching menacingly above his red-rimmed and all-too-tired eyes like very ugly and unkempt twin falcons about to strike. He had his gun out on the table in front of him and a copy of Frieda's offer unfolded, sitting there next to a cup of coffee that had probably been warm much earlier this afternoon.

I was pushed into a steel chair and then double-handcuffed to the chair. If they had time, I'm sure they would have bolted the chair to the floor and soldered it into place. And then maybe wrapped some logging chain around me.

Lacking time to do all that, six guys stood and pointed guns at me.

My cellphone and my other, much pinker candy-cellphone with a two-dollar bill taped to it and my magical feather and my plastic knife were sitting on the table, too. Parts of the feather were drifting back and forth, like there was a breeze in the room that only it could detect.

I gave Ladislav my most winning smile. "Evening, detective."

"What the fuck are you doing, Poole?"

"Probably leaving, sir. There's a car outside that's going to take me to the airport, and you'll never see me again, so I wanted to say goodbye. Why do you ask?"

"Who the fuck is protecting you, Royden? What's going on?"

"Ah. So, finally, we get to the point in the investigation when you want my help again."

"Tell me what's going on here, you little shit."

"I'd really like to. But the real question is, how many of your men in this room are ready to be let in on the truth?"

"The fuck is that supposed to mean?"

"You know what I'm talking about, detective. The truth. The truth about you and me and that weekend in Cabo San Lucas with those hookers it turned out weren't actually girls. When we got the matching tattoos. Man, that was fun. I still can't believe you did all those tequila shots and still managed to wrestle that goat into submission."

I winked at him. To give him his credit where credit is due, Detective Ladislav did not shoot me at this point. He didn't even walk around the desk and punch me in the face.

I mean, I probably would have hit me for that.

Instead, those dark eyes of his narrowed, and he told everyone to leave the room.

There was a sort of moment, there for a bit, where everybody wanted to ask if he was serious, but nobody wanted to be the first one to say something. So I piped up again, "Guys, seriously, you are going to love this story. We stole a boat and ramped it up a dock and into a hotel at one point. It was like if Michael Bay had directed *The Hangover*. But with way more nudity."

Ladislav waved at them dismissively. Suddenly, the guys got the point: I was going to sit here and bullshit until they left. And after they were out of the room, well, maybe, just *maybe*, the esteemed Detective Ladislav was going to beat the shit out of me in a way that is not technically allowed by city ordinance anymore.

The door clicked shut. Now, it was just me and Ladislav.

"Talk to me, Poole."

"Seriously? Because this involves that witching-hour bullshit that you *so* don't believe in. Are you ready to hear it, or do you want me to be an asshole a little bit more? Maybe even threaten you with the repercussions of not letting me get into that car so helpfully provided by the nice people at the nameless federal agency that came and visited me today?"

"Fuck. I've got a lot of work to do tonight, Royden. And you have a ride to catch. Now, you had a reason for asking for me before you vanish into some shiny black luxury car, and I want to know what it is."

"Oh, so the car really is out there? I wasn't actually sure about that one. Seemed like an odd play to make on their part to not actually have a car, but it's nice to confirm the thing's existence."

"You're getting very close to having me throw you in it myself."

"Yeah, yeah, I know, you've got a big workload tonight. There was a big drug bust out in the 'burbs today, from what I heard. Something like thirty kids getting shipped here tonight, huh?"

"That's correct."

"Sure, yeah, you don't even wonder how I heard about that. I mean, since it happened just after I was done with visiting hours and there's no way I could possibly have gotten the heads-up. Oh, but you probably assume that I got a call on my cellphone—and nevermind the fact that I shouldn't have had my cell on me, and you don't know how I got it."

"Where the fuck are you going with this?"

"I'm trying to tell you that it's all connected, asshole. Look, mister detective: the mayor of MacSherman Hollow, where this little bust took place, is the same guy you had a missing persons report for the other night, am I right?"

He looked uncomfortable. "Yes."

"But then he showed up again with some iron-clad alibi. Probably one involving a few very young cops? All right. So I'm telling you this right now: Those kids are being sent here to kill me. Right now, they're being loaded down with weapons, just like that little plastic knife right there on your desk, which will not set off metal detectors, and they're going to show up here to kill me. They'll rip this place apart, if they have to."

"That's not going to happen. No one would do that."

"Says you. I say different. These kids have watched the new Batman, Bourne, and Bond films a couple too many times, and they think those are gritty and realistic. I'll bet my left nut that they've got tactical munitions coming here with them that can melt through steel bars like they were fucking Jell-O and automatic rifles designed to punch holes in cement just like power weapons do in video games. This is the ultimate fantasy for the Columbine Kid who was weened, in diapers, in front of big, dumb 90s action-movies and raised on the *Saw* franchise. These boys are going to march in with guns blazing. And I'm their target."

"You're a fucking paranoid lunatic."

"Oh, sure I am. But here's a fun game that I want you to try: click open that folding plastic hunting knife there on the table, the one that's about as sharp as a folded-up Denny's napkin, and stab yourself in the hand with it."

He looked at me, warily. His eyes flicked to the gun right next to him, just for a second, and then to the folded-up knife, and then back to me. He didn't say anything.

"Come on, detective. I'd do it myself, but you're not letting me out of these handcuffs or near that knife to try it. Look, it's just like that trick I do with the coffee where it disappears into my palm into Jangladesh, only it's going to be weirder."

Without taking his eyes off me, Ladislav slowly spread the knife open. His thumb flicked across the soft, dull blade as if he was testing it, and then he paused.

"You lost all the feeling in that thumb, didn't you? Don't worry, it'll come back."

"You've got to be fucking kidding me."

"Yep. I'm kidding. Ha ha ha. That's a magic knife you're holding there, detective. And there are more like it. Swords, too, and handguns, and grenades and large-caliber rifles and unless I miss my guess, probably flame-throwers. I haven't tried out the grenades, yet, but I'll bet they're awesome. Probably fling you through the air like you're on a trampoline and shoot numbness-pellets in every direction."

He rubbed his thumb. "How does it work?"

"You're asking the wrong guy. I don't do really fancy sorcery. I'm just in this gig for the chicks. But the fact of the matter is that the thing right there in your hand is the least of the weapons forged out of fairytale stuff by a fairytale warlock. There's a king out there with a whole army of acne-scarred young men armed with this shit, some of which can be switched to deadly mode, and thirty or more of them are on their way here to collect me. Some will be dressed as cops."

His gaze narrowed at me. "Why are you telling me this?"

"What, seriously? Dude, you think I want to see a bunch of cops get killed or something? Man, you do not have a very high opinion of me. Ugh. For the last time, I'm one of the good guys, asshole. I'm trying to keep you and your men from getting shot up and blown away and then covered up as some sort of gas-line explosion or something."

"You really, honest-to-god, think that the people who want you would be willing to blow up an occupied police station?"

"To cover for the fallout of their plan being revealed? Oh, yeah. The really scary part is that the people that the Gug-Mayor of MacSherman Hollow and Mr. Alexandros, AKA Gregory Howsgrove, are reporting back to would *insist* on it, the creepy old Forgotten fucks."

"Fine. And you're saying they have the means to do this?"

"Yep. The people at the top of this little organization, like the guy who used to be Fadey Bohdan, are crazy, and they've recently switched from being local nutbags with a multi-year plan to multinational-level nutbags with decades-long plans. And their foot soldiers are living out the dream of every guy who spent a day at the arcade pumping quarters into a shoot-'em-up instead of making out with girls, way back in junior high. This is going to happen—unless I stop it."

He clicked the knife closed. "How are you going to stop it, then?"

"We're going to pull a bait-and-switch. The guys out in the car, who are supposed to be taking me to the airport, are working for the men in MacSherman who are sending a squad in here to kill me. If I get in that car, the kids will turn around and go back home. Just you watch. You'll get a phone call from the Mayor of MacSherman, saying that he's had a change of heart after hearing from a bunch of parents, and he doesn't want them incarcerated overnight up here after all. He'll make room, locally, sorry for the fucking inconvenience."

"Then you're getting in that car."

"Not so fast. Because I have reason to believe that the car is also a trap because there's no way they would let me get on a plane and fly to the Dominican Republic knowing that I could teleport back to town. I get in that car, they kill me."

"You're losing me, here."

"All right, let's try this: you go ahead and read that letter sitting next to you. Really read it. Put every ounce of your energy into telling me what, precisely, the name of the federal agency written on there is. After that, we're going to talk about how to get me out of this building without alerting the men in the car outside, and how you're going to send the Boy-Goat Brigade back to MacSherman Hollow once they get here, but not until right then. Now read that paper. *Intently.*"

And then, I admit to my deepest regret and shame, I sat back and watched Detective Ladislav give himself a massive heart attack.

It honestly sounded like his heart burst in his chest.

I didn't think that was going to happen.

Oops.

CHAPTER 59

Ladislav went red in the face, tried to swallow a few times, grabbed his chest with his right hand, and leaned over the table with a low wheeze that went up an octave and then stopped.

His left arm hung limply at his side.

Fuck.

I did not see that coming. This was not part of the plan.

With a grunt, I tried to bust open my handcuffs.

Nothing doing.

After a moment, all I had to show for my efforts was a couple of bruised wrists. Apparently, three sets of cuffs between my hands and another two latching me to my chair was a stretch beyond my limits. It's like that old saying: I can pick up one person easily enough, and he could maybe pick *me* up, but I'll be damned if we could pick each other up at the same time and the both of us fly to the moon.

Come to think of it, is that an old saying?

Sounds like it. Or maybe I'm just going into panic and am now making up folksy-sounding aphorisms and observations. Oh, man, this sucks. Sucks, sucks, sucks.

Fuck.

And everything was going so well.

I squirmed around in my seat, listening to Ladislav die. He needed medical attention, and I needed out of this fucking chair and out of this fucking police station and quite possibly out of the fucking country. I went ahead and bruised my wrists again, making a nasty *clang* sound. Ow. You know, at times like this, I wish that I was tall enough to have my feet touch the ground when I'm chained to a chair. If I was, like, Shaq's size or something, I could just lean forward and walk away.

Lacking anything better to do, I thrashed around and twisted in my seat and yelled obscenities.

The soundproofing in the conference room took care of most of the evidence that I had even tried, but my squirming got the chair to move a little, which was nice. It wasn't in the direction of the door or of Ladislav, unfortunately, but just sort of wopperjawed from where I was before. That sucked. Still, taking this as a good omen, I tried squirming a little more, throwing all of my weight in the direction of Ladislav's table and the phones sitting there.

I succeeded in flipping myself onto the floor, not-quite-face-first.

Ow.

"Dammit! Fuck! Phone!"

There was a clicking sound from up on the desk. I would have missed it, except that I'm a pretty heavy smoker and I was out of breath after my exertions and as such was not making much sound any more. I listened and considered: that was unmistakably the *click* of a cellphone flipping itself open.

"Candy phone?"

Nothing. Fuck, fuck... I tried to remember what Cleon had told me. What he had written on the $2 bill.

"Uhhh... Call-Anywhere Phone?"

Another click, as the thing shut itself and opened again.

"Call-Anywhere Phone, dial 911 for me!"

I heard the tones go off, and then a soft and haunted woman's voice. "Time of calls remaining: two minutes."

Shit, I had to make this quick.

There was a ring. Two rings.

A dispatcher picked up. "911, what's your emergency?"

"I've got a police detective here going into cardiac arrest while questioning a suspect! I'm downtown at the police station, in a secure conference room on the third floor! Send EMTs or call the station attendant on duty or something! He's dying, here!"

"Sir, may I have you name?"

"I'm the fucking suspect! Detective Ladislav is dying! Seriously, I can't have this guy croak, here, while he's questioning me! Fucking get somebody up here!"

"Sir, I need you to calm down!"

"Fuck you! Phone, end call!"

There was a click. Okay, so that should get somebody hustling along. But I had one other thing I needed to do, and I didn't have a lot of time. I crossed my fingers and hoped to god this would work.

"Call-Anywhere Phone, dial Magic-Eatin' Jim, Duke of the Big Rock Candy Mountain."

A blur of sounds, like an old-school modem dialing a hundred-and-one digit number. Then a soft, not-quite-woman's voice. "Time of calls remaining: one minute thirty-two seconds."

The whole room got colder as vents of winter wind started blowing in through the earpiece, and I could hear the howl of a dark space on the other side of death gnawing at the line. Drifts of snowflakes and ash started wafting off the table.

A buzz of static. "Royden? Royden, buddy, is that you?"

I almost started crying. I choked back the tightness in my chest. "Yeah, Jimbo, it's me. Can you hear me all right?"

"Oh, yeah. You sound warm. It's all real dark here, and I can't see nothing."

"I'm... I'm so sorry for getting you killed, Jim."

"Oh, it wasn't nothing. Not like last time, when I was starved to death. This was real quick-like, and at least the girls were pretty."

"You... you've died before?"

"Oh, yeah. It was real terrible. But then I wandered around and followed the smell of hamburgers, and I found the Boxcar Court, and it was all right, after all."

"I'm... wow. I'm happy to hear that, Jim."

"Yeah, I'm looking for the court again right now. Maybe might take me a while to find it, but I'm pretty sure it's around here somewhere."

"That makes me really happy, Jim."

"Me too. It's nice to talk to somebody. And just chatting kinda makes me warmer and less hungry. That's real nice."

There was a low beeping sound, like what my phone makes when it's almost out of batteries.

"Jim, real quick, do you know a girl named Wendy? Missing a front tooth, calls herself the Queen of Cocagne?"

"Oh, yeah! She's a sweetie-pie! Real pretty and real nice, and... heck, I might dare say I'm in *love* with her!"

"I can trust her?"

"Heck, yeah! I'd trust her better than anybody I ever met! You tell her I said hey, okay?"

"Will do, Jim. Will do."

Another beep. Softer this time, but longer. An accompanying crackle. Dying battery or dying connection or both.

Dammit.

"Hey, Jim, one other thing. You know a red feather that Wendy sometimes carries around?"

"Yeah! She got that magic tickle-tickle feather, makes a man sneeze or giggle or fall down and soil his drawers. Why, she make you embarrass yourself with it?"

"No, she gave it to me."

"Oh, you're gonna love it! You just go *tickle-tickle* and brush it on something, and then you just watch what happens!"

The wind on the line suddenly increased in intensity, and the room got cold enough to give me goose bumps. I heard the plastic of the phone start to crack. Even with my cheek pressed to the carpet, I could see gusts of stained snow blowing into the air above the desk.

"I gotta go, Jim. I'm... I'm glad you picked up. I was worried that the magic might not work since I didn't have anything on me that you like. You know, like a hamburger of something."

"What do mean, Royden? I like *you*! You're my friend, and you bought me all those beers."

I couldn't even help it. I started giggling. "Jim, you didn't even get to drink those beers."

He seemed to consider. "Well, hell, there's plenty of beers I never got to drink. But not many of them was bought for me by a friend. Hey, look, I'll see you—"

And then, with a sharp crack and a final gust of cold wind, the little pink cellphone on the desk detonated into a thousand shards of brittle plastic. A rain of them, some coated in ice, spattered to the floor and bounced off the walls. If the phone had been next to my ear, I'm pretty sure one of them would have lodged into my brain and killed me.

No shit, it would have been better to call during the 25th.

Maybe then I would have actually had time to say something worth fucking saying.

I lay there, with tears running down my face and snow falling into my hair, and took a deep breath and tried not to let out a sob.

And then the door burst open and a group of cops rushed in, one of them carrying a first aid kit.

Oh, thank god.

CHAPTER 60

I semi-sat in the chair I was still cuffed to with my cheek pressed against the carpet and tears in my eyes, and I watched Ladislav regain consciousness as nitroglycerin burned away under his tongue. He was gray and sweating and very unhappy, and then he stood up and one of the cops tried to help him. He pushed the guy away and lost his balance, making him even angrier.

He looked at me, and I saw a glint in his eye that I hadn't seen in what had felt like a very long time. Now, it seemed like it was only yesterday. I hadn't seen that look since almost a year ago, when we shared that cigarette on top of the Sideways reflection of a building that was torn down back in the 70s, watching schools of iridescent fish swim through the flooded parts of town that don't exist during the daylight hours. Trembling and breathing heavily, he struggled to come down from shooting an ogre in service to the Warrior-Princes of Builg sixteen times in the chest before I killed it with an iron poker.

When he made the decision to write me off as dead. To try to pretend that nothing had happened. To forget about the Forgotten and to ignore and pave over the Hole behind Midnight.

That mad, hard look was back. He was a sane man who had just seen insanity and understood it for what it really was.

He had read, and truly comprehended, the words of a *GOD*.

Unaware that he was breaking inside, the cops tried to hustle him out of the room and down to an ambulance outside. He looked at me, and I did my best to shrug my shoulders and smile.

"You need me to send those boys from MacSherman Hollows back to the 'burbs once they get here, don't you?"

"Yep."

"But you need me to let them take their sweet-ass time getting here and back there, don't you?"

"Yes, sir. Unless I'm entirely mistaken, they'll show up to be put through processing a little before midnight, with the assumption that they can chase me Sideways once the Witching Hour starts. They'll be stronger and their gear will work better on the other side of the curtain, I'm pretty sure, and they won't have to worry about collateral damage as much, or about getting caught. Right about then, I hope to already be in MacSherman to perform a rescue and kill the bad guys. It'll be a lot easier for me if the tower guards are all here."

"This is the last time I see you, Poole. You get the fuck out of my town when you're done with this shit."

"Got it, sir."

He pointed at two guys, and then indicated me on the floor. "Get him out of the chair, get him out of the cuffs. Give him his things back. Give him anything he wants. And then get him, discreetly, the fuck out of this station. Throw him in the trunk of an unmarked car, if you have to, and drive him anywhere but here."

"I'd actually like to go to the airport, if that's alright with you. See I have this theory about—"

"Whatever. And when those cops from MacSherman get here, tell them in no uncertain terms that we had a jailbreak earlier tonight and that Royden Poole is on the lam and that we can't hold the kids. Pull a gun if you have to. And offer to give them escort back to the 'burbs, but be willing to take no for an answer."

"Thanks, detective."

"Fuck you, Royden."

And then he was gone, out the door, down the stairs, and off to the hospital where he would be best served to sit still for a week, but would probably be leaving within the next forty-eight hours, the stubborn bastard.

Still, it was nice to hear him use my first name for once.

INTERLUDE TWO: ON AIRPORTS

I hate airports.

Just thought you should know.

CHAPTER 61

Anyway, these were the things I was thinking about while in the trunk of the unmarked cop car, heading out to the airport. Not the most fun way to travel, but I hope that I won't surprise you when I admit that I've had worse. And it's one of the too-few times that my size is an advantage, which is nice.

On the way, I made some deductions. I rolled some theories around in my head. I went through my stuff and I kicked the lid of the trunk a few times to see if I could pop myself out, assuming that I needed to. Nope. Well, there went that.

After going through the things the cops handed back to me when we left, I noticed that I was low on cigs. Again? And where was my gun? And my wallet? Fuck!

I strongly considered suing the city.

Then I remembered that, oh, shit, my carton of smokes was in my backpack. And my backpack was in Cleon's vault. And my gun had been taken by Prince Gug. And my wallet was snatched by those bitches in service to Frieda. Dammit. All I had now was my magic feather and my cellphone and my plastic knife and a few cigarettes that would hardly last me until midnight, let alone through midnight-oh-one, several hours and possibly even days later.

But I did have my Yankees cap back, so that was nice.

I tried to get the cops to stop at a gas station and buy a pack of smokes, but they said no-go.

Didn't want to let me out of the trunk. Dicks.

So I practiced with the magic feather from Wendy, and I made a certain startling discovery: I could make myself sneeze, 100% of the time, every time, just by brushing it up under my nose and saying the words *tickle-tickle*.

Whacked my head on the lid of the trunk pretty bad, trying to fight off a sneeze that ended up getting the better of me anyway.

I failed to see how that would be in any way useful to me until I casually tried tickling other things. In quick succession, I made my eyes start watering like I had a face full of pepper-spray, forced my whole body to spasm into a cringing ball by flicking it along my armpits or belly, and popped both of my ears, which is apparently the ear-equivalent of sneezing.

I also brought myself to orgasm when I flicked it across my dick. Yeah, it worked even over the fabric. Yeah, it worked more than once.

Oh, come on. You would have tried it, too.

Now, at least, I understood what Magic-Eatin' Jim meant by asking if Wendy had made me embarrass myself.

CHAPTER 62

Icleaned myself up as best I could there in the cramped dark of the trunk.
Thank god that my magic shirt is so long. Hell, it covers all the way down
to my knees.

We got to the airport, and I was pulled out of the trunk and walked by my
cops toward the special security entrance. I wished I could have been escorted
by Lieutenant Krabaowski and Officer Merrick, just to make things come sort of
full-circle, but these things were simply not in the stars.

Next time, for sure.

At the security station, I bluffed my way through very well, thank you, using a
few lines that I had been working on in the trunk. They all hinged on a suspicion
I had about Fred and Anita Baghaamrita, and something I had said to Cleon.

"Agent James Jangladesh. I'm a translator with the special security attache to
a federal taskforce currently investigating a private domestic flight from here to
Miami, intended for a connecting flight to the Dominican Republic. Take me to
someone who can show me the departure gate in question, and let's not make a
big scene out of this."

If I had been asked, I would have told them that I spoke Arabic and Farsi
and Urdu and whatever-the-hell other languages I needed to pretend to be
able to translate, that I had been fired by President Bush for being gay and
ugly or something, and that I was being called back into service by the Men in

Black hanging out by the plane to Miami because of extreme national security concerns, but I didn't have to. Hell, I barely even had to use any mind trick mojo to inform people, firmly, that they didn't have to see my ID.

I really wished that I had my stunner shades because I would have looked awesome, but those were in my backpack.

Without hesitation, I was hustled through a whole bunch of security and through a whole bunch of locked doors toward the special part of the airport for private charter planes. People apologized to me a lot, too. Got the fuck out of my way.

Yep, even with heightened security detail. Yep, that little badge with *GOD* written on it had been used here today.

My guess was, even without having to check with Ladislav there on his hospital bed, that he hadn't had any luck tracking down where the mysterious "Mr. Alexandros" had obtained the elevator-combination to Fadey Bohdan's penthouse apartment. Because if he had gotten to the bottom of it, he would have told me. And even without having to call the front desk of Le Palace Resplendent and give myself away, I was pretty sure that the building had a copy of the floor-code... but no, they didn't happen to know the combination to the safe in the penthouse bedroom.

And no, they could not tell me that information.

There was only one person I could think of who might have the big-dick-swinging authority to obtain the floor-code from the front desk. And that was somebody who used to be worshiped.

And that was Frieda Fucking Baghaamrita.

And s/he, in her dual aspects, was here at the airport tonight waiting to see if I would get on that goddamn plane.

Interesting.

I was walked to a remote and lonely checkpoint five layers deep behind regular security, and I glanced up at the sweating TSA guard standing by the private side door to the terminal. Now that I knew what to look for, I could see he had the classic near-panicked glaze to his eyes of somebody who has recently seen a badge they don't ever want to see again.

He looked even paler under the flickering fluorescent light against the off-beige paint.

Yeah, even traveling through an airport with some authority sucks. Just one indistinguishable mass of corridors. Well, at least I didn't have to take off my velcro sneakers or hand over my lighter.

I glanced through a very narrow window crisscrossed with steel wires, and I could barely make out a pair of people in black suits and shades holding hands and trying to be inconspicuous standing next to a small check-in desk, well separated from other gates.

Bingo.

I told the security guys to fuck off using the Voice of Kings, and once I was alone, I checked the clock on my cell. Almost 8:00. I sat down on the floor, lit a cigarette, and made a phone call.

"Royden? You all right?"

"Hey, Cleon. I'm fine. Out of jail. I want to bounce a few things off you. Is this a bad time?

"Well, I got a date here in a little bit."

"... what, seriously?"

"Hell's yes, seriously! I met a cutie nurse at the hospital today, and I asked her out to dinner. She gets off at 8:30."

"Jesus. We have a rescue to perform tonight! With breaking and entering and everything!"

"Not until midnight."

"Lord. Aren't you, like, almost ninety or something?"

"You watch your mouth. I'm barely sixty, you little dumbass. Plenty of juice in me, still. And I'm not apologizing for going on a date to your stripper-sniffing little self—I damn well might get killed tonight, and I might have damn well gotten killed last night, no thanks to you, and I'll go on a date if I damn well please."

"Fine, sorry. So where are you going on this date?"

"None of your damn business. So where are you at, and what do you want to know?"

"Um, well, I'm at the airport. I'm about thirty yards away from Fred and Anita, in their little two-fer-special guise, and I'm in the stairwell of a special security portion of the building that I'm pretty sure she and he don't really understand."

"Nice. And what the hell do you think you're doing?"

"The thing is, I had a thought, and I followed a hunch, and..."

I realized that I didn't know how to say this. I soldiered on.

"Well, it turns out that I was right. And now, because it happens so rarely, I don't know what to do next."

He belly-laughed, and it was so wonderful to hear after my shitty day that I actually started smiling, too.

"Okay, all right, so you called old Cleon. I've got a minute: let's hear this hunch of yours."

"I got to thinking that the only person who could have gotten the floor-code that Alexandros used to enter Fadey Bohdan's apartment without leaving a trail a mile wide and ten miles long would be Frieda. Because of that badge marked *GOD* and her ability to write her name in a way that gives people who stare at it heart attacks."

"I'm going to pretend that you haven't kept me in the dark all through this case and simply agree with you."

"Eesh. Sorry. Again. About the whole in the dark thing."

"Save it. But yes, that sounds like the sort of information that a former god could obtain. Enough people sacrifice enough oxen to a spirit, then that spirit can make people get out of the way when it wants to. And she is, after all, the only demi-god on the payroll of Bastard Greg that we know of, and the only deity I can think of who would stoop to work with him. Always in it for herself."

"Okay, so my point is, I was asking you earlier if she was playing both sides of this. I think there's a third variable in play, maybe. She's telling me one thing and then telling me another, and now it seems like there's even more she isn't telling me. And now I've checked here at the airport, and yep, she's here."

"Wait, back up. Why are you checking on the airport?"

"It has to do with Fred and Anita's offer. They came to me, after the Forgotten Kings Society had already given Bastard Greg and the Usurper of Cocagne the rights to move against the city, and s/he made me an offer on behalf of the two kings in full view of a scribe. That means that the scary bastards in the FKS are watching what the people in Paese dei Balocchi are doing."

"Okay, fine."

"Which means that they, the bad kings, can't just kill me if I accept the offer. It would be stupid to try because they know how paranoid I get and how dangerous I am when I'm cornered, but even if they were pretty sure that they could pop me in the back of the skull with a small-caliber, silenced pistol when I got in the car and then dump my body in a reservoir, that's against the rules. And the rules are protecting them right now."

"Right. They're trying to play nice, because they've moved against that old bag, the Forgotten Queen of Scythia. She can't tell anybody without losing face, but she's going to be watching them."

"Right. So, they make me an offer and then hope that I won't take it. Then, when I don't take it, they send a squad of boy-goats to come kill me. They win, I lose, they blow up a police station, and they satisfy all the conditions of their 'strength of arm' agreement with the Forgotten while also impressing the old fuckers."

"Great, Royden. Very impressive stuff. So why, then, are you at the airport again?"

"Well, because Frieda told me not to accept the offer. And you pointed out that doing that would make me want to accept it. And if there's one person who knows me as well as you do, it's her. And also Tama, maybe. But, whatever. Plus, the more I think about it, the offer was good; the King of Cocagne barely knows me, but he was able to push half my buttons with temptations, and while Bastard Greg wants to kill me, it would grant the King of Cocagne symbolic power for me to embrace a hedonistic paradise that he offered me."

"You're really losing me here, Royden. Did I mention that I have a date coming up?"

"Okay, how about this: There are plans in place for me to take the offer and deal with me that way."

"Got it."

"So what are those plans? Can't kill me in the car. But if they actually take me to the airport, what happens then? They probably have to assume that I'm investigating things, especially if Anita told them that I kept my cellphone. They know I could contact you."

"You're losing me."

"When those guys came over to grab you last night, did they look around for any prepared summoning circles or a bounded domain that you could maybe jump to?"

"Yeah. Didn't look hard enough to find the vault-vault with all my movies and shit, but yeah. They checked."

"Well, I know that the King of Majooj was there. And he's all about slippery escape-magic like domain sand. He probably could have sensed it, even through the warded door. Couldn't sense your movies, but he wasn't looking for them."

"Fair enough. What's the point?"

"So they know for a fact that you didn't have a prepared space ready for yourself, to pull a trick like running through a doorway and jumping back to Happy Happy VCR. And then, miraculously, last night you did just that."

"Okay. Yeah, that happened."

"And it won't take them long to check the place and find the residue of the jump. Even a semi-competent diviner could do it."

"Right."

"And you're not there. You're... what, staying at your niece's place or something?"

"What? You think I'm going to bring a cutie nurse back to a shithole like my niece's place? Hell, no. I went ahead and rented the nicest hotel room I could find. I paid cash and checked in under the name Denzel Washington, too, plus put a scryer biting hex on the door, so don't you worry about the boy-goats finding me."

"Great. Okay, so... so here's my question. Was there any way that you found, after I asked you about it this afternoon, that the bad kings could prevent me from using that dirt I marked as domain last night?"

"Nope. I mean, I just have to put it somewhere and you can hop through it tonight at midnight. It's good for another six sunrises."

"One other question: is there any way last night that I could have established domain for you, but not for myself?"

"Nope. A king can, and must, claim territory for himself. That's how it works, symbolically. A benevolent king could claim territory for himself as well as for an allied nation in one swoop, but nobody lands on a deserted strip of shore, sets down the flag of a rival and says, 'Before the Almighty, I dedicate this place in the name of my neighbor, Bob, who is a dick.' Can't happen."

"Damn. Just as I thought. So, they can't let me live. They know what I did, and they know I know it. They have to kill me, Cleon. If I take their offer to fly to the Dominican Republic, they still have to find a way to kill me. Because I could come back. Any time in the next six days, and they can't have that."

"Shit."

"What do you think?"

"What do I think, Royden? I think that, to summarize, the bad kings can't kill you because the FKS is watching, but they have to kill you so you can't spill the beans to the Forgotten or interfere with their plan. Your hope hinges on being important to the FKS, and you're not. Hell, half of the very few who even know about you probably want to kill you themselves. And if you had just said that to begin with, I could be off the phone by now."

"And they have to kill you, too."

"Okay, now I see why you called me."

Just then, the door to the security area opened up, and a skinny blond kid somewhere between the ages of, I don't know, maybe seventeen and twenty-two walked into the stairwell with a cigarette in his mouth and a lighter in his hand.

He was wearing a long leather trench coat over a partially obscured t-shirt that appeared to be printed with a roaring wolf's head and this: "She put you in the Friend Zone? Put her in the RAPE ZONE."

And yes, he had some acne scars.

Boy-goat.

Probably.

I flying-tackled him.

CHAPTER 63

The kid fought just about the way I expected him to. Like a guy who has played a whole lot of video games where he shoots people in the face, specifically. Unfortunately, he didn't have the advantage of having his gun out, and he started the fight with me about six feet away from him and closing all-too rapidly.

In my opinion, once I had my hands on him, his best bet would probably have been to not freak out quite so damn much and to just very calmly get that gun out and use it, considering that I wasn't armed and wasn't hoping to be.

Or maybe he should have yelled louder. I mean, the high-pitched squeak didn't really carry through the fireproof door and the muzak and the planes taking off a few feet away. But either way, the flailing didn't help very much at all.

Anyway, total elapsed fighting time—about two seconds.

So, sure, he lost. In his defense, I have a much lower center of gravity, a much higher pain tolerance, superior strength, more experience in a fight, and I'm much, much meaner. It's like when my grandma used to beat the shit out of my older brother.

Suddenly I was on top of a very frightened and sweaty young man, now sporting a broken wrist from where he had swung it at me, with me sitting on top of his chest—left hand jammed into his mouth and part way down the back of his throat and my right hand holding onto the butt of his plastic gun through his leather coat. He was sort of lying on top of one of his own legs, with the knee fractured or at least sprained, and his head against the wall. The other leg was inconsequential because I was putting weight on it.

The door clicked shut. I heard my dropped phone make a little bit of noise as Cleon was asking me what the fuck had just happened.

I looked at the kid. His nose was bleeding, and my fucking heart just totally went out to him since my nose was still broken. His eyes were very wide, and he was hyperventilating. I locked my gaze with his. Wasn't hard, since I was the center of his world.

"*Calm down.*"

He sure wanted to.

His body rebelled, but he did his best.

"Good. You have a chance to survive this, little man. Do you know who I am?"

He nodded, as uncomfortable as it was with my hand down his throat and my unwashed mass on top of him.

"I'm going to take my hand out of your mouth, and I want you to tell me who I am."

I pulled my hand out and glanced at it. Damn. Cut myself on one of his teeth pretty good.

"You're Big Jimmy. The Jangladesh. The Hindu midget-god."

I slapped him, hard enough to make his eyes go watery. He made a little gasp. He wasn't expecting that.

"Yeah, I should have mentioned, you don't use that word. Only I get to say *midget*. It's like the N-bomb, got it?"

He nodded. While he was nodding, I slipped my hand into his jacket and popped out the gun, which I pointed at him while I stood up and walked over to my cellphone.

"—the fuck? Royden?"

"Right here. I just beat up a boy-goat. We're going to have to change time-tables, here."

"... okay."

To the kid, I said, "Okay, so we've established that I'm mean. And that I'm quick. And that I'm a... wait, did you say that I'm a god? Wait, wait, don't tell me. Cleon has *got* to hear this."

I kept the gun trained on the kid as I glanced out the window to make sure that no one else was joining the party. Nope, everyone was still over there, but now I noticed that a lot of the travelers on this flight were guys in late high school and early college. Interesting.

They were much more subtle than Fred and Anita.

Out of curiosity, I checked to see what kind of gun I had just earned. Yep, a pocket-sized *Paese dei Balocchi* special with the setting clicked to "smiley-face." I narrowed my eyes at the kid, and it clicked over to "frowny-face." He gulped; I turned on the speakerphone and set it on the ground as I dropped into a crouch next to him.

"All right, then, fella. You tell the nice phone here what you told me about me being a god."

He stammered, "You're, he's... a god. The old Hindu mi... uh, little person god of trickery. Hero-guard of some holy planet. The demon-slayer. King of Giggling Self-Loathing."

I pointed the gun at the kid, and he shut up pretty emphatically. Just to be sure, I stuck the gun in his mouth.

"Cleon, what the fuck is he talking about?"

Over the phone, "You mean to tell me that the King of Majooj thinks that Royden here is Vamana? The Fifth Avatar of Vishnu?"

"Who?"

"Well, he's also described as an Avatar of Ganesha, instead."

"... who?"

"Lord. You are the worst Hindu, the worst magical detective, and without a doubt the very *worst* magical Hindu detective in the history of ever, Royden."

"Oh, this again? Just because I haven't read up on all the Vedas and whatever, I'm a bad Hindu. Well, man, fuck you. I totally skimmed the Kama Sutra, and I would have kept reading if I had known that there was stuff in there about me being a god and stuff."

"You're not a god, you idiot. If your older brother was Indra, Lord of the Devas, Master of Weather and War instead of, for example, a dentist in Sacramento, I'd lend this stupid theory more credence. The kid is referring to a deity from the Puranic texts, who also shows up in the *Guru Granth Sahib* of Sikhism. Can't fucking believe you've never read it."

"Give me the CliffsNotes."

"Vamana was a very tricky dwarf indeed."

"Good to know. And he slayed some demons?"

"You mean 'slew.' And no, not specifically that I know of. He did trick a powerful asura into granting him a request wherein he then fucked the guy over using magic, but it ended up with the guy's redemption, if I remember correctly. And the guy wasn't a demon, to begin with. Asuras are a whole different thing, and way more complex although I can see the confusion. I think that maybe our enemies are as bad at theology as you are."

"Huh."

The kid with the gun in his mouth had that look like he was getting to be a little more at ease. And "at ease" is bad. It leads to people not paying attention.

I pulled the gun out.

"Alright, motherfucker, say *midget* one more time."

"... uh..."

"Say it. Say. It."

"Midge-"

I shot him.

Oh, don't get nervous. I clicked it to the "smiley-face" mode and popped him in the chest three times with little *phoof* sounds. Then I put my gun into my jacket pocket, handcuffed myself to the kid as he went limp, and started walking out of the building the way I came in.

"It's pronounced spondyloepiphyseal dysplasia for you, white boy."

The kid's jacket let him slide him along the floor very nicely, thank you. Gotta love a well-polished floor and a leather coat.

Did I mention that one of my requests from the po-po was a set of handcuffs? Okay, I actually didn't ask because I was worried that the answer would be "no."

So I stole a set from the trunk. Actually, two sets.

Cleon said, as I clicked him back from speaker mode, "The fuck was that sound?"

"Sorry about that. I'm leaving the airport. My blond carry-on had to be tranquilized. So, where's my connection to this god, other than my height and my trickery and my giggling self-loathing?"

"You ain't that tricky, son. It's probably a little fable cooked up by somebody with a hard on for totemic theory to explain your good luck. And the giggling self-loathing is totally new to me and to this myth, except that it describes you so well. Hell, might even be a fiction set in play by Frieda since we're imagining her playing both sides."

"Makes as much sense as anything. Until further notice, I'm going to imagine her playing the two kings, but also playing both against me."

"Good call. And to be perfectly honest, Royden, it's honestly not impossible that you're channeling a trickster-god without knowing it. Stranger things have happened."

"Awesome."

"Don't get too excited. Vamana has something like four temples that I can think of, and most of them are dedicated to other deities, too."

I heard him flipping a book open. Oh, of course Cleon takes a set of books with him to a fancy hotel. Rolling my eyes, I took the time to walk past a half-dozen guys who were more than somewhat confused at my comportment. The dead-looking kid I was dragging behind me was a factor, I think. Also, I hadn't shaved in a few days. I nodded at these people as I walked past, listening to my silent phone like I had the President on the line, and hoped that I still looked official.

"ALL IS WELL, GUYS."

That was official enough. They went back to ignoring me.

"Royden?"

"Still here."

"Okay. Yeah. I've got the Thrikkakara Vamanamoorthy Temple, dedicated solely to Vamana, and that's about it. And I can't find any in the Rajasthan State that you could call on."

"Wait, you're looking up the temples?"

"Yeah. To see if any of them are in what used to be Jangladesh. Which would explain you channeling him. And no, none of them are."

"Guess I'll have to do with just the pair of national tiger reserves. I swear, ever since they expanded the Ranthambore back in '91, I've been a goddamn dynamo of action."

"Shit. You were barely out of short-pants in '91, asshole."

"I'm still *in* short pants, Cleon."

"Ha. Regarding your vaunted combat prowess, though; so we're actually, really thinking of charging head-long into Paese dei Balocchi to rescue Garrick Heldane tonight?"

"Yep. And now that I've a captured boy-goat, we're going to have ourselves a good map of the place."

"That's great, Royden. He's going to be able to tell us all sorts of useful stuff that I couldn't—because while I was tortured there last night I didn't make any notes what-so-ever."

"You're being sarcastic, Cleon. That's not helpful. Look, you go enjoy your date and stay well off the radar. Things are going to get wonky, here, because somebody is bound to notice when this blond kid doesn't come back from his smoke; security is going to go up a few notches once he's reported as missing, and with my luck, the assholes at the police station are going to fuck up and tell the kids from MacSherman Hollows that I've left the building if the 'burb-vans call ahead and ask."

"So where does that leave you?"

"Well, I'm hoping that the guys at the station are afraid enough of Ladislav that they do their jobs right. And I can't think of a good, plausible reason for 'burb-cops to call the station and ask about me. But just to be on the safe side, as soon as I've got you off the line I'm going to call old Lieutenant Krabowski and tell him to get his shit in order. And then, I think, I'm going to call Fred and Anita and bluff them that the cops are telling me that I can't leave to get in their car."

"Interesting play. She'll be able to call the car that's waiting for you and confirm that you haven't been sent out, yet. She won't know who to believe once she starts looking for our blond boy-goat. Sounds like a solid plan. Or, at least, a plan."

I passed another security checkpoint, took a left, and started heading outside. The kid made a sound, so I stopped and emptied a few more shots into him as casually as possible.

Luckily, I was still in special security areas.

"This is nothing for you to worry about."

I got some weird looks, and then they passed.

"What?"

"Nothing. Yes. A plan. Yeah, or something like it, at least. I figure that I've got just about enough time to get in a cab and take off before Fred and Anita start flashing their badges and getting the skinny on the dark-skinned midget walking out of here with an unconscious kid. That will put plenty of chaff in the air, and maybe start causing these assholes to make some mistakes. Which would be nice."

"It's sort of sad that we need to count on them making mistakes, isn't it?"

"Yep. And I just thought of one that I've made, sadly. When fucking Fred and Anita call the police station, I'm just going on hope that they can't use their command-magic over the phone to get the truth."

"Actually, I can confirm that. There's a reason that gods show up in person and write things down and send floods and set bushes on fire and stuff. Calling over a phone is too indirect. Frieda should have no more luck telling the cops what to do over a landline or cell, and making it stick, than Great Yahweh did in telling Moses to deliver that message to Pharaoh to let his people go."

"Interesting. So it seems that Fred and Anita will have to drive across town to get the lowdown on my breakout?"

"Yep. Or write it on a sheet of paper and have it delivered by a acne-ridden teenager. The interesting thing will be to see what she does. You still think she's playing more than both sides?"

"Yeah."

"Man, watching what she does next would be helpful."

"Yeah, kinda. But I can't see how not reporting these things would help her at all."

"Hm. But she didn't tell the boy-goats and their kings that you had your cellphone and would know about the bust in the 'burbs. Damn. Times like this, I wish that we could trace the bitch's phone calls or plant a bug on whatever she's driving these days. Like something out of a movie."

"Yeah, we'd have rope and stuff and rappel down buildings."

"And you would be played by somebody good looking."

"Fuck you. Okay, so I'm going to jump in a taxi with this boy-goat, and I'm going to head anywhere that Fadey Bohdan doesn't own, and I'm going to call Krabowski and get him straightened out. And then I'm going to talk to this blond kid, and I'm going to make some crank phone calls to the bad guys."

"Well, I'm going to go get laid."

"Sweet. I'll call you if anything interesting happens."

I hung up, and I walked out into the rain with my blond kid along for the ride.

And that's when I remembered that Frieda's fucking goddamn handmaidens had taken my wallet.

I didn't have a nickel on me.

Dammit.

CHAPTER 64

There's a whole world of difference between dragging a guy down a hallway of polished linoleum floors and dragging a guy through a street. Even if he's really skinny like this fucker was. Not wanting to pull my limp hostage across cement and asphalt and such, I flipped him up onto my shoulder in a fireman's carry and started hobbling my way from the special security entrance toward the taxi stand.

Or, at least, I tried to.

Damn, the fucker was unwieldy. And my hope was that my back would hold until we got to the car, but either way this was less than subtle. Oh, how I do I get myself into these things?

My plan, so you know, was to find a friendly cab driver, hopefully with a turban or something and just about my skin tone, and beg him to help a brother out.

I do a pretty good distressed Punjabi accent, and a little bit of mojo would no doubt help my case.

Just about the time that my passenger got annoyingly heavy and I realized that I couldn't walk while holding him up, I shifted him slightly on my shoulder and something fell out of the kid's front coat pocket that I hadn't checked yet. Ah, neat. A big bag of cocaine.

Right there on the sidewalk.

I put the kid down on top of the bag, considered shooting him a few more times and then thought better of it, at least right here by the main entrance and exit with all the people around, and then I checked a few more of his pockets.

Oh, look. A wallet full of hundreds.

Well, that solves any number of problems.

CHAPTER 65

In the cab, smashed between the door and my passenger, I tried to make some crank calls, but everyone's phone was apparently busy: Fred and Anita, Lieutenant Krabowski, and... well, that's it, actually.

Dammit, my plan sucks.

Anyway, a few big fat tips and a few big fat lies about my airsick friend later, I found myself sitting in a very small, poorly-lit hotel room just off the interstate, where you can hear the planes take off through the thin drywall and watch the high-beams of the big rigs out on the cloverleaf across the way next to the truck stop cut angles through the unwashed, rain-streaked windows every few seconds.

Smoking accommodations, of course. One bed.

Checkout at 10:00 am.

Full tab, paid in cash.

I even got the guy behind the counter to sell me two cigarettes, right out of his pack, for five bucks. Menthol, and *ew*, but I needed them for something special I had in mind.

We got up to the room.

The kid's eyes went wide when I pulled myself out of the cuffs: Lacking a key, I burst my end of the handcuff off, flowering around my wrist, in the most supernatural way I could manage. I pulled his coat off him, re-cuffed him across his lap with my other stolen set, and shot him in the chest one last time before I got the room ready.

This included getting a pair of Cokes from the vending machine up the hall, getting a bucket full of ice from the machine, washing my face briefly, and taking a piss.

I hadn't taken one of those in what felt like *way* too long.

While I was in there, I put the kid's coat on the sink. Yep, his cellphone was in his jacket pocket. Big, fancy thing with no buttons: just a flat screen that told me it was locked when I poked at it. The rest of his coat felt just a bit 'lumpy,' for lack of a better term, so I left it sitting. Too many things in too many pockets to check right now.

Walking back into the room, I considered. After a second, I pushed him, in the room's single chair, against the back wall, there in the corner. The kid got to sit, slumped in his t-shirt and jeans in the lumpy semi-loveseat, and I got to sit on the bed, legs crossed, because I hate leaning on the edge and feeling short.

I leaned over and idly pulled a worn, yellow-stained phone book out from a drawer in the nightstand, set it on my lap next to the gun, and looked at the kid.

"TELL ME EVERYTHING YOU KNOW."

The kid blinked at me and scowled.

"Well, it was worth a shot. Now, it's the hard way."

I popped my neck and looked over the room one more time. Then I lit up a cig, casting a meaningful glance at the two cigs from the desk-guy, which were sitting on the bed, along with the ice bucket and a washcloth, right next to my ashtray.

"So, what's your name, man?"

He said nothing.

"Oh, okay. You probably can't talk yet, because of the paralyzing gunshots and all. I get that. The darts, that's what they do. Okay, so I'm just going to call you Chaz, okay?"

He did nothing. I flicked some ash into the glass tray.

"Okay. Here's what we're going to do, Chaz. If you make me real happy, I'm going to use this phonebook here to order us some pizzas. I'm going to walk over to that phone there by the bed, and I'm going to call up and have a pie delivered to the front desk. Whatever kind you like. I don't think that they have room service here, but I'll go get it from the front desk. No worries there."

I winked at him. No response. Well, he did kind of squint at me.

"You know, I always like that, when I'm in a hotel: get something real greasy delivered, hot and spicy maybe, thin-crust or deep-dish or stuffed or something exotic, and eat it right out of the box right there in bed. Just so you know, I'm going to get pepperoni and sausage with bacon and onions. I love that."

He was trying to do nothing, say nothing, give nothing away, but this tactic of mine was not what he was expecting. Good.

"Okay, so maybe you don't like that. Not everybody likes onions; some people like olives or sardines or whatever. But that's okay. I'll get you your own pizza, too. I'm feeling generous; I'll even shoot for some hot-wings if that's what you want. Garlic bread. Cheese sticks. Call them right up and have it delivered. I'll even give you this Coke I bought, because there's nothing in the world like a good cold Coke out of a vending machine with hot, greasy pizza, unless maybe it's a Kickapoo Joy Juice. You ever had one of them? Mmm-mmm-mmm. Damn good. Then we could watch some TV, maybe. I'll even splurge for one of the pay-per-view movies."

The kid did not look like he believed me.

I nodded like I sympathized, then checked the time: almost 8:30.

Good. I gestured to my two cigarettes.

"And then, maybe you and me can have a smoke together. It's a simple pleasure, but there's something about a good cigarette right after a hot, greasy meal with a cold drink while sitting there watching a movie. Especially in bed, and I know you're not supposed to do that, but just this once I think it would be all right. These sheets are probably flame-retardant, right? So you and me, we can sit here and smoke and bullshit and watch a movie. Maybe even get some beers. Who knows? I mean, I got stuff to do later, but it's not like I'm driving or anything."

At this point, he didn't believe me even a little bit.

That was okay.

I took a drag off my smoke, and I watched his eyes follow it. Yeah, he was nic-fitting, now. He had been craving a smoke even before I jumped him. His muscle-control was coming back as the paralysis from the dart wore off, and he was trying to hide it... but as a long-time smoker, I could see him getting ready to start needing that cancer-stick.

"Mmm. Man, that's good. You know, I'll tell you, Chaz, I try not to smoke in my apartment because then everything stinks like cigarettes. But, if I'm being honest, I also hate going outside, out on the porch or the balcony, and having one there. Makes me miserable, like I'm somehow less of a person while all the good kids are inside having fun, you know, without their drugs. And it's cold. Or hot. And then I miss what's on TV, or whatever, because the smoke took too long, and then... that's why I love hotel rooms. That's what I'm saying. That is what I'm saying to you, Chaz. You can smoke right in bed, if you want. Take a shit in the shower, jerk off in the pillow-case. Who gives a fuck, right?"

He looked at me like he was wondering where I was going with all of this. Trying not to show his confusion.

"Wait... are you about ready to talk, buddy? Because, seriously, Chaz, I've just been killing time, here, until your mouth starts working again. Are we about at that point? Like, can you nod?"

He nodded.

"Great. Okay, so to tie it all back together, here: I'm going to use this phone book, and this phone, and then this Coke bottle, and then that television, and then these cigarettes. In that order. If you make me happy, well, we've covered that: pizza, soda, movies, smoke, fun. Maybe beer. We'll wind up, you and me, hanging out like best buddies until I gotta take off at midnight. You got that?"

He nodded.

"You'll stay here, in this room, but I'll even leave that big bag of cocaine here, too. And then you'll never see me again. Hell, you can leave right after I do, if you want. Take my pizza home with you, call a cab, take off. Are we on the same page, Chaz?"

He nodded again.

"Cool. Now, to be clear, that's if I'm happy. If you don't make me happy, first I'm going to beat you with this phone book. It's pretty good size, and I could probably break your jaw, but I might not do any serious damage. You'll live. Then, if I'm still unhappy, I'm going to smash your fucking face open with this phone. I love hotel phones, because they're always real heavy. You ever notice that?"

He did not nod, just stared, but I sort of pretended that he did.

"Real hefty fucker. Good swing to it. Probably so people don't, you know, steal them. Although that's probably not such a problem anymore, like it was in the 70s. Now, as I may have mentioned, the best thing about hotels is that I don't have to give a shit what gets stained or broken or messy. And that phone, well, it's probably not as hard as your cheekbones or your orbital socket or your skull, so it might get broken. But you know what? I'm willing to find out. Now, if after I've used the phone, I'm still not happy, do you remember what comes next? After the phone book and the phone, it's..."

His eyes clicked to the Coke bottle.

"Oh, that's right, the Coke bottle. Do I have to tell you what I'm going to do with that Coke bottle?"

He shook his head.

"Okay. Because... it'll be bad. And you're going to be really sad because there's nothing in the world worse than laying there with a broken jaw and a busted up face, with your teeth loose, and maybe an eye hanging out, and then that Coke... well, it would just be awful."

His eyes widened, and he reflexively tightened his grip on the arms of the chair. Good.

"Now, Chaz, you're a smart boy. You're probably wondering what I'm going to do with the TV. And the truth is, nothing fancy. I'm just going to tip it over on to you and break your spine. I'm going to drag you over, right next to that TV, and you, with a bottle still rammed up your ass and a broken-open head are going to have your back shattered. And you will never walk again. Shitting in a bag for the rest of your natural life. With no teeth. Maybe missing an eye."

I took another drag of my smoke.

"And that's just miserable. I don't want to break the TV. I want to sit here and watch one of those pay channels I can't afford at home. I love those, especially later at night. They always show great stuff where they preface it with warnings of 'Explicit Sexual Content' and 'Nudity' and 'Adult Language.' Oh, I love that. I've loved it ever since I was a kid, when my dad used to take me on business trips, and I would pretend that I was real tired, and I wanted to stay in. 'Viewer Discretion is Advised'... man, there is nothing sweeter than being advised to have viewer discretion."

I locked eyes with him.

"And then, if I'm still not happy, I'm going to use these cigarettes. You're going to be lying on the floor, back broken, asshole ripped open, face shattered into un-recognition, and then I'm going to start burning you. Just a little bit at a time. Now, with your spine severed, you know, you might not be able to really feel it. But I think you could smell it, probably."

I took a deep drag.

"Man. Little pinkie-nail-sized black spots, just burned all into you. Just hideous divots, right into your meat. Dozens of them. All over. And if you're not blind by that point, well, then these first two are going in those baby-blues."

I gestured at the two Menthols from downstairs.

I squinted as I exhaled.

"You ever have a real bad cigarette burn, Chaz? On your dick, or in your eye, maybe?"

And then I flicked my lit cig right at his face.

He jumped up like I'd jabbed him with a taser. I pulled the gun, and he calmed down, with his eyes locked on me.

"Oh, you're up. Ready to talk. Great. Let's do this. Have a seat."

He didn't want to sit down.

"You want to sit down, man. Because you sit down, or I will put you down. We'll start the conversation here with you unable to talk because you're paralyzed, and I assure that I will get very fucking unhappy very fucking quickly. You might not regain the ability to speak until after I've gotten done with the phone book and the phone and then popped this twenty-ounce bottle halfway up your colon and heading north."

I gestured with the gun for him to sit.

"So, the choice is yours. Have a seat."

He did so, tense and nervous with eyes flicking to the door. I was between him and it. I picked up the phone book.

"Okay. So, what's your name?"

He did nothing. And then he muttered: "Fuck you."

That was a mistake.

CHAPTER 66

Chaz made it all the way through the book, just to about the point that my arm was getting tired, spitting a series of profanities at me.

I hadn't mentioned that I was going to shoot him in both kneecaps right before I started swinging, which caught him off guard and made him fall down when he jumped at me.

Again, a mistake on his part.

When I was done with the book, I went and got the phone.

"Hey. What's your name, man?"

"Fuck you."

Oi. I hate this.

I yanked the cord out of the wall, wrapped it around my fist, and picked up the whole jangling thing in one hand.

"Man, you should have taken the pizza."

CHAPTER 67

I was hoping that my blond friend would decide to talk before I had to pop him with the phone. And I was also hoping that he wouldn't make me hit him in the face. As it was, it only took one whack, right across the bridge of the nose, before he was interested in chatting.

"Oh, ow, fuck! Jesus! I give! Fuck, fuck!"

"Cool. What's your name, man?"

"My name is Rick!"

"Well, all right. Nice to meet you, Rick."

I walked away. He was on the floor by this point, so I leaned against the bed and set the phone down on the comforter with a little ringing sound. I looked him over as I fished another cigarette out of my pack and lit it: a black eye and all, and his face was puffy, and that broken wrist from a while earlier didn't look too good, and his nose had seen better days. But he was going to be fine.

I tried not to show that I was on the verge of throwing up.

I flipped his wallet open.

"Oh, yeah... 'Rick short for Richard.' Says that right here on your ID. Don't know why I didn't think of that before."

He glared at me, and I scratched the side of my face, there against my stubble, with the gun.

"Okay, then, Rick. I want you to tell me everything you know about those two people in the suits from the airport. The guy and the girl, holding hands with their sunglasses on."

"You mean the God of Futa?"

"Sure, that's a good place to start. So, you know that the two of them are one person, then. What else can you tell me?"

"Her name is Frieda or something. Has a temple full of evil spirits in the Sideways, where they drink blood and wine and ambrosia and have weird dick-girl orgies or whatever."

"Yep. That's about right."

I set my gun down on the bed. Then I filled the washcloth full of ice, twisted it around into a simple ice pack, picked up my gun, and tossed the bundle to Rick.

"That's for your face. Okay, so keep going with this thing about Frieda. It's just getting interesting."

"What's there to say? She's one of the pets of the King of Demons. We stay out of his way, which means that we stay out of her way."

"Ah. Back up: what's a *futa*?"

"It's Japanese. Short for *futanari*. It means 'woman with a big penis.' Like a she-male, kinda, but with big boobs. There's all sorts of weird porn, if you Google it. Drawings, mostly."

"Ah. And, let me get this straight: she's the god of this deviant little sub-fetish."

"Yeah."

"Okay. So when people jerk off, looking at pictures of that on the Internet, she's getting power. Okay. *Frieda, futa*... yeah, there's a link."

"... link?"

"Sorry, just talking to myself. Here, have a Coke—you earned it."

He flinched, and I set the bottle on the floor on its side. Then I rolled it over to him, as gently as possible.

"Now, the King of Demons. What's he look like?"

"Well, he can shapeshift."

"Hm. You mean, like just turn into stuff, or sometimes he's wearing different bodies?"

He considered that.

"I guess he can look different. I've never actually seen him transform, if that's what you mean."

"That *is* what I mean, Rick. Man, we're really doing well, here. Pizza-well. Now, I wish I hadn't unplugged this phone. All right, so tell me more about this King of Demons."

"Well, for a long time, he looked like this real skinny tall guy with kind of a beard. Dark hair. Somebody told me he was Lebanese or like from Lebanon or whatever. Kind of creepy eyes. Now, he looks different, but you can still tell that it's him."

"Okay, that's interesting. And I'm going to want to know about that. But real quick, you ever hear the name *Gregory* around him? Or *Greg*? Maybe something like *Bastard Greg* or *Mr. Howsgrove* or something like that?"

"Nope."

"All right, that's fine. Probably doesn't want you guys to know his real name. You ever hear the name *Majooj*?"

"Uh, yeah. It means 'demons.'"

"Yes. Yes, it does. You know where it comes from?"

"Like, from Jews. *Jews*, *Jooj*. *Majooj*. That sort of thing."

"Oh. Got it. Somebody really is bad at this. Now, see, here's the thing: these questions I've been asking, they're not so bad, are they?"

"... nope."

"All right. And for that reason, I feel real bad about kind of beating the shit out of you. Because the thing is, you don't work for the King of Demons, do you?"

"No."

"You basically work for somebody who kinda knows the King of Demons, don't you? Somebody who's probably a lot more entertaining, would be my guess."

He got nervous, but he spoke up anyway. "Yep."

I lied, "Well, I don't need to know about him. He's, what? The King of Fun? King of Good Times?"

"Yeah."

"Great. And I'll bet you that he likes watching you guys enjoy yourselves: knocking shit over, fucking some sluts, playing video games, whatever. Eating some chocolate. Has a lot of cocaine to offer, I'm sure."

The kid nodded. I smiled, like I was in on the joke.

"Hell, he's probably the King of Cocaine, huh?"

The kid nodded again, and his eyes showed a certain sympathy with me. Oh, good.

"All right, so sometimes good times and demons kind of overlap. I get that. You know because it's all fun and games until somebody loses an eye—and then it's fucking hilarious, am I right?"

Rick wanted to laugh, and then he was thinking about how I had threatened to knock his eye out and also burn it. Oops.

I tried a different tactic.

"Hey, you know how every really good joke starts?"

Rick started to grin because he knew this one. I leaned forward like I was going to share a conspiracy and then looked over both of my shoulders with exaggerated caution. "Okay, so these two black guys and a rabbi are fucking this chick..."

He laughed. I laughed, too, and pointed the gun at the ceiling.

"Alright, Rick. We're kicking ass, here. Really making good time. Hell, we might get that pizza, yet. I've got a cellphone, after all. Now, this next part is going to sound kind of weird, but I gotta ask: Has your boss ever talked about how he intends to kill the King of Demons?"

"Yeah, actually."

"Hm. The reason I ask, is because I gotta kill that fucker. I'm a demon-slayer, that's what I do. You know this. Now, I have no quarrel with your boss although obviously I'm enough of an asshole to kidnap one of his guys and beat the shit out of him and be a real douchebag about it. The thing is, I don't know this King of Good Times, and if I can find out how your boss was intending to kill the King of Demons when their partnership was over, that saves me some time."

"Okay."

"So let's talk demon killing. You go first."

"Well, the thing is that the King of Demons has all these pets. These, like, spirits that follow him around and do whatever he tells them to and stuff. And some of them are really fucked up, like something out of a really gross horror movie or video game."

"Oh, dude, I love video games."

"Right. So, like, all these demons are from the Sideways. And, like, King Humbert says that when he's done getting what he wants from the demons, the boy-goats are going to kill the King of Majooj."

Rather than ask the stupid questions: like "what?" or "how?" or "what does

King Humbert want from the demons?" or even "who in the fuck is King Humbert?"—since I had a pretty good theory—I casually pointed my gun back down, away from the ceiling and right at Rick.

"Continue."

"Okay, so, all the demons he has are controlled by symbols or something. Like these medallions, like on a big charm bracelet or necklace or something. The King of Demons can make them, and then they give him power over the spirit. All the members of the brigade have one, from when we drank beer mixed with the blood of a summoned demon, and it has some of the demon goat's hair, and we carry it and it lets us transform into demon-men during the Midnight Time."

"Ah. Makes sense. Like a loup-garou with elements of Olaus Magni Gothus's old Livonian shapeshifters. Interesting."

He stared at me.

"Yeah, sorry, still talking to myself. History nerd. Please continue. We were on the topic of magic charms."

"If they're broken, the spirit goes free. And the medallions for the things that *he* controls are all worn by the King of Demons. So, when the time is right, we'll hold him down and break all his little talismans."

"That's a really good plan, Rick. Can I see your talisman?"

"It's in my coat pocket."

That was an outright lie he was telling me. Good.

"Ah. Which means it's in the bathroom. Got it. Well, I'll take a look at it later. Now, what I want to know is real simple. Does the King of Demons hang out at your clubhouse all the time? Like, does he spend most of his waking hours at the Paese dei Balocchi and sleep there, or does he have his own place?"

"No, he hangs out there. He has a room and everything."

"All right. So, where in your plan to kill him do you drag him outside first?"

His eyes went wide. He stammered. I cut him off.

"Yeah, no, I'm aware of the fact that he can't be killed while on his home turf. That's the rule: competent secret kings can't be slain while they're within their kingdoms, except by another claimant to the throne. And my guess is that your little rotting skatepark has been designated in the Sideways as official soil of Majooj and Cocagne. And since I figure that nobody else is claiming Majooj and nobody else has the balls to channel that particular totem, that means that he's unkillable by you douchebags. Am I getting close?"

Rick nodded. I sat and thought for a second and flipped my phone open.

"Great. And I'll bet dollars to donuts that Bastard Greg has a plan in place for killing King Humbert. Now, I just want to know one more thing. Ethan Milsborough is a member of the Boy-Goat Brigade, and he got real close to whacking me. So do you know the name *Officer Merrick*, of the city PD?"

His eyes got wide enough to scare me, and he licked his lips, and then he bolted for the door. Quick little bastard.

I shot him a few times in the back, and he grunted and sort of fell as he yanked the door open and slipped out. And then, as I observed that he wasn't falling over the way I hoped he would, I noticed that his fingers were crossed behind his back.

Damn.

Took him some effort, too, with his hands cuffed in front of him like that. Twisted all around to get those there.

I bolted up, ran to the door, and watched him take a hard right around a hallway toward the fire exit and the stairs.

I slammed the door shut, locked it, dead-bolted it, sprinted to the bathroom, grabbed Rick's coat, and hauled ass toward a window.

Then I jumped out, aiming for a soft car hood.

CHAPTER 68

As I fell, I cursed myself for not having gotten another room in the motel. That would have been way more fun than this, but there was, after all, a slight chance that Rick could maybe do something very fancy that I wasn't expecting and then bring a crew of boy-goats to the room to shoot the shit out of me.

That meant that I had to leave.

And since I didn't want to have to explain myself at the front desk, I had to go out the window. Dammit.

Second story drop to the pavement, but I landed on the hood of an old Ford Fiesta and the power of my empire cushioned the rest of my fall, which was nice.

Then, as casually as possible, I walked across the parking lot to a Denny's, took a table, ordered a coffee, and checked Rick's coat for that fucking goat-spirit-talisman.

A little bit of rooting around confirmed my suspicions: he had it on him all along.

Just as I had been hoping.

Now I can know where all of you are, you little bitches.

Then, feeling drained, I took a deep breath, rolled over in my head what I had done the last few hours, and tried not to puke.

Succeeding, I then closed my eyes and tried not to hate myself.

"Well, at least I know what I need to know."

Deep breaths.

Then, secure in my booth with a view of the parking lot, I called Lieutenant Krabowski.

He picked up after a few rings, and I realized that I was actually pissed that it took so long. Damn, I need to get used to the fact that not everyone answers my calls as quickly as Detective Ladislav.

"This is Krabowski."

"Hi. What are you wearing?"

"Jesus. What gives, Poole? I'm busy."

"I'm certain that you are, lieutenant. I'm just calling casually to ask about those vans full of kids from the 'burbs. How are they?"

"Oh, no, that got canceled. They're heading home."

"Of fucking course they are. By the by, I wanted to inform you that your partner Officer Merrick is one of the villains."

"Huh?"

"You won't get any of this, but the reason he's been so nervous around me is because he's been trying to figure out how to kidnap me and turn me over to his fellow demon-blood-drinking boy-goats without tipping his hand or getting killed by me."

"What?"

"Shut up. It's just like Ladislav was watching Cleon to see if I would ever pop my head up again. There were boy-goats under orders of King Humbert watching Cleon and Detective Ladislav in order to catch me. But they couldn't insert somebody close enough to watch Ladislav, so they got someone to partner up with you because you know me."

"You aren't making any sense, Poole."

"Sure, I am. Just like I'm certain that Officer Merrick has the rest of the night off. Tell me I'm wrong."

"... you mean James? His mother is sick."

"Oh, I'm sure she is. Just to be on the safe side here, I'm going to figure out how to track his medallion. But here's the thing, and I can't believe that I didn't tumble onto it before: there's only one person I can think of who knows about Cleon and about Ladislav who has been part of this since the beginning and who would have reasons to suspect that I'm not really dead. Someone who could help the King of Majooj organize a response within minutes of me getting on this case."

"What? Who?"

"Yeah, you don't know her. But she's got a big dick, and she would just love you. Anyway, I'll talk to you later, lieutenant."

I hung up. And then I sat there and I tried to remember what I had been thinking when I walked to Frieda's place with Magic-Eatin' Jim. Was her bar really the only place I could have gone? Or was there some mojo working? Had I been *drawn* there? Like by a big, magnet-style version of my "I'm in charge" power?

I closed my eyes and retraced my steps. Shit. Yeah, I remember feeling like I could... could literally think of *nowhere else to go.*

... and then Magic-Eatin' Jim patted me on the back. Fuck. And then he burped. Fuck. And then the compulsion was gone, but we were already at the bar. Fuck.

Fuck, fuck, fuck.

I didn't know she had power like that, and I'm not sure where she got it. Well, there was only one question, now: how long had she been pulling the strings on this?

My coffee arrived. I stared at it.

I poured truly copious amounts of cream and sugar into it, until it was lighter than I was. Significantly sweeter, too.

I took a sip.

And then, funny enough, I actually thought of another question to go along with the first one.

CHAPTER 69

R*ing, ring.*
      Pick up, you bitch.
      Click.
"This is Anita."

Yes. Finally, something goes right.

"Hi. So, what are you and Fred the King of?"

A pause. Oh, this was nice. I almost wanted her to hang up and lose her power, this was so sweet.

"... I'm..."

"Huh. You don't want your empire anymore?"

"I'm the Queen of Magog, you little shit."

"Oh, wow, that's super for you. What with your demon-girls and all, it even makes sense. Heck, there's two of you, Fred and Anita. Gog and Magog. And your plan, with the taking over of America, it's awesome. Really stellar stuff. I can see why you want Bastard Greg out of the way, though. Let me guess, you're looking to make a play for the throne, and you need me to whack him."

"I should have killed you when I had the chance."

"I get that a lot. Actually, once I whack him for you, you're *really* in the clear. Everybody, including the Forgotten Queen of Scythia, thinks that the Red Jew of Magog is dead. And that lets you go back to hiding and lurking and planning, possibly as the lying-royalty of something else, secretly channeling Majooj. Which is your totem. You could maybe even get the title of 'Forgotten' out of that. Clever."

"I have armies. They will strike you down."

"You have jack and shit until the 25th, bitch. Okay, so let me explain your plan to you, in case you were wondering: You coordinated the entire alliance of Poacher-King Humbert and Bastard Greg because you needed the Jar of Shifting Souls. That explains how two idiots stumbled into such power, even, and into such convoluted plans. Only immortals think like that, after all. And you need that jar to act subtly in the waking world because your mortal translation is kind of a shitty giveaway, magic ID or not. You just aren't as smart when you're split into two minds. It's kind of sad, really."

"You should have taken the deal. Gone to the islands."

"Oh, what makes you think that I didn't?"

"We know that you escaped the mortal prison. And that you came to the air port. And stole Richard."

Yes, she said it as two words: *Air. Port.* It was adorable.

"Yep. I'm a real Richard-stealer."

"What are you laughing about?"

"Nothing."

"Why are you laughing!?"

"This is all just so goddamn funny. You're the femme fatale, the big villain, and you can't even threaten me very well right now because you're split right through the center of your brain. It's almost tragic."

"Is it, Royden? Then let me ask *you* a question: do you remember how we met?"

"... yes?"

"When was it?"

"... oh, fuck. Fuck me."

"Yes."

"Shit, no."

"That's right. I was working with the Warrior-Princes of Builg, and I very nearly killed both you and Detective Ladislav before you escaped. But you've forgotten all that because it is now within my power to cause such things, as befits my totem. I will make you forget this conversation, too, with the coming of the nether. And many other things, besides. I have no reason to fear you, Royden, because I can make you dance to my tune."

"Not until midnight, you can't."

"Until then."

She hung up on me.

Oh, dammit, I really needed to call Cleon. I sincerely hoped that he was still at dinner and not watching a movie or something. Or, you know, actually getting laid.

That would be awkward.

CHAPTER 70

He picked up. I didn't give him time to yell at me.

"Cleon, fucking Anita is the villain! She was working for the Warrior-Princes of Builg, and she hexed us or something to make us forget, but I know how to kill her!"

"I'm sorry?"

"She's afraid of Bastard Greg, and it's all because he has this, like, a medallion thing that can control her or something. There's only one person who could knife him to death in his sleep, there in his domain, and that's another claimant to the throne. So she's the Queen of Magog, and that means she could do it, and she would. But she can't, because he has her medallion, so she took a risk to set me on his tail. And that's a hell of a risk! And that means that she's vulnerable. So now all I need is some way to kill Greg, and we can win this!"

I paused. Then I continued.

"Well, him and King Humbert. Him, too."

"Hmm."

"Cleon?"

I heard Cleon lean the phone away from his mouth and excuse himself. I could hear soft music playing in the background and him walking to somewhere private. Crap. Sounded like a really nice dinner.

"Royden, I am at a very nice dinner. I am wearing a goddamn suit. With a tie. I am going to get laid tonight. Do you understand that?"

"Yes. Sorry, Cleon."

"All right, now I've told Nurse Lacy that my emotionally troubled grandson called. Right now, I look sensitive and sweet, but if this takes long she's going to think that my family is fucked up, and that's not sexy. So make this good."

"Wait. Her name is Nurse Lacy?"

"Hell yes, and she's a redhead in her thirties, and she has those cutie 1950s cat-style glasses I like, and so help me god I will kill you if you fuck this up for me."

"Okay. What are you going to tell her?"

"I will make up a damn story about you setting yourself on fire, if I have to. You have five minutes. Go."

And so, for the first damn time in a long damn time, I told Cleon everything. From the beginning.

CHAPTER 71

It took way longer than five minutes, but Cleon was up to speed.

Finally.

"It's Baphomet."

"Huh?"

"Oh, Royden. You are a goddamn idiot. Baphomet is the goat-demon they're using. Back in the late 1100s, he showed up in some Occitan poems. He's this pseudo-historical monster that anti-Freemasons tried to link with the French Templars and a bunch of other shit from the 1300s and later. He's the Satanic goat with the big curly horns and the star drawn on his forehead. He's our boy."

"Wait, yeah, Baphomet. Didn't, like, Aleister Crowley have a bunch of stuff on him? Union of opposites, the leaping goat as the symbol of liberty or something? The arcane androgyne, maybe?"

"Yes. I think. Sounds right, and fits the paradigm. Look, Royden, I do not have my goddamn books on me right now. I'm standing next to very fancy bathrooms at a very fancy restaurant, pretending that you, my fictional nephew, have set your little self on fire and hoping that Nurse Lacy isn't getting too bored and eating all the damn bread."

"I love how you call her Nurse Lacy, like that's her legal name or something. Do you have her call you Crazy Old Cleon?"

"Don't call me again unless you're actually on fire. When the damn midnight hour hits, you slip the waking world and then you hop, skip, and jump your little butt to the domain dirt I've got sitting in my vault-vault. Then we're going to take Miss Molly for a drive. Do you understand me?"

"Yep."

"I'll meet you there."

"Thanks, Cleon."

"And get the hell out of the area. What are you, nuts, sitting in a diner? They're gonna hunt you down any minute."

"Well, no, my assumption is that Rick will be too freaked out from the kidnapping to go back to anybody. At least not right away. I'm keeping an eye out in case he comes here, but I haven't seen him. He doesn't have his wallet, and his cellphone is sitting in this coat right next to me. He's in handcuffs and all beaten up, and he can't call the cops. He's probably trying to figure out where to go next, and I'm going to track him. I need a mirror to do that. It's what you were saying about how it would be awesome to be able to put a tracer on Fred and Anita."

"Yeah, you do that. Baphomet, mirror. Now, you do remember how to call down a spirit, right? How to tune your eyes to it? I mean, I did teach you *something* useful, right?"

"Hanging up now, Cleon. Enjoy your meal. And the sex."

"Oh, I intend to."

He hung up. Lovable old scamp.

CHAPTER 72

Upon thinking about it just a little more, I decided to take Cleon's advice and go hide. Also, I needed a mirror. I picked up my coffee, walked to the bathroom and locked myself in a stall.

I checked my cellphone—little before 10:00 pm. Well, that was good. It was going to take me at least five minutes to call up the spirit of Baphomet, and I wanted to get a chance to chat briefly.

Sitting on the toilet, I started riffling through Rick's coat pockets hoping that he had something on him useful for the purposes of spirit summoning. Something besides the cellphone and the giant bag of cocaine, obviously, which were already part of the plan.

Chalk, maybe. Candles. A rosary and an iron dagger and lump of wax in the shape of a saint, perhaps.

Flower petals and twigs and bird-bones. Goat hair.

These things, sadly, were not to be.

I did, however, find a little one-hitter pipe and a good-sized bag of weed, along with a hip flask and a baggie full of Viagra and something that for one second I imagined to be another folded, magic hunting knife from Paese dei Balocchi until I actually looked at it, and then for a second I thought it was a dildo. But no.

It was big, made of curved, slick plastic like a pistol grip, and studded with little rubber dots. It was the handle to something, with a little slit on the top next to the hand-guard and a matte-black button pressed into the side with a stylized lotus on it.

It felt *super cool.*

With my heart racing, I exhaled and pointed it away from my face and pressed down on the button.

Ca-click. Sha-slack. Buzz-zzz.

The whole thing flicked open, and suddenly it weighed more, and a little engine was throbbing inside the handle like I was holding an electric razor or a vibrating control pad.

I was holding a taser-wreathed chain-katana, all made of pure bad-assery. It was three feet of unfolded plastic in a gentle curve, marked along the side with images of dragons. The leading edge of the blade was a blur of tiny hooks like shark teeth buzzing back and forth and spitting blue sparks in a spiral whirl.

The room filled with the smells of ozone and hot plastic, and I tried not to start hyperventilating.

Awesome.

I turned slowly in the stall, admiring the thing and trying to force myself to press the button to make it turn off. A little bit of the blade tagged the door, and part of the door died.

As in, like, the paint curled back, blistered with heat, and then the steel came open like it was rusting and then it turned to blackish ash and then inexplicably the hinges on the door came loose and the whole thing hung there with an inch-wide, five-inch-long gash ripped into it with smoke pouring out.

Holy shit.

I did everything I could not to scream, roll my eyes back with my tongue flopping out of my head, charge out the door and run through the Denny's knocking shit over and hacking tables in half.

In my mind's eye, I could see it: steaming-hot pots of coffee exploding as I swung my blade through them, glass doors blowing off their hinges and shattering as I ran past, and the sounds of police sirens in the distance as I sprinted up the road plunging my awesome chain-sword into the engines of cars before the whole thing roars into a blossom of flame and flips, end over end, above my head.

I took a deep breath, closed my eyes, and then let a lungful of air out. Slowly. It felt jagged, catching in my throat, like I was coming down from a high.

Woah. Potent magic.

With my eyes still closed, I started feeling around on the handle for an off-switch. And then my index finger ran across a trigger that had popped out of the handle, and I knew in my heart of hearts that if I pulled it, my sword would start shooting flaming ninja stars when I swung it.

Trying to stay calm, I found the little pressed-in button that had turned the thing on and clicked it again. I felt, as much as heard, the whole blade fold up with a *shlack-click* sound and secure itself inside the handle again. It almost sounded disappointed.

I opened my eyes and started breathing regularly again.

Stuffing the sword handle into my pocket, I checked the time. It was now 10:05. Holy shit, I had been standing there with my blade out, fighting the urge to wreck some havoc for almost ten minutes. And as I put my cell away, my fingers worked their way back around the handle and I had to will myself to let go. My hand started shaking involuntarily.

Fuck me running, I felt like I was trying to convince myself not to boot up a favorite video game or not to surf for porn at three in the morning. Or not to have a beer.

Jesus.

Fortunately, I have a cure-all for that monkey on the back. I lit a smoke, sat down on the toilet, and thought about calling Tama.

The shakes began to subside.

Then I stood up, walked out the door, crossed the little hallway to the ladies' room and walked in.

"Hello? Janitorial. Anybody in here?"

Nope. Awesome.

I threw the deadbolt.

Time to get to work.

CHAPTER 73

For those following along at home and taking notes, summoning up a spirit is remarkably easy work. Anyone who has ever fucked around with a Ouija board for a bit and gotten a weird response has done it. Folks all over the world, some of them as skeptical as you can get on this side of a professional debunker's conference, have stories about feeling an unseen presence in the room.

Okay, sure, at least half the time it's a momentary misfire of the temporoparietal junction, and that feeling of being watched is just your own dumbass brain suggesting helpfully to you that maybe, just maybe, your body is occupying multiple phase states simultaneously, and you're actually over there, too. And in the case of nearly 4 million people in the US who think they've been abducted by aliens or seen a ghost walk through their room in the middle of the night, it might just be sleep paralysis mixed with some bland malfunction of the temporal lobe.

And then again, sometimes it's a fucking spirit.

And while getting a spirit to show up is pretty easy, the hard part is getting the fucker to actually be in any way useful.

There are several steps to calling up a spirit, chatting with a spirit and getting the spirit to do what you want it to do, and the problem is that the steps get exponentially harder to do with each level of usefulness. Sort of like the differences between opening a webpage, editing a webpage, and building your own web browser, I suppose.

So, no, for the record, I don't know how to bind spirits and make them do my bidding like the King of Majooj does. I also don't know how to properly "translate" a spirit from the nether of the 25th into a physical body in the waking world like Frieda does. And I sure as hell don't know how to bind spirit energy into objects and make them magical the way Pale Alberich apparently does.

Then again, I don't know how to build a cellphone, either. But I do know to make a phone call, and since Cleon gave me the name *Baphomet*, I was hoping that I could muddle through a very simple summoning and that the demon goat would be inclined to talk because I'm such a nice guy and we have similar enemies.

First things first, I spread all of my ingredients on the tiled floor. I was going to want to change my lighting up a little bit here in a moment, but for now, the fluorescent bulbs overhead were just fine for prep work. I considered trying to clean off the floor a little, since a women's bathroom in a Denny's is a pretty disgusting place to cast a spell, but I decided after a moment that maybe a demon goat would prefer a few stray stains, hairs, wadded-up towels, and bits of used toilet paper.

Not like I had any cleaning supplies on hand, anyway.

Man, this plan seemed iffy.

Okay, so now I needed some components.

I started rummaging through my shit, and came upon the Viagra. Okay, little round blue pills... that might make a good bounded space for the summoning, especially for a sex demon. One at a time, I laid them out in a small circle.

Then I poured a copious amount of cocaine in the center and began cutting it into lines with Rick's debit card, forming a messy star shape in the middle, in rough approximation of the star on Baphomet's head.

That took a few minutes. While doing so, I repeated what very few phrases I know in Occitan.

Once I had a star and a circle, I dropped the Occitan. Other than the days of the week and what I'm pretty sure is "I would like the soup," I can't say much. Then, intoning the name of Baphomet and a few words in Latin, which I'm almost certain mean something like "You are invited," I sparked the one-hitter and dropped it into the center of the drug circle.

Smoke kept running out of the pipe, almost like incense.

It was working.

Fuck, yes.

With a lighter in each hand, I ran over and slapped the light-switch off using my elbow; as the room clicked to black, I flicked both lighters.

Deep red flame, like a blood-slick road flare, jumped from each of them. The room filled with a smell of sulfur, hot morning breath, and very expensive, hydroponic weed.

I sat down on the floor, cross-legged in front of the star, and set the two lighters down on either side of the circle. Letting go of them, the flames guttered for a moment and then magically kicked up again. I fished Rick's fancy cellphone out of my pocket and dropped it in the center on top of the smoking pipe. Light began to shine from the phone, dimly, and I watched the "locked" sign suddenly flash to "unlocked," and then a weird dial tone kicked up along with the smell of burning plastic.

I unscrewed the flask and flicked a few drops of liquid across the circle as I repeated the name of Baphomet; where the drops struck, the cellphone started to blister and warp, and smoke trailed out.

That's when I realized that the flask was full of ambrosia.

Holy shit.

Doing my best not to lose my cool, "Lord Baphomet, who is so called for *baphe* and *metis*, meaning 'absorption of knowledge'; who by the Atbash is translated as 'Sophia' the Greek for wisdom; he who is male and female united and thus the soul beyond the threshold, I call upon you."

Light shifted across the front of the cellphone.

The name *BAPHOMET* appeared.

Calling...

I rubbed my eyes and tried to focus on seeing the unseen, like adjusting your gaze to note the semen spots on a dirty nudie-booth window instead of looking right through it.

The phone picked up.

"You have called mighty Baphomet, mortal—the balance of the Tao and the unity of opposites—to this Denny's. I answer."

His voice emanated from the phone, and also from right in front of me. I glanced up, and a huge, horned goat head with a shining, bloody star carved across his scalp was glaring at me from the mirror above the sinks. In the reflection, I could see huge, human-like hands pressed upon the countertop, and curving, furry batwings stretching from his shoulders to fill the darkness of the stalls. Okay, so far, so good.

I also noticed that he had dozens of bites taken out of him all along his arms and chest and neck, each one of them like a chomp out of an apple. Some were scabbed and dark like needle tracks, some were fresh and leaking glowing-white pus. There were even bite marks on his horns.

"Speak, mortal. Do not gawk."

"Lord Baphomet, I ask to know who has harmed you."

"I shall answer. I am harmed by foul little mortals who drink blood stolen from vessels filled with a trifle of my essence. Boys, playing at men, who mingle this blood with beer and semen and wear upon their talismans fur taken from my violated effigies."

"Hm. Rick didn't mention that there was any semen in the magical blood-beer."

"Oh, probably not. That's pretty fucked up, you have to admit."

I stared at the goat-demon, and he shrugged.

"So, we can... speak informally?"

"Yeah, no problem. I'm a little messed up from that ambrosia you used, to be honest, and I was just doing the whole 'ye olde' thing since you seemed so into it and stuff."

"Great. Thanks. I'm really bad at the formalities. I keep wanting to tell Forgotten Kings that they're a credit to their race."

"Me too, man. I'm a spirit of freedom from society's convention. I'm made of the desire to scream 'Hail Satan' during a big church service, to wear a swimsuit to a funeral and a suit and tie to the beach. Boys wearing eyeliner, girls rocking chain-wallets. That sort of thing."

"All right, so... look, I'm going after the guys who are fucking with you. There's a summoner, called Bastard Greg the Kitty-Cat Killer, but you might know him by a different name."

"Yeah, the fucking King of Majooj. What a flaming dickhole."

"Absolutely. He's the worst."

"So what can I do for you, guy?"

"Why don't you tell me everything you know about the boy-goats and their swiped magic?"

"Got it. Okay, so these kids, they've been calling me up and forcing me to fill living vessels for a few months now. I show up pissed off, get bound into the flesh of a symbolic goat that they've got tied up and bound within a hedge-circle, and then they rape and kill the thing and steal some of my power through the blood."

"Like a... symbolic sacrifice?"

"No, no, they're not worshiping me. They're symbolically *killing* me. Eating me. Or drinking, I guess. They get a goat, carve a star into its forehead, and then force me to occupy it and bone me up the ass. Then, when they kill it, the blood has some of my power. Mix it up in a mug of home-brew beer with a little bit of spooge from their ookie-kookie games, and they can manifest my flesh as their own."

"Damn. Pretty complex stuff."

"You're telling me. Nobody has pulled anything like this in years. Centuries, maybe. Somebody did their homework. But the master of the boy-goats, the King of Cocagne or something, he's not the one running the ritual."

"I figured that. It's Greg."

"Yeah. What I don't get is why this Majooj guy is even doing this. It's not even his army. And there's a reason that people don't drink demons any more: it's a totally punk-ass move and unstable... and it fucking pisses us off, and he ought to know that I've got dangerous friends on my side of the Near Sideways."

"About that—why haven't you moved against him?"

"He's got protections. Pretty damn potent protections. But it's just mortal stuff, at the end of the day: spells and tricks and wards against my direct influence on him, and a lot of other spirits, as well. But he has to know that one day, he's gonna slip up or somebody like you is going to summon me up and ask me for information, and then he's going to be well and truly fucked."

"Huh. Well, maybe he has a safeguard in—"

And just then, the phone on the floor beeped.

It said *Incoming call: Jimbo.*

Baphomet and I stared at it.

"Fuck. You should take that call, man."

"You don't mind?"

"No. But you really, really need to end your call with me because I'm about to kill you."

And then the monster in the mirror shattered through the glass.

CHAPTER 74

I dropped and lunged forward, snatching the smoking-hot phone out of the drug circle and spraying pills in every direction. Scrambling toward the door, I knocked over one of the lighters; the room went pitch black except for the glow coming off my assailant's bites as he leaped over my head and smashed into the stalls.

"I'm so sorry, man! I'm under compulsion! This really sucks! Don't forget that the door is locked!"

His voice was fading already, but Baphomet is a potent spirit. He spun in place, eyes flashing with blue fire, and I could barely make out the words *DISSOLVE* and *CONGEL* written on his right and left palms, respectively. He growled and swung a hand at me, and the steel stall door he connected with disintegrated, spraying out in a sputtering arc like it was made of sizzling jelly.

"Fuck me."

"I know, man! Run! I can't stop!"

I needed to get the fuck out of this summoning space.

NOW.

I jumped up and hauled ass to the door, using the light of the incoming call to guide me. I kicked the deadbolt open, yanked the door ajar, and spun through the doorway. A weight like a freight train made of beef smashed into the other side.

I answered the phone as another shoulder check smashing into the door cracked the frame, and the roar on the other side stopped.

"Rick's phone. Royden speaking. Rick isn't available right now."

"Fuck you, you Jap nigger faggot fuck."

"Officer Merrick? Is that you? Oh, right, your first name is James. Man, I was really hoping this was my other, much more awesome friend who is also nicknamed *Jimbo*. He's dead, but sometimes we chat on the phone, which is pretty great."

"I'm going to fucking murder your nigger-faggot midget ass."

"Well, all the luck in the world to you."

I hung up and glanced around at the rest of the Denny's, where a lot of people were staring at me.

"Wrong number. And don't go in that bathroom—they're out of toilet paper."

I walked to the door, lighting a cigarette and trying to think. Before I got a chance, a series of headlights angrily cut across the parking lot with a squeal of tires. Three vehicles all pulled into the parking lot at high speed; one of them was a white van with recent duct-tape-based repairs and *Free Candey* written on the side.

Okay, looks like I called down the wrath of the boy-goats an hour or so ahead of schedule.

I turned and ran the other direction.

Booking it out the emergency exit door of the restaurant as fast as I could, I barely heard the sound of my new stolen phone ringing again over the fire alarm going off. I glanced at it: *King of Demons*. Still running, I answered.

"Hello. This is Royden Poole, sitting poolside in the Dominican Republic. How may I direct your call, Greggie?"

"You've fucked up for the last time, little man. I'll have you in chains before me by midnight."

Still sprinting, feeling cold rain slapping into me and letting it clear my head as best it could get cleared.

"Yeah, yeah, I've heard it before."

I stopped, ducking behind a bush and trying to figure out where I was. Dammit, still in the parking lot? I decided to kill time while I caught my breath.

"So, pretty good response time for the boy-goats. Just real quick, let me guess—Rick made a collect call at a pay phone somewhere and called up the cavalry to hit the hotel. But you didn't know that I was in the bathroom of the Denny's until I made contact with the demon you've been farming. Am I close?"

"Yes. Now, if you'd be so kind as to indulge me a question: your stubby legs and smoker's lungs cannot carry you very far or very fast. I simply wonder if you even know how to drive a car. Do you?"

"Nope. Can't even reach the pedals except on fancy shit."

"I have you now, Mr. Poole. Give up, and my men will simply subdue you before you are brought to me. Struggle further, and I cannot guarantee that they will not vent their frustrations upon you. I do not require that you possess your arms, legs, tongue, eyes, cock, or anal virginity when I make you my court's fool."

"Huh."

Man, I really wanted to say something clever. I felt around in my pockets a little bit. And then... oh, shit.

Well, there was something I had stolen from somebody with a plan to kill the King of Majooj. Neat.

"Is that all you have to say, Mr. Poole? Just 'huh'?"

"Actually, I was going to say that they aren't even *your* men. You don't even *have* any men. All you have is your demons, and some of them are a damn sight less loyal than you might think they are. You should ask Frieda what she's the queen of, some time. That, and I hope these boys are up for a fight. See you at midnight, motherfucker."

I hung up and dropped the phone in a puddle. Then I pulled out the hip flask of ambrosia, unscrewed the top, and took a deep swallow.

It tasted like a bolt of lightning, and my ears popped. Every inch of my skin a cold fire, like I was walking out of a cave I'd been in my whole life, only to just then see the most beautiful sunset in the world, and everything went bright gold.

"HEY, ASSHOLES! I'M OVER HERE!"

CHAPTER 75

I don't remember much of the next hour and a half, so I'll keep it brief. I mostly remember the overwhelming sensation of a massive erection and my whole body humming with hot tears of joy streaming down my face, and me flexing my shoulders like I was trying to get angel wings to unfurl from my back.

At one point, I was convinced that I had three sets of wings, all made out of bright thunder.

And I kept yelling.

I remember that pretty clearly.

Other than that, these are the things I can best recall.

Seen: me charging the boy-goats across the parking lot, swinging my new chain-katana and screaming and laughing.

Overheard: someone shouting, panicked, about calling the cops, and me mentioning, loudly, that at least one cop was already here, and his name was Jimbo Merrick! Come on down!

Remembered: that my plan had initially been to take a swig of the ambrosia to give me enough *oomph* to run away and maybe hail a cab using my mojo; that getting into a fight was seriously a bad idea... but by then, I'd already committed to it.

Seen: a bunch of shattered glass and at least one car on fire; a lot of streetlights zigging and zagging past me making funny shapes.

Overheard: the sounds of someone yelling "he went that way"; me belting show tunes as I ran and drank more swigs from my hipflask. I think that I was shouting parts of "The Surrey with the Fringe on Top" from *Oklahoma!*, but I couldn't really be sure, and if I was, I have no idea why.

Remembered: puking from exhaustion after sprinting a couple of miles and then hiding and then sprinting again; later, trying to relight the cigarette that had been in my mouth when I puked in the gutter, and which was now pretty darn soaked through. Eventually, I gave up.

At one point, I was thinking that it would be awesome if there was a big fat guy in a diaper running right behind me, like on *Jackass*.

Also remembered: throwing my hand up in the air and screaming *"CAB!"* with every ounce of my energy, successfully pulling in a taxi despite the fact that I was running along the side of a freeway at the time.

And it's also entirely possible that none of that even happened, except for maybe the cab bit.

Because I also pretty clearly remember getting laid at some point in there, and I'm damn certain that *that* didn't happen.

Point being, there's a good reason that people don't get into fights while well and truly fucked up on ambrosia.

Although I suppose it worked out for me.

CHAPTER 76

I sat in the backseat of the cab, my stomach empty of ambrosia and everything else, coming down off a world-class adrenaline rush mixed with a drunk-on like I had never felt before. I think I had a broken toe. My feet hurt, my throat burned, both of my arms ached, my head was throbbing. I felt like I had jammed icepicks into each knee, thigh, and hip, and I was having trouble keeping my eyes open.

"... New York?"

The guy in the front seat, the cabbie, was talking to me.

"Sorry, what?"

"I said, hey, man, so you from New York or something?"

"No. I'm from around here. Why?"

"Oh, I just see that you got that Yankees cap on. Don't see a lot of those except on New Yorkers. My brother lives up there, so I was just wondering."

"Yeah, okay. Whatever. No, man I just like the Yankees. I mean, I'm not one of those guys who cried when Steinbrenner died, but I can't say that I wasn't a little choked up. Dude was legend."

"Cool. You a big baseball guy, then?"

"Nope. Couldn't even tell you anybody who plays on the team. I guess I just like the Yankees because everyone else hates them so much."

"Okay. That's cool."

"Not really. I'm actually just kind of a dick that way. Why, who do you like?"

"Well, I grew up in KC, so I still root for the Royals."

I started laughing. I couldn't help it.

"What? Hey, fuck you, man."

"No, no, it's cool. I just know a lot of people who wear Royals caps and jackets and shit, but I've never met anybody who was really into them."

"Wearing a Royals cap but not really into the team? That doesn't... well, whatever."

"It's because of the crown on the logo, man. And the colors, with the gold and everything. I just know some people who are into that shit. Them and the Sacramento Kings."

"All right. You got some weird friends, man."

"I didn't say they were my friends. Hey, look, could you pull over at a gas station or something? I gotta take a piss."

We stopped, and I hopped out and ran inside the nasty little fill-up joint.

See, the thing is that I did actually have to piss, but my main reason for wanting to get the fuck out of the car had to do with the fact that I didn't have any goddamn money on me.

I vaguely remembered using Rick's debit card to cut those lines of cocaine into a star pattern. And to do that, I had pulled his wallet full of hundreds out of my pocket and set it next to me on the floor. And then I had run the hell out of that bathroom, in the dark, like there was a demon trying to chomp down on my ass. Because, of course, there actually had been a demon trying to chomp down on it.

But the end result is that I didn't have a fucking dime on me. Not one. Because my wallet had been snagged by those bitches at Frieda's place.

Dammit.

I went into the bathroom, washed my face, and caught a glimpse of myself in the mirror. Damn, I looked awful. And apparently, I had a nasty cut on my face, which I hadn't noticed until now but which, upon being poked at, started to hurt like a motherfucker.

"Ow."

Then I looked at my cell. Holy shit, almost 12:00.

I walked back out into the convenience store, pulled a soda out of the fridge, snatched a fistful of beef jerky sticks, and strolled casually back to the bathroom; I closed the door softly, making sure that it didn't lock behind me. Then I sat down on the toilet, drank my soda, and stared at my cell, watching the numbers creep into the high 11:50s. I lit a smoke, closed my eyes, and waited for the world to shift underneath me.

I almost fell asleep.

And then everything changed and the memory-potential universe lurking below our own yawned open. I plunged backward into the Hole behind Midnight.

Heading for Cleon.

CHAPTER 77

I couldn't have picked a better spot to pop through into the Nether Time if I had done it on purpose; of all the bathrooms I had hunkered down in over the course of the evening, this one was by far the least well attended.

The whole room shifted and broke. I closed my eyes and breathed in unnatural air, letting my exhaustion run out of me in thin rivulets. The sounds of scampering cockroaches clicked up a few decibels.

Yes, they live on the other side of the curtain, too.

Couldn't tell you why.

I pushed the door of the bathroom open and found myself standing in the ribcage of a gutted, skeletal convenience store: the ceiling hung over me in a patchwork, like the shattered sternum of some decaying giant, letting the weird light of the 25th Hour sky play across the crosshatchings of linoleum and peeling concrete floor. A cold wind blew through the broken walls where the beer and cigarettes would be kept, and drifts of ash and soiled wrappers skittered around in little whirlwinds between the empty, gaping shelves. Stray dogs, lost and on the prowl, started barking in the distance.

Taking a sip of my stolen soda, I took a moment to consider the questions of a place with so much emotional investment in the products and so little investment in the actual building.

Deep stuff.

The walls of the women's room across from me were solid and stained, but the door itself had faded away to only a pitted frame; blackish grass poked up through the white dirt smeared along the floor of the restrooms, and then the automatic condom machine behind me started laughing a little bit, just to itself.

That's when I heard the howls and yawps of the boy-goats in the distance, and the clop of cloven hooves sprinting inhumanly fast on asphalt.

From a few blocks away, "RUN, YOU FUCKING SHIT-NIGGER-FAGGOT FUCK! I'm gonna teabag your corpse!"

"Huh."

The condom dispenser spoke up, "Yo. Yo, hey, my man. I think they're talking about you, dude."

"Yeah, probably. Hey, real quick, are goats known for a keen and unerring tracking instinct?"

"Dunno. Sounds to me like they're getting closer, man. I hope you don't mind if I watch while they fuck you up."

"About that. Tell them I left."

I stepped through the doorway again and thought of Cleon's vault, sending an emphatic message to the cosmos that I, the King of Jangladesh, was going home through this door.

The universe humbly obliged.

CHAPTER 78

Cleon was right. I do suck at casting spells.

The room shifted again. My broken nose started bleeding, and I felt like I had been punched in the back of the head. My eyes watered, and then my knees dopped out from underneath me. I barely caught myself, and then I started breathing heavily.

"You forgot to put any stone or dirt from ancient Jangladesh into the mix. You're lucky that the shit under your fingernails counts, or the ritual never would have worked."

I looked up, still on all fours, to see Cleon, his head freshly shaved bald, crouched in the corner wearing a tactical vest and a set of goggles, calmly reading an old, leather-bound book by candlelight with a futuristic assault rifle propped up next to him. I lay down, cheek against the floor.

"Cleon, I don't own any dirt from Bikaner, or even from Rajasthan. Hell, I've never even been to India."

He stood, "Well, now I know what to get you for Christmas."

I rolled over onto my back, "Ha. So, how was your date?"

"It was goddamn fantastic. And that's all I'm gonna say about it."

"Get laid?"

"Yep."

"Huh. So, does Nurse Lacy have any friends?"

"None that I would inflict you upon. Come on, let's get rolling."

"Give me a second. I'm kinda... really fucked up."

"Yeah, you smell like it. Is that puke on your shirt?"

"Yep. Came by it honestly, too. I was running from boy-goats."

"We get done with this, you're taking a shower."

"Oh, please, dear gods, let that be so. Extra hot. With bubbles."

"Showers don't do bubbles, Royden. You're thinking of baths."

"I want one of those, too."

Still lying on my back, I watched him walk over and start pulling videocassettes off the shelves, seemingly without rhyme or reason.

"So, uh, Cleon... are we going to watch a movie or something before we kill these guys? Because I might fall asleep."

He didn't bother to look at me. "Sleep? Shit, not if you're watching any of this. I got more than half of *Blues Brothers 2*, a bunch of damn good shots from *Ghostbusters 3*, the raw cut of the original Eric Stoltz *Back to the Future*, a whole fuck-load of the test footage from the Nicholas Cage *Superman*, and an hour of Michael Caine and Robert Redford doing Hitchcock's 1967 *Kaleidoscope*. It's even scarier than *Psycho*, I'm telling you. And the main character is the serial killer from *Shadow of a Doubt*. The best one, though, is probably the thirty-minute short of *Alien 3* by William Gibson with him and Lance Henricksen and some sound guys reading the thing on a private stage."

"Wow. I'd love to see that sometime."

"Oh, you ain't never gonna see *shit*. I offered to let you watch *Kaleidoscope* with me five years ago, and you said no, and then you got all huffy because I wouldn't give you the damn Demi Moore/Bruce Willis sex tape. And now you don't get to watch fucking nothing. You been asking me forever, and you can keep on asking me forever, and the answer is no."

"So... we're not watching a movie?"

"Dumbass. These ones I'm grabbing here aren't for entertainment purposes. These particular bastards all have the remnants of exorcisms bound into them: nasty blights, curses, sorrows, afflictions, demonic possessions, all the ugly stuff I ever pulled off a king or queen with the coin to pay for a black tape to pull a hole off their soul. They're weapons, now. I'm going to unleash hot, holy hell on Bastard Greg and on that fucker King Humbert and especially on Frieda-fucking-Baghaamrita."

I paused.

"I'm sorry, *who*?"

He grinned at me. "Damn, that girl works quick. *Baghaamrita*—name evolved from an apocryphal, androgynous Phrygian-Turkish sex and wine deity called Baghak; later adapted, post-Rome, as Bacchus, with the Greek myths of Dionysus; mix that with the Sankrit word *Amrit* for 'nectar of immortality,' or ambrosia, and you have a very evil and cunning old bitch indeed."

"... and her first name is Frieda. Sounds like *futa*, means chicks with dicks. Oh, fuck, she's good."

"Yep. A very insidious, precise memory short circuit."

"Shit. Shit, shit, shit. So how the fuck come did you not get tagged by her mindwipe?"

"Because I'm a goddamn professional. You have underestimated the sneakiness of the vault-vault. I've been down here since before the clocks went funny, and her mojo can't reach down here. She doesn't know that it exists, and so it doesn't... at least for purposes of her spells and such."

"Damn."

"Yep. Reading up a bit on *Pinocchio*, too. In the original Italian. You know, like somebody trying to solve a case like this *should* be doing."

"Fuck. If I don't stand up, put on a vest, and grab a gun, you're going to lecture me about this forever, aren't you?"

"Yep. Also, just so you know, there's a crew of boy-goats upstairs waiting for us. We're going to have to shoot our way out to Miss Molly."

"Where is she parked?"

"Right out back."

"Fuck. Then let's go."

CHAPTER 79

I should mention that Cleon's car, Miss Molly, isn't really a car at all. She's actually an amalgamation of car-related hopes, dreams, rose-tinged reminiscences, and burning, burning yearning.

Cleon tells me that she looks a lot like a 1957 Cadillac Coup de Ville convertible, except bigger and with just a little bit of a 1967 El Dorado and some 1958 Plymouth Fury sort of mixed in, along with a 1969 Ford Mustang Boss 302 GT and a 1966 Thunderbird, heavy on the chrome with a pink-red paint job that he can only describe as "neon hot cherry."

But I'm not much of a car guy. All I know is that she's beautiful. A convertible. Always topless, too, because the rain is just too much of a pussy to fall on her.

Anyway, I don't actually remember closing my eyes and falling asleep, but apparently I did.

I was awoken quite rudely when Cleon dropped a heavy plastic bag from Salvation Army on my chest.

"Up and at 'em, asshole."

"Fuck, fuck, fuck, I'm awake. You're a dick, Cleon."

"Good. Put this on."

He kicked at the object now sitting on my chest, and it took a second for me to register what it was.

In short, it was a fresh, white plastic grocery bag from the Salvation Army looped on a woven leather cord, clipped shut with a Church of Jesus Christ of Latter-day Saints nametag emblazoned with the name *Elder Smith* and containing an oddly shaped video cassette, still held in a tight wrapper.

"The fuck is this?"

"Medallion of protection, you ass. The tape is fresh Betamax; it'll eat any kind of nasty magic anybody cares to throw at you. It should keep us safe from Frieda's mindwiping until the tape itself runs out—we'll have about two hours once we walk out the door of the vault-vault."

"Why the Mormon nametag bit?"

"Because if you want to keep something from getting infected with all the nasty, oozing badness roiling out of slutty demon girls, you want to wrap it in plastic and call it Mormon. Now get up and load up. You want the assault rifle, the grenades, the handguns, or a little of each?"

"Why so you ask me these foolish questions, Cleon?"

"Two apiece it is, then."

The guns fit well. The rifles were a tad big, maybe, but serviceable—like they were designed for ten-year-old African child soldiers.

The grenades felt great, especially once I found the tiny dials on the side that let you set them to "lethal." Love that frowny-face.

And, since you asked, my new bulletproof vest fit like a secondhand prom dress, hanging all the way down to my knees.

I put my aviators on. Stunna-time.

CHAPTER 80

We opened the door that says TV Man Wasn't Here, and a little click sounded from inside each of our medallion-bags. The tapes started running, recording Frieda's bad mojo off the universe—right past us and into the nether of the magical Betamax tapes snuggled against us.

It was very spiritual and profound.

Then the shooting started.

Then the screaming.

There really isn't much to say about our fight out of Happy Happy VCR—there were only six of them and there were two of us. We knew the terrain, we knew the objective, and we had the element of significant surprise over the defenders, who were most certainly *not* expecting the pair of us to come busting out of a previously unknown basement behind an invisible door, guns already blazing. They didn't even know they were in a fight until it was almost over.

My only stray observation might be that boy-goats are pretty goddamn quick and pretty goddamn tough to hurt.

But automatic gunfire, well used, shuts down just about anyone.

Plus, I'm bulletproof from the neck down.

And on a couple of odd occasions during the thirty or so seconds that the fight lasted, some of our assailants tried holding a hand behind their backs or something, right there in the middle of the gunfight, and that weirded me out. I flying tackled at least one guy doing that.

Grabbed him and vented a frustration or two.

But they weren't exactly ready for us, and so, we won.

Handily.

Go, us.

CHAPTER 81

Miss Molly was waiting for us behind Happy Happy VCR, already purring like a smoldering kitten.

God, I had forgotten how pretty she is.

She almost looked like she was pulsing, there under the shifting god-hemorrhage of unlight running out of the splintered sky above with traceries of neon silver and electric liquid sexy running across her.

Whitewall tires gleamed in reflection on the stark pavement.

The rain on the Nether Side just isn't ballsy enough to fall on her. It gets all shy and awkward at the last second and stammers, stumbling away when it gets close to fall instead in extra-dense sheets around me.

By the time I limped up to Molly, Cleon had already slid across her hood and jumped behind the wheel; something cool and soft and bluesy and dark yet somehow fast and ready and raw and so juicy sweet started pouring out of Molly's trembling subwoofers.

Her door unlocked for me and rolled open like a beautiful older woman uncrossing her legs under an ankle-length dress with a slit running up the side to just below the top of her thigh.

"Hurry your ass up! We're burning Betamax, here."

"I think I tore a tendon or a hamstring or something in my fucking leg, Cleon. Give a guy a freaking break."

"Save it for the tropical vacation at the end of all this bullshit. And if you fall asleep on me while we're driving out there, so help me god I will slap you awake. Scout's honor."

"Also, my hip really hurts. And I have a toothache."

"Tell someone who gives a damn."

"Can we stop for nachos?"

"No. Now is wartime. Game face."

"Got it, Cleon."

I eased into the car.

We took off at just under the speed of very fast, very smooth sound and accelerated quite briskly.

CHAPTER 82

True to his word, Cleon slapped me awake.

The night outside the car was whipping past on all sides in the tattered demi-form of a million little glow-bug lights that seemed almost like hallucinogenic highway signs, umber lo-glow from a bank of thigh-high fog and Christmas lights rolling back and forth through the woods.

They weren't, of course. This was bat-shit country.

Nothing out here has real names.

We were going hurry, hurry, hurry.

"Fuck, fuck, I'm up."

"Good. We're almost there."

"You think they have bathrooms? I have to piss again."

"We piss after we win. Those are the rules. That's how America won WWII, after all."

"You're making that up, Cleon."

"Am I? I can never remember anymore. Hey, that totally reminds me, did I ever tell you about when I banged that one chick and then took a piss in her backseat when she wouldn't let me leave until I got her off?"

"This again?"

"Oh, I told you this?"

"Yeah, Cleon. I heard all about it, like, the third time we hung out. You always tell this story before you get into big fights, too. As I recall, you were going down on her and everything, and you were both drunk, and you got real mad that she wouldn't let you 'come right back' after the sex, so you just whipped it out and went. Took a leak in her shoes, as I recall. And, of course, that's all total bullshit. You wrote that in a journal once and then left it on your nightstand to see if anybody was going through your stuff because you're a weird, paranoid bastard."

"Damn. It's such a good story."

"Yeah, it's really genius. It reminds me why I call you my mentor."

"Yeah. Keeping you awake, though."

"Which is great. And now, I really have to pee. It's ambrosia-pee, so it burns with magic of many kinds."

"Hold it. It builds character."

"More like it builds freaking bladder cancer. And you're one to talk about character-building exercises. That piss story is awful, and I notice that there's a garbage bag in the back seat full of loose cigarettes."

"I won those playing poker."

"Yeah?"

"Against hobos. Don't you judge me."

"Ew. And while we're on the subject, how exactly are we planning to deal with Bastard Greg and King Humbert once we get to them?"

"How do you mean?"

"You know, the villains?"

"I'm aware of them."

"Cleon, we know that Paese dei Balocchi is named as their domain, so they can't be killed while on it. What are we gonna do here—incapacitate them with stun darts and drag them out into the parking lot to kill them by stomping on their heads?"

"Actually, the parking lot, the street outside and even the township itself might be part of the domain, too. They're got the mayor of the city in their pocket and an army. No telling how deep this goes."

"You're not making me feel better, Cleon."

"I can see that."

"So, what's our plan?"

"Well, I was kind of hoping to get them to just step down."

He leaned over and popped the glove compartment.

It was stuffed full of pink and yellow toy ponies.

"You're a madman, Cleon. That's the stupidest trick ever."

"It's worked before. Abdication is abdication. A horse, a horse..."

"Stop that."

"You know, I had a thought about why the bad kings have been calling you a demon-slayer-god to their troops."

"Oh, really?"

"Yep. You've been building all kinds of consensus power recently, getting under people's feet and stomping through the carefully manicured gardens of multi-part world-domination plans. That sort of action leads to belief, and belief inevitably leads to potency around here, especially when even Forgotten royalty are watching. Hell, you're toting a sorcery-gun and wearing knee-length magical armor with an army of monsters arranged against you. "

"Woo. Go, me."

"Shut up. I'm making a point."

"Sure. Got it. So, Cleon, what does that have to do with me and demon slaying, specifically?"

"Nothing. But this way, a bunch of randy boy-goats with vivid, ADHD, pop-culture-choked teenage imaginations are painting you in their heads as a minor, no-name Hindu deity with a focus on demons, instead of as a hardboiled dick with a gun and an attitude. That's a strike against you. Demon slayers tend to get bested by the demons they fight in the long run or to become one of the same thing that they fight. Your subsequent fall will be all the more totemically significant when you grovel before their masters."

"Fuck. The work of Frieda, no doubt."

"No doubt at all. That bitch is clever."

"And old and mean. Speaking of her clever moves, how long have we got until these Betamax tapes run out?"

"You've got about an hour left. A little more. Me, I've got maybe forty minutes, tops."

"What? How is that possible?"

"I caught a shot to the head earlier from one of the boy-goat's guns, right after we busted out the TV Man door. Didn't even sting, but I heard the tape speed up like it was on fast forward for a few seconds while the medallion ate the magic off that dart. Rang my bell a little."

"Oh, shit. Then how come... "

"Your aegis-shirt caught all the damage when you got shot, and this toy body armor soaks up the velocity of super-darts just fine unless somebody really knows what he's aiming for. But I'd be a dead man without the medallion."

"Wait... so we're invincible until the tapes wear off?"

"Quite the opposite, actually. We can still die via any other means, just like you hurt your leg back there—it's just that raw magic can't affect us. But it does make the tapes go faster. Much faster, actually. And when these tapes run out, and they're gonna, we'll forget that Frieda even exists. And then she'll kill us at her leisure."

"Cleon, we're so fucked."

"Yep. Oh, and look. The welcome wagon is here."

That's about when I saw the roadblock: three dozen heavily armed boy-goats arranged around three parked police SUVs and one revving, angry Free Candey Van, a forty-foot-tall Gug looming behind in the shadows over the scene, and a pissed off clown sprinting right at us.

"Fuck this. Cleon, can Miss Molly still jump?"

"Chicken have lips?"

"I'll take that as a yes. I'm getting out. Meet me there."

CHAPTER 83

Cleon slammed on the brakes and kicked Miss Molly into a power slide, like something out of a movie designed to make Michael Bay blush after shitting himself.

I hunkered way down in my seat, waited until I guessed we had made enough of a rotation for my side of the car to be pointed back down the highway and lunged out the side of the door with my backpack hugged tight to my chest, weapon clutched in a fist.

I hit the pavement very hard and very fast, ears ringing, shoulder first, and came up in a somersault onto one knee with a pistol belching hot death from my hand. Cleon pitched a duffel bag out of the top of the car; it crashed to the ground two blocks up ahead in a wide spin of rocketing plastic armaments out across the road. Then I watched the taillights of Miss Molly recede faster and faster from me in a streak of red lighting as a hail of muzzle flashes erupted from the roadblock ahead.

Canio de Pogo, my tenacious clown, was on me like a cannonball.

We smashed backward across shattering asphalt, his legs kicking in the air with the force of his inhuman speed, and I spared a happy thought that this stupid monster was so obsessed with murdering me that he hadn't even bothered to try to kill Cleon or his beautiful, beautiful ride.

Love you, Miss Molly.

I pushed the barrel of my gun deep into Canio's stomach and pulled the trigger as fast as I could, watching flapping, whining chunks of wet, brightly colored, rapidly deflating balloon-intestines spray out of his back. I took a moment to consider the fact that my amazing aegis had just kept the shock of hitting the pavement from turning me into short, ugly road-pasta, like hot human *kasha hrechana zi shkvarkamy*.

The ground out here on the Gone Way Highway, after all, is just as magical as the enchanted levels of speed that Miss Molly is capable of.

Thank you, Garrick.

The bag around my neck gave a vicious scream, matching note-for-awful-note the intensity of my assailant, moving at eight-times fast forward as Canio de Pogo's fingers broke and ran in rivulets trying to choke me.

Very glad that I hadn't just died as stupidly as I'd lived, I shot him several more times, backed up, and finally stood upon shaking knees, surveying the ripped-up landscape.

We definitely left a large mark, like something out of one of Cleon's stupid over-the-top Japanese cartoons. I had rolled a half block or more when I hit the ground, digging chunks out of the pavement with my back and shoulders, and Canio had flying-tackled me backward another thirty yards up the highway into a newly made ditch. Damn.

Speaking of that particular killer clown, Canio de Pogo was now missing most of his mid-torso region; his legs held on to his madly-working shoulders only with lengths of wet black rope, and he was crawling toward me with both shattered hands outstretched, clawing at the earth and hissing.

I stared at him. "I'm getting sick of killing you, asshole."

He calmed down for one moment and then looked right at me. His lips peeled back to show black teeth, and his throat opened, and without a single movement of his lips, rotten air spilled out, "See you at home, sweetheart."

He took a bullet-dart to the center of the skull, and then he detonated in a spray of busted noisemakers, wet confetti, cold gore, and orange tufts of cotton candy with bits of silvered razor blades jammed in it. It all clattered to the ground in a hail twenty feet wide.

Ew.

I looked up the road where Miss Molly was at a slight angle, some thirty feet off the ground, blazing like a leaping tiger and illuminated from below by a mass of gunfire as she cleared the roadblock.

On the other side, hauling back to swat her from the sky, stood the terrible form of Gug, Son of Gog, four fists raised to strike.

Fuck that.

I rushed up the road toward the exploded duffel bag in the street and howled with everything I had.

"FACE ME, GUG!"

Yep, that did it.

His grotesque face, which had once been dominated primarily by a slick gash approximately seven inches long from north to south, was now a vertical, weeping gorge of flesh four feet tall and half-again as wide, full of fangs.

All turning toward me and slavering further open in abject rage.

Shit.

CHAPTER 84

The next few seconds somehow *clenched* against time.

The moment of Gug's distraction was all it took.

Miss Molly and Cleon were past the still-flashing line of defense, and Gug's arms whistled through empty air as every bit of his attention focused on me, and a roar echoed across the hills from the pit of a stomach deeper than hell.

I heard, as much as felt through the road, two hot sets of shrieking whitewall tires impact the shuddering street ahead and a screech of rubber burning on asphalt. Miss Molly's bright taillights flashed as she snaked through the trees beyond, heading over the horizon toward Paese dei Balocchi and the war to come.

I was suddenly preoccupied with five stories of angry flesh and hair lurching toward me. And the wall of mutated warriors before him, rushing me in foaming fury. And a haunted van careening in front of all of them, headlights lowering into a determined stare as it crashed ahead like a fifty-five-hundred-pound nose tackle.

Sprinting toward my dropped weapons cache, I realized that I wasn't going to make it before the Free Candey Van got there.

It was a block from me, maybe, and closing fast.

So close, so close, so close...

It clipped me as I tried to leap sideways, hitting my shoulder with a sickening thud and spinning me ass over teakettle. Once again, four hundred dollars of stolen stripper money I gave Garrick Heldane saved my fucking life.

I smashed into the ground, every part of me aching all over again, as the fucker careened by, spun, and prepared to charge me once more.

I spit out half a tooth, my head swimming. The van revved.

As I stood, the ringing in my ears drowned out some of the revs, now faster and somehow more playful. Suddenly it lunged forward.

It was having fun.

The side doors opened and a goggle-clad boy-goat leaned out, holding a very awesome-looking, very high-tech flame-thrower dripping something smoldering green.

This was going to be a problem.

Then, I had an idea.

I yanked a grenade from its attachment on the shoulder strap of my vest and felt something click deep down inside it as I pulled the pin with my teeth. I whipped the bitch, underhand, as far and high as I could.

"FREE CANDEY VAN! CATCH!"

Dear god, I still can't believe that worked.

The van braked in a cloud of hot, suddenly vaporized asphalt and rubber, popped a wheelie, and reversed while still on its rear wheels. It blew backward, angling left and then right, still on its "hind legs." The hood kicked open just as the grenade descended.

Three point shot, right at the buzzer.

A wash of flame rocked the entire vehicle. Both front windows, along with the windshield, blew out in a spatter of glass, and smoke started pouring from the now-blackened husk of steel.

"Good boy."

Another hiccup of flame engulfed the Free Candey Van, this time a deep chartreuse and acrid from the back seats, and a burning figure tried to emerge.

He didn't get far. Goat fur is highly flammable.

Free Candey Van coughed and revved once, fitfully, angled itself slightly on two popped front tires, and glared at me with the one half-broken headlight still shining from its destroyed face. I rushed up to the first automatic weapon lying on the ground, shouldered it and sighted.

BEEEEEEEEEEEEEEEP.

"Yeah. That's why I had you play your music so loud, last time."

It lunged at me. Too slow.

I sprayed the whole front end with high-velocity, screaming plastic, and watched the thing disintegrate.

Free Candey Van had the decency to actually fly backward, flip over on to its back, and catch fire once I was done.

That was pretty great.

Then the ground around me erupted into a hail of gunfire.

The rest of the Brigade was on me, now.

CHAPTER 85

I turned and raised my assault rifle, kicking a wave of rounds back at the horde as they closed.

Darts, screaming and leaving nothing more than wet stains of jelly in their wake, rattled off my face, neck, and arms, and I could hear the tape on my chest howling in fits and starts of agony. It reminded me of my older brother trying to fast forward through all the boring parts where people talk during those rare nights when he was allowed to choose the family movie. Big fan of action flicks, my brother.

No wonder this reminded me of him.

I squeezed the trigger and focused, and the first line of assault withered.

"I'M BULLETPROOF, YOU STUPID FUCKS! HA! YES, YES, I AM YOUR DEATH! I AM COME FOR YOUR DEMON-SOULS! ALL IS LOST TO YOU, BOY! FLEE! FLEEEEE! FLEE BEFORE MY TERRIBLE MIGHT!"

That took care of most of the second line.

Away they went, breaking formation and hopping on their mutated legs into the woods, weapons abandoned behind them.

Deserters: gotta appreciate 'em when they're on the other side.

Just then, a grenade detonated about two feet from me.

I flinched, and felt my tape-medallion go up an ugly octave for a second.

Unfortunately, the third line was the cavalry.

Three SUVs, loaded down for war, raced toward me, and a giant clomped behind them with murder on his mind.

A heavily muscled, tattoo-sleeved boy-goat in a Hurley hat was climbing out of the ruined, bullet-ridden windshield of the closest SWAT vehicle, stepping onto the hood. In a quick motion, he drew from the scabbard on his back a massive, thickly rune-laid, two-handed plastic greatsword, wreathed in some kind of black flame.

His footing was surprisingly sure. Like a goat, you might say.

His sword was awesome. Didn't know they had those.

His snarl was foaming, and his eyes were wild.

Surf that van, bad man-goat.

The thing sped closer, ramping over the bodies of the fallen while the driver leaned out of his window and popped wild suppressing fire into the street with the plastic uzi clutched in his left hand. The guy on the hood crouched low, and I could just barely make out the writing on his black t-shirt, stretched tight over the body armor he wore and the cords of demon-muscle underneath: "Bloody Panties Posse."

I ignored the driver.

Dropping the assault rifle, I dug into my pockets. In one swift motion, I flicked open my lightning chain-katana and palmed the magic feather into my left hand. I got as low as I could.

"Let's do this."

And then he was on me.

I dodged his swing. And I didn't hit him, either.

I, however, was actually swinging for the engine block of his SUV.

The resultant impact of my katana with the vehicle's iron-churning, gasoline-igniting heart was intense, just as I had expected.

Feeling like my arm was going to come out of its socket, I slashed out and carved through most of the engine, back through the wheel well and the top of the front tire, across the passenger side door as it sped past me, into and out the other side of the back door, and all the way back to the gas tank before I lost my grip.

The gas tank and my sparking chain-katana didn't get along.

Both of them detonated.

As I flew backward in a shock wave of superheated steel and rapidly self-annihilating fuel, I listened idly to the tape hanging from my neck devouring up backlashes of speed-magic that should have torn my arm into an unrecognizable mass of butchered meat from about the bicep on down.

This time, when I landed, I stayed down.

Ow.

I looked up, blinking tears out of my eyes, numb from the impact, and watched the SWAT vehicle I'd gutted swing wide, clip another of the vans, and then both of them spin end over end, still on fire.

The third and final SUV pulled to a stop, and it disgorged a half-dozen boy-goats armed to the teeth. I tried to pick myself off the ground, see straight, or grab hold of a weapon, failing quite miserably on all counts. But I could still talk.

"Heh. You boys want some of this?"

One kid, ugly even for a boy-goat, wore a t-shirt reading "Shut up before this rape turns into a murder." He leveled a sniper rifle at my head as he strode toward me, the buckles of his pants jingling. "Yeah, you gonna yiff in hell, fur-fag."

"What the fuck is that supposed to mean?"

"**Leave it. It is mine.**"

All of us looked up at once.

What I had mistaken, foolishly, for a very ugly tree sprouting out of the middle of the road about thirty yards behind the boy-goats was, in fact, one of Gug's legs. It moved.

The world shook as it came back down.

He was hunched, like a vast Quasimodo or killer ape, and his four hands dug furrows in the earth. Something thick, stubby, pink, hairless, and obscene jutted from his loins like a warped third thigh, winking at me as it stabbed into the night air above his pendulous gut.

I took the opportunity to check my holdout pistol. Still there, tucked into the front of my drawers.

Gug towered over the scene, stink rolling down in a warm miasma from the mass of wet flesh at the top of his building-sized bulk.

"As you wish, great Prince Gug of Majooj."

"**Indeed. It is to keep my mortal magistrate-body safe at all costs, and it must see to the defense of the king's keep from that filthy nigger and his sorcerous auto-carriage. Leave here; go and slay them both.**"

"Yes, Your Majesty."

I looked the kid dead in the eye as he walked away.

"Coward. And what's with the homophobia, man? Uncool."

He spat at me.

The crew got back into their SUV, and for one moment, I saw the well-dressed, eerily comatose form of the city's mayor with a look of abject horror plastered across his slack and drool-smeared face, buckled into the backseat like he was a little kid.

A pair of katanas in black sheaths crossed over his lap.

And then the vehicle was full, and they sped away.

"Hey, guys, see you back at Paese dei Balocchi, okay?"

And then, before I could think of anything else semi-clever to say, the massive, filth-matted, hairy-palmed hand of Gug scooped me up.

It was unpleasant.

CHAPTER 86

He flipped me over, the dick. I was dangling by my backpack some forty-odd feet above the ground, my legs and arms kicking as wildly as they were able, considering how massively exhausted I was.

"Hey again, Gug."

"Where are its signs and weapons and tricks now, slave?"

"Right here."

With my right hand, I drew the holdout pistol from my waistband, flicked the safety, and pumped a dozen shots directly into Gug's face.

He yawned, and a finger significantly bigger than my torso reached up and casually flicked the weapon away.

Nearly broke my wrist, and spun me hard on my axis, so that I could really appreciate seeing the weapon smash itself into nothingness a dozen yards below. I thought about the grenades still hanging from my shoulder strap and then immediately thought better of it.

"Its weapon, slave?"

"I mean, uh, back in the van. Uh, let me go get 'em, and I'll give you a fight. What do you say, hombre? You feeling lucky?"

He considered me with one bright pink, bloodshot eye, now grown to about the size of my skull while pus from divots like burst pimples leaked from the minuscule gunshot wounds in his face. The stink coming from his cavern of a mouth seethed, like a bucket of week-old Mexican seafood left next to a space heater to curdle.

"**Helpless.**"

"Yeah. Wait, let me guess—that makes two of us. You can't even get back into your stolen human body without the Jar of Shifting Souls. So now, you gotta stay like this, all naked, ugly, and fat, until you can meet up with your buddy Bastard Greg. Boy, that's embarrassing."

"**It is quite lucky, slave. Its generous king, my master Gog, bids his servant, Gug, to keep this slave alive, so it might dance and sing and caper and be raped for his amusement.**"

"Fuck you."

He laughed.

"**It will, Gug thinks, survive for some time in his belly.**"

And with that, I was jammed into the thing's maw.

Gug peeled me from my backpack with a slurp, like a sweet from a wrapper, and I could hear the bag clatter to the ground as I slid past, in dawning blackness, something halfway between a bruised, messy cervix and a deeply infected uvula. I could feel the world shift as Gug turned and a peal of distant thunder as he began to walk. Then everything was upside down and backward in the acrid, bubbling dark.

It felt like I slid down and down and down for a long damn time.

I kept expecting a splash. None. Eventually, I just stopped.

Suddenly, I was very glad that I had accepted Wendy's generous offer of a magic feather that makes people embarrass themselves.

Unwrapping my fingers from the tiny token still clutched in my left hand, I dug out one of my spare lighters.

Flick your Bic.

The flame was less than impressive, and the air in here was damp and dangerously low on oxygen, but it was enough to temporarily survey my surrounding, such as they were.

I was stuck in a tube that smelled like hot vomit and rotten meat.

The flame guttered out, and I was left with nothing but the sound of my tape running, clicking along like it was on forward scan, trying to pull the magic of this thing's flesh-dissolving juices into itself.

That was okay. I was getting sick of looking at this asshole's upper digestive tract, anyway.

Well, here went nothing.

"Tickle tickle, motherfucker."

Everything around me seized as I drew the feather back and forth along his stomach wall, and the crashes of his footfalls stopped for a single moment. Severe cramps, nausea, and intense stomach distress: the bad-food equivalent of sneezing, I should hope.

"Tickle tickle, I said."

The walls tightened, I moved a little further up, and Gug's center of gravity shifted. Unless I missed my guess, he was now hunched over and moving toward his knees in worship to the porcelain god.

"*TICKLE TICKLE, FUCKER.*"

What I was going to do once he puked me up, of course, I had no idea. Then the whole world shifted, and suddenly I was sliding rapidly, feet first, back in the direction I had just come up from.

Ew. Looks like I'm heading out the back door.

Time to make like a rusty fishhook, I decided.

Now, there's a reason that I always keep a sharp knife on me. And yet, suddenly, I was really pissed at myself that I hadn't picked the fucking thing back up, after I threw it at the wall of my apartment two days ago, back when I was mad at Garrick Heldane, which somehow in my current position felt like years upon years distant.

Digging into my pockets, I came up with... a spoon?

Where the fuck was that from?

Oh, right, from the Denny's earlier.

When I took my coffee to the bathroom. I jammed it in my pocket before I started playing with the katana.

Heh.

And mom said that my kleptomania would only get me in trouble.

I summoned every bit of crown and throne and dust, every bit of eldritch might I had, and jammed the semi-sharp-edge into the wall.

Then I flicked around the wound with the feather.

"*Tickle tickle, demon shit; hope this fucking hurts a bit.*"

The wound seized up, quivered, and then gushed: jetting a geyser of stinking, rank, red-hot ichors, the just-discovered wound-equivalent of ejaculation and explosive diarrhea.

The walls twitched and I dropped yet again, into a swampy morass of something indescribably foul, my shoes filling with hot, wet, and semi-solid corruption, and then everything got smellier and tighter and darker and much, much faster, and I lashed out in every direction that I could with the spoon and the feather in the poisonous quicksand.

Thank all the gods, I managed a quick breath before I went down hell's own waterslide. Also, I may have let go of some grenades.

Pins pulled, of course.

CHAPTER 87

Leaving out the backside of Prince Gug was, and I say this with all truthfulness and sincerity, somehow even worse than going in the front.

The drop at the end was only ten feet, at least, so that was nice.

I hit the ground and crashed to my knees, blood and shit and worse raining down all around me, and I rolled.

Trying to wipe my face clean of the sick clots of horror that stuck to me, surging forward in a half crouch, half crawl I gasped for sweet, clean air and struggled to my feet. Then I turned to see my foe.

That's when the grenades went off.

Once more, and for the last time, the aegis saved my damn life.

I was blown backward, while the giant was doubled over with anguish and shock, spurts of still-steaming lifeblood running freely from his anus, his legs a ruin of matted hair and thick masses of half-digested meals clumped with black blood.

And then fire, detonating in clean and spiteful bursts, leapt out of his bowels, and from the earth at his feet, and from a few other places somewhere inside of him where he was still bleeding.

Ow, indeed.

He screamed, and spun, and rushed at me with suicidal rage as his body broke, and I couldn't even move as his fists, each like a freight train of fur and foot-thick bones, descended in a tsunami.

All I could manage to do was to flinch.

And all four of his arms shattered against me.

Every finger, every tendon, every wrist, broken like glass.

He collapsed, panting and in shock, and the shirt I wore beneath my armor unraveled in a shimmering spool with quiet, golden dignity.

It dropped into a wide circle at my feet, and then, with a twinkling like candles being blown out, it was no more.

Gug was little more than a red-brown ruin, now.

I walked away, limping, and picked up the closest piece of heavy automatic weaponry that I could find: a 50-caliber rail cannon dropped by a fleeing or gunned-down boy-goat.

I could barely lift it.

"See, this is what you get for fucking with me."

"Slave, Gug will rape its mothe—"

I shot him in the skull.

Then I turned my attentions up the road.

I started jogging toward MacSherman Hollows.

CHAPTER 88

Paese dei Balocchi wasn't tough to find. It was lit up like the 4th of July, every light in the place on and the parking lot around the squatting toad of a building bathed in orange light and full to the brim with cars. Sounds from it echoed across the empty streets in the Middle of Midnight in this dead-end zone of sleepy festering-sprawl of 'burb.

I stood in the darkness of the woods across the road.

And I watched.

Snipers on the roof, at least five two-man teams making sweeps.

The building and the lights and the crowd reminded me, quite idly, of the opening night of *LotR* when I went to the multiplex with Tama.

I let that memory—especially the part where I almost got my ass stampeded by douchebag nerds—fill me with rage. Rage was a poor substitute for strength at this late an hour, but I took what I could get.

Crossing the parking lot, ducking between cars, the building started to loom more and more like a fortress.

And then the commotion started.

It wasn't me, I swear.

Whitewall tires squealed as Miss Molly came rocketing around a corner, and shots started blazing back and forth as the boy-goats tried in vain to track her, hurt her... something. Anything.

They had very little luck.

She was a shark in a swimming pool.

Great white at feeding time.

16-cylinder Jaws.

I watched one poor, dumb bastard fling himself into her path from between two rows of Jeeps and eat, for his trouble, a ton and a half of polished steel to the midsection going eighty miles an hour. she reversed on a dime and then accelerated over him, whipping a snappy bootleg on his torso in the process.

Visibly in shock, his companion hastily retreated, firing a short series of three-round bursts that seemingly bothered Molly no more than a swarm of wasps might bug a semi.

Her fog lights flared at me once, and she idled up with a purr.

The passenger door popped open.

Her radio crackled once as I climbed in, smearing demon-shit onto her white leather upholstery, and she took off again at high speed just as our presence was beginning to draw more of a crowd.

"Uhh... sorry about the mess, Molly."

She ignored me.

The radio crackled once again, and the station dial spun, and then Cleon's voice came echoing through, along with the sounds of gunshots.

"Royden! All right, you made it!"

"Can you hear me, Cleon?"

"Yes, dummy!"

"All right, cool. Just wanted to check. Sorry that I'm a little late to the party, but I'm bringing some party favors: I got a big-ass gun, and Free Candey Van, Prince Gug, and Canio de Pogo are all down and out."

"Canio? The clown? Nope, he's running around in here."

"Fuck. Will that stupid monster just not stay dead?"

"I have a plan for that. But, look, I'm gonna need you to get down here in a quickness. I'm not doing well; I'm pinned at the moment, and I've got maybe five minutes left of this medallion-tape, tops."

"Shit."

"So, how much Betamax have you got left?"

"Cleon, I have no idea. I'm not really trained to gauge the length of tape left on an enchanted VCR tape."

"God, you're hopeless. Alright, so Miss Molly is gonna bring you around to the loading docks, and you need to meet me on the bottom floor of the building. Paese dei Balocchi can get kind of, you know... wonky, but you should be able to take the lift straight down, got it?"

"Lift?"

"It's kind of like an elevator, but... hell, you'll see."

"Meet you there."

CHAPTER 89

Miss Molly and I looped around the parking lot once, drove out onto the empty streets and whipped three blocks up, jogging across an intersection before speeding back and running around the side of the massive, decayed off-white skate park and paintball facility in about the amount of time it took to say the words.

There was a small, tightly clustered contingent of heavily armed boy-goats and what I might call "goat-hounds" waiting for us.

They were doomed from the start.

They should have had a tank.

Or an aircraft carrier.

I stood up in the back seat, wind whipping in my hair, my feet braced against the black garbage bag full of loose cigarettes, with my mighty new 50-cal propped on the passenger side headrest, and I let loose some sweet holy fucking hell.

Miss Molly smashed into everything that hadn't gotten out of the way by the time we pulled up, then idled in revving neutral just long enough for me to clumsily climb up onto the loading dock bay, keeping an eye on the still-snarling half of a weird, horn-headed hybrid of a pit bull and rabid goat trapped under her back wheels.

Then she took off fast enough to leave a contrail and sparks.

I rushed up to the big metal doors and slid them up.

Now *this* was definitely not up to code.

Inside the huge building, echoing steel rafters, like in a high school basketball court, ran across a pitted, rusty steel ceiling hundreds of feet overhead. Walkways connected with the tiny platform in front of me led to dozens of zigzag towers, bridges, stair-steps, hammocks, tree-forts and less-identifiable structures all hanging by groaning chains, held up by exposed orange girders jutting from the floor, or plugged in to each other by loops of wobbling cable.

If I rushed forward, I would plummet maybe thirty stories straight down into a vast swimming pool with an orgy of waterslides running from it. To my immediate left and right there were easily thirteen or more different directions to go: up, down, around, sideways, or off to the nook where a mall-food-court-style nacho, hot-dog and fruit-smoothie snack-bar was incongruously sitting next to a bungee-jumping station, which was next to a bunch of lawn chairs facing a blank wall.

A single laptop computer on a broken end table, set right next to a beanbag chair, was attached to a stolen projector, still with "Property of MacSherman Hollows Elementary" written on it.

The projector was running amputee anal-fisting on the wall.

On the other side of me, of course, was a wooden lemonade-style stand apparently offering free shots of bourbon, roofies, and ecstasy.

And two different roller coaster tracks looped through all of it.

It was hot in here and damp and smelled like a locker room.

The so-called "lift" was, it seemed, just a five-foot-by-five-foot steel plate right in front of my current platform with a remote control on a long rubber cord sticking out of one corner with two buttons on it like a piece of industrial equipment: up and down.

Of course there was no safety rail.

I got onto the thing and hit the down button just in time; a set of sprinting reinforcements for the slain "doormen" got just barely into range, running up into the gaping maw of the building's loading dock as I began my descent into madness. I was understandably a little anxious about the massive recoil on my new gun, and I wasn't willing to return fire while standing in such a precarious position.

Darts flew around me.

I dropped to a squat and flipped them off.

And then the lift went down and down and down.

The lift was bolted to a chain-lined groove on the far wall of a screaming madhouse that stretched as far as the eye could see—an artificial rainforest throbbing with buzzers, toys, music, games, food, entertainment, flashing lights, climbing equipment, and ramps.

It was Dave & Buster's on acid.

Six Flags on speed.

A massive, sprawling, "Timmy (Age 6)'s Ultimate Cool Mansion, drawn on graph paper with crayon" on steroids.

Also, on crack cocaine

And the lift kept going down and down and down, and just as I saw that the swimming pool had naked, bruised women handcuffed to the walls of the shower area and to the sun-chairs, I heard the clip-clop of goat hooves descending the stairs on all sides of me.

I shouldered my weapon, dropped to my stomach, checked my sights through the haze of steam, and began opening fire at my pursuers.

The lift went down even further, and slowly the walls of the many "ground level" buildings scattered throughout the demiplane began to grow up and around me until I was looking almost straight up while I fired.

After a few more moments, with chunks of scaffolding and other unsafe building materials crashing down around me, the lift descended to the floor and stopped—and just as I was about to leap off, it lurched and began to creep further and further down.

Into the dark, where gunshots echoed, and down to Cleon.

CHAPTER 90

A nd so, I reached the bottom floor.

I passed three levels on my way down beneath the showroom of Paese dei Balocchi, and these were cramped sub-basement affairs, reminiscent of my trip into the special security sections of the airport: white tiles over bare concrete, simple metal prefab walls with unadorned steel doors pressed into them, and long tubes of florescent bulbs hanging by chains to bathe everything in an ugly greenish-white.

Upon reaching each level, I announced my presence with several seconds of intense artillery bombardment.

On the bottom floor, level −4 by my count, they were waiting for me behind chest-high concrete road barriers.

Seeing this, I pitched half a dozen grenades into the hallway and pressed the Up button.

The big gun wasn't the only thing I looted from the boy-goats.

The whole floor hiccupped.

My second trip down to level −4 was much quieter.

Pushing my way through the clouds of smoke and stepping over still-sputtering debris, I started calling out for Cleon.

The first figure to emerge caught a face full of my new two-handed sword, and he went down in a pile of burning, skull-opened agony.

"Cleon?"

The thing on the floor screamed and kicked goat-legs at me.

Its shirt said "Fine, call the cops. I'll rape them, too."

It was not Cleon.

I flicked the thing's charred blood to the ground as the many runes running the length of my great blade hummed at me.

"Cleon!"

From up ahead, pushing out of the last of the smoke, I heard gunfire and saw a trail of arcane destruction that could only be the result of a pissed off Mr. Quiet on the prowl.

A single goat monster lay up against one wall, swollen now to the size of a VW Bug and bright purple, his skin chafed and bloody where it had ripped through his body armor in rapid expansion.

Next to him was a broken-open Betamax cassette, a blown-out firecracker neatly duct taped to it. "Eat Me" was written, elegantly, in black magic marker on the silver adhesive.

Many other improvised Betamax-curse-based explosives littered the hallway, especially once I turned the corner and looked up and down the T-junction at the halls beyond. There were boy-goats here, dead in all manner of ugly and unseemly predicaments: some of them weeping shards of jagged salt and bloody tears from now-sightless eyes, some of them paralyzed with violent tremors and mumbling backwards, and at least one of them apparently turned into loose sandstone with a surprised look on what was left of his face.

Ten yards away, a shadow crept along the ground and then stood.

I drew down, and it looked up at me, its phantom face an insectile and quivering thing of mandibles and ghostly, clacking pincers.

It was Kafkaesque as shit.

"Did you brush your teeth, little boy?"

"Yep."

"Good."

It walked through the wall. I took a right at the end of the hall, and then paused at the next intersection, trying to figure out where those sounds were coming from.

"Cleon!"

More gunfire. Fuck, where was he?

A roar from my left signaled the approach of another boy-goat. He raced at me, a pair of automatics outstretched before him, flashing an eerie and unwholesome yellow in the ugly dull-green light.

My sword swiped the mass of roaring rubber from the air without pause in a casual back swing, and I closed with him in a hop by bringing the blade around in a power drive from over my right shoulder into his ribcage through a new route I made where his clavicle used to be.

The blade dug in, and he stopped twitching after a single heartbeat.

"Cleon, dammit!"

Heading down the hallway toward the shots I had heard, I kicked around another corner.

A door hanging open.

I peeked in, and I heard a groan.

Blade passed to my left hand, I flipped on the lights with my right; a single bare bulb on a chain flicked to life, illuminating a small white workroom spattered with blood and hair clots and teeth and less-identifiable things. A workbench to the left held an assortment of razors, a sawed-off baseball bat, dental implements, a lead pipe, a wrench, several box cutters, a bullwhip, a mass of wire hangers, and some things I didn't want to look at.

In the middle was a chair and...

"Garrick!"

He did not look good. His chin pressed to his chest, shoulders constricted with pain, face a darkened mass of bruises and scabs barely visible in the shadows behind the tangled curtain of hair hanging from his skull in greasy strands, matted with sweat and blood and dirt. He looked, in point of fact, about like I felt.

"... Roy... Roy...?"

"Shit. Yeah, yeah, it's me, Roy-Roy. Fuck, fuck, fuck. Okay, let's get you out of here. Shit, I'm not sure if I can carry you."

"Royd... you should have... "

"Say what?"

I stepped closer, glancing back out toward the hallway. The fight sounded far away but coming our way rapidly.

Christ, of course they're heading toward me now.

"CLEON! I've got wounded!"

"Royden, you should..."

He had his hands cuffed behind him, slumped in his chair. I leaned in close and tried to gauge the depth of his strength and of his various wounds. Breathing shallowly, like his whole chest was in pain. Two broken ribs? Three, maybe? All of them?

"Okay, buddy, can you walk? We're gonna take a walk, okay?"

"Wrong... question, Royden. You should... "

I leaned in as close as I could, feeling the faintest breaths of his hot breath on my cheek.

"What's that, big guy?"

His right hand suddenly swung around from behind the chair and caught me square, hard and sharp, solid in the temple. My blade clattered to the ground. A foot lashed out, then, huge and heavy and booted in slick-oiled snakeskin with steel toes, and smashed me hard right in the nuts as I began to collapse.

His voice still a whisper: "You should have asked me what I was the king of, you dumb shit. Sneak attack, motherfucker."

From the ground, I drew down and shot him. He didn't mind.

He stood, grinning, popping the fingers of his right hand.

"Still holding my breath there, fucktard. And I still have my fingers crossed behind my back. That makes me ally-all-come-free for your faggy freeze-tag gun. Dumbass."

His voice was hoarse and new, but suddenly, I recognized it.

"The King of Fucking Majooj."

"In the flesh. The new flesh. As always, Mr. Poole."

He casually kicked the gun from my hand and then brought his left hand around to blast me in the nose.

Right on top of the break.

Fuck.

Everything went to stars and flashing lights for a second.

When I came to, he had me by the throat, dangling three feet off the ground, eye to eye with his arm fully extended like I weighed about as much as a half-sack of groceries.

He flipped his perfect hair back with a grin, and I saw that the bruises and cuts across his face were all stage makeup. He had dozens of fetishistic icons, scored with demon faces, hanging from necklaces.

"I simply have to ask, Royden. Did you really, honestly not figure out how the guns and swords worked? How to trick their sullen bites, like I did right in front of you the very first time we met? Did you even bother to see an oracle about this?"

I tried to talk, "... you... suck."

"Yes, always with the quick wit, Mr. Poole. Any last words?"

I wrapped both of my hands around his forearm, and did my best to squeeze it until it shattered.

Nothing doing. He was thick with power, like my midnight assault on his fortress had somehow given him even more strength.

As the king of terror, actually, it really might have.

I struggled, and he loosened his grip just enough to let me breathe.

"What about Frieda? She still claiming queenhood over Majooj?"

"... who?"

"Fuck."

"Ah, fine last words. Now, I suppose, we're done with hearing you talk. I'll have Canio take you to be humbled, shaved, and muted, and we can begin my celebrations almost immediately. In fact, let us perhaps begin your disrobing process right now. I do so hate holy symbols."

He yanked my Betamax medallion off.

The leather snapped.

It bit my neck hard enough to draw blood.

Someone stepped into the doorway, and I felt myself give up.

"Royden!"

Shit on me, it was Cleon.

I take back what I said about giving up.

Garrick's, or rather Gog's, eyes went wide, his free hand went behind his back as he took a deep breath, and he shifted slightly to use me as a small human shield between him and the door.

I heard a series of soft *ppfft* sounds. They felt like somebody put out a series of cigarettes on my spine and shoulders. I went totally limp.

Gog snuffed, without exhaling too much, "You... you do realize that you just shot your friend several times in the back, don't you?"

"Oops."

My head lolled to the side as the King of Majooj smugly angled me to peer over my shoulder, and I saw that Cleon had the gun in his left hand and a look in his eye that I know all too well.

It's the look that he gets right before checkmate.

"You're not very good at this, are you, Mr. Quiet?"

"Guess not. Alright, everybody do-si-do."

His right hand came up, and a small ceramic vase sitting in his palm started glowing with a look like the aurora borealis.

"NO!"

"Yep."

And then I blacked out as my soul left my body.

CHAPTER 91

An eternity passed.
It took no time at all.
It was a very deep white.
And a very bright black.
And everything in-between.

CHAPTER 92

The next thing I knew, I was laying on my side, blinking into the ugliest, saddest face I had ever seen.

It looked a lot like the one I see in the mirror every morning, but slack and weak and bruised and bloody and stained with smoke and shit. It was lumpy and discolored, and I could see with great clarity as I stood up to a great, great height that it was attached to a rude parody of a person.

I was very tall, now.

Someone far below was yelling my name.

"Royden!"

I turned, and a much shorter, older version of Cleon was looking at me with pathetic fear in his eyes.

"Royden, is that you?"

He pointed his gun at me, and it was no trouble at all to simply reach out and take it from him before he could pull the trigger.

I had never, in all my life, felt so good.

"Royden? Christ! ROYDEN!"

"Yes, Cleon?"

My voice sounded terrific.

My legs long and strong.

Nothing hurt, nor could.

I flexed every muscle I had and stared down at strong, exquisite hands built for shaping wood and plucking songs from sad guitars and running over smooth and nubile, trembling skin in the dark.

A cold, dark heat stirred in my loins, far below, and something powerful and hot pushed against my thigh.

"Royden! Speak to me!"

I glanced back at little old Cleon and saw his confusion.

It delighted me and made me want to break him.

"And what would you have me say?"

"Asshole! What are you the king of?"

"I? I am Royden Poole, the King of Jangladesh."

And with that, the dust of Majooj drained out of the body I wore, and I was filled to the brim once more with my own heart.

The amulets on my chest shattered, each and every one of them.

A million nomads cheered for me and rattled their blades.

This made me fall down.

"Royden?"

"Fuck. Yeah. Okay, so, Cleon, I think that I have some proof that totemic magic isn't as bullshit as you think it is."

"You scared me, cock knocker."

I sat up slowly, surveying the room from a height I was much more comfortable with. The body I had grown up using was lying there, crying softly, and not doing much else.

And I still felt fucking great.

"So, Cleon, the soul of Bastard Greg... he's in there?"

I looked at my body. It shuddered, and then I did.

"Yep. But he can't claim his empire right now, so his mojo is entirely kaput. Plus, I think pretty much his whole nervous system is shot through with paralysis, pain, and shock."

"Good. Welcome to my world, Greggie."

I stood up, getting used to an entirely new set of muscle memory and a body literally a million times better than I had ever felt before.

"Sorry about shooting you in the back."

"No harm, no foul. You're a goddamn genius, Cleon."

"I've been accused of worse."

"So what's the next plan? We track down King Humbert of Cocagne and put an end to the whole bloody mess?"

Cleon looked at me and cocked his head to the side in that way he does when I've just said something stupid.

"Yes?"

"You forgot. Where's your Betamax medallion, Royden?"

"Oh. Yeah, uh, Gog pulled it off me and dropped it, I think. It was just about out of time anyway although it did stop a shitload of bullets. Well worth the investment. Wait, here it is. Can I put it back on, you think? It does have, like, a few more minutes on it, right?"

"Yeah. Ten to twenty minutes, maybe."

"Cool."

Cleon took the thing, made a pass over it with his hands and muttered something, retied the leather cord, and handed it to me.

I looped it over my neck.

"Again, yes?"

"Frieda Baghaamrita."

It clicked. So did the tape.

"Oh fuck, that evil bitch! Cleon, I hate her."

"Yeah. Me too. Look, I'm almost out of time on my tape. I've been fighting guerrilla style to keep from getting hit and cannibalizing bits of recording space off other Betamaxes, but it's a losing proposition. We gotta find her now and hit her real fucking hard."

"Got it."

Gunfire started echoing up and down the hallway, along with a whole lot of screams.

"Huh."

"Uh, Cleon, aren't we the only ones in here breaking shit?"

"To my knowledge."

"So, what do you think that is?"

He kicked a glance at the mass of shattered amulets at my feet.

"I think the demons of Magog are off their leashes."

CHAPTER 93

We tied my prone body, now host to a mostly harmless Poole/Gog, to the room's chair, wrapping it solidly in duct tape and stuffing a dirty sock in Poole/Gog's mouth, also quite securely duct taped.

I came up with his new name, by the way.

And I was still thinking about the implications of having a new body and my awesome strength. And my newfound appreciation for how short Cleon is as we armed up and headed back into the fray.

We moved up the corridor, and I was quite pleased to discover that I could now wield my greatsword in my left hand alone with the big 50-cal in my right hand without any difficulty.

The first intersection was clear except for some corpses of boy-goat chewed on by what appeared to be a feral death clown.

We pressed on.

"So... how tall are you, Cleon?"

"That's your question? Jesus wept, Royden. You're not wondering where Frieda is or whether I'm going to be able to put you back in your own body or about whether you'll even want to go back or what that will really mean for you or what, exactly, we're going to do with Bastard Greg's soul once I have time to figure out how to use this damned jar properly or where, in fact, Garrick Heldane's spiritual component is being held or how we're going to get the jar back to the Forgotten Queen of Scythia without her killing us because we're the only witnesses to her fuck up or how we're going to find the body of Fadey Bohdan and kill it like she asked us to or even, for God's own sake, how we're going to survive this?"

"Answer the question."

"I'm five foot eight. Fuck you."

"You seem really little."

"You're a prick, Royden."

There were gunshots up ahead, and we marched toward them.

This is because we're crazy people.

We rounded another corner, and the hunched insect-man-ghost I had seen earlier was standing in the hallway again. It blinked at me, and gnawed at the hunk of boy-goat visible through its hands.

"Cleon, do you know this guy?"

"Yep. He's the Talking Cricket, man. Pinocchio killed him with a hammer, but he keeps showing up as a shade."

"From the original story, I assume?"

"Yes, it's much darker."

"I caught that. What's he doing here?"

"I summoned him. He hates naughty children."

"Did you eat your veggies, little boys?"

We answered in unison, "Yes."

"Good."

It dropped into a crouch and scuttled away through a wall.

The corner suddenly erupted into a mass of retreating boy-goats, all emptying shots into something we couldn't see. And then the corridor behind us filled with the sound of a nasty howl from a raw throat that could only belong to Canio de Pogo.

Coming fast. Far away, but closing.

"Huh. You want the front or the back?"

"You take the clown, Royden."

"Oh, I always get the clown!"

Cleon grinned just a little too manically for my taste as he looked up the hallway, pulled a pink plastic cellphone from his pocket, and flicked it open. It beeped; I saw a bit of bill taped to it and a scrawl of ink.

"Wait. You made two of those?"

"Two? Fuck you, I'm a professional. Why make one when you can have a twelve for a mere dozen-times the price?"

"So what are you doing now?"

"Calling in reinforcements. Now deal with your killer clown like a man, and let me do my sorcerer's work. Call-Anywhere Phone, dial me up Wendy-called-Tiger-Lily, Queen of Cocagne."

Then he threw the fucker up the hallway like a grenade.

It rattled to the ground, ringing, as a mass of black, pin-stripe suit with curling spider legs, vast and hairy, jutting from the shoulders and a slender man without a proper face hanging within it came shuffling around the corner.

The arms of the torso began to wave, boneless and long.

A detachment of boy-goats backed up in noisy, stinking panic, emptying round after round into the slim black figure in his cloak of limbs. He opened his not-ever-a-mouth to reveal a place of infinite aching blood and electronic distortion moans, and then his shapeless head began twisting and flickering back and forth like a guttering candle-flame.

The bullets didn't seem to bother him.

There was a click from the floor.

And then Wendy came exploding out of the cellphone like Athena blowing out the top of Zeus's skull, dreadlocks and bare, callused feet and a surprisingly conservative nightie flickering and flapping behind her in a shriek of a war-whoop.

She landed about five feet away in a crouch, hands balled into little fists, and spared a glance over her shoulder at us, shooting a gap-toothed grin through her inexpertly applied warpaint.

"How, paleface."

"How, indeed?"

She smirked, took a deep breath, crossed her fingers and put them behind her back, and began kicking shins, pulling hair and punching boy-goat in the kidneys as the mass descended on her.

Cleon looked up at me, which was a really weird feeling: "What do you mean, 'how?'—this is her dominion too, Royden."

"Right. Oh, yeah, so she can step to it. I get that. But how did she know about the thing with the guns—"

And then, like a rocket, Canio de Pogo was on me.

He hated me so much that *I* could taste it.

We wrestled, then, as he closed upon me and went in to pin me to the ground, smearing me with grease paint and knocking my blade aside. For the first time, I truly saw how grotesquely and unutterably deformed he really was—so bloated and squat and awful.

And I felt how fast he was, the ultimate chasing nightmare always a little quicker than you, no matter how hard you run or fly or climb.

And I felt his strength, too. That hideous strength.

Not as strong as me, though. Not in this body with my throne and crown.

I crushed his limbs as he tore at me, and I wrapped steely fingers around his fat throat. I lifted him with blood running from my wounds and began to mash the life out of him.

He stared at me with those cavernous, cadaverous sockets, blood leaking from them in a torrent. His mouth opened wide, too wide, and an echo ran out: "Oh, no. I never, ever die, boy. You know that."

From beside me, "Yeah, but you'll never be live again, either."

And then the clown vanished into the black tape exorcism of the Betamax that Cleon pressed against the thing's sticky, fleshy scalp.

The cassette roared, bulged for a moment, and then went still.

"Admit it, you've been waiting to say that this whole time."

"Maybe. So, looks like the path is clear."

I stood up, stunned again at how little I hurt, and glanced up at the now-naked form of Wendy waving to us with a blood-streaked hand from the top of a pile of wrenched-open corpses.

"Hey, you fellas sure know how to show a girl a good time!"

"What happened to your night-gown?"

"Monsters ate it. Happens a lot, and I like it better nakie. Now, if you'll please and thank you, pass the potatoes, excuse me, I'm gonna go kill my fucking husband."

"Husband?"

She grinned, let out a war-whoop, and ran away.

"Dammit, Cleon, I knew that we couldn't trust her!"

"Yeah, there's that. Maybe she was speaking metaphorically. But either way, she'll be able to find King Humbert in here since she's tapping into the same dust, and now we just have to follow her bloody footprints to be sure that she finished the job. Then we can go home."

"Huh. Good call."

"I'm a genius. You said it yourself."

We started walking.

We got to the corner.

We stepped over the corpses.

We turned and kept right on walking, now following a blood-splattered trail of tiny footprints.

Cleon nudged me, "So, now, who is this chick?"

I glanced up the hallway where Frieda Baghaamrita was standing in a long black dress with a plastic handgun and a sly smile.

"Huh? But—"

"I just wish this was a real gun, Royden."

That's when I realized that Cleon's tape had run out.

"Shit, get down! She's the villain!"

Frieda raised her weapon; I shoved Cleon out of the way and took a deep breath with fingers crossed behind my back.

She shot well. Very well, in fact.

Her bolt smashed directly into the plastic-wrapped medallion hanging around my neck, shattering it utterly, then punched into my chest, where it stopped as if it had forgotten where it was going and promptly bounced harmlessly away.

A dark wave called amnesia washed over me, and I remember thinking for one second that Frieda was an evil, clever bitch.

CHAPTER 94

I had no idea what that meant, and I promptly forgot it.

I took stock of the situation.

There I stood, having just not died from being shot in the chest.

Confused, huddled over Cleon, I looked up.

A beautiful brunette was rushing up to the two of us, looking very frightened and pale and holding a smoking gun in both hands.

Okay, this was different.

CHAPTER 95

O h, my god! I'm so sorry I shot at you! I didn't know who you were, and I've been so, SO scared! My kings, forgive me!"

I looked at Cleon. He was unharmed although he seemed a little shaken up. He straightened, shrugged, and I shrugged back.

Then, after another glance to our new guest, I gestured for Cleon to do all the talking because I've never been particularly good with hot women who don't enjoy my unique brand of extra-rude sarcasm.

My best bet here would be to play the strong, silent type.

Also, I was suddenly feeling a little bit out of it, like I had missed something very important. And it was on the tip of my tongue.

And man, oh man, this girl was pretty.

Trying not to blush, I reached down and picked up the weapons I had dropped when she startled us. Then I started looking around for more monsters. None, fortunately.

Cleon, meanwhile, wasted absolutely no time in pouring on the kingly charm. He bowed low and courtly and took the girl's hands as she set the gun at his feet.

"No... no worries, young lady. No harm done. I am merely Mr. Cleon Quiet, the King of Urartu, this is... my associate, and we are at your esteemed service. But who are you, if I may be so bold as to ask?"

"Why, I'm Princess Anastasia, the Forgotten of the USSR!"

She shuddered then, as if she was going to faint right there.

Thank god that she didn't, of course, because we were both too stunned to do any damn thing as all.

"Oh. No shit?"

I gave Cleon a meaningful nudge to keep it together.

His eyes wide, he nudged me back with the same meaning.

"No, I suppose not. No... shit, indeed. No, I've been the captive of the terrible and monstrous King of Majooj for some time now and owe you both a great deal of gratitude. He was, I think, looking for a way to symbolically tie my lands to his own!"

That made some sense, actually.

Something about a conversation I had with Cleon about doing almost the same thing, except with America.

Then a nasty sinus headache started to hit, which I blinked away by pressing a thumb to my temple, and by the time I was paying attention again, Anastasia was kissing Cleon on the cheek.

"Alright, then, Your Majesty, let's get you out of here. My... silent manservant and I will escort you to safety."

Oh, so I'm his manservant, now?

I want a pay raise.

Also, my headache and disorientation were starting to fade.

"Please do, kind kings! Whatever treasures you desire, I assure you, will be yours, and more! But I think that we must not dally, for your naked friend, the Queen of Cocagne, has gone to war with her husband, has she not?"

"Yeah, there's that. That's also kind of at the top of the list. All right, manservant, let's go kick some of this guy's ass, huh?"

I nodded as grimly as possible.

"Go, my brave ones! I shall be safe here, I think. The demons of Majooj cannot harm me, for I have these few medallions I stole from him, my captor, and this gun so recently and errantly used on you shall protect me from the boy-goats!"

Then she got on her tiptoes and kissed me on the cheek.

It was awesome.

CHAPTER 96

We tracked the bloody footprints.

When they stopped, Cleon spoke to the floor itself and produced a more elaborate version of the spell I used to track Kynan with his shoes.

We soldiered on, down and down.

We tromped through the sub-basements, heavily armed.

We encountered little to no resistance.

Although we found over a dozen things ripped in half by Wendy.

One of them was a giant half-goat, half-boar made of bricks.

We stepped over its corpse.

I looked to Cleon. "So... rescuing a princess? That's good, right?"

"That's actually, technically, the very, very BEST, my young student Royden. Plus, this job just got significantly easier."

"How do you figure?"

"Now, we don't have to worry at all about the Forgotten Queen of Scythia or the rest of the society. One of the elder secret royalty is here and, most importantly, rescued by us. We can call upon Koloksai, Lady of the Sun, right after we've dealt with King Humbert with violent force, which fulfills the commandments of the Forgotten King of Gurankalia, and then we're home free."

"Yeah?"

"Yeah."

"Because, what... the Queen of Scythia can't just totally kill us outright with another member of the FKS here?"

"Well, okay, she can."

"Not making me feel better, Cleon."

"But she won't. She'll be able to save significant face, now: The real folks to be embarrassed by this will be whoever is claiming the title of Forgotten King and Queen of the USSR these days since they lost a whole daughter—or at least a girl claiming that in their court—and the fact that the Forgotten Queen of Scythia got burgled of some bauble won't even make a ripple. Then, when she uses the Jar of Shifting Souls to set everything right, like the deus ex machina of the King of Athens and Queen Hippolyta at the end of *Midsummer's,* she'll actually be gaining a boatload of power."

"Which means that we're doing her a favor. She'll owe us."

"Okay, so then maybe she'll kill us after all."

"Not helping, Cleon."

We reached the end of the glowing footprints.

We were now in a hallway another three floors down, a place I had taken to calling level −7, and the air here was chilly and damp.

In front of us, the hallway reached to two giant golden doors pounded into the steel, with *Feel* and *Good* etched into them.

"Shit. I know where we are."

"Is that right?"

"You're a smart-ass, Royden."

"I learned it from watching you, short guy."

"This part of the building curls around and hides in itself. I couldn't find it earlier, but it's the place they brought me to be tortured. It's a full-on, honest-to-god throne room."

"Dear god, who has a fucking throne room in this day and age?"

"Assholes, Royden. You know that. And for the record, I'm pretty sure that there's a throne in Cahokia that fits your tight new butt just about perfectly."

I glared at him.

"What's that supposed to mean?"

"Nothing. But you do have a much nicer ass, now."

"Let's go in there and see what's happening."

"Ruin somebody's day. After you."

CHAPTER 97

There was brief game of monkey-in-the-middle.

We lost.

Cleon and I probably should have been tipped off by the fact that Wendy's footprints stopped a few yards before the doors.

On my knees before the Throne of Cocaine, my weapons cast to the side and my stomach reeling, all I could think was that meeting a cute brunette sure screws with my head.

"Mr. Poole, Mr. Poole, oh, indeed, indeed, it's a pleasure to finally make your acquaintance! I've heard all about you, I must say! And what a delight to see you looking so very fine!"

Man, this guy's fake Cockney accent was getting to me.

I looked up as best I could, my neck straining with the effort and cold sweat pouring down my face. I glanced to the side, where Cleon was turning a dangerous color of dark red as he danced a merry jig.

Blood was running from his feet. Red shoes.

"Likewise, gracious King Humbert."

"Oh, that's better! Yes, it is and yes it is! No more of the naughty f-bombs, now, is there? Simon says, my friend, to stand up, take two steps forward, and look around!"

I did, and immediately wished that I hadn't.

What a shithole.

The room was decked out in plasma TVs playing pornography, carpeted with thick pillows in a million different colors—all spattered with the white streaks of dried semen—and studded with short, ionic-style pillars bearing plates of chocolate and honey-glazed cakes topped with mounds of drifting nose candy.

And in the center of it all, a gold-toothed idiot in a tracksuit and a shiny top hat was sitting in a lawn chair on top of a huge pile of sand studded with plastic pails, tiny shovels, cigarette butts, broken beer bottles, and a variety of lingerie, idly playing with a megaphone and a TV remote.

The Jar of Shifting Souls was sitting in his lap.

Cleon was going to die because he had refused to hand it over.

On guard between me and the King of Cocaine stood a seven-foot-tall pink toy bunny, like a grizzly with button eyes the size of dinner plates.

It had a human-head-sized hole right in the middle of its barrel-like chest, with pinkish stuffing oozing out of it and dozens of wet, grasping human hands and throbbing scores of human phalli protruding like bones, but it didn't seem to care much.

In the far corner, I saw Wendy being held down by a twelve-foot-tall blue stuffed bear, and I hoped to Christ that they were just wrestling.

"Ooo, Pedo-Bear love Loli!"

Ech. Didn't sound like it.

He laughed. "My child-bride, she thinks of herself as a big, strong Injun girl. Well, me-sum called Big Chief Choke-a-Ho of the Slap-a-Bitch tribe, and she gonna get fucked inside out tonight. "

This plan was not working, and I needed a new one.

"Thank you for letting me stand, King Humbert."

"Yes, yes! Now, that rude jig will dance that rude jig until his rude jig heart pops in his bleeding chest, like, but I think that you, my little cockweasel, will get to answer me some questions. Shall we play a game, then?"

"Oh, Christ."

"Very impolite, Mr. Poole. Simon says, punch yourself in the face."

The impact broke both a knuckle and a cheekbone.

"FUCK!"

"Two for flinching."

By the time I got done hitting myself, I was on the floor again.

My mouth was full of blood, and I was out of breath.

"You're an addict, Mr. Poole. That makes you mine. You've spent your last dollar, more than once, begging to be made dead, free of dread free will, to lose yourself in fun and games. You're my bitch, sir."

"... you are wise, King Humbert."

"See? That's not so hard now, is it? Now, Simon says, answer me this question: have all the spirits controlled by Gregory Howsgrove been let loose and free to run their demon hearts wild?"

Through gritted teeth, "Yes."

"Ah. Good. Can't get in here, but that will cause a delightful bit of mess to watch on the telly. Now, another: has he been slain?"

"No."

"Damn. More's the bother. But, I reckon, I do 'fink, that he might just be in *your* body now, now isn't he, Mr. Poole?"

"Yes."

"Ah! Then perhaps I'll make him my dancing slave in lieu of you. Oh, and isn't that a tasty dish to set before a king?"

He paused.

"I asked you a question, Mr. Poole."

"Ah, yes. Why yes, Your Majesty, that is, in fact, a tasty dish to set before a king. Very much so. Delicious, even."

"Ha! Fun, fun fun, and who wants a toke? Oh, I do, I do! Now, then, Mr. Poole, I think that I would like to let *you* ask me a question!"

"Your Majesty?"

"Ooh, yes, a grand question! Yes, I am, I am Your Majesty. Now ask, ask, ask another!"

"Okay. What's your endgame, here?"

"Why, immortality, of course! Power, fame, drugs, money, women! I'll fiddle, like Nero, as the American Empire burns, and I'll name my horse to the Senate like Caligula! Incantatus!"

I very barely stopped myself from informing this ignorant fuck that Caligula's horse was actually named *Incitatus*.

"A... fine name for a horse, Your Majesty."

"A learned man! Ah! Well, I'm quite impressed, and I'm going to bugger it up the ass first, too! Another question! This is fine preparation for my Good Morning America interview!"

I thought for a moment.

I needed him off-guard.

"How many boring people does it take to screw in a lightbulb?"

"..."

"Give up?"

"How many?"

I shrugged. "One."

He shrieked with delight.

"You are funny, Mr. Poole!"

"Funny looking, sir. Yes."

"Ask another!"

"So, how many madmen does it take to screw in a lightbulb?"

His eyes lit up. "Oh, how many?"

"Why, to get to the other side, of course!"

"Hee-hee! Another!"

"Okay. Oh, you'll like this one: how many women with PMS does it take to screw in a lightbulb?"

"How many, how many?"

"Four."

He frowned. "..."

"I said FOUR, asshole."

"... and why—"

"Because it just *does*, okay? God!"

"Hee-hee-hee! Oh, this is fun! Another!"

Oh shit, this could go on forever.

"I will, Your Majesty. First, I needs buy more Laffy Taffy. May I go get some? I'll be right back."

"Ha! Yes, you are funny! Why, I'm going to keep you as my very own! In fact, you're being such a good boy and great sport that I'm actually going to grant you a request, yes. Any request your heart desires. Indeed, yes, any request except for your freedom or for my death. Laffy Taffy? A cigarette? A poke at my old lady? The bear will be done, soon. Perhaps a sniff or a slurp or a bit of a gamble? I'll let you fight any man I own and let you win, as well. What do you say?"

"Hmm. Gracious and wise King Humbert, I ask only that you allow my friend Cleon to stop his dancing and to speak with me."

"Wot's that? Oh, 'ell, son, didn't you ever play *Risk* as a kid? Flip the board and storm off pissed? You're supposed to screw your neighbor over rightly and forthrightly. Mercy, no, is no fun at all. Request denied."

"King, what about the game Mercy? Surely, you like that one."

"Oh, right, where you twist a cunt's arm all about and around until she screams mercy? Oh, you've got me there!"

"Your Majesty is too kind."

"Alright, I'll allow it this once. Court nigger, on account of mercy, Simon says... stop dancing and speak to your friend!"

Cleon collapsed to the floor and started mumbling.

"May... may I speak with him, King Humbert?"

"No. But he may speak with you. Ha-ha! Speak, nigger!"

His breath was coming in ragged gasps now, and he climbed uncertainly to a trembling knee.

"Royden?"

I nodded, keeping an eye on the throne.

"I ever told you why I tell that stupid story about peeing in a girl's backseat to people?"

King Humbert laughed.

Under my breath, "Not sure this is the time, Cleon."

"It's because, I think, that I just want to be sure that... that they know about the worst thing that I ever did. And that they hear it from me, and not from somebody else or something."

I couldn't help it.

"You didn't even do that shit, Cleon."

"What if I did?"

I looked to King Humbert, who seemed both fascinated and very, very stoned. It looked like he was going to allow this exchange.

"That's really not important right now, I think."

"Okay, but even if I didn't do it, me writing it in a journal so that a person would read it and think that I did it is... pretty crazy, right?"

"Not necessarily. Look, can we talk about this some other time?"

"You're my best friend, Royden. And I just want you to know that I tell people that story when I want to know if I can trust them, and also when I'm comfortable with someone enough and want them to know, without me having to say it, that I'm kinda crazy, sometimes. And because, if I die, I want them to set the record straight about me."

"What?"

"You know. If I die."

"If you die, I'm going to tell everyone that you pissed in that girl's backseat, Cleon. And that you then lied about it, but only *after* writing about it in your journal to catch snoopers, which is crazy."

"Fuck you, Royden."

"See, now you're not allowed to ever die."

"Fine. Hell with it. A horse, a horse."

We both looked at King Humbert.

"Eh?"

Cleon continued, "A horse, a horse."

Under my breath, "Is a horse, of course..."

The king grinned, "Of course, of course!"

I bit the bullet, "My kingdom, my kingdom..."

Humbert shouted, "My kingdom for a horse!"

Cleon grinned, "It's yours, fucker. Fair trade, fair deal."

He yanked his backpack around, and then he tossed it.

A bag full of pink, plastic ponies fell onto the sandcastle of the Throne, at the feet of the bunny. The big bunny fell down.

All the dust of Cocagne ran out of Humbert.

His power broke. His spells failed.

The amulets around his neck burst, and I heard Wendy rip the stuffed bear in half with her bare hands.

The shade of the Talking Cricket appeared upon the Throne, looking pissed off and whispering about math homework.

Simon Humbert didn't know what to say.

I knew.

He should have said that he was the King of Cocagne.

And he most certainly should have held his breath and crossed his fingers behind his back.

Failing that, he should have run.

Before he got a chance to do any of that, I shot him in the skull.

And then Wendy kicked his corpse into an ugly smear.

CHAPTER 98

We called in the cavalry.

Within moments, it seemed, the place was being turned upside down by servants of Koloksai, Lady of the Sun, who even deigned to show up herself, looking young and blonde and hot and *fabulous* in a dress only partially stained with the fresh heart's-blood of a virgin. And by servants of the Forgotten of the USSR, and by many, many gold-draped slaves in service to Urukagina of Lagash. And by several dozen score of assorted hangers-on, inquisitors, informants, wet-works men, sycophants, ass kissers, yes men, aura readers, self-proclaimed "modernity experts," diviners, oracles, and all the other filthy flotsam and jetsam eternally associated with the unlimited power of the Forgotten Kings Society.

We were assured that everything would be put right.

We were assured, furthermore, that justice would be served.

We were assured, above all, that nothing untoward had happened.

And that we sure as hell better not say different to anyone.

These people can all kiss my hairless little brown ass.

And yes, for the record, I was asked very repeatedly if I was certain that I wanted to be placed back into my "birth body," as the Lady of the Sun kept referring to it. And when I insisted that she return my friend Garrick Heldane from his current body, a badly beaten, three-legged pit bull, to his own and me to mine, she took that as a favor done for me.

Patching my broken midget body up, of course, was extra.

Which meant that now, I owed her.

Which, funny enough, is the best position to be in once you've gotten the attention of one of the Forgotten, because she's far less likely to kill me until I pay back what I owe.

I'm an investment, I suppose, and she didn't get so damn old and so damn powerful by wasting her investments.

Well, not without some hard consideration first.

The one and only good part of the night was when Anastasia, very nearly in tears, hugged Cleon and me and told us to be good.

And she called me Royden.

Which was weird, now that I think about it, because Cleon never said my name in front of her.

My brain hurt too much to think about it.

Eventually, they let us leave.

CHAPTER 99

The secret time hidden there within the folds of Mostly Midnight finally bled out and collapsed into exhausted nothing while Cleon and I were walking through the darkened streets of MacSherman Hollows, and we slid without a word back into the shadows of the waking world.

If I were a little better at casting spells, of course, we could have kept ourselves on the Nether Side and just stepped back to the vault-vault.

But that trip would have hurt, for one, and the only benefit to that would have been that we would be at Cleon's place.

Where there was only one bed.

So instead, we had to walk.

We were way too tired to give a fuck.

A crappy hotel downtown took a couple of bucks from us, and we passed out with our clothes still on.

It was the best sleep I had all week.

EPILOGUE

As you may recall from much, much earlier in the book, I do not care much for prologues. In fact, I hate them.

I do not feel the same way about epilogues.

There I stood, in the remnants of my apartment, going through what little bits of garbage and detritus my overzealous neighbors hadn't already stolen, smoked, shat upon, or otherwise soiled in my absence, trying to decide what to take with me as I fled and what to simply abandon, when I realized that it was almost midnight.

Again.

A long day of sleeping until five in the afternoon, getting a cab into town, and then dodging the police half the day does that to you.

I let it pass, staring in grim wonder at the clock on my stove as it crept up to the Secret Time, refusing to let myself get pulled back in.

Click.

There.

Midnight oh one, just like it was a minute ago.

A feeling like the plane finally touching down again after a long trans-oceanic flight settled into me, and I let out a sigh of relief.

My cellphone went off, buzzing like crazy.

I wandered over to it.

Lord have mercy. Seven new messages.

I checked them, weary with disdain for my life.

The first was, of course, from the Forgotten King of Gurankalia, in his position as liaison amongst the Elder Equals to the Long Hour holds of Alone We Are Kings, informing me that my presence was politely requested in connection to a number of pressing questions regarding my indirect involvement with possible inappropriate and potentially illegal behavior within the waking world.

This, I promptly deleted.

If my presence were actually desired, the Forgotten would have sent Corporate-Owned Jesus to come and get me.

This was nothing more than a thinly veiled and semi-snide offer to allow me the pleasure and honor of crawling in front of a masked, star-chamber tribunal to beg, weep, gnash my teeth, tear my hair, and cry out for help from the all-powerful Forgotten.

If they deigned, after my first rounds of gifts and presentations of evidence, to hear my side of everything, they might even stoop to aid me in the discovery of some justice.

Which would mean that I owed them, of course.

And not in a good way.

I would owe all of them.

Their polite request for my company was an opportunity for me to give them a less-polite, point-blank refusal, so I could save face amongst AWAK by not being a tattletale running to mommy while also allowing the Forgotten the much-loved opportunity to pursue their own blood vendettas and witch hunts using my crisis without the burden of my expert, eyewitness testimony.

Dicks.

The second message, infuriatingly, was to inform me that Garrick and Tama were officially being wed.

A combined mingled bridal/baby-shower was planned.

Long Hour hold, tomorrow night, just after 11:60.

Gifts accepted, bride registered at Neiman Marcus.

Wedding to follow. Date not yet set, but keep your calendar open.

I let myself roil and burn and twitch in the knowledge that if I were a much less decent human being, that would be my wedding and my kid and even my gifts from fucking Neiman Marcus.

I made a note not to go to this shower or to the wedding or to the reception. And if I did go, to not go drunk.

Or, you know, not *too* drunk.

Or, just maybe, get very, very, dangerously drunk.

And then I hated myself.

The third message was from Garrick Heldane, asking me as coldly as possible to be his best man since I had saved his life and all.

The fourth message was from Tama, asking me not to accept.

The fifth message was from Garrick, rescinding the offer.

The sixth message was from Tama, asking me to be the unofficial date of her fat cousin who would not be in the bridal party.

This is what passes for her charity.

The seventh and by far the most interesting message of the night was from Alone We Are Kings: a coronation was to be held for a member of the Forgotten, and the whole of AWAK was invited to attend a banquet feast in the honor of the new Forgotten Queen of the USSR.

We would all, of course, be seated outside the festival hall proper with the servants, but the entire event was still quite the commotion. And some select few lesser kings might be allowed inside, it was hinted, during the actual coronation.

Squabbling for that honor was sure to be fierce.

That wasn't in the message, by the way.

They didn't have to say it.

There was to be, the message went on, a jousting tournament, as well, and a grand melee. And a few tests of skill in the arts of magic for the delight of guests, and a showing of rare and exotic discoveries from the Sideways.

Dress, it seemed, was to be formal mourning black, in deference to the recent and untimely passing of Queen Anastasia's most beloved and dearest-departed Symbolic Mother.

Interesting. Curious, one might say.

And just then, my cellphone rang in my hand.

Cleon.

"Yes?"

"Where in the fuck are you, son?"

"In my apartment. I keep thinking that I'm forgetting something. But I'm not sure what. And where are you, exactly?"

"Outside, in the car, bored to tears. Come on. Vacation awaits. First stop is Utah to deliver your ambrosia. Then, I'm thinking Vegas."

"Vegas?"

"Vegas."   Ω

ABOUT THE AUTHOR

Clinton J. Boomer, known to his friends as "Booms," resides in the quaint, leafy, idyllic paradise of Macomb, Illinois, where he attended 4th grade through college. He began writing before the time of his own recollection, predominantly dictating stories to his ever-patient mother about fire monsters and ice monsters throwing children into garbage cans.

He began gaming with the 1993 release of Planescape, which shaped his Jr. High years, and he was first published professionally in the Ennie Award winning *Pathfinder Chronicles: Campaign Setting* from Paizo Publishing—after placing in the Final Four of Paizo's inaugural RPG Superstar competition.

Boomer is a writer, filmmaker, gamer, and bartender. His short comedic films, the D&D PHB PSAs, have been viewed more than one and a half million times. A member of the WereCabbages creative guild, he is a frequent freelance contributor to Rite Publishing, Legendary Games, Sean K. Reynolds Games, Paizo Publishing, Reality Deviants Press, Zombie Sky Press, and the Hellcrashers setting. *The Hole Behind Midnight* is his first novel.

Boomer is currently the happiest he has ever been in his whole life.

Preview of the next Royden Poole novel by Clinton J. Boomer:

THE THIRTEENTH IMPOSSIBILITY

—another story of the 25th Hour—

COMING SOON

CHAPTER 1

Mr. Poole, it is truly a pleasure."

"Oh, well I'll just bet that it is."

So here I goddamn sit with a gun pointed at my face, plopped in a fucking hot tub with a grinning Italian immortal so fat that his cellulite has cellulite, watching the greasy bastard drip chunks of mostacholi or some such thing into the water, wiggling, and giggling.

On a beach, no less.

Under the full moon, hanging above a black ocean, watching the whole thing cascade into the 25th Hour, along with an entire mansion and the manicured grounds spread beneath. Sliding, cold and polished and brilliant bone white. And all the king's horses and all the king's men ride with him into the Nether Time to a realm of fantasies.

I hate hot tubs.

No one takes people my size seriously, but the worst offenders of the bunch, other than the people who design buses and grocery stores, are the fuckers who should really know better: the people who build waterslides, jet skis, hot tubs, and other such "fun" things.

Their discourtesy to me is epidemic.

You know, like I wouldn't enjoy being able to sit down without drowning my own ass right about now. Christ.

Every time he drops a fistful of food, the water level rises.

"Hungry, Mr. Poole?"

"No. Grabbed a bite on the way here."

"A-ha. Very funny. I was told that you have quite the sense of humor, and I see that it's true. So Mr. Poole, I assume that you must be wondering why I've begged your presence here tonight."

"There's that. Also, I'm wondering why you specifically asked for me naked and beaten up."

"A simple precaution, Mr. Poole. That is all. You're quite well known in many circles as a dangerous man, and I'm afraid that I allow only my own sworn men into my presence while clothed in any way. Too much trouble with concealed weapons, you know."

"Great."

"To put my guests at ease, though, I prefer to be naked as well."

"Super. So, then, we can look forward to many future instances of seeing each other's junk, I suppose."

"A possibility that does not bother me over-much. Still, you have not yet asked me who I am. Surely, you are curious?"

"Not particularly. While I was waiting after the manhandling, I heard one of your men refer to you as Mr. Kama. Roughly translated from modern Sanskrit, that means something akin to 'sensuality' or even 'sexual fulfillment.' It's one of the things that the Buddha specifically renounced en route to his Awakening, but Kama is also a famous child-god. Since you're observably Mediterranean instead of Hindu, though, I'll guess that it's a clever word play."

The tubby fucker smiled a lot more, shifted his not-inconsiderable weight, and I'm pretty sure he got a chubby somewhere way down there under the rolls of fat and the surface of the all-but-boiling water.

I tried not to glance downward in any way.

"Tell me more, Mr. Poole."

"Meh. It's probably a play from the Greek word *eros*—a word with a similar and similarly untranslatable meaning and a nickname for Cupid. My guess is that you go by the first name of Ascanius, ancestor of Romulus and last noble son of Troy, and that you're calling yourself the King of Latium, Lavinium, or Albalonga—Virgil mentioned Cupid taking that form to inspire the love of Dido in the *Aeneid*."

"Well, aren't you clever, Mr. Poole."

It wasn't a question.

And all of my pre-interrogation preparation on the bastard hadn't paid off as handsomely and impressively as I might have liked.

But I'm a prick and a show-off, so I had to answer anyway.

"Yep. I sure am. But it helps that you have the words *annuit cœptis* emblazoned on an iron plate, there on the wall above the bar. From the reverse of the Great Seal of the United States, there above the eye in the pyramid and the thirteen steps, and an original line from your namesake, Ascanius. Lovely, stirring, and a great quote."

"Yes. And I assure you, Mr. Poole, that 'he' does indeed 'approve my undertakings.' But you misread my title, sir. Yes, Ascanius was known as Euryleon when amongst the Greeks, but in surviving the Italian Wars and the advances of the Etruscans, in founding of the cities of the Alban Hills, he became Julus, first of the Gens Julia, from which sprang the Caesars themselves. I, Cupid, am Protogenoi—yet, also, the son of Venus and of Mars, and am a being of passionate, acquisitive aggression."

"Oh."

"Yes."

"So, what are you the king of?"

Now it was his turn to have to answer.

He grinned wider than I think was healthy.

"I am, in fact, the Forgotten King of Rome and of all its many holdings. Rightful and True King of all that does dwell between Venus and Mars, between whore Aphrodite and her whoremaster, Ares, and her cuckold husband, crippled Hephaestus. King, then, of all the Earth, and of humanity, and of machines and hearts and hatred, of blood and blade and the world, the great Magnus Rex Mundi made flesh."

Two tiny wings like the hands of pale, chubby children appeared above his pimpled shoulders, frantically flapping. The bastard rose about an inch in the water, and I think his foot touched mine.

I shrank back, on guard, and watched the man standing next to us track my skull with his gun very slightly and efficiently.

I decided to be polite.

"And what, precisely, do you want from me?"

"You are going to help me to impale someone on Morton's Fork, Mr. Poole. Do you know what that means?"

"Shit. I think so. It means that you're going to give someone two identical, equally horrible options. No matter which one they choose, they're screwed."

"Indeed. Yes, they will be forced to choose between death and dishonor or dishonor and death. Oh, it will be lovely."

His eyes got kinda dreamy, and I'm pretty sure that he farted.

The bubbles in the hot tub made it hard to tell.

I pressed on.

"Do you mind if I ask whom I'll be screwing over, sir?"

"Not at all. My cousin, the beast Frieda Baghaamrita."

"Never heard of her."

"Oh, but you have, Mr. Poole. Oh, but you have."

And then he giggled a whole lot. And then he started splashing in the water and shaking. And then he started doing a high-pitched thing with his voice that sounded like helium-huffing geese honking their way toward orgasm, and that was not the last time I strongly considered throwing caution to the wind and just strangling billionaire media-mogul Julian Kama to death with my bare hands.

Unfortunately, the man next to me with the gun, the crisp British accent, and the very, very nice—if slightly old-fashioned—suit had already proven himself at least slightly invulnerable.

Mostly while he was beating the living shit out of me earlier.

I glanced up at him while Cupid, the King of Rome, rubbed his hair-rimmed, bright pink nipples.

"So, what is your ass the king of?"

"Ruddygore, sir, and Knight of Rome."

"Cool. Nice bowler cap."

Now I had a whole lot of questions for Cleon.

As if that was something new.   Ω

SPECIAL THANKS

Very special thanks are due, and well past overdue:
Ashavan Doyon, Lou Agresta, Christopher Yono, Samuel L. Berry, Ryan Sykes,
Uri Kurlianchik, Matt Haertjens, Darrin Drader, Karen Terry, Mysi & Craig
Finlay, Trent M. Martin, Jake Desalvo, Jordan Bryan, The Sye, Jessica Leigh,
Erik "The Viking, Big-E, Chops, or The Red" Liljewall for use of his smoking-
section, and most especially to Matt Banach and to Doug Billingsly.
Thank you, thank you, one and all.

The author wishes to thank and to acknowledge
each and every one of the WereCabbages,
the people who let David Bowie throw a baby in the air,
Ms. Bailey Jay, the Linetrap,
Yozora and all his monsters,
/d/,
Bill Hicks, the Original (and best) Goat-Boy,
Vincent Joseph, Stephen Francis, & Kevin James
of Model Stranger,
everyone drinking Downstairs at The Café, and
Al and the girls at Big Al's in Peoria.
This one is for you.

PRAISE FOR
CLINTON J. BOOMER

"Okay, I just finished Clinton Boomer's book, *The Hole behind Midnight*... it was fantastic, and I'm not just saying that because he cut his gaming teeth on Planescape... I'm saying it because the book was fast, profane, full of joy, deeply intelligent, and just a lot of damn fun to read. Oh, and the cover says "For Adults Only." Yeah. Keep that in mind."

—Colin McComb

"*The Hole behind Midnight* reads like the fevered brainchild of Warren Ellis and Kenneth Hite. Smart, dark fun."

—Matt Forbeck

"*The Hole behind Midnight* is relentlessly, kinetically, amorally creative. It's like Neil Gaiman, Warren Ellis, and an issue of Nintendo Power all met in an alleyway and did unspeakable things to each other."

—Robert Brockway

"... a story that breaks all of the rules of reality with magic and mystical badassery but isn't above sharing its regular morning ritual of rolling over, surfing the net, and having a good fap. I like... reminds [the reader] of Darren Shan's *Demonata* series... <3 <3 <3"

—Holly Long

"*The Hole behind Midnight* is Raymond Chandler meets Douglas Adams by way of a fantasy nerd's fever dream. And it's *awesome*."

—Daniel O'Brien

"*The Hole behind Midnight* is an incredibly fucked up book, and I mean that in the best way possible. It is viscerally, violently WRONG on so many levels, but at the same time, it has the same inescapable internal logic of an acid trip or a fever dream. Imagine if Humphrey Bogart was a foul-mouthed, magic-wielding dwarf, chasing a Maltese Falcon, which happened to be a dangerous magical talisman capable of making you bleed from every orifice and that the people after him were cannibal cultists and those flying monkey-things from *The Wizard of Oz*. *The Hole behind Midnight* is stranger than even that. Based upon this work, I feel I can state without fear of contradiction that Clinton Boomer is a dangerous sociopath, albeit a high-functioning one. I fear he may be stalking me. If I am found dead in a compromising position with a bloodstained copy of his novel near my corpse, you can be sure that he is to blame."

—Erin Palette

"I am aware that reading this is an option."

—Cody Johnston

"Imagine a hysterically profane and kinetic collision between the worlds of those twin masters of American Fantasy, Neil Gaiman and Max Hardcore. Boomer's audacious debut novel is full of swagger, punk energy, piss, and vinegar, just like Royden Poole, his diminutive, rage-and-cigarettes-fueled gutter-wizard protagonist. A refreshingly raunchy respite for fans of modern fantasy that have outgrown flying schoolboys and lovesick Mormon vampires."
—Richard Rittenhouse

"... awesome."

—Michael Kortes

"Holy fuck balls... I like where this is heading. Great inspiration for some eerie songs... "

—Vincent Joseph

"... had me laughing out loud. And I don't do that when I read... [A] bit obscene and probably unnecessary. But in a good way. I think. I just don't know if the bestsellers list is ready for dickgirls... "

—Jake "The Snake" Desalvo

"Book rules. Put it in your mouth."

—Steve Barry

"... love the cast of characters, particularly Cleon, the Free Candey Van, Wendy, and Magic Eatin' Jim. Seriously, when [SPOILER OMITTED], it actually brought a bit of a tear to my eye. I like the unlikeable yet likable main character. I like that, although he is a little person, the character had a lot more going on than that, and it wasn't a endless source of slapstick comedy. Same thing with his ethnicity. The setting and tone hits a particular sweet spot for me. I'm always interested in various religions and mythologies and this book is loaded with so much of that. I also love me some pop culture, so all of that was great too... And by the way, how loud of an 'Aw, hell no!' did I let out when the [SPOILER OMITTED]? A very, very loud one. Ouch, it stings!"

—Rebecca Elson

CPSIA information can be obtained
at www.ICGtesting.com
Printed in the USA
FSOW03n0142230218
44611FS